THE CLAY SANSKRIT LIBRARY

FOUNDED BY JOHN & JENNIFER CLAY

WWW.CLAYSANSKRITLIBRARY.ORG

WWW.NYUPRESS.ORG

Artwork by Robert Beer.
Typeset in Adobe Garamond at 10.25 : 12.3 +pt.
Editorial input from Dániel Balogh,
Tomoyuki Kono, & Peter Szántó.
Printed and Bound in Great Britain by
TJ Books Limited, Cornwall on acid free paper

HANDSOME NANDA BY AŚVAGHOṢA

TRANSLATED BY

LINDA COVILL

NEW YORK UNIVERSITY PRESS
JJC FOUNDATION
2007

First Edition 2007

The Clay Sanskrit Library is co-published by
New York University Press
and the JJC Foundation.

Further information about this volume
and the rest of the Clay Sanskrit Library
is available on the following websites:
www.claysanskritlibrary.org
www.nyupress.org

ISBN 978-0-8147-1683-0

Library of Congress Cataloging-in-Publication Data
Aśvaghoṣa
[Saundarananda. English & Sanskrit]
Handsome Nanda / by Asvaghosa ;
translated by Linda Covill. - 1st ed.
p. cm. – (The Clay Sanskrit Library)
In English with Sanskrit (romanized) on facing pages;
includes translation from Sanskrit.
Includes bibliographical references and index.
ISBN 978-0-8147-1683-0
1. Gautama Buddha - Friends and associates - Poetry.
2. Nanda - Poetry. 3. Buddhist poetry - Translations into English.
4. Asvaghosa-Translations into English.
I. Covill, Linda 1962– II. Title.
BQ905.N2A713 2007
294.3'4432–dc22 2007003642

CONTENTS

CSL CONVENTIONS

SANSKRIT ALPHABETICAL ORDER

Vowels:	*a ā i ī u ū ṛ ṝ ḷ ḹ e ai o au ṃ ḥ*
Gutturals:	*k kh g gh ṅ*
Palatals:	*c ch j jh ñ*
Retroflex:	*ṭ ṭh ḍ ḍh ṇ*
Dentals:	*t th d dh n*
Labials:	*p ph b bh m*
Semivowels:	*y r l v*
Spirants:	*ś ṣ s h*

GUIDE TO SANSKRIT PRONUNCIATION

a	b*u*t
ā, â	f*a*ther
i	s*i*t
ī, î	f*ee*
u	p*u*t
ū, û	b*oo*
ṛ	vocalic *r*, American p*ur*dy or English p*re*tty
ṝ	lengthened *ṛ*
ḷ	vocalic *l*, ab*le*
e, ê, ē	m*a*de, esp. in Welsh pronunciation
ai	b*i*te
o, ô, ō	r*o*pe, esp. Welsh pronunciation; Italian s*o*lo
au	s*ou*nd
ṃ	*anusvāra* nasalizes the preceding vowel
ḥ	*visarga*, a voiceless aspiration (resembling English *h*), or like Scottish lo*ch*, or an aspiration with a faint echoing of the preceding vowel so that *taiḥ* is pronounced *taih*^{i}
k	lu*ck*
kh	blo*ckh*ead
g	*g*o
gh	bi*gh*ead
ṅ	a*n*ger
c	*ch*ill
ch	mat*chh*ead
j	*j*og
jh	aspirated *j*, he*dgeh*og
ñ	ca*ny*on
ṭ	retroflex *t*, *t*ry (with the tip of tongue turned up to touch the hard palate)
ṭh	same as the preceding but aspirated
ḍ	retroflex *d* (with the tip of tongue turned up to touch the hard palate)
ḍh	same as the preceding but aspirated
ṇ	retroflex *n* (with the tip

	of tongue turned up to touch the hard palate)
t	French *t*out
th	ten*t h*ook
d	*d*inner
dh	guil*dh*all
n	*n*ow
p	*p*ill
ph	u*ph*eaval
b	*b*efore
bh	a*bh*orrent
m	*m*ind
y	*y*es
r	trilled, resembling the Italian pronunciation of *r*
l	*l*inger
v	*w*ord
ś	*sh*ore
ṣ	retroflex *sh* (with the tip of the tongue turned up to touch the hard palate)
s	hi*ss*
h	*h*ood

CSL PUNCTUATION OF ENGLISH

The acute accent on Sanskrit words when they occur outside of the Sanskrit text itself, marks stress, e.g. Ramáyana. It is not part of traditional Sanskrit orthography, transliteration or transcription, but we supply it here to guide readers in the pronunciation of these unfamiliar words. Since no Sanskrit word is accented on the last syllable it is not necessary to accent disyllables, e.g. Rama.

The second CSL innovation designed to assist the reader in the pronunciation of lengthy unfamiliar words is to insert an unobtrusive middle dot between semantic word breaks in compound names (provided the word break does not fall on a vowel resulting from the fusion of two vowels), e.g. Maha·bhárata, but Ramáyana (not Rama·áyana). Our dot echoes the punctuating middle dot (·) found in the oldest surviving forms of written Indic, the Ashokan inscriptions of the third century BCE.

The deep layering of Sanskrit narrative has also dictated that we use quotation marks only to announce the beginning and end of every direct speech, and not at the beginning of every paragraph.

CSL PUNCTUATION OF SANSKRIT

The Sanskrit text is also punctuated, in accordance with the punctuation of the English translation. In mid-verse, the punctuation will not alter the *sandhi* or the scansion. Proper names are capitalized. Most Sanskrit metres have four "feet" *(pāda):* where possible we print the common *śloka* metre on two lines. In the Sanskrit text, we use French *Guillemets* (e.g. *«kva saṃcicīrṣuḥ?»*) instead of English quotation marks (e.g. "Where are you off to?") to avoid confusion with the apostrophes used for vowel elision in *sandhi*.

Sanskrit presents the learner with a challenge: *sandhi* ("euphonic combination"). *Sandhi* means that when two words are joined in connected speech or writing (which in Sanskrit reflects speech), the last letter (or even letters) of the first word often changes; compare the way we pronounce "the" in "the beginning" and "the end."

In Sanskrit the first letter of the second word may also change; and if both the last letter of the first word and the first letter of the second are vowels, they may fuse. This has a parallel in English: a nasal consonant is inserted between two vowels that would otherwise coalesce: "a pear" and "an apple." Sanskrit vowel fusion may produce ambiguity. The chart at the back of each book gives the full *sandhi* system.

Fortunately it is not necessary to know these changes in order to start reading Sanskrit. For that, what is important is to know the form of the second word without *sandhi* (pre-*sandhi*), so that it can be recognized or looked up in a dictionary. Therefore we are printing Sanskrit with a system of punctuation that will indicate, unambiguously, the original form of the second word, i.e., the form without *sandhi*. Such *sandhi* mostly concerns the fusion of two vowels.

In Sanskrit, vowels may be short or long and are written differently accordingly. We follow the general convention that a vowel with no mark above it is short. Other books mark a long vowel either with a bar called a macron (*ā*) or with a circumflex (*â*). Our system uses the macron, except that for initial vowels in *sandhi* we use a circumflex to indicate that originally the vowel was short, or the shorter of two possibilities (*e* rather than *ai*, *o* rather than *au*).

When we print initial		before *sandhi* that vowel was	
	â,		*a*
	î or *ê*,		*i*
	û or *ô*,		*u*
	âi,		*e*
	âu,		*o*

ā,	*ā* (i.e., the same)
ī,	*ī* (i.e., the same)
ū,	*ū* (i.e., the same)
ē,	*ī*
ō,	*ū*
āi,	*ai*
āu,	*au*
’, before *sandhi* there was a vowel *a*	

FURTHER HELP WITH VOWEL SANDHI

When a final short vowel (*a*, *i* or *u*) has merged into a following vowel, we print ’ at the end of the word, and when a final long vowel (*ā*, *ī* or *ū*) has merged into a following vowel we print ” at the end of the word. The vast majority of these cases will concern a final *a* or *ā*.

Examples:

What before *sandhi* was *atra asti* is represented as *atr’ âsti*

atra āste	*atr’ āste*
kanyā asti	*kany” âsti*
kanyā āste	*kany” āste*
atra iti	*atr’ êti*
kanyā iti	*kany” êti*
kanyā īpsitā	*kany” ēpsitā*

Finally, three other points concerning the initial letter of the second word:

(1) A word that before *sandhi* begins with *ṛ* (vowel), after *sandhi* begins with *r* followed by a consonant: *yatha” rtu* represents pre-*sandhi* *yathā ṛtu*.

(2) When before *sandhi* the previous word ends in *t* and the following word begins with *ś*, after *sandhi* the last letter of the previous word is *c* and the following word begins with *ch*: *syāc chāstravit* represents pre-*sandhi* *syāt śāstravit*.

(3) Where a word begins with *h* and the previous word ends with a double consonant, this is our simplified spelling to show the pre-*sandhi*

form: *tad hasati* is commonly written as *tad dhasati*, but we write *tadd hasati* so that the original initial letter is obvious.

COMPOUNDS

We also punctuate the division of compounds (*samāsa*), simply by inserting a thin vertical line between words. There are words where the decision whether to regard them as compounds is arbitrary. Our principle has been to try to guide readers to the correct dictionary entries.

EXAMPLE

Where the Deva·nágari script reads:

कुम्भस्थली रक्षतु वो विकीर्णसिन्दूररेणुर्द्विरदाननस्य ।
प्रशान्तये विघ्नतमश्छटानां निष्ठ्यूतबालातपपल्लवेव ॥

Others would print:

kumbhasthalī rakṣatu vo vikīrṇasindūrareṇur dviradānanasya /
praśāntaye vighnatamaśchaṭānāṃ niṣṭhyūtabālātapapallaveva //

We print:

kumbha|sthalī rakṣatu vo vikīrṇa|sindūra|reṇur dvirad'|ānanasya
praśāntaye vighna|tamaś|chaṭānāṃ niṣṭhyūta|bāl'|ātapa|pallav" êva.

And in English:

"May Ganésha's domed forehead protect you! Streaked with vermilion dust, it seems to be emitting the spreading rays of the rising sun to pacify the teeming darkness of obstructions."

"Nava·sáhasanka and the Serpent Princess" I.3 by Padma·gupta

INTRODUCTION

'Handsome Nanda' (*Saundarananda*) is a story of religious conversion by an early Indian poet about whom we know very little. The poem's colophon identifies him as the Buddhist monk Ashva·ghosha, a teacher, great poet and eloquent speaker. It also tells us his mother's name and that he lived in Sakéta, now Ayódhya in the modern Indian state of Uttar Pradesh. Informed guesses based on paleography, linguistic style and apocryphal biographical data place him in the early second century CE. Unlike many Buddhist works of Indian origin, 'Handsome Nanda' was not translated into Tibetan or Chinese, nor does it seem to have inspired any commentaries; it would be lost to the world but for H. SHASTRI's fortunate discovery of the complete Sanskrit text in a Nepalese library in 1908. Such unpopularity is entirely unwarranted: beautiful in form and engrossing in content, it succeeds both as a work of poetry and as a Buddhist spiritual biography.

The legend related in 'Handsome Nanda' was widely known and is easily told: once upon a time in the city of Kápila·vastu there was a young man named Nanda who was very much in love with his pretty wife. One day the Buddha comes to Nanda's house for alms but leaves empty-handed. Nanda goes after him, having first promised his wife that he will return while her recently-applied cosmetics are still damp. But the Buddha nevertheless leads Nanda to the monastery, where he is unwillingly ordained. Nanda is unhappy with his life as a monk and longs to go home to his wife. Hearing of this, the Buddha takes him to heaven and shows him the *apsaras*es, a group of ravishingly beautiful celestial nymphs. Nanda immediately forgets all about his wife and is filled with desire for the nymphs. The Buddha promises the nymphs to Nanda if Nanda perseveres in his life as a monk. Nanda agrees, but on hearing from the Buddha's disciple Anánda that his enjoyment of the nymphs would be a temporary and not a permanent reward, he approaches the Buddha, releases him from his pledge, and asks to hear the *dharma*, the Buddha's teachings. The Buddha responds to his request at length, after which Nanda begins meditation practice and soon achieves liberation. The poem concludes with a glimpse of Nanda setting out to preach the *dharma* in his turn.

Ashva·ghosha's 'Handsome Nanda' is the longest, most complex and most convincing formulation of a popular legend that engaged the Buddhist imagination for many centuries. The versions range chronologically from the very early Pali *Udāna* (3.2.21–24)[1] to Sinhalese versions of the 14th century, and stylistically from the simple prose narrative of the Pali *Jātaka* (182) to the highly developed poetical form of Ksheméndra's Sanskrit version included in the *Bodhisattvāvadānakalpalatā*. The early *Udāna* version, which gives a simple, repetitive account of Nanda's unhappiness and his visit to heaven, was subsequently elaborated and interpreted by Dhamma·pala in his *Udāna* Commentary (*Udāna Aṭṭhakathā* 3.2). Dhamma·pala inserts an independent episode at the beginning of the story in order to relate the circumstances under which Nanda joined the order, and to provide convincing motivation for Nanda's lack of enthusiasm for the celibate life of a monk. The *Dhammapada* Commentary (*Dhammapada Aṭṭhakathā* I.9.i) recounts the Nanda story as an explanation for two verses in the

Dhammapada (13–14) that have traditionally been associated with Nanda. Nanda himself is held to be the author of two verses of the *Theragāthā* (157–158), and the *Theragāthā* Commentary (*Theragāthā Aṭṭhakathā* 2.31–34) additionally provides a partial version of his story. There are, too, several Chinese and Tibetan versions of the story. The Nanda story has also attracted the attention of artists and sculptors. Notably, it is depicted on the left wall of Cave XVI at Ajanta; the fresco of Súndari fainting in distress, painted in muted colours and showing a despondent peacock, has become known as "The Dying Princess." The museums at Lucknow and Mathura contain engraved panels of the Kushána period showing Nanda handing his wife a garment and holding a mirror for her.

Despite Ashva·ghosha's debt to traditional material, his work is unique and compelling. He uses the familiar characters and plot of the Nanda legend as a foundation on which to construct a work of complexity and depth. Since the poem presents Nanda's spiritual biography, the emphasis falls on internal events and psychological nuance rather than external action and incidents of plot. Nanda's flow of thought is brilliantly traced: his indecision as he is torn between desire for his wife and respect for the Buddha, his initial passivity and emotional dependence that slowly shade into personal responsibility and self-determination, his solipsistic daydreaming that is eventually replaced by concentrated meditation, and his maturing insight into his own condition are all conveyed with precision and sensitivity—so much so, indeed, that one intuits that the plight of the vacillating hero of 'Handsome Nanda' has a personal resonance for Ashva·ghosha. Perhaps he too was torn between his celibacy-demanding faith and a beloved woman; maybe he too attained a measure of equanimity only after a period of inner conflict.

Poetry or Proselytism?

'Handsome Nanda' is a curious mixture: a generous helping of Buddhist didacticism flavored with a zesty narrative, the lip-smacking nymphs of heaven, a bitter-sweet love story and the condiments of *kāvya*. *Kāvya*, a refined and rather fastidious type of literary Sanskrit, is marked by such features as varied poetic meters, ornate descriptive passages, numerous figurative expressions, euphonic blend of sound, and the purposeful evocation of aesthetic delight. Ashva·ghosha uses these *kāvya* features frequently and skillfully, but they are always subordinate to his message. The real purpose of the poem, we are told in the final two verses, is not to entertain us but to bring us tranquillity. Thus he makes of the *kāvya* form a bribe, a sweetener on which his audience can suck while simultaneously digesting less palatable Buddhist teachings. Ashva·ghosha's commitment to Buddhist ideals and to their propagation among his audience and readership is obvious from both 'Handsome Nanda' and from his other great poem, 'The Life of the Buddha' (*Buddhacarita*). He has no wish merely to entertain his hearers, but to change their lives.

As might be expected of a work with proselytizing ambitions, a substantial proportion of 'Handsome Nanda'—around a quarter of the total length—is given over to instruction in meditation, teachings on eating and sleeping, warnings against sensual excess and so forth. Extensive though these didactic passages are, they contain much to interest scholars in the field of Buddhist Studies and to stimulate Buddhist practitioners, such as Ashva·ghosha's unexpected opinion that it is better to sleep than to engage in inappropriately selected meditation practices (16.78). Furthermore, these passages are rich in figurative language, with vivid similes and engaging comparisons which do much to counteract the tendency to preachiness, and which render abstract and potentially dull topics lively, vivid and concrete. Who could forget the injunction to eat as mindfully and ungreedily as parents who, lost and starving in a desert, are forced to eat their child (14.13)? Or, in a passage asserting the impermanence of the body, the likening of an old person's body to a stick of sugar-cane with all its juices squeezed out, tossed to the ground to dry before it is thrown out for burning (9.31)?

Nanda and the Buddha

The poem's central theme is conversion, a movement away from an inferior condition of worldliness to a superior condition of spiritual perfection and enlightenment. This drama of spiritual re-orientation is centered in the character of Nanda, the Buddha's younger half-brother. Nanda is endowed with certain physical characteristics that are shown to impede his psychological development—he is young, strong and exceptionally good-looking (2.58–59). Not only does he take his current vitality and robustness for granted, but his general appreciation of physicality leads him to over-estimate the worth of sensual pleasure. Nanda's specific problem is a strong sexual appetite or, to use the prevalent Buddhist metaphor, "thirst." His sexuality is portrayed both through his interaction with his wife Súndari in Canto 4 and through his incontinent desire for the *apsaras*es in Canto 10.

Nanda's initial preoccupations hardly conform to the Buddhist ideal of dispassion and non-attachment, yet by the end of the poem he has attained liberation (17.60) and experiences unparalleled bliss (17.65–66). Several forces act on Nanda to facilitate this remarkable transformation from libertine to liberated man. To weaken Nanda's specific fixation with the physical and emotional pleasure to be found in a sexual relationship, an unnamed monk makes an extended attack on female appearance and character, some of it splendidly anti-romantic and anti-*kāvya* in tone (Canto 8). Then, in an effort to correct Nanda's assumption of physical invincibility, the same monk stresses the frailty of the human body and its vulnerability to old age and sickness (Canto 9). Anánda, one of the Buddha's foremost disciples, tries to prove to Nanda that a heavenly rebirth is ultimately as unsatisfactory as any other, since it offers no permanent refuge (Canto 11). Above all, and offsetting Nanda and his constant hankering for sensual gratification, is the figure of the Buddha, the perfected man who experiences no likes or dislikes and who neither seeks out pleasant sensations nor avoids unpleasant ones. It is the Buddha's active intervention that produces the most profound and lasting change in Nanda's life.

Decisive and goal-oriented, the Buddha is always present to persuade, assist, exhort and even coerce Nanda on his journey, sometimes so radically that the imputation of a forced conversion is difficult to avoid. First there are the events described in Canto 5—the Buddha noticing Nanda in the throng of enthusiastic followers and disappearing down a side-road to shake off the crowd whilst retaining Nanda, handing Nanda his begging bowl to make it difficult for him leave, then stepping into Nanda's path to block his exit, and finally turning him over to Anánda to be manhandled towards tonsure. Secondly, the Buddha purposefully increases Nanda's suffering by exposing him to the *apsaras*es, an experience that makes him burn with a desire so fierce that he begs the Buddha to save his life (Canto 10). Ashva·ghosha defends the Buddha mainly on the grounds that Nanda's own passivity and dependent personality demand the Buddha's initiative (verses 5.15–18 for instance). Fundamentally, Nanda must be brought to liberation by the Buddha because he would have been unable to attain it on his own. However, while the Buddha precipitates Nanda's conversion, it does not really take hold until Nanda's own volition gathers sufficient strength. Nanda becomes increasingly able to direct his own salvation from Canto 12 onwards, and in Canto 17, with its aggressive language and military metaphors, we see the final stage in the metamorphosis from Nanda's passive acceptance of the Buddha's interventionist policy to his active control of his own spiritual future. For Ashva·ghosha, it seems, motivation and volition pass from the master to the disciple by degrees.

Conversion Metaphors

Nanda's conversion, which is no single sharply-defined moment of revelation but a long-term process of spiritual growth, is underpinned by several important metaphors, each of which reflects Nanda's initial state, his final state, and a converting action which produces the change from the former to the latter. For instance, Nanda in the early stages of his conversion is portrayed as a wild or ruttish elephant, but once he is approaching liberation, he is likened to a well-trained war elephant. The converting action effecting this transformation is conceived as the capture of the elephant and its submission to a rigorous training programme. More pervasive still is the metaphor of Nanda as a sick man whose primary symptom is passion. The medical scenario of a patient cured of his disease by the medicine dispensed by a doctor provides an excellent conceptual model for Nanda relieved of existential suffering by the teachings of the Buddha. Not all the medical allusions pertain to Nanda alone; the famous penultimate verse (18:63) designates me, and all other readers and auditors of 'Handsome Nanda,' as patients, because we have ingested the medicine that is bottled in this poem. The familiar Buddhist metaphor of the path is also frequently encountered. Here, the Buddha appears as a guide who knows the path and its destination, while his instructions serve as a map. When Nanda strives to realise the Buddha's teachings within his life, he is portrayed as following the path towards the destination of liberation (17.41, for instance), but as long as he fails to do so, he is depicted as a traveler separated from his caravan, wandering in the undemarcated wilderness, as in 5.40.

Metaphors such as these narrate not just Nanda's conversion, but also his characteristic passivity and the subsequent requirement for the Buddha to function as a catalyst. Ashva·ghosha foregoes matter-of-fact reporting of the Buddha's intervention, preferring to tussle with the possibility that Nanda's conversion may be considered too forceful. His justification for the Buddha's strong-arm tactics is conveyed in part through metaphors which regularly stress present pain for future gain. The elephant metaphor delivers the message that the removal of the elephant from its native habitat and its subjection to strict discipline are necessary in order to transform the once wild creature into a noble fighting machine. The medical metaphor in particular provides a persuasive justification for the Buddha's vigorous intervention in Nanda's life, presenting Nanda as a recalcitrant patient who doesn't know what is good for him, and the Buddha as a skilled physician who is obliged to inflict short-term suffering on his patient in order to save his life. Not only do the metaphors record the facilitation of Nanda's conversion by the Buddha, they also bring out the fact that Nanda's conversion, superficial to begin with, does not begin to take hold until he takes charge of his own path to liberation, a change of heart which is surely difficult to convey. The path metaphor, for instance, provides an impressive image of a large vehicle turning round (12.5), while the medical metaphor portays Nanda's evolution from a disobedient patient who refuses to take medical advice to a patient who acknowledges that he is gravely ill and adapts his attitude accordingly. The metaphors are particularly useful in delineating such inner, psychological action.

Ashva·ghosha uses metaphor to concretise psychological events and abstract concepts as familiar everyday objects and occurrences, thus making vivid and visible the essentially private and invisible drama of conversion that is played out in Nanda's heart and mind. The metaphors are always explanatory rather than merely decorative in function: they explain the conversion of Nanda and his reorientation to the Buddhist goal of liberation, thereby revealing Ashva·ghosha as a truly Buddhist poet who is urgently concerned with the dissemination of his message.

The Buddhist Context

To comprehend the poem, it is vital that the reader accept it on its own terms, giving at least temporary credence to the Buddhist values that permeate it. Chief of these is the view of 'Handsome Nanda' that detachment is better than attachment, and that human love and sexuality are the chief obstacles to the attainment of serenity and equanimity. Hence Nanda's emotionality is a major character flaw, his sensuality a defect that prohibits his attainment of the goal of liberation. These flaws must be eradicated in him if his story is to have a happy ending in the Buddhist sense—that is, if he is to escape from the turmoil of samsara and attain the calmness of nirvana, the state of liberation. Since this state of liberation is an escape from relentless rebirth and redeath, it is often qualified in the poem as *amṛta*, deathless.

'Handsome Nanda' is largely accessible to the general reader without further technical knowledge. While it does contain many references to specifics of Buddhist thought, these are annotated where necessary, and the interested reader is directed to the bibliography at the end of this section. For the moment, a few broad remarks will suffice to place the story of Nanda in its Buddhist context.

Samsara is the relentless cycle of rebirth and death, repeated over and over again. Rebirth can occur in various realms—among humankind, or among animals, gods or other non-human beings. This concept is important for understanding Cantos 10 and 11. Thus the divine *apsaras*es are available as sexual playmates only to those who are reborn in heaven. They are not available to Nanda in his human form, in his current life. To win them, Nanda must earn a rebirth as a god, and it is this that he resolves to do at the end of Canto 10. Asceticism was held in high regard, and was commonly believed to be rewarded with an afterlife filled with refined sensual delights of a heavenly standard. Hence the Buddha is able to make a deal with Nanda—ascetic practice and celibacy in this life in return for celestial sex in the next (10.59). Amazingly, Nanda appears to be unaware that heaven is included in samsara, and when informed of this fact, he is devastated (12.4). Everything within samsara (including such happy lives as Nanda's and Súndari's at the beginning of Canto 4, including even the lives of the gods in heaven) is unsatisfactory and liable to suffering (*duḥkha*). The only sure refuge from *duḥkha* is liberation from the entire cycle of samsara, a liberation which occurs only through strict adherence to and understanding of the *dharma*, that set of eternal truths propounded by the Buddha.

A Note on the Edition and Translation

My translation is based on JOHNSTON's critical edition of the *Saundarananda* published in 1928 by the Oxford University Press. I have translated *tathāgata* as "the realized one," but left *sugata* as it is due to lack of suitable equivalents. Liberation, Buddhism's *summum bonum*, is often referred to in the poem as *śreyas*, the best, which I have rendered "Excellence." I have left the word *dharma* untranslated, in the hope that this very frequent word will take on various shades of meaning according to context. *Saṃsāra*, the ongoing cycle of life after life, has also been left untranslated. *Duḥkha*, that fundamental Buddhist concept and the first of the well-known Four Noble Truths, I have generally translated as "unsatisfactoriness" or "suffering." *Śīla*, the cornerstone of Buddhist moral development, expounded in the first half of Canto 13 with an underlying metaphor of cleanliness, has been rendered as "moral self-restraint."

This book is for Niki, with love.

Acknowledgments

Grateful thanks are due to Harunaga Isaacson for the input of the electronic text, and to Richard Gombrich, Lawrence McCrea, Patrick Olivelle, David Smith, and Somadeva Vasudeva for suggestions of emendations and help with tricky passages.

Bibliography

Johnston, E.H. (ed.) (1928). *The Saundarananda of Aśvaghoṣa*. London: Oxford University Press.

Johnston, E.H. (trans. & ed.) (1936). *Aśvaghoṣa's Buddhacarita or Acts of the Buddha*. New Delhi: Munshiram Manoharlal, pp. xiii–xcviii.

Olivelle, P. (trans.) (2007). *The Life of the Buddha (Buddhacarita)*. New York: New York University Press and JJC Foundation.

Rahula, W. (1959) *What the Buddha Taught*. Oxford: Oneworld.

Shastri, Haraprasad (1909). 'The Recovery of a Lost Epic by Aśvaghoṣa.' *Journal of the Asiatic Society of Bengal*, 5, pp. 165–6.

NOTES

1 References to Pali texts are to the editions of the Pali Text Society.

INVOCATION

oṃ namo Buddhāya!

Homage to the Buddha!

CANTO 1
A DESCRIPTION OF KÁPILA·VASTU

1.1 Gautamaḥ Kapilo nāma munir dharma|bhṛtāṃ varaḥ
babhūva tapasi śrāntaḥ Kākṣīvān iva Gautamaḥ,
aśiśriyad yaḥ satataṃ dīptaṃ Kāśyapa|vat tapaḥ
āśiśrāya ca tad|vṛddhau siddhiṃ Kāśyapa|vat parām,
havīṃṣi yaś ca sv'|âtm'|ârthaṃ gām adhukṣad Vasiṣṭha|vat
tapaḥ|śiṣṭeṣu śiṣyeṣu gām adhukṣad Vasiṣṭha|vat,
māh'|ātmyād Dīrghatapaso yo dvitīya iv' âbhavat,
tṛtīya iva yaś c' âbhūt Kāvy'|Āṅgirasayor dhiyā.
1.5 tasya vistīrṇa|tapasaḥ pārśve Himavataḥ śubhe
kṣetraṃ c' āyatanaṃ c' âiva tapasām āśramo 'bhavat.
cāru|vīrut|taru|vanaḥ prasnigdha|mṛdu|śādvalaḥ
havir|dhūma|vitānena yaḥ sad" âbhra iv' ābabhau.
mṛdubhiḥ saikataiḥ snigdhaiḥ kesar'|āstara|pāṇḍubhiḥ
bhūmi|bhāgair a|saṃkīrṇaiḥ s' âṅgarāga iv' âbhavat.
śucibhis tīrtha|saṃkhyātaiḥ pāvanair bhāvanair api
bandhumān iva yas tasthau sarobhiḥ sa|saroruhaiḥ.
paryāpta|phala|puṣpābhiḥ sarvato vana|rājibhiḥ
śuśubhe vavṛdhe c' âiva naraḥ sādhanavān iva.
1.10 nīvāra|phala|saṃtuṣṭaiḥ svasthaiḥ śāntair an|utsukaiḥ
ākīrṇo 'pi tapo|bhṛdbhiḥ śūnya|śūnya iv' âbhavat,
agnīnāṃ hūyamānānāṃ śikhināṃ kūjatām api
tīrthānāṃ c' âbhiṣekeṣu śuśruve yatra nisvanaḥ,
virejur hariṇā yatra suptā medhyāsu vediṣu
sa|lājair mādhavī|puṣpair upahārāḥ kṛtā iva,
api kṣudra|mṛgā yatra śāntāś ceruḥ samaṃ mṛgaiḥ
śaraṇyebhyas tapasvibhyo vinayaṃ śikṣitā iva,

THE SAGE KÁPILA Gáutama was a great upholder of 1.1
dharma. As rigorously ascetic as Kakshívat Gáutama, as ceaselessly fixed on burning asceticism as Káshyapa, he achieved the highest success through its development. He milked his cow for sacrificial milk, like Vasíshtha, and like him too milked speech for his disciples, trained in asceticism. He was like a second Dirgha·tapas in high-mindedness, a third to Kavya and the son of Ángiras in wisdom.

On the bright slopes of the Himalayas this sage of exten- 1.5
sive austerities had his ashram, the domain and abode of asceticism. It was a place of lush and springy grass, sweetly wooded with creepers and trees, seeming cloud-like in its permanent veil of sacrificial smoke. With portions of its grounds soft, sandy, smooth or carpeted with yellow *késara* flowers, it was like a body anointed with unguents. The ashram stood, as though with kinsfolk, amid lotus lakes famed as sacred bathing places, clear, pure and wholesome. With forest avenues all about, bursting with fruit and flowers, the ashram glowed and flourished like a prosperous man.

The ashram seemed deserted, yet was crowded with as- 1.10
cetics, self-contained, calm and quite without avidity, content to live on wild rice and fruit. Here one heard only the sound of fires receiving offerings, peacocks crying, and water splashing in the sacred bathing pools. Here the deer slept in the sacrificial compounds, seemingly made into offerings along with dried rice and *mádhavi* flowers. Here even the smaller animals roamed peaceably alongside the deer, as though they had learned discipline from the ascetics who gave them shelter.

saṃdigdhe 'py a|punar|bhāve viruddheṣv āgameṣv api
pratyakṣiṇa iv' âkurvaṃs tapo yatra tapo|dhanāḥ,

1.15 yatra sma mīyate Brahma kaiś cit kaiś cin na mīyate
kāle nimīyate somo na c' â|kāle pramīyate,

nir|apekṣāḥ śarīreṣu dharme yatra sva|buddhayaḥ
saṃhṛṣṭā iva yatnena tāpasās tepire tapaḥ,

śrāmyanto munayo yatra svargāy' ôdyukta|cetasaḥ
tapo|rāgeṇa dharmasya vilopam iva cakrire.

atha tejasvi|sadanaṃ tapaḥ|kṣetraṃ tam āśramam
ke cid Ikṣvākavo jagmū rāja|putrā vivatsavaḥ,

suvarṇa|stambha|varṣmāṇaḥ siṃh'|ôraskā mahā|bhujāḥ
pātraṃ śabdasya mahataḥ śriyāṃ ca vinayasya ca.

1.20 arha|rūpā hy an|arhasya mah"|ātmānaś cal'|ātmanaḥ
prājñāḥ prajñā|vimuktasya bhrātṛvyasya yavīyasaḥ,

mātṛ|śulkād upagatāṃ te śriyaṃ na viṣehire,
rarakṣuś ca pituḥ satyaṃ yasmāc chiśriyire vanam.

teṣāṃ munir upādhyāyo Gautamaḥ Kapilo 'bhavat
guru|gotrād ataḥ Kautsās te bhavanti sma Gautamāḥ,

eka|pitror yathā bhrātroḥ pṛthag|guru|parigrahāt
Rāma ev' âbhavad Gārgyo, Vāsubhadro 'pi Gautamaḥ.

śāka|vṛkṣa|praticchannaṃ vāsaṃ yasmāc ca cakrire,
tasmād Ikṣvāku|vaṃśyās te bhuvi Śākyā iti smṛtāḥ.

Here the ascetics practiced asceticism as if they could see
its effectiveness right in front of their eyes, even though
their escape from further rebirth was uncertain and their
scriptures inconsistent. Here some contemplated God, none 1.15
committed transgressions, *soma* juice* was measured out at
the right time and no one died at the wrong time. Here the
ascetics, disregarding their bodies and following their own
understanding of *dharma*, distilled asceticism as though delighting in their labor. Here the sages, their minds straining heavenwards, so greatly exerted themselves that they seemed to do violence to *dharma* with their passion for asceticism.

Now one day certain princes of Ikshváku's lineage came
to the ashram, desiring to live in that domain of austerity, the dwelling of those luminaries. They were tall like
golden columns, lion-chested and strong-armed, potential
vessels of wide fame, majesty and self-regulation. The wor- 1.20
thy princes, large-natured and wise, could not stomach the
rank that had come to their unworthy, fickle-minded and
foolish younger half-brother as his mother's dowry, and observing their father's vow, had retreated to the forest.

The sage Kápila Gáutama became their guru, and because of their guru's clan, they who had been Kautsas became Gáutamas, just as Rama had become a Gargya and Vasu·bhadra a Gáutama because of their attendance on different gurus, though the two were brothers and had the same father. And since they made a dwelling roofed with *shaka* trees, the sons of Ikshváku were known on earth as Shakyas.

1.25 sa teṣāṃ Gautamaś cakre sva|vaṃśa|sadṛśīḥ kriyāḥ
munir ūrdhvaṃ kumārasya Sagarasy' êva Bhārgavaḥ,
Kaṇvaḥ Śākuntalasy' êva Bharatasya tarasvinaḥ,
Vālmīkir iva dhīmāṃś ca dhīmator Maithileyayoḥ.
tad vanaṃ muninā tena taiś ca kṣatriya|puṃgavaiḥ
śāntāṃ guptāṃ ca yugapad brahma|kṣatra|śriyaṃ dadhe.

ath' ôda|kalaśaṃ gṛhya teṣāṃ vṛddhi|cikīrṣayā,
muniḥ sa viyad utpatya tān uvāca nṛp'|ātmajān:
«yā patet kalaśād asmād a|kṣayya|salilān mahīm
dhārā, tām an|atikramya mām anveta yathā|kramam.»
1.30 tataḥ «paramam» ity uktvā śirobhiḥ praṇipatya ca
rathān āruruhuḥ sarve śīghra|vāhān alaṃkṛtān.

tataḥ sa tair anugataḥ syandana|sthair nabho|gataḥ
tad āśrama|mahī|prāntaṃ pariciksepa vāriṇā.
aṣṭā|padam iv' ālikhya nimittaiḥ surabhī|kṛtam,
tān uvāca muniḥ sthitvā bhūmi|pāla|sutān idam:
«asmin dhārā|parikṣipte nemi|cihnita|lakṣaṇe,
nirmimīdhvaṃ puraṃ yūyaṃ, mayi yāte triviṣṭapam.»

tataḥ kadā cit te vīrās tasmin pratigate munau,
babhramur yauvan'|ôddāmā gajā iva niraṅkuśāḥ.
1.35 baddha|godh"|âṅgulī|trāṇā hasta|viṣṭhita|kārmukāḥ
śar'|ādhmāta|mahā|tūṇā vyāyat'|ābaddha|vāsasaḥ,
jijñāsamānā nāgeṣu kauśalaṃ śvāpadeṣu ca
anucakrur vana|sthasya Dauṣmanter* deva|karmaṇaḥ.

Afterwards, the sage Gáutama performed their rites in 1.25
keeping with those of his own lineage, as Bhárgava did for the young Ságara, as Kanva did for bold Bhárata the son of Shakúntala, and as wise Valmíki did for the wise sons of Máithili. At one and the same time the forest emanated tranquillity and security, the respective glories of the brahmin and the kshatriya, because of the sage and those warrior heroes.

One day, wishing to ensure their prosperity, the sage took a vessel containing water, flew up into the air and said to the princes: "Follow me in due order, and do not pass beyond the boundary marked out by the drops which will fall to
earth from this vessel of inexhaustible water." "Very well," 1.30
they replied, bowing their heads respectfully, and mounted their finely decorated chariots drawn by swift horses.

Then flying in the air, and followed by them in their chariots, he sprinkled a boundary of water drops round the ashram grounds. The sage mapped out the area like a checkered board made yet lovelier by these happy marks, then stood still and said to the princes: "When I have gone to heaven, build a city here, within this sprinkled boundary, where your wheels have stamped a groove."

In the course of time the sage passed away, and then those heroes wandered with youthful unrestraint, like elephants
without guiding hooks. With their great quivers bristling 1.35
with arrows, their fingers protected by leather straps, their bows extended in their hands and the arrows drawn back, they sought to prove their hunting skills among elephants and wild beasts, in imitation of the godlike deeds of the son of Dushyánta when he lived in the forest. The ascetics

tān dṛṣṭvā prakṛtiṃ yātān vṛddhān vyāghra|śiśūn iva,
tāpasās tad vanaṃ hitvā Himavantaṃ siṣevire.
tatas tad āśrama|sthānaṃ śūnyaṃ taiḥ śūnya|cetasaḥ
paśyanto manyunā taptā vyālā iva niśaśvasuḥ.

atha te puṇya|karmāṇaḥ pratyupasthita|vṛddhayaḥ,
tatra taj|jñair upākhyātān avāpur mahato nidhīn,
1.40 alaṃ dharm'|ârtha|kāmānāṃ nikhilānām avāptaye
nidhayo n' âika|vidhayo bhūrayas te gat'|ârayaḥ.
tatas tat|pratilambhāc ca pariṇāmāc ca karmaṇaḥ
tasmin vāstuni vāstu|jñāḥ puraṃ śrīman nyaveśayan.

sarid|vistīrṇa|parikhaṃ spaṣṭ'|âñcita|mahā|patham
śaila|kalpa|mahā|vapraṃ Girivrajam iv' âparam,
pāṇḍur'|âṭṭāla|sumukhaṃ suvibhakt'|ântar'|āpaṇam
harmya|mālā|parikṣiptaṃ kukṣiṃ Himagirer iva.

veda|vedāṅga|viduṣas tasthuṣuḥ ṣaṭsu karmasu
śāntaye vṛddhaye c' âiva yatra viprān ajījapan,
1.45 tad|bhūmer abhiyoktṝṇāṃ prayuktān vinivṛttaye
yatra svena prabhāvena bhṛtya|daṇḍān ajījapan,
cāritra|dhana|sampannān sa|lajjān dīrgha|darśinaḥ
arhato 'tiṣṭhipan yatra śūrān dakṣān kuṭumbinaḥ.
vyastais tais tair guṇair yuktān mati|vāg|vikram'|ādibhiḥ
karmasu pratirūpeṣu sacivāṃs tān nyayūyujan.
vasumadbhir a|vibhrāntair alaṃ|vidyair a|vismitaiḥ
yad babhāse naraiḥ kīrṇaṃ Mandaraḥ kiṃnarair iva.

noticed that in growing up the princes had reverted to nature, like young tigers, and so they abandoned the forest and retreated to the Himalayas. When the princes saw the ashram empty of ascetics, their hearts were empty too. In their warm grief they hissed like snakes.

Then, their actions being meritorious, and upon the attainment of their maturity, they located great treasures at the site upon the advice of those in the know,* abundant 1.40
treasures of all kinds, arousing no enmity, and enough to fulfill the goals of *dharma*, wealth and pleasure.* Because of those treasure-troves and the fruition of their karma, they could now use their building acumen and erect a glorious city on that site.

It had a moat as broad as a river, wide boulevards which straightened and curved and, as if it were another Giri·vraja, ramparts so great as to almost serve as mountains. It had a fine frontage of white watch-towers and a well laid out center of shops surrounded by crescents of mansions, like a Himalayan valley.

Here they had brahmins, learned in the Vedas and Vedángas and engaged in the six permitted occupations,* recite prayers for peace and prosperity. Here by their own au- 1.45
thority they raised a victorious army of soldiers, drafted to turn back invaders from their land. Here they settled respectable householders of wealth and good character, who were modest, far-sighted, brave and industrious. They appointed counsellors to suitable posts according to their various merits, such as wisdom, eloquence and courage. Crowded with wealthy, orderly, knowledgeable and modest citizens, the city seemed like Mándara filled with *kínnaras*.

yatra te hṛṣṭa|manasaḥ paura|prīti|cikīrṣayā
śrīmanty udyāna|saṃjñāni yaśo|dhāmāny acīkaran,
1.50 śivāḥ puṣkarinīś c' âiva param'|âgrya|guṇ'|âmbhasaḥ
n' ājñayā cetan"|ôtkarṣād dikṣu sarvāsv acīkhanan,
mano|jñāḥ śrīmatīḥ praṣṭhīḥ pathiṣ' ûpavaneṣu ca
sabhāḥ kūpavatīś c' âiva samantāt pratyatiṣṭhipan,
hasty|aśva|ratha|saṃkīrṇam a|saṃkīrṇam an|ākulam
a|nigūḍh'|ârthi|vibhavaṃ nigūḍha|jñāna|pauruṣam,
saṃnidhānam iv' ârthānām ādhānam iva tejasām
niketam iva vidyānāṃ saṃketam iva sampadām,
vāsa|vṛkṣaṃ guṇavatām āśrayaṃ śaraṇ'|âiṣiṇām
ānartaṃ kṛta|śāstrāṇām ālānaṃ bāhu|śālinām.
1.55 samājair utsavair dāyaiḥ kriyā|vidhibhir eva ca
alaṃcakrur alaṃ vīryās te jagad|dhāma tat puram;
yasmād a|nyāyatas te ca kaṃ cin n' âcīkaran karam
tasmād alpena kālena tat tad" âpūpuran puram.
Kapilasya ca tasya ṛṣes tasminn āśrama|vāstuni
yasmāt te tat puraṃ cakrus tasmāt Kapilavāstu tat.
Kakandasya Makandasya Kuśāmbasy' êva c' āśrame
puryo yathā hi śrūyante tath" âiva Kapilasya tat.
āpuḥ puraṃ tat Puruhūta|kalpās
te tejas" āryeṇa na vismayena
āpur yaśo|gandham ataś ca śaśvat
sutā Yayāter iva kīrtimantaḥ.
1.60 tan nātha|vṛttair api rāja|putrair
a|rājakaṃ n' âiva rarāja rāṣṭram,

To please the citizens, the princes gladly commissioned magnificent fame-winning sites and designated them as public gardens. They had lovely lotus pools dug in every 1.50
quarter, with water of the finest quality, not because they were asked to, but because they were noble-minded. On the surrounding roads and in the woods they established splendid first-rate lodges, most welcome, complete even with wells.

The city itself was crowded with elephants, horses and chariots, yet it was not in confusion nor disorder. Its wealth lay open to the needy, while learning and courage were closely tended. It was like a storehouse of wealth, like a repository of brilliance, like a temple of the sciences, like a meeting-place of the accomplishments. It was a homing-tree for the virtuous, a refuge for the vulnerable, an arena for the learned and a tethering-post for the strong.

The heroes embellished that city, the glory of the world, 1.55
with assemblies, festivals, patronage and rites; and since they never raised unjust taxes, in no long time they populated the city, named Kápila·vastu because they had built it on the ashram of the seer Kápila. Just as the cities built on the hermitage-sites of Kakánda, Makánda and Kushámba were named for them, so was it named for Kápila.

The princes protected the city in a manner befitting 1.60
much-invoked Indra, with vigor and nobility, but without arrogance, and won for themselves the perpetual scent of glory like the renowned sons of Yayáti. But though they conducted themselves royally, the country could not reach full brilliance without a king, just as the night sky can-

tārā|sahasrair api dīpyamānair
anutthito candra iv' ântarīkṣam.
yo jyāyān atha vayasā guṇaiś ca teṣāṃ
bhrātṝṇāṃ vṛṣabha iv' âujasā vṛṣāṇām;
te tatra priya|guravas tam abhyaṣiñcann
Ādityā Daśa|śata|locanaṃ div' îva.
ācāravān vinayavān nayavān kriyāvān
dharmāya n' êndriya|sukhāya dhṛt'|ātapatraḥ
tad bhrātṛbhiḥ parivṛtaḥ sa jugopa rāṣṭraṃ
Saṃkrandano divam iv' ânusṛto Marudbhiḥ.

Saundaranande mahā|kāvye Kapilavāstu|varṇano nāma prathamaḥ sargaḥ.

not reach full brilliance when the moon has not yet risen, though a thousand stars twinkle.

Now just as the leader of a herd of bulls is marked out by his strength, so was the eldest of the brothers marked out by his seniority and good qualities; and with affection for this eldest brother they consecrated him king, as the Ádityas did thousand-eyed Indra in heaven. Virtuous, disciplined, politic and pious, he bore the royal umbrella for the sake of *dharma* and not to gratify his senses. With the support of his brothers he guarded his realm as Indra with his retinue of Maruts guards heaven.

End of Canto 1: A Description of Kápila·vastu.

CANTO 2
A DESCRIPTION OF THE KING

2.1 TATAḤ KADĀ cit kālena tad avāpa kula|kramāt
rājā Śuddhodhano nāma śuddha|karmā jit'|êndriyaḥ,
yaḥ sasañje na kāmeṣu śrī|prāptau na visismiye
n' âvamene parān ṛddhyā parebhyo n' âpi vivyathe,
balīyān sattva|sampannaḥ śrutavān buddhimān api
vikrānto nayavāṃś c' âiva dhīraḥ sumukha eva ca,
vapuṣmāṃś ca na ca stabdho dakṣiṇo na ca n' ārjavaḥ
tejasvī na ca na kṣāntaḥ kartā ca na ca vismitaḥ.
2.5 ākṣiptaḥ śatrubhiḥ saṃkhye suhṛdbhiś ca vyapāśritaḥ
abhavad yo na vimukhas tejasā ditsay" âiva ca.
yaḥ pūrvai rājabhir yātāṃ yiyāsur dharma|paddhatim
rājyaṃ dīkṣām iva vahan vṛtten' ânvagamat pitṝn.
yasya su|vyavahārāc ca rakṣaṇāc ca sukhaṃ prajāḥ
śiśyire vigat'|ôdvegāḥ pitur aṅka|gatā iva.
kṛta|śāstraḥ kṛt'|âstro vā jāto vā vipule kule
a|kṛt'|ârtho na dadṛśe yasya darśanam eyivān.
hitaṃ vipriyam apy ukto yaḥ śuśrāva na cukṣubhe
duṣ|kṛtaṃ bahv api tyaktvā sasmāra kṛtam aṇv api.
2.10 praṇatān anujagrāha vijagrāha kula|dviṣaḥ
āpannān parijagrāha nijagrāh' â|sthitān pathi.
prāyeṇa viṣaye tasya tac|chīlam anuvartinaḥ
arjayanto dadṛśire dhanān' îva guṇān api.

AFTER SOME time a king named Shuddhódana, pure in conduct and controlled in senses, one day came to the throne through familial succession. He was not preoccupied with sensuality, nor arrogant in winning sovereignty, nor contemptuous of others by reason of his own success, nor did he quail before his enemies. He was mighty, courageous, learned and wise, as well as bold, politic, serious-minded and fair of face; handsome but not obstinate, pleasant but not insincere, energetic but not impatient, active but not overbearing. 2.1

When his enemies challenged him in battle, he did not 2.5
shy from fierceness, nor from generosity when his friends approached as supplicants. In his wish to follow the foot-path of *dharma* trodden by previous kings, he modeled his conduct on that of his ancestors, treating his kingship as a consecration. Thanks to his good government and protection, his subjects slept soundly, undisturbed, like children in their father's lap. No one who came to see him, whether accomplished in learning or weaponry or born to the nobility, failed to achieve his goals.

He listened even to disagreeable advice without agitation; he overlooked the greatest wrong-doing and remembered
the smallest service. He upheld the humble, and held off 2.10
his family's foes, held his hand out to the wretched, and held back drifters from the path. Those within his realm generally followed his moral self-restraint; they looked as though they were earning virtues like money.

adhyaiṣṭa yaḥ paraṃ brahma na vyaiṣṭa satataṃ dhṛteḥ
dānāny adita pātrebhyaḥ pāpaṃ n' âkṛta kiṃ cana.
dhṛty" âvākṣīt pratijñāṃ sa sad|vāj" îv' ôdyatāṃ dhuram,
na hy avāñcīc cyutaḥ satyān muhūrtam api jīvitam.
viduṣaḥ paryupāsiṣṭa vyakāśiṣṭ' ātmavattayā,
vyarociṣṭa ca śiṣṭebhyo mās' īṣe candramā iva.
2.15 avedīd buddhi|śāstrābhyām iha c' âmutra ca kṣamam;
arakṣīd dhairya|vīryābhyām indriyāṇy api ca prajāḥ.
ahārṣīd duḥkham ārtānāṃ dviṣatāṃ c' ōrjitaṃ yaśaḥ;
acaiṣīc ca nayair bhūmiṃ bhūyasā yaśas" âiva ca.
apyāsīd duḥkhitān paśyan prakṛtyā karuṇ'|ātmakaḥ;
n' âdhauṣīc ca yaśo lobhād a|nyāy'|âdhigatair dhanaiḥ.
sauhārda|dṛḍha|bhaktitvān maitreṣu viguṇeṣv api,
n' âdidāsīd aditsīt tu saumukhyāt svaṃ svam arthavat.
a|nivedy' âgram arhadbhyo n' âlikṣat kiṃ cid a|plutaḥ;
gām a|dharmeṇa n' âdhukṣat kṣīra|tarṣeṇa gām iva.
2.20 n' âsṛkṣad balim a|prāptaṃ n' ârukṣan mānam aiśvaram;
āgamair buddhim ādhikṣad dharmāya na tu kīrtaye.
kleś'|ârhān api kāṃś cit tu n' âkliṣṭa kliṣṭa|karmaṇaḥ;
ārya|bhāvāc ca n' âghukṣad dviṣato 'pi sato guṇān.
ākṛkṣad vapuṣā dṛṣṭīḥ prajānāṃ candramā iva;
parasvaṃ bhuvi n' âmṛkṣan mahā|viṣam iv' ôragam.

He studied high religious knowledge, his resolution never ceased, he was generous to worthy recipients, and he did no evil. He carried out his promises rigorously, as a good horse carries the burden it has accepted, since he would not have wished to live a moment longer were he ever to deviate from telling the truth. He honored the wise yet radiated self-possession, and delighted the learned like the harvest moon. With his intelligence and his education, he knew what was 2.15
appropriate both for this world and the next; with constancy and vigor he guarded his senses as well as his subjects.

He removed their sorrows from the suffering, and from his enemies he removed their mighty reputations; he covered the earth with his good government and great fame. His was a compassionate nature, which welled up when he beheld suffering; but greed could never drive him to damage his reputation with improperly attained wealth. Staunchly loyal and affectionate to his friends, even if they had failings, he did not take from them but cheerfully gave to each according to his need.

He would not eat unless he had first bathed and made an offering to worthy persons; nor did he milk the earth unjustly, as a thirsty man might overmilk a cow. He made 2.20
no untimely offering, and did not develop lordly pride; he applied his intellect to the scriptures for the sake of *dharma*, not for renown. He did not pass harsh sentence on those few who had done wrong, even when they deserved it; and his noble nature did not permit him to conceal the qualities of a good man, even if he were an enemy. His fine appearance drew the gaze of his subjects as does the moon; as if it were

n' âkrukṣad viṣaye tasya kaś cit kaiś cit kva cit kṣataḥ,
adikṣat tasya hasta|stham ārtebhyo hy a|bhayaṃ dhanuḥ.
kṛt'|āgaso 'pi praṇatān prāg eva priya|kāriṇaḥ
adarśat snigdhayā dṛṣṭyā ślakṣṇena vacas" âsicat.

2.25 bahvīr adhyagamad vidyā viṣayeṣv a|kutūhalaḥ,
sthitaḥ kārta|yuge dharme dharmāt kṛcchre 'pi n' âsrasat.
avardhiṣṭa guṇaiḥ śaśvad avṛdhan mitra|sampadā;
avartiṣṭa ca vṛddheṣu n' âvṛtad garhite pathi.

śarair aśīśamac chatrūn guṇair bandhūn arīramat;
randhrair n' âcūcudad bhṛtyān karair n' âpīpiḍat prajāḥ.
rakṣṇāc c' âiva śauryāc ca nikhilāṃ gām avīvapat;
spaṣṭayā daṇḍa|nītyā ca rātri|sattrān avīvapat.
kulaṃ rāja'|rṣi|vṛttena yaśo|gandham avīvapat
dīptyā tama iv' ādityas tejas" ârīn avīvapat

2.30 apaprathat pitṝṃś c' âiva sat|putra|sadṛśair guṇaiḥ;
salilen' êva c' âmbhodo vṛtten' âjihladat prajāḥ.

dānair ajasra|vipulaiḥ somaṃ viprān asūṣavat;
rāja|dharma|sthitatvāc ca kāle sasyam asūṣavat.
a|dharmiṣṭhām acakathan na kathām a|kathaṃkathaḥ;
cakra|vart" îva ca parān dharmāy' âbhyudasīṣahat.
rāṣṭram anyatra ca baler na sa kiṃ cid adīdapat;
bhṛtyair eva ca s'|ôdyogaṃ dviṣad|darpam adīdapat.

a poisonous snake upon the ground, he never laid hold of the property of others in his land.

No one anywhere in his kingdom cried injury from others, for his bow signified to the downtrodden that safety was at hand. He let his gentle gaze and soft words fall not only on those that had previously done him service, but
also on those offenders who submitted to him. He had no 2.25
interest in sensuality, but studied many sciences, keeping to *dharma* as it was in the golden age and not straying from it even in rough times. He continually grew in virtue, and he thrived on the success of his friends; he followed his elders, but would not proceed along a censured path.

He subdued his enemies with his arrows, and gladdened his kinsmen with his merits; he did not goad his servants by referring to their weaknesses, nor did he oppress his subjects with taxes. He cultivated the whole earth through his protection and valor, and with his transparent administration of justice he fostered overnight sacrifices. By his conduct as a king-seer he sowed the fragrance of fame in his family; he scattered his enemies with his radiance as the sun
scatters darkness with light. He glorified his ancestors with 2.30
virtues that befit a true son; and like a cloud with its rain, he gladdened his subjects with his conduct.

The brahmins pressed *soma* juice because of his continuing generous patronage; and the corn came to seasonable harvest because of his adherence to his royal *dharma*. He did not make unrighteous speeches, nor did he give voice to doubts; and like a true wheel-turning emperor he inspired his enemies to turn to *dharma*. He did not oblige his people to pay anything other than rightful taxes; and he

svair ev' âdīdapac c' âpi bhūyo bhūyo guṇaiḥ kulam;
prajā n' âdīdapac c' âiva sarva|dharma|vyavasthayā.

2.35 a|śrāntaḥ samaye yajvā yajña|bhūmim amīmapat;
pālanāc ca dvijān brahma nir|udvignān amīmapat.
gurubhir vidhivat kāle saumyaḥ somam amīmapat;
tapasā tejasā c' âiva dviṣat|sainyam amīmapat.
prajāḥ parama|dharma|jñaḥ sūkṣmaṃ dharmam avīvasat;
darśanāc c' âiva dharmasya kāle svargam avīvasat.

vyaktam apy artha|kṛcchreṣu n' â|dharmiṣṭham atiṣṭhipat;
priya ity eva c' â|śaktaṃ na saṃrāgād avīvṛdhat.
tejasā ca tviṣā c' âiva ripūn dṛptān abībhasat,
yaśo|dīpena dīptena pṛthivīṃ ca vyabībhasat.

2.40 ānṛśaṃsyān na yaśase ten' âdāyi sad" ârthine,
dravyaṃ mahad api tyaktvā na c' âiv' âkīrti kiṃ cana.
ten' ârir api duḥkh'|ārto n' âtyāji śaraṇ'|āgataḥ;
jitvā dṛptān api ripūn na ten' âkāri vismayaḥ.

na ten' âbhedi maryādā kāmād dveṣād bhayād api,
tena satsv api bhogeṣu n' âsev' îndriya|vṛttitā.
na ten' âdarśi viṣamaṃ kāryaṃ kva cana kiṃ cana;
vipriya|priyayoḥ kṛtye na ten' âgāmi nikriyāḥ.

energetically excised the arrogance of enemies using just his regular troops. More and more did his family shine through his own good qualities; and he had no need to compel his subjects, since they were all established in *dharma*.

When occasion demanded, he was an untiring worship- 2.35
per, arranging for the place of sacrifice to be measured out; and due to his protection, the twice-born could offer their prayers unhindered. This gentle king had the gurus mete out *soma* juice at the appropriate times according to injunction while by his austerity and brilliance he diminished the army of his enemies. Knower of the highest *dharma*, he ensured that his subjects lived within the subtleties of *dharma*; and because his subjects understood *dharma*, he ensured that they in due course would dwell in heaven.

He would not employ an unrighteous man in difficult times, even one who seemed the obvious person; nor, out of affection, would he promote an incompetent friend. He burned up his proud enemies with his luster and splendor, and he brightened the earth with the shining lamp of his
fame. He always gave to those in need, not for the sake 2.40
of his reputation but from benevolence, and even when he had distributed great largesse he did not boast of it. Even an enemy in trouble who came to him for help would not be turned away; and he did not become proud, though he conquered arrogant enemies.

He transgressed no moral boundary, whether out of desire, hatred or fear, and though pleasures were available to him, he did not cultivate sensuality. Under no circumstance was any kind of irregularity observed in him; and in his obligations to either friend or enemy he never resorted to deceit.

ten' âpāyi yathā|kalpaṃ somaś ca yaśa eva ca
vedaś c' âmnāyi satataṃ ved'|ôkto dharma eva ca.
2.45 evam|ādibhir a|tyakto babhūv' â|sulabhair guṇaiḥ
a|śakyaḥ śakya|sāmantaḥ Śākya|rājaḥ sa Śakra|vat.

atha tasmiṃs tathā kāle dharma|kāmā divaukasaḥ
vicerur diśi lokasya dharma|caryāṃ didṛkṣavaḥ.
dharm'|ātmānaś carantas te dharma|jijñāsayā jagat
dadṛśus taṃ viśeṣeṇa dharm'|ātmānaṃ nar'|âdhipam.
devebhyas Tuṣitebhyo 'tha bodhisattvaḥ kṣitiṃ vrajan,
upapattiṃ praṇidadhe kule tasya mahī|pateḥ.

tasya devī nṛ|devasya Māyā nāma tad" âbhavat,
vīta|krodha|tamo|māyā Māy" êva divi devatā.
2.50 svapne 'tha samaye garbham āviśantaṃ dadarśa sā
ṣaḍ|dantaṃ vāraṇaṃ śvetam Airāvatam iv' âujasā.
taṃ vinirdidiśuḥ śrutvā svapnaṃ svapna|vido dvijāḥ
tasya janma kumārasya lakṣmī|dharma|yaśo|bhṛtaḥ.

tasya sattva|viśeṣasya jātau jāti|kṣay'|âiṣiṇaḥ
s'|âcalā pracacāl' ôrvī taraṅg'|âbhihat" êva nauḥ.
sūrya|raśmibhir a|kliṣṭaṃ puṣpa|varṣaṃ papāta khāt,
dig|vāraṇa|kar'|ādhūtād vanāc Caitrarathād iva.
divi dundubhayo nedur dīvyatāṃ Marutām iva;
didīpe 'bhyadhikaṃ sūryaḥ śivaś ca pavano vavau.
2.55 tutuṣus Tuṣitāś c' âiva Śuddhāvāsāś ca devatāḥ
sad|dharma|bahumānena sattvānāṃ c' ânukampayā.

He drank *soma* juice in conformity with ritual and took care of his good name, with constant recall of the Vedas and also of the *dharma* as directed by the Vedas.

Never deficient in rare qualities such as these was that 2.45
king of the Shakyas, who with his capable feudatories was as unconquerable as Indra.

Now at that time the *dharma*-loving denizens of heaven, hoping to see *dharma* in action, traversed the world in all directions. Moving over the earth with a wish to know its *dharma*, the *dharma*-beings saw this king whose nature was particularly given to *dharma*. The bodhisattva then proceeded from the Túshita gods to earth, resolving to take birth in the family of the king.

The king had at that time a queen named Maya, free from anger, mental darkness and duplicity, like the goddess Maya
in heaven. She in due course saw in her sleep a six-tusked 2.50
white elephant, mighty as Airávata, entering her womb. When brahmins versed in dreams heard about this dream, they foretold the birth of a prince, a bearer of honor, majesty and *dharma*.

At the birth of this excellent being who sought the end of the cycle of birth, the wide earth with its mountains shook like a vessel tossed on the waves. A rain of blossom unwilted by the sun's rays fell from the sky, as though from the trees of Chitra·ratha's forest when shaken by the trunks of the elephants at the corners of the world.* In the sky drums resounded as though the Maruts were gaming; the
sun blazed beyond measure and a fair wind blew. The gods 2.55
of the Túshita and Shuddhavása heavens rejoiced out of reverence for the true *dharma* and out of fellow feeling

samāyayau yaśaḥ|ketuṃ śreyaḥ|ketu|karaḥ paraḥ
babhrāje śāntayā lakṣmyā dharmo vigrahavān iva.

devyām api yavīyasyām araṇyām iva pāvakaḥ
Nando nāma suto jajñe nity'|ānanda|karaḥ kule.
dīrgha|bāhur mahā|vakṣāḥ siṃh'|âṃso vṛṣabh'|ēkṣaṇaḥ
vapuṣ" âgryeṇa yo nāma sundar'|ôpapadaṃ dadhe.
madhu|māsa iva prāptaś candro nava iv' ôditaḥ
aṅgavān iva c' ân|aṅgaḥ sa babhau kāntayā śriyā.

2.60 sa tau saṃvardhayām āsa nar'|êndraḥ parayā mudā,
arthaḥ saj|jana|hasta|stho dharma|kāmau mahān iva.
tasya kālena sat|putrau vavṛdhāte bhavāya tau
āryasy' ārambha|mahato dharm'|ârthāv iva bhūtaye.
tayoḥ sat|putrayor madhye Śākya|rājo rarāja saḥ
madhya|deśa iva vyakto Himavat|Pāriyātrayoḥ.

tatas tayoḥ saṃskṛtayoḥ krameṇa
nar|êndra|sūnvoḥ kṛta|vidyayoś ca,
kāmeṣv ajasraṃ pramamāda Nandaḥ
Sarvārthasiddhas tu na saṃrarañja.
sa prekṣy' âiva hi jīrṇam āturaṃ ca mṛtaṃ ca
vimṛśañ jagad an|abhijñam ārta|cittaḥ
hṛdaya|gata|para|ghṛṇo na viṣaya|ratim agamaj
janana|maraṇa|bhayam abhito vijighāṃsuḥ.

for all living things. To him whose banner was fame came the bearer of the banner of Excellence, the supreme one, radiating calm splendor like *dharma* incarnate.

As kindling gives rise to fire, so the younger queen too gave birth to a son named Nanda, a bringer of constant joy to his family. He was long-armed and wide-chested, with the shoulders of a lion and the eyes of a bull—and he bore the epithet "handsome" due to his superlative looks. He was like the onset of springtime in his pleasing loveliness, like the rising of the new moon, or like the god of love* in human form.

The king brought up the two with much joy, just as 2.60
great wealth in good hands fosters *dharma* and pleasure. In time his two good sons grew up to do him credit, just as *dharma* and wealth bring profit to a gentleman with ambitious projects. Between his two good sons the king of the Shakyas stood resplendent like the middle country between the Himalayas and the Vindhya mountains.

The two princes gradually grew in refinement and learning, but while Nanda for ever idled away his time in pleasures, Sarvártha·siddha was not so colored. For he had seen an old man, a sick man and a corpse, and heart-sore he pondered how the world took no cognizance of these things. With his heart moved to compassion, he took no pleasure in sensuality, but instead wished to destroy the perils of birth and death that lay all around him.

2.65 udvegād a|punar|bhave manaḥ praṇidhāya
sa yayau śayita|var'|âṅganāsv anāsthaḥ
niśi nṛ|pati|nilayanād vana|gamana|kṛta|manāḥ
sarasa iva mathita|nalināt kalahaṃsaḥ.

Saundaranande mahā|kāvye Rāja|varṇano nāma
dvitīyaḥ sargaḥ.

Distressed, he set his mind on freedom from rebirth and decided to go to the forest. Like a goose leaving a lake of bruised lotuses, he left the king's palace at night, indifferent to the beautiful women sleeping in it. 2.65

End of Canto 2: A Description of the King.

CANTO 3
A DESCRIPTION OF THE REALIZED ONE

3.1 TAPASE TATAḤ Kapilavāstu
hayalgajalrath'|âughalsaṃkulam
śrīmad a|bhayam anurakta|janaṃ
sa vihāya niścita|manā vanaṃ yayau.
vividh'|āgamāṃs tapasi tāṃś ca
vividha|niyam'|āśrayān munīn
prekṣya sa viṣaya|tṛṣā|kṛpaṇān
an|avasthitaṃ tapa iti nyavartata.
atha mokṣa|vādinam Ārāḍam
upaśama|matiṃ tath" Ôḍrakam
tattva|kṛta|matir upāsya jahāv
ayam apy a|mārga iti mārga|kovidaḥ.
sa vicārayañ jagati kiṃ tu
paramam? iti taṃ tam āgamam,
niścayam an|adhigataḥ parataḥ
paramaṃ cacāra tapa eva duṣ|karam.
3.5 atha n' âiṣa mārga iti vīkṣya
tad api vipulaṃ jahau tapaḥ.
dhyāna|viṣayam avagamya paraṃ
bubhuje var'|ânnam amṛtatva|buddhaye.
sa suvarṇa|pīna|yuga|bāhur
ṛṣabha|gatir āyat'|ēkṣaṇaḥ,
plakṣam avaniruham abhyagamat
paramasya niścaya|vidher bubhutsayā.
upaviśya tatra kṛta|buddhir
acala|dhṛtir adri|rājavat,
Māra|balam ajayad ugram atho
bubudhe padaṃ śivam a|hāryam a|vyayam.

Then leaving behind the safe and splendid city of Kápila·vastu, loved by its citizens, crowded with numbers of horses, elephants and chariots, he went to the forest with his heart set on asceticism. 3.1

He noticed that the sages held varying doctrines concerning asceticism and that they followed a variety of practices, yet were still miserable for want of sensual experience. So he turned away, concluding that asceticism was unreliable. Then, still bent on truth, he became the disciple of Aráda, who spoke of liberation, and likewise of Údraka, who inclined to quietism. But in his wisdom concerning paths he left them, aware that theirs were not the right paths. Of the many doctrines in the world, he pondered, which one was supreme? Not meeting with answers elsewhere, he began strenuous asceticism after all. Then, ascertaining that 3.5
this was not the path, he abandoned that extreme asceticism too. He understood that the practice of meditation was best, and he ate good food to prepare himself for comprehending deathlessness.

With his golden arms as thick as a yoke, his bull-like gait and elongated eyes, he came to a fig-tree intent on discovering the highest certain knowledge. Resolutely sitting there, as unmovingly constant as the king of the mountains, he conquered Mara's fierce forces and awoke to the happy, unalterable and imperishable state.

avagamya taṃ ca kṛta|kāryam
amṛta|manaso divaukasaḥ
harṣam a|tulam agaman muditā,
vimukhī tu Māra|pariṣat pracukṣubhe.
sa|nagā ca bhūḥ pravicacāla,
huta|vaha|sakhaḥ śivo vavau,
nedur api ca sura|dundubhayaḥ,
pravavarṣa c' âmbu|dhara|varjitaṃ nabhaḥ.

3.10 avabudhya c' âiva param'|ârtham
a|jaram anukampayā vibhuḥ
nityam amṛtam upadarśayituṃ
sa Varāṇasī|parikarām ayāt purīm.
atha dharma|cakram ṛta|nābhi
dhṛti|mati|samādhi|nemimat
tatra vinaya|niyam'|āram ṛṣir
jagato hitāya pariṣady avartayat.
«iti duḥkham etad, iyam asya
samudaya|latā pravartikā,
śāntir iyam, ayam upāya» iti
pravibhāgaśaḥ param idaṃ catuṣṭayam
abhidhāya ca tri|parivartam
a|tulam a|nivartyam uttamam
dvādaśa|niyata|vikalpam ṛṣir
vininend Kauṇḍina|sa|gotram āditaḥ.
sa hi doṣa|sāgaram a|gādham
upadhi|jalam ādhi|jantukam,
krodha|mada|bhaya|taraṅga|calaṃ
pratatāra lokam api ca vyatārayat.

When they recognized that he had accomplished his task, the deities in heaven, whose minds were set on deathlessness, felt boundless joy and delight, but Mara's followers were hostile and agitated. The earth with its mountains quaked, an auspicious wind blew, the drums of the gods reverberated, and it began to rain from a cloudless sky.

After perceiving the highest, ageless truth, the lord in 3.10
his compassion made his way to river-encircled Varánasi to reveal enduring deathlessness to its citizens. And among the people assembled there, for the welfare of the world, the seer set in motion the wheel of *dharma*, whose hub is truth, whose rim is constancy, thought and meditation and whose spokes are the rules of the Vínaya.*

"This is suffering, this is the network of causes producing it, this is its pacification, this is the means." Thus the seer separately set forth the highest fourfold truth which is unequaled, incontrovertible and supreme, with its three divisions and twelve connecting statements, and he guided to insight firstly a man from the Kúndina clan. For the seer had passed over the fathomless sea of faults—which is watered by conditioned existence, which has anxious thoughts for fish, and which is disturbed by waves of anger, desire and fear—and he carried the world across too.

3.15 sa vinīya Kāśiṣu Gayeṣu
bahu|janam atho Girivraje
pitryam api parama|kāruṇiko
nagaraṃ yayāv anujighṛkṣayā tadā.
viṣay'|ātmakasya hi janasya
bahu|vividha|mārga|sevinaḥ
sūrya|sadṛśa|vapur abhyudito
vijahāra sūrya iva Gautamas tamaḥ.
abhitas tataḥ Kapilavāstu
parama|śubha|vāstu|saṃstutam
vastu|mati|śuci śiv'|ôpavanaṃ
sa dadarśa niḥ|spṛhatayā yathā vanam.
a|parigrahaḥ sa hi babhūva
niyata|matir ātman' īśvaraḥ,
n' âika|vidha|bhaya|kareṣu kim u
sva|jana|sva|deśa|jana|mitra|vastuṣu.
pratipūjayā na sa jaharṣa,
na ca śucam avajñay" âgamat.
niścita|matir asi|candanayor
na jagāma duḥkha|sukhayoś ca vikriyām.
3.20 atha pārthivaḥ samupalabhya
sutam upagataṃ Tathāgatam,
tūrṇam a|bahu|turag'|ânugataḥ
suta|darśan'|ôtsukatay" âbhiniryayau.
Sugatas tathāgatam avekṣya
nara|patim a|dhīram āśayā
śeṣam api ca janam aśru|mukhaṃ
vininīṣayā gaganam utpapāta ha.
sa vicakrame divi bhuv' îva
punar upaviveśa tasthivān,

After guiding many people to insight in Kashi, Gaya and Giri·vraja, he wished to show favor also to his ancestral city, and so with supreme compassion he made his way there. For just as the risen sun dispels darkness, so Gáutama with his sun-like appearance dispelled the dark ignorance of sensual people who followed a number of different paths. 3.15

Then he saw Kápila·vastu all around him, with its gracious gardens, famed for its beautiful architecture and pure in its financial and intellectual life, but he looked without longing, as though at a forest. For restrained in his thoughts and master of himself, he was without appurtenances, not even of family, countrymen, friends or property, which engender all sorts of anxieties. He felt no pleasure when revered, nor was he hurt by slights. Unperturbed by violent sword or luxurious sandalwood, he remained unaltered in sorrow or happiness.

Hearing that his son had become a realized man, the king was so eager to see him that he set out hurriedly attended by few horses. The Súgata noticed that the king had arrived in an excitable state and full of expectations and that the rest of the people had tearful faces, so with the intention of guiding them to insight he rose up into the air. 3.20

He walked in the air as though on the earth, and then stopped and sat down, then lay down, his mind immoveable. He multiplied himself into many forms and then be-

niścala|matir aśayiṣṭa punar
bahudh" âbhavat punar abhūt tath" âikadhā.
salile kṣitāv iva cacāra
jalam iva viveśa medinīm.
megha iva divi vavarṣa punaḥ
punar ajvalan nava iv' ôdito raviḥ.
yugapaj jvalañ jvalana|vac ca
jalam avasṛjaṃś ca megha|vat
tapta|kanaka|sadṛśa|prabhayā
sa babhau pradīpta iva sandhyayā ghanaḥ.

3.25 tam udīkṣya hema|maṇi|jāla|
valayinam iv' ôtthitaṃ dhvajam,
prītim agamad a|tulāṃ nṛ|patir
janatā natāś ca bahumānam abhyayuḥ.

atha bhājanī|kṛtam avekṣya
manuja|patim ṛddhi|sampadā
paura|janam api ca tat|pravaṇaṃ
nijagāda dharma|vinayaṃ vināyakaḥ.
nṛ|patis tataḥ prathamam āpa
phalam a|mṛta|dharma|siddhaye
dharmam a|tulam adhigamya muner
munaye nanāma sa yato gurāv iva.

came just one again. He walked on water as though on the earth, and he sank into the ground as though into water. He rained like a cloud in the sky, and he shone like the newly-risen sun. Simultaneously blazing like a fire and giving water like a cloud, he was radiant with light like molten
gold, like a cloud at twilight. Looking up at him as at a raised 3.25
standard hung about with a filigree of gold and jewels, the king's rapture was unbounded, and his subjects bowed in reverence.

Then, perceiving that his psychic accomplishments had made the king a suitable recipient for instruction and perceiving also that the townsfolk were well-disposed to him, the Teacher proclaimed the *dharma* and the discipline. The king then acquired the first fruit for the complete attainment of the deathless *dharma*,* and since he had acquired the unequaled *dharma* from the sage, he bowed to the sage as to a guru.

bahavaḥ prasanna|manaso 'tha
janana|maraṇ'|ārti|bhīravaḥ
Śākya|tanaya|vṛṣabhāḥ kṛtino
vṛṣabhā iv' ânala|bhayāt pravavrajuḥ.
vijahus tu ye 'pi na gṛhāṇi
tanaya|pitṛ|mātr|apekṣayā
te 'pi niyama|vidhim ā maraṇāj
jagṛhuś ca yukta|manasaś ca dadhrire.

3.30 na jihiṃsa sūkṣmam api jantum
api para|vadh'|ôpajīvanaḥ.
kiṃ bata vipula|guṇaḥ kula|jaḥ
sadayaḥ sadā, kim u muner upāsakaḥ!
a|kṛś'|ôdyamaḥ kṛśa|dhano 'pi
para|paribhav'|â|saho 'pi san,
n' ânya|dhanam apajahāra tathā
bhujagād iv' ânya|vibhavādd hi vivyathe.
vibhav'|ânvito 'pi taruṇo 'pi
viṣaya|capal'|êndriyo 'pi san,
n' âiva ca para|yuvatīr agamat
paramaṃ hi tā dahanato 'py amanyata.
an|ṛtaṃ jagāda na ca kaś cid,
ṛtam api jajalpa n' â|priyam.
ślakṣṇam api ca na jagāv a|hitaṃ,
hitam apy uvāca na ca paiśunāya yat.
manasā lulobha na ca jātu,
para|vasuṣu gṛddha|mānasaḥ.
kāma|sukham a|sukhato vimṛśan,
vijahāra tṛpta iva tatra saj|janaḥ.

Then many eminent sons of the Shakyas, pure-minded, virtuous and as wary of birth, death and disease as bulls of a forest fire, went forth as wanderers. Even those who stayed at home out of consideration for their children or parents accepted the restraints of the precepts until death, and they
kept them assiduously. Those who had made their living 3.30
through butchery no longer injured any living creature, even tiny ones. And oh, how gentle always was the man of noble family, with his abundant good qualities, and even more so the lay disciples of the sage!

Even the man of unremitting labor poorly remitted, not lightly tolerating humiliations from others, even he did not carry off the goods of others, for he shrank from others' wealth as from a snake. Even the man of money and youth, with his senses itching for action, even he did not approach the wives of others, for he considered them more dangerous than fire.

No one told an untruth, and even if something was true, no one made it nasty gossip. No one, even slyly, said anything hurtful to others, and even when speaking to others' benefit, no one told tales. No man ever suffered mental yearnings, with greedy thoughts about other people's riches. Good folk took sensual pleasures to be a source of discomfort, and lived as though they were satisfied without them.

3.35 na parasya kaś cid apaghātam
api ca sa|ghṛṇo vyacintayat,
mātṛ|pitṛ|suta|suhṛt|sadṛśaṃ
sa dadarśa tatra hi parasparaṃ janaḥ.
niyataṃ bhaviṣyati paratra
bhavad api ca bhūtam apy atho
karma|phalam api ca loka|gatir
niyat" êti darśanam avāpa sādhu ca.
iti karmaṇā daśa|vidhena
parama|kuśalena bhūriṇā
bhraṃśini śithila|guṇo 'pi yuge
vijahāra tatra muni|saṃśrayāj janaḥ.
na ca tatra kaś cid upapatti|
sukham abhilalāṣa tair guṇaiḥ.
sarvam a|śivam avagamya bhavaṃ
bhava|saṃkṣayāya vavṛte na janmane.
a|kathaṃkathā gṛhiṇa eva
parama|pariśuddha|dṛṣṭayaḥ
srotasi hi vavṛtire bahavo
rajasas tanutvam api cakrire pare.
3.40 vavṛte 'tra yo 'pi viṣameṣu
vibhava|sadṛśeṣu kaś cana
tyāga|vinaya|niyam'|âbhirato
vijahāra so 'pi na cacāla sat|pathāt.
api ca svato 'pi parato 'pi
na bhayam abhavan na daivataḥ;
tatra ca susukha|subhikṣu|guṇair
jahṛṣuḥ prajāḥ kṛta|yuge Manor iva.

The people in their fellow-feeling never even dreamed of harming others, for they saw each other as mother, father, child, friend. They also attained the proper insight that actions will inevitably bear fruit in a future state, that they do so in the present, and that they have done so in the past, and that passage to another world is certain. Though virtue was lax in that declining age, with the help of the sage the people lived according to the ten great rules of conduct which are so highly meritorious. 3.35

No one there wanted a happy rebirth as a reward for his virtues. People understood that all existence was harmful, therefore they were intent on the cessation of existence, not on its continuation. Even the householders were free from doubt, and their views were lofty and pure; for many were stream-entrants,* while others had minimized their passions. Even those who had been preoccupied with harmful 3.40 things, such as luxury, now spent their time content with charitable giving and the rules of the Vínaya, and never swerved from the right path. Nor did anyone fear harm from himself, from others or from fate; the people there rejoiced in great ease, abundant in provisions and virtue, as in the golden age of Manu.

iti muditam an|āmayaṃ nir|āpat
Kuru|Raghu|Pūru|pur'|ôpamaṃ puraṃ tat
abhavad a|bhaya|daiśike maha"|rṣau
viharati tatra śivāya vīta|rāge.

iti Saundaranande mahā|kāvye Tathāgata|varṇano nāma
tṛtīyaḥ sargaḥ.

So with the great dispassionate sage living there, pointing it to safety for its own good, the city rejoiced, free from disease or calamity, like the cities of Kuru, Raghu or Puru.

End of Canto 3: A Description of the Realized One.

CANTO 4
HIS WIFE'S REQUEST

4.1 MUNAU BRUVĀṆE 'pi tu tatra dharmaṃ
dharmaṃ prati jñātiṣu c' ādṛteṣu,
prāsāda|saṃstho madan'|âika|kāryaḥ
priyā|sahāyo vijahāra Nandaḥ.
sa cakravāky" êva hi cakravākas
tayā sametaḥ priyayā priy'|ârhaḥ
n' âcintayad Vaiśravaṇaṃ na Śakraṃ
tat|sthāna|hetoḥ kuta eva dharmam.
lakṣmyā ca rūpeṇa ca Sundar" îti
stambhena garveṇa ca Mānin" îti
dīptyā ca mānena ca Bhāmin" îti
yato babhāṣe tri|vidhena nāmnā.
sā hāsa|haṃsā nayana|dvirephā
pīna|stan'|âtyunnata|padma|kośā;
bhūyo babhāse sva|kul'|ôditena
strī|padminī Nanda|divākareṇa.
4.5 rūpeṇa c' âtyanta|manohareṇa
rūp'|ânurūpeṇa ca ceṣṭitena,
manuṣya|loke hi tadā babhūva
sā sundarī strīṣu nareṣu nandaḥ.
sā devatā Nandana|cāriṇ" îva
kulasya nandī|jananaś ca Nandaḥ
atītya martyān anupetya devān
sṛṣṭāv abhūtām iva bhūta|dhātrā.
tāṃ Sundarīṃ cen na labheta Nandaḥ
sā vā niṣeveta na taṃ nata|bhrūḥ,
dvandvaṃ dhruvaṃ tad vikalaṃ na śobhet'
ânyonya|hīnāv iva rātri|candrau.
Kandarpa|Ratyor iva lakṣya|bhūtaṃ
pramoda|nāndyor iva nīḍa|bhūtam

THOUGH THE sage was in the city teaching the *dharma*, 4.1
and though his near relations honored the *dharma*, Nanda stayed in his palace with his wife, making love his only concern. For Nanda was fitted for love, and so lived united with his beloved like a *chakra·vaka* bird with its mate. In this situation he thought of neither Váishravana nor Shakra, let alone the *dharma*. She was known by three different names: Súndari for her charm and beauty, Mánini for her stubbornness and disdain, and Bhámini for her sparkle and willfulness.

She seemed a lotus-pool in womanly form, with her laughter for swans, her eyes for bees and her swelling breasts as budding lotus calyxes; still more did she shine after the
sun-like Nanda had arisen in her own family. With her 4.5
captivating beauty and manner to match, in the world of humankind she,Súndari, was the loveliest of women and he, Nanda, the happiest of men.* The Creator had made them greater than mortals, though not yet gods—she, walking the Nándana gardens like a divinity, and Nanda, bringer of joy to his kin. If Nanda had not won her, Súndari, or if she, arch-browed, had withheld herself from him, then the pair would surely have appeared impaired, like the night and the moon without each other.

Blind with passion, the couple took their pleasure in each other, as though they were the targets of Kandárpa and Rati, as though they were a home to joy and rapture, as though

praharṣa|tuṣṭyor iva pātra|bhūtaṃ
dvandvaṃ sah' âraṃsta mad'|ândha|bhūtam.
paraspar'|ôdvīkṣaṇa|tat|par'|âkṣaṃ,
paraspara|vyāhṛta|sakta|cittam
paraspar'|āśleṣa|hṛt'|âṅgarāgaṃ
parasparaṃ tan mithunaṃ jahāra.

4.10 bhāv'|ânuraktau giri|nirjhara|sthau
tau kiṃnarī|kiṃpuruṣāv iv' ôbhau,
cikrīḍatuś c' âbhivirejatuś ca
rūpa|śriy" ânyonyam iv' ākṣipantau.
anyonya|saṃrāga|vivardhanena tad
dvandvam anyonyam arīramac ca,
klam'|ântare 'nyonya|vinodanena
salīlam anyonyam amīmadac ca.

vibhūṣayām āsa tataḥ priyāṃ sa
siṣeviṣus tāṃ na mṛj"|āvah'|ârtham;
sven' âiva rūpeṇa vibhūṣitā hi
vibhūṣaṇānām api bhūṣaṇaṃ sā.
dattv" âtha sā darpaṇam asya haste
«mam' âgrato dhāraya tāvad enam
viśeṣakaṃ yāvad ahaṃ karom' îty»
uvāca kāntaṃ sa ca taṃ babhāra.
bhartus tataḥ śmaśru nirīkṣamāṇā
viśeṣakaṃ s" âpi cakāra tādṛk.
niśvāsa|vātena ca darpaṇasya
cikitsayitvā nijaghāna Nandaḥ.

they were a vessel for arousal and satiety. With eyes only for each other's eyes, they hung upon each other's words and rubbed off their cosmetics through caressing each other, so mutually absorbed was the couple. They were resplendent 4.10
in their play like a *kínnari* and a *kímpurusha* standing in a mountain waterfall intent on love, as though wishing to outdo each other in beauty and splendor. The couple gave each other pleasure by exciting passion in each other, while in languid moments they teasingly inebriated each other by way of mutual entertainment.

At one time he arranged her jewellery on her, not to make her lovelier, but to do her a service; for she was so adorned by her own beauty that it was she who lent loveliness to her jewels. She put a mirror into his hand and said to her lover, "Just hold this in front of me while I do my *vishéshaka*,"* and he held it. Then, looking at her husband's mustache, she made up her *vishéshaka* just like it, but Nanda blew on the mirror to remedy this.

4.15 sā tena ceṣṭā|lalitena bhartuḥ
śāṭhyena c' ântar|manasā jahāsa
bhavec ca ruṣṭā kila nāma tasmai
lalāṭa|jihmāṃ bhrukuṭiṃ cakāra,
cikṣepa karṇ'|ôtpalam asya c' âṃse
kareṇa savyena mad'|ālasena.
pattr'|âṅguliṃ c' ârdha|nimīlit'|âkṣe
vaktre 'sya tām eva vinirdudhāva.
tataś calan|nūpura|yoktritābhyāṃ
nakha|prabh"|ôdbhāsitar'|âṅgulibhyām
padbhyāṃ priyāyā nalin'|ôpamābhyāṃ
mūrdhnā bhayān nāma nanāma Nandaḥ.
sa mukta|puṣp'|ônmiṣitena mūrdhnā
tataḥ priyāyāḥ priya|kṛd babhāse
suvarṇa|vedyām anil'|âvabhagnaḥ
puṣp'|âtibhārād iva nāga|vṛkṣaḥ.
sā taṃ stan'|ôdvartita|hāra|yaṣṭir
utthāpayām āsa nipīḍya dorbhyām.
«kathaṃ|kṛto 's' îti!» jahāsa c' ôccair
mukhena sācī|kṛta|kuṇḍalena.
4.20 patyus tato darpaṇa|sakta|pāṇer
muhur muhur vaktram avekṣamāṇā,
tamāla|pattr'|ārdra|tale kapole
samāpayām āsa viśeṣakaṃ tat.
tasyā mukhaṃ tat sa|tamāla|pattraṃ
tāmr'|âdhar'|âuṣṭhaṃ cikur'|āyat'|âkṣam,
rakt'|âdhik'|âgraṃ patita|dvirephaṃ
sa|śaivalaṃ padmam iv' âbabhāse.
Nandas tato darpaṇam ādareṇa
bibhrat tadā maṇḍana|sākṣi|bhūtam

She smiled to herself at her husband's cheekiness and playful little game, but furrowed her brow as though annoyed, and with her left hand, languorous with wine, she threw the lotus from behind her ear at his shoulder. Then she smeared some of her make-up on his face and half-closed eyes. 4.15

Nanda, in a pretence of fear, bent his head to his lover's lotus feet—feet encircled with swaying anklets, with toes brightened by their shimmering nails. His head blossoming with loosened flowers as he begged his lover's pardon, he resembled a *naga* plant overburdened with flowers, bending over its golden pedestal in the breeze.* She pressed him close in her arms and raised him up, making the strands of her pearl necklace lift off her breast. "What are you doing?" she cried laughingly, as her earrings were pushed sideways from her face.

While she finished applying the *vishéshaka* to her cheeks, damp with *tamála* paste,* she kept looking at her husband's face as he held the mirror in his hand. Her own face, with its *tamála* paste, lips touched with red and eyes extending to her hair, seemed a moss-bedecked, crimson-tipped lotus settled by bees. 4.20

So Nanda dutifully held the mirror which bore witness to her act of adornment, and as he squinted to watch her maquillage, he observed his lover's mischievous face. Nanda

viśeṣak'|âvekṣaṇa|kekar'|âkṣo
    laḍat|priyāyā vadanaṃ dadarśa.
tat|kuṇḍal'|ādaṣṭa|viśeṣak'|āntaṃ
    kāraṇḍava|kliṣṭam iv' âravindam
Nandaḥ priyāyā mukham īkṣamāṇo
    bhūyaḥ priy"|ānanda|karo babhūva.
  vimāna|kalpe sa vimāna|garbhe
    tatas tathā c' âiva nananda Nandaḥ,
Tathāgataś c' āgata|bhaikṣa|kālo
    bhaikṣāya tasya praviveśa veśma.

4.25 avāṅ|mukho niṣ|praṇayaś ca tasthau
    bhrātur gṛhe 'nyasya gṛhe yath" âiva.
tasmād atho preṣya|jana|pramādād
    bhikṣām a|labdhv" âiva punar jagāma—
kā cit pipeṣ' âṅga|vilepanaṃ hi,
    vāso 'ṅganā kā cid avāsayac ca,
ayojayat snāna|vidhiṃ tath" ânyā,
    jagranthur anyāḥ surabhīḥ srajaś ca.
tasmin gṛhe bhartur ataś carantyaḥ
    krīḍ"|ânurūpaṃ lalitaṃ niyogam
kāś cin na Buddhaṃ dadṛśur yuvatyo
    Buddhasya v" âiṣā niyataṃ manīṣā.

made his sweetheart happier than ever when he watched her face, the edge of its *vishéshaka* smudged by her earrings so that it seemed a lotus nibbled by a *karándava* bird.

While Nanda was thus enjoying himself in his palace, which was like a celestial palace, the Tathágata, the realized one, entered his home for alms, since it was the time for his alms-round. Looking downwards and without ask- 4.25
ing for anything, he stood in his brother's house as he would in the house of any other person. But he went away again without obtaining any alms because of the household's preoccupation—one woman was grinding body-unguents, another was perfuming clothes, one was preparing a bath, and others were weaving fragrant garlands. The Buddha came to the unavoidable conclusion that the housemaids were so busy carrying out frivolous tasks related to their master's dalliance that none of them noticed him.

kā cit sthitā tatra tu harmya|pṛṣṭhe
gavākṣa|pakṣe praṇidhāya cakṣuḥ
viniṣpatantaṃ Sugataṃ dadarśa
payoda|garbhād iva dīptam arkam.
sā gauravaṃ tatra vicārya bhartuḥ
svayā ca bhakty" ârhatay" ârhataś ca,
Nandasya tasthau purato vivakṣus
tad|ājñayā c' êti tad" ācacakṣe:
4.30 «anugrahāy' âsya janasya śaṅke
gurur gṛhaṃ no bhagavān praviṣṭaḥ,
bhikṣām a|labdhvā giram āsanaṃ vā
śūnyād araṇyād iva yāti bhūyaḥ.»
śrutvā maha"|rṣeḥ sa gṛha|praveśaṃ
satkāra|hīnaṃ ca punaḥ prayāṇam,
cacāla citr'|ābharaṇ'|âmbara|srak
kalpa|drumo dhūta iv' ânilena.
kṛtv" âñjaliṃ mūrdhani padma|kalpaṃ
tataḥ sa kāntāṃ gamanaṃ yayāce.
«kartuṃ gamiṣyāmi gurau praṇāmaṃ.
māṃ abhyanujñātum ih' ârhas' îti?»
sā vepamānā parisasvaje taṃ
śālaṃ latā vāta|samīrit" êva.
dadarśa c' âśru|pluta|lola|netrā
dīrghaṃ ca niśvasya vaco 'bhyuvāca:
«n' âhaṃ yiyāsor guru|darśan'|ârtham
arhāmi kartuṃ tava dharma|pīḍām.
gacch', ārya|putr', âihi ca śīghram eva
viśeṣako yāvad ayaṃ na śuṣkaḥ.
4.35 saced* bhaves tvaṃ khalu dīrgha|sūtro
daṇḍaṃ mahāntaṃ tvayi pātayeyam;

However, one woman at the top of the palace had glanced at a side-window, and she had seen the Súgata emerging like the radiant sun from a cloud. Taking into consideration her master's deep respect for the enlightened one as well as his worthiness and her own devotion to him, she approached
Nanda to tell him, and spoke at his permission: "The Blessed 4.30
One, the guru, entered our house, presumably as a favor to you. He received no alms, no conversation, and no seat, and so he is going away as though from an empty forest."

When he heard that the great seer had come to his house, found no hospitality and left again, he trembled, seeming, with his bright decorations, garments and garlands, like a tree of Paradise swaying in the wind. Putting his hands together in the shape of a lotus, he raised them to his forehead and asked his wife if he might leave. "I would like to go and pay my respects to the guru. Will you let me?" She held him close and shivered like a wind-stirred creeper encircling a *shala* tree. Looking at him with her rolling eyes filled with tears, she sighed deeply and replied:

"You wish to leave in order to see the guru, and I ought not to hinder you in your duty. Go, my dear husband, but
come back quickly before my *vishéshaka* dries. If you are late, 4.35
I will punish you severely; as you lie sleeping, I will keep waking you up by brushing against you with my breasts, but then refuse to talk to you. But if you hurry back to me before my *vishéshaka* is dry, I will hold you in my arms, bare of ornaments and still damp with unguents." Her voice shook

muhur muhus tvāṃ śayitaṃ kucābhyāṃ
vibodhayeyaṃ ca na c' ālapeyam.
ath' âpy an|āśyāna|viśeṣakāyāṃ
mayy eṣyasi tvaṃ tvaritaṃ tatas tvām
nipīḍayiṣyāmi bhuja|dvayena
nir|bhūṣaṇen' ārdra|vilepanena.»
ity evam uktaś ca nipīḍitaś ca
tay" â|sa|varṇa|svanayā jagāda.
«evaṃ kariṣyāmi. vimuñca, caṇḍi,
yāvad gurur dūra|gato na me saḥ.»
tataḥ stan'|ôdvartita|candanābhyāṃ
mukto bhujābhyāṃ na tu mānasena.
vihāya veṣaṃ madan'|ânurūpaṃ
satkāra|yogyaṃ sa vapur babhāra.
sā taṃ prayāntaṃ ramaṇaṃ pradadhyau
pradhyāna|śūnya|sthita|niścal'|âkṣī,
sthit" ôcca|karṇā vyapaviddha|śaṣpā
bhrāntaṃ mṛgaṃ bhrānta|mukhī mṛg" îva.
4.40 didṛkṣay" ākṣipta|manā munes tu
Nandaḥ prayāṇaṃ prati tatvare ca,
vivṛtta|dṛṣṭiś ca śanair yayau tāṃ
kar" îva paśyan sa laḍat|kareṇum.
chāt'|ôdarīṃ pīna|payodhar'|ōruṃ
sa Sundarīṃ rukma|darīm iv' âdreḥ
kākṣeṇa paśyan na tatarpa Nandaḥ
pibann iv' âikena jalaṃ kareṇa.
taṃ gauravaṃ Buddha|gataṃ cakarṣa
bhāry"|ânurāgaḥ punar ācakarṣa.
so '|niścayān n' âpi yayau na tasthau
turaṃs taraṅgeṣv iva rāja|haṃsaḥ.

as she spoke, and she embraced him. "I will," he replied. "Now let me go, my little vixen, before the guru has gone too far."

So she let him go from her arms which were scented with sandal from her breast, but she did not let him go in her mind. He set aside the clothes suited to love-making, and made himself presentable for paying his respects. She contemplated her departing lover, her face troubled and her eyes empty and unmoving in her preoccupation, like a doe standing with ears pricked up and chewed grass falling
from her mouth as she watches the stag wander off. With 4.40
his thoughts taken up by his wish to see the sage, Nanda hurried his departure, then lingered with a backward glance at her, like an elephant watching a playful she-elephant. But a glance at Súndari, her waist compact between her swelling breasts and thighs like a golden fissure in a mountain, could no more satisfy Nanda than drinking water with one hand.

Reverence for the Buddha drew him on, love for his wife drew him back again. He hesitated, neither going nor staying, like a king-goose pushing forwards against the waves. However, once she was no longer in his sight, he came briskly out of the palace, only to hang back again, his heart

a|darśanaṃ t' ûpagataś ca tasyā
harmyāt tataś c' âvatatāra tūrṇam,
śrutvā tato nūpura|nisvanaṃ sa
punar lalambe hṛdaye gṛhītaḥ.
sa kāma|rāgeṇa nigṛhyamāṇo
dharm'|ânurāgeṇa ca kṛṣyamāṇaḥ,
jagāma duḥkhena nivartyamānaḥ
plavaḥ pratisrota iv' āpagāyāḥ.

4.45 tataḥ kramair dīrghatamaiḥ pracakrame
«kathaṃ nu yāto na gurur bhaved» iti
«svajeya tāṃ c' âiva viśeṣaka|priyāṃ
kathaṃ priyām ārdra|viśeṣakām» iti.
atha sa pathi dadarśa mukta|mānaṃ
pitṛ|nagare 'pi tathā|gat'|âbhimānam
daśa|balam abhito vilambamānaṃ
dhvajam anuyāna iv' āindram arcyamānam.

Saundaranande mahā|kāvye Bhāryā|yācitako nāma
caturthaḥ sargaḥ.

contracting, at the sound of her anklets. Kept back by his passion for love, and drawn forward by his attachment to *dharma,* he proceeded with difficulty, being turned about like a boat going upstream on a river.

Then setting out with long strides, he thought "The guru 4.45
can't possibly not be gone by now!" and "Perhaps I'll be able to hug my darling girl, whose love is so special, while her *vishéshaka* is still wet."

Then on the road he saw him of the ten powers,* free from pride even in his father's city, and with all arrogance similarly gone, stopping everywhere and being worshipped like Indra's banner in a procession.

End of Canto 4: His Wife's Request.

CANTO 5
NANDA IS MADE TO ORDAIN

5.1 ATH' ÂVATĪRY' âśva|ratha|dvipebhyaḥ
Śākyā yathā|sva|rddhi gṛhīta|veṣāḥ,
mah"|āpaṇebhyo vyavahāriṇaś ca
mahā|munau bhakti|vaśāt praṇemuḥ.
ke cit praṇamy' ânuyayur muhūrtaṃ,
ke cit praṇamy' ârtha|vaśena jagmuḥ,
ke cit svakeṣv âvasatheṣu tasthuḥ
kṛtv" âñjalīn vīkṣaṇa|tat|par'|âkṣāḥ.
Buddhas tatas tatra nar'|êndra|mārge
sroto mahad|bhaktimato janasya
jagāma duḥkhena vigāhamāno
jal'|āgame srota iv' āpagāyāḥ.
atho mahadbhiḥ pathi sampatadbhiḥ
sampūjyamānāya Tathāgatāya,
kartuṃ praṇāmaṃ na śaśāka Nandas,
ten' âbhireme tu guror mahimnā.
5.5 svaṃ c' âvasaṅgaṃ pathi nirmumukṣur
bhaktiṃ janasy' ânya|mateś ca rakṣan
Nandaṃ ca geh'|âbhimukhaṃ jighṛkṣan
mārgaṃ tato 'nyaṃ Sugataḥ prapede.
tato viviktaṃ ca vivikta|cetāḥ
san|mārga|vin mārgam abhipratasthe
gatv" âgrataś c' âgryatamāya tasmai
nāndī|vimuktāya nanāma Nandaḥ.
śanair vrajann eva sa gauraveṇa
paṭ'|āvṛt'|âṃso vinat'|ârdha|kāyaḥ
atho nibaddh'|âñjalir ūrdhva|netraḥ
sa|gadgadaṃ vākyam idaṃ babhāṣe:
«prāsāda|saṃstho bhagavantam antaḥ|
praviṣṭam aśrauṣam anugrahāya,

THEN THE SHAKYAS, their clothes befitting their wealth, got down from their horses, chariots and elephants, while merchants came from their large stores, and overcome by devotion to the great sage, they bowed low. After honoring him, some followed him for a short while, others had to leave due to the demands of their work, while some stood outside their houses with their hands folded in respect and their eyes absorbed in gazing at him. Then the Buddha walked along the royal highway, making his way with difficulty through the stream of greatly devoted people there, as if through a streaming monsoon river. Because of the large numbers on the road flocking to offer homage to the realized one, Nanda was not able to pay his respects, but he was pleased by the guru's eminence. 5.1

Wishing to dismiss his own disciples whilst fostering the devotion of people of other persuasions, and intending also to catch hold of Nanda who was already turning towards home, the Súgata set out along a different route. When the judicious knower of the right path reached an isolated road, Nanda went in front and bowed down to him, the foremost man, who was free of the desire for pleasure. Walking slowly and respectfully, with one shoulder covered by his garment and his body in a semi-stoop, Nanda joined his hands in a gesture of reverence, raised his eyes, and stammered out these words: 5.5

"When I was in my palace, I heard that the Blessed One had favored us with a visit, so I have come in a hurry, indignant with the attendants of my large household. It

atas tvarāvān aham abhyupeto
   gṛhasya kakṣyāṃ mahato* 'bhyasūyan.
tat sādhu sādhu|priya mat|priy'|ârthaṃ
   tatr' âstu bhikṣ'|ûttama bhaikṣa|kālaḥ.
asau hi madhyaṃ nabhaso yiyāsuḥ
   kālaṃ pratismārayat' îva sūryaḥ!»

5.10 ity evam uktaḥ praṇatena tena
   sneh'|âbhimān'|ônmukha|locanena.
tādṛṅ nimittaṃ Sugataś cakāra
   n' āhāra|kṛtyaṃ sa yathā viveda,
tataḥ sa kṛtvā munaye praṇāmaṃ
   gṛha|prayāṇāya matiṃ cakāra.
anugrah'|ârthaṃ Sugatas tu tasmai
   pātraṃ dadau puṣkara|pattra|netraḥ.

tataḥ sa loke dadataḥ phal'|ârthaṃ
   pātrasya tasy' â|pratimasya pātram
jagrāha cāpa|grahaṇa|kṣamābhyāṃ
   padm'|ôpamābhyāṃ prayataḥ karābhyām.
parāṅ|mukhas tv anya|manaskam ārād
   vijñāya Nandaḥ Sugataṃ gat'|āstham,
hasta|stha|pātro 'pi gṛhaṃ yiyāsuḥ
   sasāra mārgān munim īkṣamāṇaḥ.
bhāry"|ânurāgeṇa yadā gṛhaṃ sa
   pātraṃ gṛhītv" âpi yiyāsur eva,
vimohayām āsa munis tatas taṃ
   rathyā|mukhasy' āvaraṇena tasya.

5.15 nir|mokṣa|bījaṃ hi dadarśa tasya
   jñānaṃ mṛdu kleśa|rajaś ca tīvram,
kleś'|ânukūlaṃ viṣay'|ātmakaṃ ca.
   Nandaṃ yatas taṃ munir ācakarṣa.

would be an excellent thing, and a kindness to me, if you, beloved of the good, best of monks, were to spend your alms-time at my house. And look, the sun is heading towards the middle of the sky, as though to remind us of the time!"*

He bowed as he spoke, his eyes raised in affection and 5.10
reverence. The Súgata, however, showed with a gesture that he did not require food, and as he had now completed his courtesies to the sage, Nanda decided to go home. But the Súgata, his eyes like lotus petals, handed him his bowl as an act of grace.

So with his lotus hands more suited to holding a bow, he devotedly took the bowl of that matchless vessel who gave it for the sake of reward in the world.* Yet at that moment Nanda realized that the Súgata had his mind on other things and was not concentrating on him, so with his head turned to keep his eye on the sage he moved away from the road, intending to go home, though he still had the bowl in his hands. Longing for his wife, he was just about to go home even holding the bowl, when the sage confused him by blocking the entrance to the street.

For the sage saw that knowledge, the seed of liberation, 5.15
was weak in him while the dirt of the defilements* was strong in him, and that his disposition tended to the defilements and to sensuality. Therefore he pressured Nanda. There are two different possibilities regarding defilements,

saṃkleśa|pakṣo dvi|vidhaś ca dṛṣṭas,
tathā dvi|kalpo vyavadāna|pakṣaḥ:
ātm'|āśrayo hetu|bal'|âdhikasya
bāhy'|āśrayaḥ pratyaya|gauravasya.
a|yatnato hetu|bal'|ādhikas tu
nirmucyate ghaṭṭita|mātra eva,
yatnena tu pratyaya|neya|buddhir
vimokṣam āpnoti par'|āśrayeṇa.
Nandaḥ sa ca pratyaya|neya|cetā
yaṃ śiśriye tan|mayatām avāpa.
yasmād imaṃ tatra cakāra yatnaṃ
taṃ sneha|paṅkān munir ujjihīrṣan.
Nandas tu duḥkhena viceṣṭamānaḥ
śanair a|gatyā gurum anvagacchat,
bhāryā|mukhaṃ vīkṣaṇa|lola|netraṃ
vicintayann ārdra|viśeṣakaṃ tat.
5.20 tato munis taṃ priya|mālya|hāraṃ
vasanta|māsena kṛt'|âbhihāram
nināya bhagna|pramadā|vihāraṃ
vidyā|vihār'|âbhimataṃ vihāram.
dīnaṃ mahā|kāruṇikas tatas taṃ
dṛṣṭvā muhūrtaṃ karuṇāyamānaḥ,
kareṇa cakr'|âṅka|talena mūrdhni
pasparśa c' âiv' êdam uvāca c' âinam:
«yāvan na hiṃsraḥ samupaiti kālaḥ
śamāya tāvat kuru, saumya, buddhim.
sarvāsv avasthāsv iha vartamānaḥ
sarv'|âbhisāreṇa nihanti mṛtyuḥ.
sādhāraṇāt svapna|nibhād a|sārāl
lolaṃ manaḥ kāma|sukhān niyaccha.

and likewise there are two alternative possibilities regarding purification: the superior man of strong motivation is self-dependent, while the man for whom faith is important is dependent on something external to himself. The superior man of strong motivation is liberated effortlessly with just the merest nudge, but the man whose mind is governed by faith attains liberation with difficulty, and only through dependence on someone else.

Now Nanda, whose mind was governed by faith, became absorbed in whomever he depended on. That is why the sage, wishing to lift him out of the mire of love, made an effort for him.

Nanda followed the guru slowly and helplessly, contorted with grief, thinking of his wife's face with its *vishéshaka* no longer wet and her restless eyes watching for him. He 5.20
had been so fond of garlands and necklaces, he had been assailed by the spring months! Now the sage led him to the monastery, which was considered the recreation ground of knowledge, and where pleasure in women was inoperative.

The greatly compassionate one saw his distress in an instant, and pitied him. He laid his hand with its wheel-marked palm on Nanda's head and said:

"Dear friend, Death is present in every situation and strikes in many ways. Before that dread time arrives, make sure your mind is composed. Hold back your restless mind from the sense-pleasures common to all, which are dream-like and insubstantial. For sensual pleasures are no more satisfying for people than oblations are for a wind-blown fire.

havyair iv' âgneḥ pavan'|ēritasya
lokasya kāmair na hi tṛptir asti.
śraddhā|dhanaṃ śreṣṭatamaṃ dhanebhyaḥ,
prajñā|rasas tṛpti|karo rasebhyaḥ,
pradhānam adhyātma|sukhaṃ sukhebhyo,
vidyā|ratir duḥkhatamā ratibhyaḥ.

5.25 hitasya vaktā pravaraḥ suhṛdbhyo,
dharmāya khedo guṇavāñ chramebhyaḥ,
jñānāya kṛtyaṃ paramaṃ kriyābhyaḥ.
kim indriyāṇām upagamya dāsyam?
tan niścitaṃ bhī|klama|śug|viyuktaṃ
pareṣv an|āyattam a|hāryam anyaiḥ,
nityaṃ śivaṃ śānti|sukhaṃ vṛṇīṣva,
kim indriy'|ârth'|ârtham an|artham ūḍhvā?
jarā|samā n' âsty a|mṛjā prajānāṃ,
vyādheḥ samo n' âsti jagaty an|arthaḥ,
mṛtyoḥ samaṃ n' âsti bhayaṃ pṛthivyām:
etat trayaṃ khalv avaśena sevyam.
snehena kaś cin na samo 'sti pāśaḥ,
sroto na tṛṣṇā|samam asti hāri,
rāg'|âgninā n' âsti samas tath" âgnis;
tac cet trayaṃ n' âsti, sukhaṃ ca te 'sti.
avaśya|bhāvī priya|viprayogas
tasmāc ca śoko niyataṃ niṣevyaḥ
śokena c' ônmādam upeyivāṃso
rāja'|rṣayo 'nye 'py a|vaśā viceluḥ.

5.30 prajñā|mayaṃ varma badhāna tasmān
no kṣānti|nighnasya hi śoka|bāṇāḥ.
mahac ca dagdhuṃ bhava|kakṣa|jālaṃ
saṃdhukṣay' âlp'|âgnim iv' ātma|tejaḥ.

The riches of faith are the very best riches, the taste of
wisdom is the most satisfying of tastes, inner happiness is
the chief happiness, and intellectualization is the sorriest of
delights. He who says what is salutary for you is the best of 5.25
friends, taking pains over *dharma* is the most excellent of
labors, working for knowledge is the best of actions. Why
be a slave to your senses? So choose the bliss of tranquillity,
which is certain, free from fear, weariness and grief, which
is neither dependent on others nor assailable by them, and
which is eternal and pure. Why endure pain for the sake of
sense objects?

Nothing befouls mankind so much as old age, no misfortune in the world can equal sickness, no danger on earth compares with death. Yet one must submit to this triad, however unwillingly. There is no fetter like affection, no torrent like desire for sweeping one away, and no fire like the fire of passion. If these three did not exist, bliss would be yours. Separation from our loved ones is a certainty, therefore grief must inevitably be incurred; even certan king-seers lost control and faltered when they went mad with grief.

So put on armor made of wisdom, for the arrows of grief 5.30
are nothing to a man ruled by patience. Just as you would
light a small fire to burn up a great heap of straw, kindle your
own courage to consume becoming, the cycle of rebirth. Just
as a snake never bites the wise man who holds herbs in his

yath" âuṣadhair hasta|gataiḥ sa|vidyo
na daśyate kaś cana pannagena,
tath" ân|apekṣo jita|loka|moho
na daśyate śoka|bhujaṃgamena.
āsthāya yogaṃ parigamya tattvaṃ
na trāsam āgacchati mṛtyu|kāle,
ābaddha|varmā su|dhanuḥ kṛt'|âstro
jigīṣayā śūra iv' āhava|sthaḥ.»
ity evam uktaḥ sa Tathāgatena
sarveṣu bhūteṣv anukampakena
dhṛṣṭaṃ gir" ântar|hṛdayena sīdaṃs
«tath" êti» Nandaḥ Sugataṃ babhāṣe.
atha pramādāc ca tam ujjihīrṣan
matv" āgamasy' âiva ca pātra|bhūtam,
«pravrājay' Ānanda śamāya Nandam»
ity abravīn maitra|manā maha"|rṣiḥ.
5.35 Nandaṃ tato 'ntar|manasā rudantam
«eh' îti» Vaideha|munir jagāda.
śanais tatas taṃ samupetya Nando
«na pravrajiṣyāmy aham» ity uvāca.
śrutv" âtha Nandasya manīṣitaṃ tad
Buddhāya Vaideha|muniḥ śaśaṃsa;
saṃśrutya tasmād api tasya bhāvaṃ
mahā|munir Nandam uvāca bhūyaḥ:

hand, so the serpent of grief does not bite the man with no preferences who has conquered his delusions about the world. Just like the warrior wearing protective armor, armed with a good bow and skilled in weapons, standing ready for battle and hoping for victory, neither does the disciplined man who encompasses the truth fear the moment of death."

That was how the realized one in his compassion for all living beings spoke to him. "Yes," replied Nanda to the Súgata in a brave voice, but with despair in his innermost heart.

At this, the great seer considered him to have become a fitting recipient of the teaching, and as he wished to rescue him from his heedlessness, he said with kindness, "Anánda,
ordain Nanda, so that he may find peace." Then the sage 5.35
of Vidéha* said to Nanda, who was crying inside, "Come." Nanda slowly went up to him and replied, "I will not become a monk." The sage of Vidéha took note of Nanda's disinclination and told the Buddha about it. The great sage also heard from him about Nanda's state of mind, and so spoke to him again:

«mayy agra|je pravrajite ’|jit’|ātman
bhrātṛṣv anupravrajiteṣu c’ âsmān,
jñātīṃś ca dṛṣṭvā vratino gṛha|sthān
saṃvinna|vitte ’sti, na v” âsti cetaḥ?
rāja’|rṣayas te viditā na nūnaṃ
vanāni ye śiśriyire hasantaḥ,
niṣṭhīvya kāmān upaśānti|kāmāḥ
kāmeṣu n’ âivaṃ kṛpaṇeṣu saktāḥ.
bhūyaḥ samālokya gṛheṣu doṣān,
niśāmya tat|tyāga|kṛtaṃ ca śarma;
n’ âiv’ âsti moktuṃ matir ālayaṃ te
deśaṃ mumūrṣor iva s’|ôpasargam.
5.40 saṃsāra|kāntāra|parāyaṇasya
śive kathaṃ te pathi n’ ārurukṣā
āropyamāṇasya tam eva mārgaṃ,
bhraṣṭasya sārthād iva sārthikasya!
yaḥ sarvato veśmani dahyamāne
śayīta mohān na tato vyapeyāt,
kāl’|âgninā vyādhi|jarā|śikhena
loke pradīpte sa bhavet pramattaḥ.
praṇīyamānaś ca yathā vadhāya
matto hasec ca pralapec ca vadhyaḥ,
mṛtyau tathā tiṣṭhati pāśa|haste
śocyaḥ pramādyan viparīta|cetāḥ.
yadā nar’|êndrāś ca kuṭumbinaś ca
vihāya bandhūṃś ca parigrahāṃś ca
yayuś ca yāsyanti ca yānti c’ âiva,
priyeṣv a|nityeṣu kuto ’nurodhaḥ?

"I, your elder brother, have gone forth from home; our brothers have followed me in going forth; and you see that our relatives who remain at home are observing vows. Now you, who have not conquered yourself—is your mind in agreement with theirs, or not? Presumably you don't know about the king-seers who smilingly withdrew to the forest. They spat out desires, clung to no miserable desires, their only desire was for peace.

What is more, you have seen the flaws of family life, and you have heard of the bliss of giving it up; yet still you have no mind to leave your home, like a death-desiring man who will not leave a place of plague. How can you be so 5.40
fixated with the wasteland of samsara* that you have no urge to venture upon the good path, even when you have been set on that very path? You are like a merchant who has wandered from his caravan!

Only a man who is so stupid that he would settle down to sleep in a house ablaze on all sides, rather than escaping from it, would be oblivious to the world burning with the fire of time, with its flames of disease and old age. It is dreadful that a convicted man being led out for execution should be drunk, laughing and babbling; so too is it dreadful that a man should be careless and contrary-minded while Death stands by with a noose in his hand. When kings and householders have gone, are going and will go forth, leaving behind their relatives and possessions, you give consideration to incidental loves!

kiṃ cin na paśyāmi ratasya yatra
tad|anya|bhāvena bhaven na duḥkham.
tasmāt kva cin na kṣamate prasaktir
yadi kṣamas tad|vigamān na śokaḥ.
5.45 tat saumya lolaṃ parigamya lokaṃ
māy'|ôpamaṃ citram iv' êndra|jālam
priy"|âbhidhānaṃ tyaja moha|jālaṃ
chettuṃ matis te yadi duḥkha|jālam.
varaṃ hit'|ôdarkam an|iṣṭam annaṃ
na svādu yat syād a|hit'|ânubaddham,
yasmād ahaṃ tvā viniyojayāmi
śive śucau vartmani vipriye 'pi.
bālasya dhātrī vinigṛhya loṣṭaṃ
yath" ôddharaty" âsya puṭa|praviṣṭam,
tath" ôjjihīrṣuḥ khalu rāga|śalyaṃ
tat tvām avocaṃ paruṣaṃ hitāya.
an|iṣṭam apy auṣadham āturāya
dadāti vaidyaś ca yathā nigṛhya,
tadvan may" ôktaṃ pratikūlam etat
tubhyaṃ hit'|ôdarkam anugrahāya.
tad yāvad eva kṣaṇa|saṃnipāto
na mṛtyur āgacchati yāvad eva
yāvad vayo yoga|vidhau samarthaṃ,
buddhiṃ kuru śreyasi tāvad eva.»
5.50 ity evam uktaḥ sa vināyakena
hit'|âiṣiṇā kāruṇikena Nandaḥ,
«kart" âsmi sarvaṃ, bhagavan, vacas te
tathā yathā jñāpayas' îty» uvāca.
ādāya Vaideha|munis tatas taṃ
nināya saṃśliṣya viceṣṭamānam

I see no feature of pleasure which would not change into something else and so bring sorrow. Therefore under no circumstances should you tolerate attachment, unless the
grief at its passing is bearable. So, dear friend, knowing that 5.45
the world flickers like a mirage, that it is kaleidoscopic like a magic trick, give up the tissue of delusions labeled 'lover,' if you are minded to cut through the snare of sorrow.

Unpleasant food that benefits your health is better than a tasty delicacy that may be bad for you. Likewise I commit you to a benign and pure path, though it doesn't please you. I truly wish to draw out your dart of passion, and have spoken severely to you for your own good, just as a nurse keeps a firm hold on a child while she takes out the clod of earth that has got into its mouth. Just as a doctor holds down a sick man while he gives him unwanted medicine, so do I as a kindness to you speak this unwelcome message with its beneficial results. Before this moment passes, before death comes, while your time of life is fit for disciplined practices, set your mind on Excellence."

When the guide, the well-wisher, the compassionate one 5.50
had spoken to him in this manner, Nanda replied "I shall do everything that you say, Lord, just as you order." Then the sage of Vidéha took hold of the writhing Nanda, held him close and led him away, and saw to it that his glorious hair was shaven from the royal umbrella of his head, while his eyes streamed with tears. As his hair was being removed,

vyayojayac c' âśru|pariplut'|âkṣaṃ
keśa|śriyaṃ chattra|nibhasya mūrdhnaḥ.
atho nataṃ tasya mukhaṃ sa|bāṣpaṃ
pravāsyamāneṣu śiro|ruheṣu
vakr'|âgra|nālaṃ nalinaṃ taḍāge
varṣ'|ôdaka|klinnam iv' âbabhāse.

Nandas tatas taru|kaṣāya|virakta|vāsāś
cint"|âvaśo nava|gṛhīta iva dvip'|êndraḥ,
pūrṇaḥ śaśī bahula|pakṣa|gataḥ kṣap"|ânte
bāl'|ātapena pariṣikta iv' âbabhāse.

Saundaranande mahā|kāvye Nanda|pravrājano nāma pañcamaḥ sargaḥ.

his tearful down-turned face looked like a rain-soaked lotus in a pond with the tip of its stalk curling away.

And later, wearing a faded garment of ochre tree-bark and depressed as a newly-captured elephant, Nanda resembled the full moon moving into the dark half of the month, at the end of the night, daubed with the light of the early morning sun.

End of Canto 5: Nanda is Made to Ordain.

CANTO 6
HIS WIFE'S LAMENT

6.1 TATO HṚTE BHARTARI gauraveṇa
prītau hṛtāyām a|ratau kṛtāyām,
tatr' âiva harmy'|ôpari vartamānā
na Sundarī s" âiva tadā babhāse.

sā bhartur abhyāgamana|pratīkṣā
gavākṣam ākramya payodharābhyām,
dvār'|ônmukhī harmya|talāl lalambe
mukhena tiryaṅ|nata|kuṇḍalena.

vilamba|hārā cala|yoktrakā sā
tasmād vimānād vinatā cakāśe,
tapaḥ|kṣayād apsarasāṃ var" êva
cyutaṃ vimānāt priyam īkṣamāṇā.

sā kheda|saṃsvinna|lalāṭakena,
niśvāsa|niṣpīta|viśeṣakeṇa
cintā|cal'|âkṣeṇa mukhena tasthau
bhartāram anyatra viśaṅkamānā.

6.5 tataś cira|sthāna|pariśrameṇa
sthit" âiva paryaṅka|tale papāta,
tiryak ca śiśye pravikīrṇa|hārā
sa|pāduk'|âik'|ârdha|vilamba|pādā.

NOW WITH HER husband having been spirited away by his respect for the Buddha, Súndari's delight evaporated and she was made wretched. She no longer seemed herself, though she stayed in the same place high up in the palace. In expectation of her husband's return, she leant from the top of the palace to watch the gateway, her breasts touching the window and her earrings hanging across her face. 6.1

As she bent down from the palace with her necklaces of pearls dangling and her ear-drops swinging, she seemed like one of the beautiful *ápsaras*es watching her lover fall from her celestial abode when he had used up his ascetically-derived credit. Her forehead broke into a sweat of anxiety, her *vishéshaka* shriveled as she panted for breath and her eyes moved around worriedly while she fretted over her
husband's absence. She merely stood, then exhausted from 6.5
standing so long, she collapsed on a sofa and lay across it with her strings of pearls scattered about and with one slipper half hanging off her foot.

ath' âtra kā cit pramadā sa|bāṣpāṃ
tāṃ duḥkhitāṃ draṣṭum an|īpsamānā,
prāsāda|sopāna|tala|praṇādaṃ
cakāra padbhyāṃ sahasā rudantī.
tasyāś ca sopāna|tala|praṇādaṃ
śrutv" âiva tūrṇaṃ punar utpapāta,
prītyāṃ prasakt" âiva ca saṃjaharṣa
priy'|ôpayānaṃ pariśaṅkamānā.
sā trāsayantī valabhī|puṭa|sthān
pārāvatān nūpura|nisvanena,
sopāna|kukṣiṃ prasasāra harṣād
bhraṣṭaṃ dukūl'|ântam a|cintayantī.
tām aṅganāṃ prekṣya ca vipralabdhā
niśvasya bhūyaḥ śayanaṃ prapede.
vivarṇa|vaktrā na rarāja c' āśu
vivarṇa|candr" êva him'|āgame dyauḥ.

6.10 sā duḥkhitā bhartur a|darśanena
kāmena kopena ca dahyamānā
kṛtvā kare vaktram upopaviṣṭā;*
cintā|nadīṃ śoka|jalāṃ tatāra.
tasyā mukhaṃ padma|sapatna|bhūtaṃ
pāṇau sthitaṃ pallava|rāga|tāmre,
chāyāmayasy' âmbhasi paṅkajasya
babhau nataṃ padmam iv' ôpariṣṭāt.
sā strī|svabhāvena vicintya tat tad
dṛṣṭ'|ânurāge 'bhimukhe 'pi patyau
dharm'|āśrite tattvam a|vindamānā,
saṃkalpya tat tad vilalāpa tat tat:

One of her women, hating to see her so tearful and distressed, suddenly began to sob and banged her feet against the palace stairs.* Hearing her noise from the stairs, Súndari quickly jumped up again, transfixed with joy and thrilling with delight in the belief that her husband had come back. She ran joyfully to the stairwell, frightening the pigeons in the eaves with the tinkling of her anklets, and without thought for the edge of her scarf which trailed on the ground. Seeing the woman she sighed, feeling cheated, and again slumped on the sofa. Her face was all of a sudden lusterless, like the sky at the onset of winter when the moon turns pale.

She sat right there with her face in her hands, suffering because she couldn't see her husband, and burning with desire and anger; she sank into the river of worry with its waters of grief. Her lotus-rivaling face rested on the hennaed stem of her hand, like a lotus bent over its reflection in the water. She considered the matter from a woman's perspective, and failed to perceive the truth, that her husband, though demonstrably passionate and attuned to her, had taken refuge in the *dharma*. Imagining all sorts of things, she lamented in various ways: 6.10

«eṣyāmy an|āśyāna|viśeṣakāyāṃ
tvay" îti kṛtvā mayi tāṃ pratijñām.
kasmān nu hetor dayita|pratijñaḥ
so 'dya priyo me vitatha|pratijñaḥ?
āryasya sādhoḥ karuṇ'|ātmakasya
man|nitya|bhīror atidakṣiṇasya
kuto vikāro 'yam abhūta|pūrvaḥ
sven' âparāgeṇa mam' âpacārāt?
6.15 rati|priyasya priya|vartino me
priyasya nūnaṃ hṛdayaṃ viraktam
tath" âpi rāgo yadi tasya hi syān
mac|citta|rakṣī na sa n' āgataḥ syāt.
rūpeṇa bhāvena ca mad|viśiṣṭā
priyeṇa dṛṣṭā niyataṃ tato 'nyā,
tathā hi kṛtvā mayi mogha|sāntvaṃ
lagnāṃ satīṃ mām agamad vihāya.
bhaktiṃ sa Buddhaṃ prati yām avocat
tasya prayātuṃ mayi so 'padeśaḥ,
munau prasādo yadi tasya hi syān
mṛtyor iv' ôgrād an|ṛtād bibhīyāt.
sev"|ârtham ādarśanam anya|citto
vibhūṣayantyā mama dhārayitvā
bibharti so 'nyasya janasya taṃ cen,
namo 'stu tasmai cala|sauhṛdāya!
n' êcchanti yāḥ śokam avāptum evaṃ
śraddhātum arhanti na tā narāṇām.
kva c' ânuvṛttir mayi s" âsya pūrvaṃ
tyāgaḥ kva c' âyaṃ janavat kṣaṇena?»

"He made me a promise that he would be back before my *vishéshaka* dries. What reason could there possibly be for my dear husband to break his promise now, when his promises are so important to him? What has caused this unprecedented change in him, who was noble, good, compassionate, always deferential to me, and open? Does he hate me? Have I behaved badly? My lover loves love and loves 6.15
me; surely his heart has hardened, since if he still loved me, he would have cared about my request and been sure to return.

My lover must have seen another woman, more beautiful than me and with finer feelings, for he has placated me falsely, and has gone away and deserted me, attached to him as I am. That devotion to the Buddha of which he spoke was just an excuse to me for leaving, since if he believed in the sage he would fear falsehood as he would a horrible death. He held the mirror as a service to me as I got myself ready, while thinking of another! If he holds it now for some other woman, so much for my fickle friend! Women who don't want to suffer such grief should not put their faith in men. Look at his former regard for me, and look at how he now deserts me in a trice as if I were just anybody!"

6.20 ity evam|ādi priya|viprayuktā
priye 'nyad āśaṅkya ca sā jagāda.
saṃbhrāntam āruhya ca tad vimānaṃ
tāṃ strī sa|bāṣpā giram ity uvāca:
«yuv" âpi tāvat priya|darśano 'pi
saubhāgya|bhāgy|ābhijan'|ânvito 'pi,
yas tvāṃ priyo n' âbhyacarat kadā cit
tam anyathā paśyasi, kātar" âsi.
mā svāminaṃ svāmini doṣato gāḥ*
priyaṃ priy'|ârhaṃ priya|kāriṇaṃ tam.
na sa tvad|anyāṃ pramadām avaiti
sva|cakravākyā iva cakravākaḥ.
sa tu tvad|arthaṃ gṛha|vāsam īpsañ
jijīviṣus tvat|paritoṣa|hetoḥ;
bhrātrā kil' āryeṇa Tathāgatena
pravrājito netra|jal'|ārdra|vaktraḥ.»
śrutvā tato bhartari tāṃ pravṛttiṃ
sa|vepathuḥ sā sahas" ôtpapāta;
pragṛhya bāhū virurāva c' ôccair
hṛd' îva digdh'|âbhihatā* kareṇuḥ.
6.25 sā rodan'|āroṣita|rakta|dṛṣṭiḥ*
saṃtāpa|saṃkṣobhita|gātra|yaṣṭiḥ
papāta śīrṇ'|ākula|hāra|yaṣṭiḥ
phal'|âtibhārād iva cūta|yaṣṭiḥ.
sā padma|rāgaṃ vasanaṃ vasānā,
padm'|ānanā padma|dal'|āyat'|âkṣī,
padmā vipadmā patit" êva Lakṣmīḥ,
śuśoṣa padma|srag iv' ātapena.

This she said and more, separated from her dear one and 6.20
suspecting him of other interests. In agitation, her attendant climbed up to the top of the palace and spoke tearfully to her:

"Though he is young, though he is good-looking, though he enjoys sexual love and is full of courtesies, your husband was never unfaithful to you; you are overwrought, and looking at him in the wrong way. Madam, do not accuse your dear husband, who is worthy of your love, and who always acts lovingly. He never notices any other woman except you, like a *chakra·vaka* bird with its mate. He wished to stay at home for your sake, he wanted to live only to make you happy; but they say that he has been ordained, his face wet with tears, by his noble brother the realized one."

Hearing this news of her husband she immediately leaped up, shaking; she clutched at her arms and screamed piercingly, like a she-elephant struck in the heart with a poisoned
arrow. Her eyes reddened and smeared with tears, and her 6.25
thin limbs wracked with burning pain, she fell down with her strings of pearls broken and in disarray, like the branch of a mango-tree breaking due to its burden of fruit. Clothed in garments of lotus hue, her face a lotus, her eyes extended like lotus petals, she was like a fallen Padma Lakshmi without her lotus,* like a lotus-wreath withered in the hot sun.

saṃcintya saṃcintya guṇāṃś ca bhartur
dīrghaṃ niśaśvāsa tatāma c' âiva
vibhūṣaṇa|śrī|nihite prakoṣṭhe*
tāmre kar'|âgre ca vinirdudhāva.
«na bhūṣaṇ'|ârtho mama samprat' îti»
sā dikṣu cikṣepa vibhūṣaṇāni.
nir|bhūṣaṇā sā patitā cakāśe
viśīrṇa|puṣpa|stabakā lat" êva.
«dhṛtaḥ priyeṇ' âyam abhūn mam' êti»
rukma|tsaruṃ darpaṇam āliliṅge;
yatnāc ca vinyasta|tamāla|pattrau
ruṣṭ" êva dhṛṣṭaṃ pramamārja gaṇḍau.

6.30 sā cakravāk" îva bhṛśaṃ cukūja
śyen'|âgra|pakṣa|kṣata|cakravākā,
vispardhamān" êva vimāna|saṃsthaiḥ
pārāvataiḥ kūjana|lola|kaṇṭhaiḥ.
vicitra|mṛdv|āstaraṇe 'pi suptā
vaiḍūrya|vajra|pratimaṇḍite 'pi
rukm'|âṅga|pāde śayane mah"|ârhe,
na śarma lebhe paricesṭamānā.
saṃdṛśya bhartuś ca vibhūṣaṇāni
vāsāṃsi vīṇā|prabhṛtīś* ca līlāḥ,
tamo viveś' âbhinanāda c' ôccaiḥ
paṅk'|âvatīrṇ" êva ca saṃsasāda.

Turning her husband's merits over and over in her mind, she gulped long breaths, choked, and jerked her forearms with their wealth of costly ornaments and her hennaed fingertips. "I have no need of ornaments now," she cried, and threw them about in all directions. Unadorned, slumping, she seemed like a creeper whose clusters of blossoms are rent. "My darling held this for me," she said, and cradled the golden-handled mirror; and forcefully she rubbed at her cheeks, as though angry with the *tamála* paste that had been so carefully applied.

She moaned loudly, like a *chakra·vaka* bird when a hawk 6.30
has wounded the tip of her mate's wing, as if to compete with the pigeons gathered on the palace roof, their throats tremulous with cooing. The couch she lay on, though decked in soft colored rugs, though decorated with cat's-eye gems and diamonds, though with feet of gold and extremely valuable, gave her no comfort in her restlessness. Beholding her husband's ornaments and clothes, and his items of amusement such as his *vina*,* she entered a state of darkness, howling loudly, and collapsing as though sinking into the mire.

sā Sundarī śvāsa|cal'|ôdarī hi
vajr'|âgni|sambhinna|darī guh" êva,
śok'|âgnin" ântar|hṛdi dahyamānā
vibhrānta|citt" êva tadā babhūva.
ruroda mamlau virurāva jaglau
babhrāma tasthau vilalāpa dadhyau;
cakāra roṣaṃ vicakāra mālyaṃ
cakarta vaktraṃ vicakarṣa vastram.

6.35 tāṃ cāru|dantīṃ prasabhaṃ rudantīṃ
saṃśrutya nāryaḥ param'|âbhitaptāḥ,
antar|gṛhād āruruhur vimānaṃ
trāsena kiṃnarya iv' âdri|pṛṣṭham.
bāṣpeṇa tāḥ klinna|viṣaṇṇa|vaktrā
varṣeṇa padminya iv' ārdra|padmāḥ,
sthān'|ânurūpeṇa yath"|âbhimānaṃ
nililyire tām anu dahyamānāḥ.
tābhir vṛtā harmya|tale 'ṅganābhiś
cintā|tanuḥ sā su|tanur babhāse,
śata|hradābhiḥ pariveṣṭit" êva
śaśāṅka|lekhā śarad|abhra|madhye.
yā tatra tāsāṃ vacas" ôpapannā
mānyā ca tasyā vayas" âdhikā ca
sā pṛṣṭhatas tāṃ tu samāliliṅge
pramṛjya c' âśrūṇi vacāṃsy uvāca:

For as her diaphragm heaved with her hard breathing like a cave's interior rent by a fiery thunderbolt, and her innermost heart burned with the fire of grief, Súndari at that moment seemed to have lost her mind. She wept, grew exhausted, yelled, fell weary, wandered about, stood still, lamented, brooded; she raged, scattered her garlands, tore at her face and pulled at her clothes.

The violent sobbing of this girl of the beautiful teeth 6.35
greatly distressed her ladies-in-waiting when they heard it, and in anxiety they climbed from inside the house to the palace roof, like *kínnaris* on a mountain-side. Distressed, they settled down next to her according to their rank and status, their downcast faces wet with tears, like lotus-pools with rain-soaked lotuses. The slip of a girl, taut with worry and surrounded by her ladies on the palace roof, seemed a sliver of moon shrouded in lightning among the autumn clouds. One woman among them, their senior in age, articulate and well-respected, stood behind Súndari and held her close. She wiped away her tears and said:

«rāja'|rṣi|vadhvās tava n' ânurūpo
dharm'|âśrite bhartari jātu śokaḥ,
Ikṣvāku|vaṃśe hy abhikāṅkṣitāni
dāyādya|bhūtāni tapo|vanāni.

6.40 prāyeṇa mokṣāya viniḥsṛtānāṃ
Śākya'|rṣabhāṇāṃ viditāḥ striyas te—
tapo|vanān' îva gṛhāṇi yāsāṃ
sādhvī|vrataṃ kāmavad āśritānām.

yady anyayā rūpa|guṇ'|âdhikatvād
bhartā hṛtas te, kuru bāṣpa|mokṣam.
manasvinī rūpavatī guṇ'|āḍhyā
hṛdi kṣate k" âtra hi n' âśru muñcet?
ath' âpi kiṃ cid vyasanaṃ prapanno—
mā c' âiva tad bhūt sadṛśo!—'tra bāṣpaḥ!
ato viśiṣṭaṃ na hi duḥkham asti
kul'|ôdgatāyāḥ pati|devatāyāḥ.
atha tv idānīṃ laḍitaḥ sukhena
sva|sthaḥ phala|stho vyasanāny a|dṛṣṭvā
vīta|spṛho dharmam anuprapannaḥ!
kiṃ viklavā rodiṣi harṣa|kāle?»

ity evam ukt" âpi bahu|prakāraṃ
snehāt tayā n' âiva dhṛtiṃ cakāra.
ath' âparā tāṃ manaso 'nukūlaṃ
kāl'|ôpapannaṃ praṇayād uvāca:

"Grief ill becomes you, the wife of a royal seer, when your husband has sought refuge in the *dharma*; for in Ikshváku's lineage the ascetics' forest is a much-desired inheritance! You 6.40
know about those wives of eminent Shakyas who go forth for liberty's sake—most of them observe a vow of chastity as though it were a passionate promise, and make their homes like ascetics' groves.

Had your husband been seduced by another woman's better looks and character, then you could let your tears run freely. What spirited and beautiful woman with a wealth of good qualities would not shed tears when her heart was broken? Or had he met with some accident (and may that sort of thing never happen) then yes, tears! For no greater tragedy befalls a nobly-born woman whose husband is for her a god. But now he is following the *dharma*, light-hearted with happiness, easy in himself, well-placed for a good result, with no accident in sight, and free from longing! Why are you distressed and weeping at this joyful time?"

Tenderly she said this, and more besides, but Súndari still could not contain herself. Then another woman told her something in confidence which better pleased her mind and which fitted the circumstance:

6.45 «bravīmi satyaṃ su|viniścitaṃ me
prāptaṃ priyaṃ drakṣyasi śīghram eva;
tvayā vinā sthāsyati tatra n' âsau
sattv'|āśrayaś cetanay" êva hīnaḥ.
aṅke 'pi lakṣmyā na sa nirvṛtaḥ syāt*
tvaṃ tasya pārśve yadi tatra na syāḥ;
āpatsu kṛcchrāsv api c' āgatāsu
tvāṃ paśyatas tasya bhaven na duḥkham.
tvaṃ nirvṛtiṃ gaccha, niyaccha bāṣpaṃ,
tapt'|âśru|mokṣāt parirakṣa cakṣuḥ.
yas tasya bhāvas tvayi yaś ca rāgo
na raṃsyate tvad|virahāt sa dharme.
syād atra n' âsau kula|sattva|yogāt
kāṣāyam ādāya vihāsyat' îti;
an|ātman" ādāya gṛh'|ônmukhasya,
punar vimoktuṃ ka iv' âsti doṣaḥ?»
iti yuvati|janena sāntvyamānā
hṛta|hṛdayā ramaṇena Sundarī sā
Dramiḍam abhimukhī pur" êva Rambhā
kṣitim agamat parivārit" âpsarobhiḥ.

Saundaranande mahā|kāvye Bhāryā|vilāpo nāma
ṣaṣṭhaḥ sargaḥ.

"You'll soon see your husband come back; he can't stay there without you, any more than a living creature exists without consciousness. I am absolutely convinced of the truth of this. Even in the lap of luxury he wouldn't be happy without you there at his side; even in awful situations, he wouldn't suffer if you filled his gaze. Calm down, stop crying, spare your eyes the release of hot tears. His feelings for you and his passion are such that he will find no pleasure in the *dharma* while separated from you. One might think that the combination of his noble birth and strength of character would not permit him to relinquish the ochre robe once he had put it on; but he put it on unwillingly, hoping for home, so what's wrong with giving it up again?" 6.45

And being comforted in this way by her young attendants at the time when her heart was stolen away by her lover, Súndari went into her palace, just as Rambha was once tended by the *ápsaras*es when she came to earth yearning for Drámida.

End of Canto 6: His Wife's Lament.

CANTO 7
NANDA'S LAMENT

7.1 LIṄGAṂ TATAḤ śāstṛ|vidhi|pradiṣṭaṃ
gātreṇa bibhran na tu cetasā tat,
bhāryā|gatair eva mano|vitarkair
jehrīyamāṇo na nananda Nandaḥ.
sa puṣpa|māsasya ca puṣpa|lakṣmyā
sarv'|âbhisāreṇa ca puṣpa|ketoḥ,
yānīya|bhāvena ca yauvanasya
vihāra|saṃstho na śamaṃ jagāma.
sthitaḥ sa dīnaḥ sahakāra|vīthyām
ālīna|saṃmūrchita|ṣaṭpadāyām,
bhṛśaṃ jajṛmbhe yuga|dīrgha|bāhur
dhyātvā priyāṃ cāpam iv' ācakarṣa.
sa pītaka|kṣodam iva pratīcchaṃś
cūta|drumebhyas tanu|puṣpa|varṣam,
dīrghaṃ niśaśvāsa vicintya bhāryāṃ,
nava|graho nāga iv' âvaruddhaḥ.
7.5 śokasya hartā śaraṇ'|āgatānāṃ
śokasya kartā pratigarvitānām;
aśokam ālambya sa jāta|śokaḥ
priyāṃ priy'|âśoka|vanāṃ śuśoca.
priyāṃ priyāyāḥ pratanuṃ priyaṅguṃ
niśāmya bhītām iva niṣpatantīm,
sasmāra tām aśru|mukhīṃ sa|bāṣpaḥ
priyāṃ priyaṅgu|prasav'|âvadātām.

NANDA KNEW no gladness; he bore the signs ordained by the teacher on his body, but not in his heart, and was discomfited by conjectures about his wife. With the flowery riches of the month of flowers, with all the assaults of the flower-bannered god,* and with the emotions habitual in the young, he lived in a monastery, but found no peace. Wretched, he stood under a row of mango-trees that were thick with settling bees. Long-armed as a chariot yoke, he contemplated his lover and stretched vigorously, as though drawing a bow. Receiving from the mango trees a rain of tiny flowers like saffron powder, he thought of his wife and gave a heavy sigh, like a newly-caught elephant in confinement. 7.1

He had removed grief from those who sought his protection, he had inflicted grief on the proud; now, leaning against an *ashóka* tree, grief rose up in him, and he grieved for his wife, who was so fond of an *ashóka* grove. When he noticed a delicate *priyángu* creeper bashfully shying away, another plant beloved by his beloved, he recalled her tearful face pale as the *priyángu* blossom, and wept. 7.5

puṣp'|âvanaddhe tilaka|drumasya
drṣṭv" ânyapuṣṭāṃ śikhare niviṣṭām,
saṃkalpayām āsa śikhāṃ priyāyāḥ
śukl'|âṃśuke 'ṭṭālam apāśritāyāḥ.
latāṃ praphullām atimuktakasya
cūtasya pārśve parirabhya jātām
niśāmya cintām agamat «kad" âivaṃ
śliṣṭā bhaven mām api Sundar" îti?»
puṣpaiḥ karālā api nāga|vṛkṣā
dāntaiḥ samudgair iva hema|garbhaiḥ,
kāntāra|vṛkṣā iva duḥkhitasya
na cakṣur ācikṣipur asya tatra.
7.10 gandhaṃ vasanto 'pi ca gandhaparṇā
gandharva|veśyā iva gandhapūrṇāḥ,
tasy' ânya|cittasya śug|ātmakasya
ghrāṇaṃ na jahrur hṛdayaṃ pratepuḥ.
saṃrakta|kaṇṭhaiś ca vinīla|kaṇṭhais,
tuṣṭaiḥ prahṛṣṭair api c' ânyapuṣṭaiḥ,
lelihyamānaiś ca madhu dvirephaiḥ,
svanad vanaṃ tasya mano nunoda.
sa tatra bhāry"|âraṇi|sambhavena
vitarka|dhūmena tamaḥ|śikhena,
kām'|âgnin" ântar|hṛdi dahyamāno
vihāya dhairyaṃ vilalāpa tat tat:
«ady' âvagacchāmi su|duṣkaraṃ te
cakruḥ kariṣyanti ca kurvate ca
tyaktvā priyām aśru|mukhīṃ tapo ye
ceruś cariṣyanti caranti c' âiva.
tāvad dṛḍhaṃ bandhanam asti loke
na dāravaṃ tāntavam āyasaṃ vā

Seeing a cuckoo alighting on the flower-decked top of a *tílaka* tree, he imagined it as a lock of his darling's hair against her white tunic as she leant from the palace. Next he noticed a cheerful *atimúktaka* creeper which had grown up entwined around the mango-tree at its side, and he thought "When will Súndari hold me like that?"

Though the orange trees bristled with buds that seemed
like gold-filled ivory caskets, they did not draw Nanda's
despairing eye, any more than if they had been trees in
a wasteland. The *gandha·parna* trees, though scented and 7.10
fragrant like a *gandhárva*'s geisha, failed to win his sense of
smell but made his heart burn, for his mind was elsewhere
and his entire being grieved. His mind was repelled by the
forest as it resounded with the passionate calls of the peacocks, the thrilling cheer of the cuckoo, and the bees sipping
at honey. Burning in his heart with the fire of passion which
arose from his wife as the firestick, which had his fancies as
smoke and his mental darkness as flames, he put composure
aside and lamented in various ways:

"Today I comprehend that men who leave behind their
weeping sweethearts to practice asceticism—and those who
have done so in the past, and those who will do so in the
future—they are doing something very difficult indeed, and
so it was in the past and will be in the future. There is no
bond in the world, whether of wood, fibre or iron, as solid
as this bond—teasing words and a face with fluttering eyes!
The former disappear when they are cut or broken, by one's 7.15

yāvad dṛḍhaṃ bandhanam etad eva—
mukhaṃ cal'|âkṣaṃ lalitaṃ ca vākyam!
7.15 chittvā ca bhittvā ca hi yānti tāni
sva|pauruṣāc c' âiva suhṛd|balāc ca,
jñānāc caraukṣyāc ca vinā vimoktuṃ
na śakyate sneha|mayas tu pāśaḥ.
jñānaṃ na me tac ca śamāya yat syān
na c' âsti raukṣyaṃ karuṇ'|ātmako 'smi.
kām'|âtmakaś c' âsmi guruś ca Buddhaḥ;
sthito 'ntare cakra|gater iv' âsmi!
ahaṃ gṛhītv" âpi hi bhikṣu|liṅgaṃ
bhrāt'|ṛṣiṇā dvir guruṇ" ânuśiṣṭaḥ;
sarvāsv avasthāsu labhe na śāntiṃ,
priyā|viyogād iva cakravākaḥ.
ady' âpi tan me hṛdi vartate ca
yad darpaṇe vyākulite mayā sā
kṛt'|ânṛta|krodhakam abravīn māṃ
‹kathaṃ kṛto 's' îti!› śaṭhaṃ hasantī.
yath" ‹âiṣy an|āśyāna|viśeṣakāyāṃ
may' îti› yan mām avadac ca s'|âśru
pāriplav'|âkṣeṇa mukhena bālā—
tan me vaco 'dy' âpi mano ruṇaddhi.
7.20 baddhv" āsanaṃ parvata|nirjhara|sthaḥ
svastho yathā dhyāyati bhikṣur eṣaḥ,
saktaḥ kva cin n' âham iv' âiṣa nūnaṃ;
śāntas tathā tṛpta iv' ôpaviṣṭaḥ.
puṃs|kokilānām a|vicintya ghoṣaṃ
vasanta|lakṣyām a|vicārya cakṣuḥ,
śāstraṃ yath" âbhyasyati c' âiva yuktaḥ
śaṅke priy" ākarṣati n' âsya cetaḥ.

own force or the strength of friends, but the snare of love cannot be undone without knowledge and cruelty. That knowledge which might make for peace I do not have, nor, being compassionate by nature, can I be cruel. I am naturally passionate, yet the Buddha is my guru; I am as if fixed to a turning wheel!

I have accepted the guise of a monk, and I am taught twice over by a guru, my brother the seer;* even so, I cannot find peace under any circumstances, like a *chakra·vaka* bird separated from its mate. Even now that incident keeps churning in my mind, when I blew on her mirror, and she, making a show of anger, laughed roguishly and said to me 'What are you doing?' The words that the lass spoke to me, her eyes brimming with tears—'Hurry back before my *vishéshaka* dries!'—those words lock up my mind even now.

This monk who meditates at ease beside the mountain 7.20
waterfall, his posture controlled, can hardly be as attached to someone as I am; that's why he sits calmly, as though quite content. As he is concentrating so attentively on the teachings, ignoring the call of the cuckoos and without his eye straying over the glories of spring, it is unlikely that a loved one is tugging at his heart. All credit to him for being firm in his purpose, who has turned back curiosity and pride, who is peaceful in himself, and whose mind is turned inward! He walks up and down without eager longings when beholding the lotus-decked water and the flowering forest

asmai namo 'stu sthira|niścayāya
nivṛtta|kautūhala|vismayāya
śānt'|ātmane 'ntar|gata|mānasāya
caṃkramyamāṇāya nir|utsukāya,
nirīkṣamāṇāya jalaṃ sa|padmaṃ
vanaṃ ca phullaṃ parapuṣṭa|juṣṭam!
kasy' âsti dhairyaṃ nava|yauvanasya
māse madhau dharma|sapatna|bhūte?
bhāvena garveṇa gatena lakṣmyā
smitena kopena madena vāgbhiḥ
jahruḥ striyo deva|nṛpa'|rṣi|saṃghān.
kasmādd hi n' âsmad|vidham ākṣipeyuḥ?
7.25 kām'|âbhibhūto hi Hiraṇyaretāḥ
Svāhāṃ siṣeve Maghavān Ahalyām
sattvena sargeṇa ca tena hīnaḥ
strī|nirjitaḥ kiṃ bata mānuṣo 'ham!
Sūryaḥ Saraṇyūṃ prati jāta|rāgas
tat|prītaye taṣṭa iti śrutaṃ naḥ
yām aśva|bhūto 'śva|vadhūṃ sametya
yato 'śvinau tau janayāṃ babhūva.
strī|kāraṇaṃ vaira|viṣakta|buddhyor
Vaivasvat'|Âgnyoś calit'|ātma|dhṛtyoḥ,
bahūni varṣāṇi babhūva yuddhaṃ,
kaḥ strī|nimittaṃ na caled ih' ânyaḥ?
bheje śvapākīṃ munir Akṣamālāṃ
kāmād Vasiṣṭhaś ca sa sad|variṣṭhaḥ
yasyāṃ vivasvān iva bhū|jal'|âdaḥ
sutaḥ prasūto 'sya Kapiñjalādaḥ.
Parāśaraḥ śāpa|śaras tatha" rṣiḥ
Kālīṃ siṣeve jhaṣa|garbha|yonim,

visited by cuckoos! Who, in the prime of his youth, could show such fortitude in the *dharma*-countering months of spring?

The temperament, disdain, gait, charm, smiles, temper, wantoness and voices of women have entranced hosts of divine and royal seers. How could they not overpower a chap
like me? For overwhelmed by desire, Hiránya·retas made 7.25
love to Svaha and Indra to Ahályа. So it is natural that I, who am only human and lacking their courage and resolve, should be bowled over by a woman! Legend has it that the Sun, roused to passion for Saránуu, was reduced in brilliance to allow pleasure with her. He became a stallion to mate with her as a mare, whereby the two Ashvins were conceived. Vaivásvata and Agni were shaken from self-control because of women, and with their minds fixed on enmity fought each other for many years. What other man on earth would not be moved by a woman?

It was through desire that the sage Vasíshtha, best of the good, took up with the low-caste Aksha·mala, and on her he begot a son, Kapinjaláda, who consumed earth and water like the sun. In the same way the seer Paráshara, who has curses as weapons, made love with Kali, born of a fish's womb. She bore him a son, the venerable Dvaipáyana, who
divided up the Vedas. And Dvaipáyana, though oriented to 7.30
the *dharma*, enjoyed a prostitute in Kashi, and he was struck

suto 'sya yasyāṃ suṣuve mah"|ātmā
Dvaipāyano veda|vibhāga|kartā.

7.30 Dvaipāyano dharma|parāyaṇaś ca
reme samaṃ Kāśiṣu veśya|vadhvā,
yayā hato 'bhūc cala|nūpureṇa
pādena vidyul|latay" êva meghaḥ.

tath" Âṅgirā rāga|parīta|cetāḥ
Sarasvatīṃ Brahma|sutaḥ siṣeve,
Sārasvato yatra suto 'sya jajñe
naṣṭasya vedasya punaḥ pravaktā.

tathā nṛpa'|rṣer Dilipasya* yajñe
svarga|striyāṃ Kāśyapa āgat'|āsthaḥ
srucaṃ gṛhītvā sravad ātma|tejaś
cikṣepa vahnāv, Asito yato 'bhūt.

tath" Âṅgado 'ntaṃ tapaso 'pi gatvā
kām'|âbhibhūto Yamunām agacchat,
dhīmattaraṃ yatra Rathītaraṃ sa
sāraṅga|juṣṭaṃ janayāṃ babhūva.

niśāmya Śāntāṃ nara|deva|kanyāṃ
vane 'pi śānte 'pi ca vartamānaḥ,
cacāla dhairyān munir Ṛṣyaśṛṅgaḥ
śailo mahī|kampa iv' ôcca|śṛṅgaḥ.

7.35 brahma'|rṣi|bhāv'|ârtham apāsya rājyaṃ
bheje vanaṃ yo viṣayeṣv an|āsthaḥ;
sa Gādhi|jaś c' âpahṛto Ghṛtācyā
samā daś" âikaṃ divasaṃ viveda.

by her foot with its tremulous anklets like a cloud is struck by a twist of lightning. Similarly Ángiras, son of Brahma, had sex with Sarásvati when his mind was encompassed with desire. From her was born their son Sarásvata, who again proclaimed the lost Vedas.

Káshyapa became obsessed with a celestial nymph, and at the sacrifice of the king-seer Dílipa he took the ceremonial ladle and poured his own streaming semen into the fire, from which Ásita arose. Though he had completed his period of asceticism, Ángada too was overcome with desire and slept with Yámuna, with whom he engendered wise Rathítara, friend to the deer. The sage Rishya·shringa, though living at peace in the forest, caught sight of the princess Shanta and fell from stability like a high-peaked mountain in an earthquake. And the son of Gadhin, who had no care for 7.35
sensory experience, rejected his kingdom and retired to the forest to become a brahmin sage; but he became smitten, reckoning ten years with Ghritáchi as a single day.

tath" âiva Kandarpa|śar'|âbhimṛṣṭo
Rambhāṃ prati Sthūlaśirā mumūrcha
yaḥ kāma|roṣ'|ātmatay" ân|apekṣaḥ
śaśāpa tām a|pratigṛhyamāṇaḥ.

Pramadvarāyāṃ ca Ruruḥ priyāyāṃ
bhujaṅgamen' âpahṛt|êndriyāyām,
saṃdṛśya saṃdṛśya jaghāna sarpān
hriyaṃ na roṣeṇa tapo rarakṣa.

naptā śaś'|âṅkasya yaśo|guṇ'|âṅko
Budhasya sūnur vibudha|prabhāvaḥ,
tath" Ôrvaśīm apsarasaṃ vicintya
rāja'|ṛṣir unmādam agacchad Aiḍaḥ.

rakto girer mūrdhani Menakāyāṃ
kām'|ātmakatvāc ca sa Tālajaṅghaḥ
pādena Viśvāvasunā sa|roṣaṃ
vajreṇa hintāla iv' âbhijaghne.

7.40 nāśaṃ gatāyāṃ param'|âṅganāyāṃ
Gaṅgā|jale 'naṅga|parīta|cetāḥ
Jahnuś ca Gaṅgāṃ nṛpatir bhujābhyāṃ
rurodha Maināka iv' ācal'|endraḥ.

nṛpaś ca Gaṅgā|virahāj jughūrṇa
Gaṅg"|âmbhasā śāla iv' ātta|mūlaḥ,
kula|pradīpaḥ Pratipasya sūnuḥ
śrīmat|tanuḥ Śantanur a|svatantraḥ.

So too did Sthula·shiras, when touched by Kandárpa's dart, lose his senses over Rambha. She refused him and, impetuous in his characteristic lust and fury, he put a curse on her.

When his lover Pramádvara lost her senses because of a snake, Ruru killed all snakes whenever he saw them and in his anger maintained neither his reserve nor his ascetic practices. The son of Budha and Ida was a royal seer, and the grandson of the Moon. He was marked by fame and virtue and had the power of the wise, but thoughts of the *ápsaras* Úrvashi drove him to a frenzy. Essentially lustful, Tala·jangha became besotted with Ménaka on a mountain-top. Vishva·vasu angrily kicked at him with his foot, like a thunderbolt striking a date tree.

When his favorite wife perished in the waters of the 7.40
Ganges, King Jahnu, his mind encompassed by disembodied Kama, dammed up the Ganges with his arms like Mainâka lord of the mountains. And King Shántanu son of Prátipa, the light of his family and splendid in appearance, shook uncontrollably when separated from Ganga, like a *shala* tree whose roots are eroded by the waters of the Ganges.

hṛtāṃ ca Saunandakin" ânuśocan
prāptām iv' ôrvīṃ striyam Urvaśīṃ tām,
sad|vṛtta|varmā kila Somavarmā
babhrāma citt'|ôdbhava|bhinna|varmā.
bhāryāṃ mṛtāṃ c' ânumamāra rājā
bhīma|prabhāvo bhuvi Bhīmakaḥ saḥ
balena Senāka iti prakāśaḥ
Senā|patir deva iv' ātta|senaḥ.
svargaṃ gate bhartari Śantanau ca
Kālīṃ jihīrṣañ Janamejayaḥ saḥ,
avāpa Bhīṣmāt samavetya mṛtyuṃ
na tad|gataṃ manmatham utsasarja.
7.45 śaptaś ca Pāṇḍur Madanena nūnaṃ
strī|saṅgame mṛtyum avāpsyas' îti;
jagāma Mādrīṃ na maha"|rṣi|śāpād
asevya|sevī vimamarśa mṛtyum.
evaṃ|vidhā deva|nṛpa'|rṣi|saṅghāḥ
strīṇāṃ vaśaṃ kāma|vaśena jagmuḥ.
dhiyā ca sāreṇa ca dur|balaḥ san
priyām a|paśyan kim u viklavo 'ham?
yāsyāmi tasmād gṛham eva bhūyaḥ
kāmaṃ kariṣye vidhivat sa|kāmam.
na hy anya|cittasya cal'|êndriyasya
liṅgaṃ kṣamaṃ dharma|pathāc cyutasya.
pāṇau kapālam avadhāya vidhāya mauṇḍyaṃ
mānaṃ nidhāya vikṛtaṃ paridhāya vāsaḥ
yasy' ôddhavo na dhṛtir asti na śāntir asti—
citra|pradīpa iva so 'sti ca, n' âsti c' âiva.
yo niḥsṛtaś ca na ca niḥsṛta|kāma|rāgaḥ
kāṣāyam udvahati yo na ca niṣ|kaṣāyaḥ,

When Soma·varman's lover Úrvashi was taken over by Saunándaki as though she were conquered terrain, it is said that his armor of good conduct was broken by mind-born Kama and that he roamed about grieving for her. And King Bhímaka, of dread power on earth, was known as Senáka because with his troops he was like the gods' general, the receiver of armies. Yet when his wife died, he died too.

Janam·éjaya wished to marry Kali when her husband Shántanu had gone to heaven. He received death from Bhishma on meeting him in battle, but he never gave up his love for her. And Pandu was cursed by Mádana to die upon 7.45
intercourse with a woman; but disregarding the death that would result from the seer's curse, he did what he shouldn't have done and slept with Madri. Many such divine and royal seers fell to women's will under the force of lust. I am weak in wisdom and inner strength; how much more despairing am I when I can't see my darling?

Therefore I will go home again, and make love legitimately, as I please. For the insignia of a monk are inappropriate for one of restless senses, whose mind is elsewhere, and who has slipped from the path of *dharma*. He who has taken the alms-bowl in his hand, who has shaved his head, who has put aside pride and put on different clothing, but who is frivolous and lacking in earnestness and tranquillity—he, like a lamp in a picture, is not really real. And a man who has departed from the household life, but from whom desire and passion have not departed, who wears the earth-hued robe but is not dirt-free, who carries a bowl but has not become a vessel of goodness—though he bears the marks of a monk, such a one is neither monk nor householder.

pātraṃ bibharti ca guṇair na ca pātra|bhūto—
liṅgaṃ vahann api sa n' âiva gṛhī na bhikṣuḥ.

7.50 na nyāyyam anvayavataḥ parigṛhya liṅgaṃ
bhūyo vimoktum iti yo 'pi hi me vicāraḥ,
so 'pi praṇaśyati vicintya nṛpa|pravīrāṃs
tān ye tapo|vanam apāsya gṛhāṇy atīyuḥ.
Śālv'|âdhipo hi sa|suto 'pi tath" Âmbarīṣo
Rāmo 'ndha eva sa ca Sāṃkṛti|Rantidevaḥ,
cīrāṇy apāsya dadhire punar aṃśukāni
cchittvā jaṭāś ca kuṭilā mukuṭāni babhruḥ.

tasmād bhikṣ"|ârthaṃ mama gurur ito
yāvad eva prayātas
tyaktvā kāṣāyaṃ gṛham aham itas
tāvad eva prayāsye,
pūjyaṃ liṅgaṃ hi skhalita|manaso
bibhrataḥ kliṣṭa|buddher
n' âmutr' ârthaḥ syād upahata|mater
n' âpy ayaṃ jīva|lokaḥ.

Saundaranande mahā|kāvye Nanda|vilāpo nāma
saptamaḥ sargaḥ.

When I think of those royal heroes who left the ascetics' grove behind and went home, I also revise my opinion that it is not right for a nobly-born man to discard the signs of a monk once they have been adopted. For the king of the Shalvas, and his son, likewise Ambarísha, Rama, Andha and Ranti·déva son of Sánkriti discarded the bark cloth of an ascetic and put on fine muslin again, and cutting off their matted locks bore the diadem once more. 7.50

So while my guru is away on his alms-round, I will put aside the ochre robe and go home, for a man bearing the honored marks of a monk while his thoughts are wavering, his reasoning impaired and his mind infatuated has no purpose in the next world, nor does he even have this world of living creatures.

End of Canto 7: Nanda's Lament.

CANTO 8
THE ATTACK ON WOMEN

8.1 Atha Nandam a|dhīra|locanaṃ
gṛha|yān'|ôtsukam utsuk'|ôtsukam,
abhigamya śivena cakṣuṣā
śramaṇaḥ kaś cid uvāca maitrayā:
«kim idaṃ mukham aśru|durdinaṃ
hṛdaya|sthaṃ vivṛṇoti te tamaḥ?
dhṛtim ehi, niyaccha vikriyāṃ,
na hi bāṣpaś ca śamaś ca śobhate.
dvi|vidhā samudeti vedanā
niyataṃ cetasi deha eva ca;
śruta|vidhy|upacāra|kovidā
dvi|vidhā eva tayoś cikitsakāḥ.
tad iyaṃ yadi kāyikī rujā
bhiṣaje tūrṇam anūnam ucyatām.
vinigṛhya hi rogam āturo
nacirāt tīvram an|artham ṛcchati.
8.5 atha duḥkham idaṃ mano|mayaṃ,
vada, vakṣyāmi yad atra bheṣajam;
manaso hi rajas|tamasvino
bhiṣajo 'dhyātma|vidaḥ parīkṣakāḥ.
nikhilena ca satyam ucyatāṃ
yadi vācyaṃ mayi, saumya, manyase;
gatayo vividhā hi cetasāṃ
bahu|guhyāni mad'|ākulāni ca.»

THEN A CERTAIN ascetic with a gracious expression came up to Nanda, who with restless eyes was yearning with the very height of yearning to go home, and he said to him in a friendly way: 8.1

"Why this face clouded with tears, which reveals the dark ignorance abiding in your heart? Steady yourself, control your agitation, for tears and tranquillity do not sit well together. Pain is of two kinds, arising either in the mind or in the body; and there are two kinds of physician, those learned in the prescriptions of their religious tradition and those skilled in medical practice. So if your illness is physical, tell a doctor all about it straightaway, because a sick man
soon gets worse when he hides his illness. If it is mental 8.5
suffering, tell me, and I will prescribe a remedy for it; for careful examiners who understand the psyche are doctors for minds filled with passion and dark ignorance. If you think you can confide in me, tell me the whole truth, dear friend, for the minds of men move in various ways, and contain many secrets that are stirred up by passion."

iti tena sa coditas tadā
vyavasāyaṃ pravivakṣur ātmanaḥ,
avalambya kare kareṇa taṃ
praviveś' ânyatarad van'|ântaram.
atha tatra śucau latā|gṛhe
kusum'|ôdgāriṇi tau niṣedatuḥ
mṛdubhir mṛdu|mārut'|ēritair
upagūḍhāv iva bāla|pallavaiḥ.
sa jagāda tataś cikīrṣitaṃ
ghana|niśvāsa|gṛhītam antarā
śruta|vāg|viśadāya bhikṣave—
viduṣā pravrajitena dur|vacam:

8.10 «sadṛśaṃ yadi dharma|cāriṇaḥ
satataṃ prāṇiṣu maitra|cetasaḥ,
a|dhṛtau tad* iyaṃ hit'|âiṣitā
mayi te syāt karuṇ'|ātmanaḥ sataḥ.
ata eva ca me viśeṣataḥ
pravivakṣā kṣama|vādini tvayi
na hi bhāvam imaṃ cal'|ātmane
kathayeyaṃ bruvate 'py a|sādhave.
tad idaṃ śṛṇu me samāsato
na rame dharma|vidhāv ṛte priyām,
giri|sānuṣu kāminīm ṛte
kṛta|retā iva kiṃnaraś caran.
vana|vāsa|sukhāt parāṅ|mukhaḥ
prayiyāsā gṛham eva yena me;
na hi śarma labhe tayā vinā,
nṛpatir hīna iv' ôttama|śriyā.»

Thus urged, and wishing to speak of his own decision, Nanda clung to his hand with his own and proceeded to a different part of the forest. Here they sat down in a cleared bower of creepers bursting with flowers, so that they seemed embraced by the tender young shoots swaying in the soft breeze. Then, intermittently overcome by deep sighs, he told the monk, who was pure in learning and speech, what he meant to do—hard words for a wise man who has adopted homelessness:

"If it is fitting in a *dharma* practitioner who is always 8.10
well-disposed to living beings, then may this benevolence of yours, who are compassionate and good, be directed towards me in my wavering! That is why I want to talk to you in particular, since you speak with forbearance, for I would not mention my feelings to a bad person with a volatile nature, however eloquent. So listen to this. To be brief, I do not enjoy the prescriptions of *dharma* without my dear girl, but am like a *kínnara*, his semen ready, wandering the mountain plateaux without his lover. I am averse to the pleasures of living in the forest, since I just want to go home; for without her I can find no joy, like a king without his sovereignty."

atha tasya niśamya tad vacaḥ
priya|bhāry"|âbhimukhasya śocataḥ,
śramaṇaḥ sa śiraḥ prakampayan
nijagād' ātma|gataṃ śanair idam:

8.15 «kṛpaṇaṃ bata yūtha|lālaso
mahato vyādha|bhayād viniḥsṛtaḥ,
praviviksati vāgurāṃ mṛgaś
capalo gīta|raveṇa vañcitaḥ!

vihagaḥ khalu jāla|saṃvṛto
hita|kāmena janena mokṣitaḥ
vicaran phala|puṣpavad vanaṃ
praviviksuḥ svayam eva pañjaram!

kalabhaḥ kariṇā khal' ûddhṛto
bahu|paṅkād viṣamān nadī|taṭāt,*
jala|tarṣa|vaśena tāṃ punaḥ
saritaṃ grāhavatīṃ titīrṣati!

śaraṇe sa|bhujaṅgame svapan
pratibuddhena pareṇa bodhitaḥ
taruṇaḥ khalu jāta|vibhramaḥ
svayam ugraṃ bhujagaṃ jighṛkṣati!

When he heard these words from the grieving Nanda, who was focused on his beloved wife, the ascetic shook his head and softly said to himself:

"How pitiful that the wayward deer has escaped from the great danger posed by the hunter, but now in his longing for the herd is about to leap into the net, fooled by the sound of singing!* Here is a bird that was enmeshed in a net, freed by a well-wisher to glide through the forest of fruit and flowers, now voluntarily trying to get into a cage! Here is a young elephant pulled out of the thick mud at a treacherous riverbank by another elephant, that wants to once more descend into the crocodile-infested river, impelled by its thirst for water! Here is a lad sleeping in a shelter with a snake, who, when woken by a mindful elder, is filled with confusion and tries to grab the fierce snake himself! 8.15

mahatā khalu jātavedasā
jvalitād utpatito vana|drumāt,
punar icchati nīḍa|tṛṣṇayā
patituṃ tatra gata|vyatho dvijaḥ!

8.20 a|vaśaḥ khalu kāma|mūrchayā
priyayā śyena|bhayād vinā|kṛtaḥ,
na dhṛtiṃ samupaiti na hriyaṃ
karuṇaṃ jīvati jīva|jīvakaḥ!

a|kṛt'|ātmatayā tṛṣ"|ânvito
ghṛṇayā c' âiva dhiyā ca varjitaḥ
aśanaṃ khalu vāntam ātmanā
kṛpaṇaḥ śvā punar attum icchati!»

iti manmatha|śoka|karṣitaṃ
tam anudhyāya muhur nirīkṣya ca,
śramaṇaḥ sa hit'|âbhikāṅkṣayā
guṇavad vākyam uvāca vipriyam:

«a|vicārayataḥ śubh'|â|śubhaṃ
viṣayeṣv eva niviṣṭa|cetasaḥ
upapannam a|labdha|cakṣuṣo,
na ratiḥ śreyasi ced bhavet tava.

śravaṇe grahaṇe 'tha dhāraṇe
param'|ârth'|âvagame manaḥ|śame
a|viṣakta|mateś cal'|ātmano
na hi dharme 'bhiratir vidhīyate.

Here is a bird flown away from a forest tree ablaze with a raging fire, that wishes to fly back there, its qualms forgotten in its longing for its nest! Here is a pheasant in a helpless 8.20
swoon of lust when separated from its mate through fear of a hawk, living in wretchedness and attaining neither resolution nor modesty! Here is a wretched undisciplined dog, full of greed but lacking decency and wisdom, who wants to feed once more on the food he has himself vomited!"

The ascetic reflected for a while, then looking at Nanda who was torn up with the anguish of passion, he spoke the following unwelcome but excellent words, intended for his benefit:

"You do not discriminate between good and bad, and your mind is encamped among the objects of the senses. You have not properly attained insight, so no pleasure in Excellence could be yours. For joy in *dharma* is not vouchsafed to a volatile man whose thoughts are not fastened to mental peace, nor to hearing, absorbing, retaining and understanding the supreme truth.

8.25 viṣayeṣu tu doṣa|darśinaḥ
paritusṭasya śucer a|māninaḥ
śama|karmasu yukta|cetasaḥ
kṛta|buddher na ratir na vidyate.

ramate tṛṣito dhana|śriyā
ramate kāma|sukhena bāliśaḥ
ramate praśamena saj|janaḥ
paribhogān paribhūya vidyayā.

api ca prathitasya dhīmataḥ
kula|jasy' ârcita|liṅga|dhāriṇaḥ
sadṛśī na gṛhāya cetanā,
praṇatir vāyu|vaśād girer iva.

spṛhayet para|saṃśritāya yaḥ
paribhūy' ātma|vaśāṃ sva|tantratām
upaśānti|pathe śive sthitaḥ
spṛhayed doṣavate gṛhāya saḥ.

vyasan'|âbhihato yathā viśet
parimuktaḥ punar eva bandhanam,
samupetya vanaṃ tathā punar
gṛha|saṃjñaṃ mṛgayeta bandhanam.

8.30 puruṣaś ca vihāya yaḥ kaliṃ
punar icchet kalim eva sevitum,
sa vihāya bhajeta bāliśaḥ
kali|bhūtām a|jit'|êndriyaḥ priyām.

Yet no joy is inaccessible to a determined man who sees the flaws in sensory experience, who is contented, pure, unconceited, and who has enjoined his mind to actions which make for peace. A greedy man delights in the luxuries of wealth, a childish man delights in sensual pleasures, but a good man delights in tranquillity and and overcomes physical enjoyments through his wisdom. 8.25

What is more, when a well-born, wise and respected man wears the honored robes, his mind does not incline to life at home, any more than a mountain bends from the force of the wind. It's the man who scorns self-reliance and independence and who craves the support of another person who would yearn for home, with all its defects, even when standing on the blessed path that leads to peace.

Were a man to again chase the bondage known as 'home' after he has come to the forest, it would be as if a released prisoner were to return to prison when misfortune strikes.
Only a man who renounces strife and then wishes to engage 8.30
in it again would be foolish enough to leave his wife who is all strife, and then with unruly senses seek her out.

sa|viṣā iva saṃśritā latāḥ,
parimṛṣṭā iva s'|ôragā guhāḥ,
vivṛtā iva c' âsayo dhṛtā,
vyasan'|āntā hi bhavanti yoṣitaḥ.
pramadāḥ sa|madā mada|pradāḥ;
pramadā vīta|madā bhaya|pradāḥ.
iti doṣa|bhay'|āvahāś ca tāḥ
katham arhanti niṣevanaṃ nu tāḥ?

sva|janaḥ sva|janena bhidyate
suhṛdaś c' âpi suhṛj|janena yat
para|doṣa|vicakṣaṇāḥ śaṭhās
tad an|āryāḥ pracaranti yoṣitaḥ.
kula|jāḥ kṛpaṇī|bhavanti yad
yad a|yuktaṃ pracaranti sāhasam
praviśanti ca yac camū|mukhaṃ
rabhasās—tatra nimittam aṅganāḥ.

8.35 vacanena haranti valgunā
niśitena praharanti cetasā.
madhu tiṣṭhati vāci yoṣitāṃ
hṛdaye hālahalaṃ mahad viṣam.

Like creepers poisonous to the touch, like scoured caves still harboring snakes, like unsheathed swords held in the hand, women are ruinous in the end. When women want sex they arouse lust; when women don't want sex they bring danger. In what way are they worthy of attention, since they bring vice and danger?

Women behave ignobly, maliciously spying out the weaknesses of others, such that kinsman is set against kinsman and friend against friend. When nobly-born men become destitute, when they behave improperly and rashly, when they recklessly place themselves in the forefront of
an army—it is because of women. They enthrall with their 8.35
charming talk, and attack with their sharp minds. Women's speech is honeyed but there is the deadliest poison in their hearts.

pradahan dahano 'pi gṛhyate,
vi|śarīraḥ pavano 'pi gṛhyate,
kupito bhujago 'pi gṛhyate—
pramadānāṃ tu mano na gṛhyate.

na vapur vimṛśanti na śriyaṃ
na matiṃ n' âpi kulaṃ na vikramam;
praharanty a|viśeṣataḥ striyaḥ
sarito grāha|kul'|â|kulā iva.

na vaco madhuraṃ na lālanaṃ
smarati strī na ca sauhṛdaṃ kvacit;
kalitā vanit" âiva cañcalā
tad ih' âriṣv iva n' âvalambyate.

a|dadatsu bhavanti narma|dāḥ
pradadatsu praviśanti vibhramam;
praṇateṣu bhavanti garvitāḥ
pramadās tṛptatarāś ca māniṣu;

8.40 guṇavatsu caranti bhartṛvad
guṇa|hīneṣu caranti putravat;
dhanavatsu caranti tṛṣṇayā
dhana|hīneṣu caranty avajñayā.

One can grasp a blazing fire, one can grasp the bodiless wind, one can grasp an angry snake—but one cannot grasp the female mind. Women have no regard for handsome looks, wealth, intelligence, lineage or valor; like hordes of crocodiles in a river, they attack without discrimination. A woman never remembers sweet words, caresses or affection. Even when coaxed a woman is flighty, so depend on her no more than you would on your enemies.

Women flirt with those who give them nothing, but become restless with generous men; they are disdainful of humble men, and highly satisfied with grandiloquent men;
they lord it over virtuous men like husbands, and submit 8.40
like children to the wicked; they are covetous of the rich and contemptuous of the poor.

viṣayād viṣay'|ântaraṃ gatā
pracaraty eva yath" āhṛt" âpi gauḥ,
an|avekṣita|pūrva|sauhṛdā
ramate 'nyatra gatā tath" âṅganā.
praviśanty api hi striyaś citām
anubadhnanty api mukta|jīvitāḥ,
api bibhrati n' âiva yantraṇā
na tu bhāvena vahanti sauhṛdam.
ramayanti patīn kathaṃ cana
pramadā yāḥ pati|devatāḥ kva cit,
cala|cittatayā sahasraśo
ramayante hṛdayaṃ svam eva tāḥ.
śvapacaṃ kila Senajit|sutā
cakame Mīnaripuṃ Kumudvatī
mṛga|rājam atho Bṛhadrathā;
pramadānām a|gatir na vidyate.
8.45 Kuru|Haihaya|Vṛṣṇi|vaṃśa|jā
bahu|māyā|kavaco 'tha Śambaraḥ
munir Ugratapāś ca Gautamaḥ
samavāpur vanit"|ôddhataṃ rajaḥ.
a|kṛta|jñam an|āryam a|sthiraṃ
vanitānām idam īdṛśaṃ manaḥ.
katham arhati tāsu paṇḍito
hṛdayaṃ sañjayituṃ cal'|ātmasu?

Just as a cow, even when herded, goes grazing from one field to another, so will a woman move on to take her pleasure elsewhere, disregarding any previous attachment. For though they enter their husbands' funeral fires, though they stick by their husbands even at the cost of their lives, women cannot bear pain and show no affection in their demeanor. Women who sometimes please their husbands in some ways, treating them as gods, please their own hearts a thousand times more with their inconsistency.

They say that Sénajit's daughter slept with an outcaste, Kumúdvati with Mina·ripu and Brihad·ratha with a lion;
there is nothing a woman will not do. Sons of the families of 8.45
Kuru, Háihaya and Vrishni, as well as Shámbara who wore armor of powerful magic, and the sage Ugra·tapas Gáutama, all encountered the dust of passion stirred up by women. This is the sort of mind that women have—ungrateful, ignoble, unsteady. How could a wise man fasten his heart to such fickle creatures?

atha sūkṣmam atidvay'|â|śivaṃ
laghu tāsāṃ hṛdayaṃ na paśyasi!
kim u kāyam a|sad|gṛhaṃ sravad
vanitānām a|śuciṃ na paśyasi?
yad ahany ahani pradhāvanair
vasanaiś c' ābharaṇaiś ca saṃskṛtam
a|śubhaṃ tamas" āvṛt'|ēkṣaṇaḥ
śubhato gacchasi; n' âvagacchasi.
atha vā samavaiṣi tat|tanūm
a|śubhāṃ tvaṃ na tu saṃvid asti te,
surabhiṃ vidadhāsi hi kriyām
a|śuces tat|prabhavasya śāntaye.
8.50 anulepanam añjanaṃ srajo
maṇi|muktā|tapanīyam aṃśukam—
yadi sādhu, kim atra yoṣitāṃ?
sahajaṃ tāsu vicīyatāṃ śuci:
mala|paṅka|dharā dig|ambarā
prakṛti|sthair nakha|danta|romabhiḥ
yadi sā tava Sundarī bhaven
niyataṃ te 'dya na sundarī bhavet.
sravatīm a|śuciṃ spṛśec ca kaḥ
sa|ghṛṇo jarjara|bhāṇḍavat striyam
yadi kevalayā tvac" āvṛtā
na bhaven makṣika|pattra|mātrayā?
tvaca|veṣṭitam asthi|pañjaraṃ
yadi kāyaṃ samavaiṣi yoṣitām,
madanena ca kṛṣyase balād,
a|ghṛṇaḥ khalv a|dhṛtiś ca manmathaḥ!
śubhatām a|śubheṣu kalpayan
nakha|danta|tvaca|keśa|romasu

So, you don't see that women's hearts are cunning, utterly duplicitous, pernicious and superficial! Do you at least see that their bodies are dirty, oozing, houses of vice? The repulsiveness adorned day by day with cleansing, clothing and decoration you, with your sight veiled by dark ignorance, perceive as attractive; you fail to undertand. Or perhaps you know in theory that their bodies are impure, but lack full comprehension, for you are engaged in a fragrant task to
allay the foulness they produce. Ointments, cosmetics, gar- 8.50
lands, jewels, pearls and gold, fine silks—if these are good, what have they to do with women? Let's analyze their inherent purity:

If your Súndari were naked, covered only by dust and mud, with her nails, teeth and hair in their natural state, she definitely wouldn't be beautiful Súndari for you then. What sensitive man would touch a woman, leaking and unclean like an old box, if she were not covered in skin, thin as a fly's wing though it is? If you know in theory that women's bodies are cages of bone wrapped round with skin, but are still strongly moved by lust, then Passion must indeed lack delicacy and constancy! You are imagining a pure beauty in impure nails, teeth, skin and long hair. You blind fool, can't you see the natural state of women and what they
come from? So understand women to be especially flawed 8.55
in mind and body, and use the strength of this recollection to hold back your roving mind which longs for home!

a|vicakṣaṇa kiṃ na paśyasi
prakṛtiṃ ca prabhavaṃ ca yoṣitām?

8.55 tad avetya manaḥ|śarīrayor
vanitā doṣavatīr viśeṣataḥ,
capalaṃ bhavan'|ôtsukaṃ manaḥ
pratisaṃkhyāna|balena vāryatām!

śrutavān matimān kul'|ôdgataḥ
paramasya praśamasya bhājanam;
upagamya yathā tathā punar
na hi bhettuṃ niyamaṃ tvam arhasi.

abhijana|mahato manasvinaḥ
priya|yaśaso bahu|mānam icchataḥ
nidhanam api varaṃ sthir'|ātmanaś
cyuta|vinayasya na c' âiva jīvitam.

baddhvā yathā hi kavacaṃ pragṛhīta|cāpo
nindyo bhavaty apasṛtaḥ samarād ratha|sthaḥ,
bhaikṣākam abhyupagataḥ parigṛhya liṅgaṃ
nindyas tathā bhavati kāma|hṛt'|êndriy'|âśvaḥ.

hāsyo yathā ca param'|ābharaṇ'|âmbara|srag
bhaikṣaṃ caran dhṛta|dhanuś cala|citta|mauliḥ,
vairūpyam abhyupagataḥ para|piṇḍa|bhojī
hāsyas tathā gṛha|sukh'|âbhimukhaḥ sa|tṛṣṇaḥ.

8.60 yathā sv|annaṃ bhuktvā
parama|śayanīye 'pi śayito
varāho nirmuktaḥ
punar a|śuci dhāvet paricitam,
tathā śreyaḥ śṛṇvan
praśama|sukham āsvādya guṇavad
vanaṃ śāntaṃ hitvā
gṛham abhilaṣet kāma|tṛṣitaḥ.

You are learned, you are intelligent, you are nobly-born, you are a worthy recipient of supreme peace; as such you mustn't in any way break the observances which you have undertaken. Better death for a nobly-born man, firm in himself and sound of mind, holding his reputation dear and wishing to be respected, than life for one whose discipline has slipped.

When a man has donned armor, has his bow at the ready and stands in his chariot, it is shameful for him to retreat from the field of battle. Likewise it is shameful for a man who has adopted mendicancy and accepted the robes of a monk to allow the horses of his senses to run away with desire. And just as it is ridiculous to practice mendicancy decked in the finest ornaments, clothes and garlands, holding a bow and with one's head full of frivolities, likewise it is ridiculous to consent to the drab robes and to eat the almsfood of others while thirstily longing for domestic pleasures.

Just as a boar would return to his dunghill when set free, 8.60
though he had been fed with good food and had slept on the finest bedding, so would a man thirsty for passion yearn to abandon the peaceful forest and go home, though he had learned of Excellence and had sipped the bliss of peace. Just as a firebrand with wind-fanned flames burns the hand that bears it, just as a snake in a rush of fury bites the foot that steps on it, just as a tiger attacks, though captured as a cub and reared in your house, just so does cohabiting with a woman cause all manner of ill.

yath" ôlkā hasta|sthā
dahati pavana|prerita|śikhā,
yathā pād'|ākrānto
daśati bhujagaḥ krodha|rabhasaḥ,
yathā hanti vyāghraḥ
śiśur api gṛhīto gṛha|gataḥ,
tathā strī|saṃsargo
bahu|vidham an|arthāya bhavati.
tad vijñāya manaḥ|śarīra|niyatān
nārīṣu doṣān imān;
matvā kāma|sukhaṃ nadī|jala|calaṃ
kleśāya śokāya ca;
dṛṣṭvā dur|balam āma|pātra|sadṛśaṃ
mṛty'|ûpasṛṣṭaṃ jagat—
nirmokṣāya kuruṣva buddhim a|tulām,
utkaṇṭhituṃ n' ârhasi!»

Saundaranande mahā|kāvye Strī|vighāto nām' âṣṭamaḥ sargaḥ.

So be cognizant of these defects that pertain to women's minds and bodies; understand that pleasure from passion flows away like the waters of a river and makes for defilement and sadness; observe that the world, flimsy as an unfired pot, is in the grip of death—make the peerless decision for freedom, and yearn no more!"

End of Canto 8: The Attack on Women.

CANTO 9
THE DENUNCIATION OF INFATUATION

9.1 ATH' ÂIVAM ukto 'pi sa tena bhikṣuṇā
jagāma n' âiv' ôpaśamaṃ priyāṃ prati;
tathā hi tām eva tadā sa cintayan
na tasya śuśrāva visaṃjñavad vacaḥ.
yathā hi vaidyasya cikīrṣataḥ śivaṃ
vaco na gṛhṇāti mumūrṣur āturaḥ,
tath" âiva matto bala|rūpa|yauvanair
hitaṃ na jagrāha sa tasya tad vacaḥ.
na c' âtra citraṃ yadi rāga|pāpmanā
mano 'bhibhūyeta tamo|vṛt'|ātmanaḥ
narasya pāpmā hi tadā nivartate
yadā bhavaty anta|gataṃ tamas tanu.
tatas tath" ākṣiptam avekṣya taṃ tadā
balena rūpeṇa ca yauvanena ca,
gṛha|prayāṇaṃ prati ca vyavasthitaṃ,
śaśāsa Nandaṃ śramaṇaḥ sa śāntaye:
9.5 «balaṃ ca rūpaṃ ca navaṃ ca yauvanaṃ
tath" âvagacchāmi yath" âvagacchasi;
ahaṃ tv idaṃ te trayam a|vyavasthitaṃ
yath" âvabuddho na tath" âvabudhyase.
idaṃ hi rog'|āyatanaṃ jar"|â|vaśaṃ
nadī|taṭ'|ânokahavac cal'|â|calam,
na vetsi dehaṃ jala|phena|durbalaṃ
bala|sthatām ātmani yena manyase.
yad" ânna|pān'|āsana|yāna|karmaṇām
a|sevanād apy ati|sevanād api
śarīram āsanna|vipatti dṛśyate.
bale 'bhimānas tava kena hetunā?
him'|ātapa|vyādhi|jarā|kṣud|ādibhir
yad" âpy an|arthair upanīyate jagat

THOUGH THE monk spoke to him in this manner, Nanda 9.1
found no peace as far as his sweetheart was concerned; he thought of her so much that, like an unconscious man, he didn't hear a word he said. Just as a sick and dying man takes no notice of the beneficient words of the doctor who wishes to treat him, so Nanda, intoxicated with his physical fitness, good looks and youthfulness, took no notice of his well-intentioned words. It is hardly surprising that the mind of one cloaked in dark ignorance should be overwhelmed by lustful inclinations, for man's perversity will come to a halt only when his ignorance is attenuated and comes to an end. Then, observing him to be caught up with his own physical fitness, good looks and youthfulness, and preparing to go home, the ascetic rebuked Nanda in order to calm him down:

"I am aware, just as you are aware, of your bodily strength, 9.5
beauty and fresh youth; but I understand, as you do not, that these three are impermanent. You think bodily strength will endure in you because you do not comprehend that the body is the living quarters of disease, helpless before old age, as loose as a tree on a riverbank, fragile as a water-bubble. The body is obviously close to failing, either from neglecting the activities of eating, drinking, resting and exercizing or from over-indulging in them. Why then are you so proud of your physical fitness?

You, body-proud, what are you thinking as you travel towards ruin? The world is pulled in by misfortune—cold, heat, sickness, old age and hunger—just as water in the hot

jalaṃ śucau māsa iv' ârka|raśmibhiḥ,
kṣayaṃ vrajan kiṃ bala|dṛpto manyase?
tvag|asthi|māṃsa|kṣataj'|ātmakaṃ yadā
śarīram āhāra|vaśena tiṣṭhati,
ajasram ārtaṃ satata|pratikriyaṃ,
bal'|ânvito 'sm' îti kathaṃ vihanyase?

9.10 yathā ghaṭaṃ mṛn|mayam āmam āśrito
naras titīrṣet kṣubhitaṃ mah"ârṇavam;
samucchrayaṃ tadvad a|sāram udvahan
balaṃ vyavasyed viṣay'|ârtham udyataḥ.
śarīram āmād api mṛn|mayād ghaṭād
idaṃ tu niḥ|sāratamaṃ mataṃ mama,
ciraṃ hi tiṣṭhed vidhivad dhṛto ghaṭaḥ
samucchrayo 'yaṃ su|dhṛto 'pi bhidyate.
yad" âmbu|bhū|vāyv|analāś ca dhātavaḥ
sadā viruddhā viṣamā iv' ôragāḥ,
bhavanty an|arthāya śarīram āśritāḥ,
kathaṃ balaṃ roga|vidho vyavasyasi?
prayānti mantraiḥ praśamaṃ bhujaṃgamā
na mantra|sādhyās tu bhavanti dhātavaḥ.
kva cic ca kaṃ cic ca daśanti pannagāḥ
sadā ca sarvaṃ ca tudanti dhātavaḥ.
idaṃ hi śayy"|āsana|pāna|bhojanair
guṇaiḥ śarīraṃ ciram apy avekṣitam,
na marṣayaty ekam api vyatikramaṃ
yato mah"|āśīviṣavat prakupyati.

9.15 yadā him'|ārto jvalanaṃ niṣevate;
himaṃ nidāgh'|âbhihato 'bhikāṅkṣati;
kṣudh"|ânvito 'nnaṃ, salilaṃ tṛṣ"|ânvito.
balaṃ kutaḥ kiṃ ca kathaṃ ca kasya ca?

season is absorbed by the rays of the sun. The body is made of skin, bones, flesh and blood; it subsists only through dependence on food. It is perpetually afflicted and in need of continuous remedial action, so why do you frustrate yourself with your assumption of physical well-being?

A man carries about this sapless excrescence and in his 9.10
longing for sensory experience is persuaded of its robustness; but he is like a man who sets out to cross the rolling ocean in an unbaked earthen pot. In my opinion the body is even more fragile than an unbaked earthen pot, since a pot, when carefully maintained, would last for a long time, but this excrescence will break down even when well-maintained.

And when the elements of water, earth, wind and fire* are always at variance with each other like contrary snakes, and they abide in the body only to do it harm, how can you, the sick type, be so confident of your vitality? Snakes can be soothed by mantras,* but the elements cannot be managed with a mantra. Snakes bite some people under certain circumstances, but the elements strike all people at all times. Though the body be long and carefully tended with good sleeping, resting, drinking and eating habits, it does not excuse even one false move and so becomes irritated like a great poisonous snake.

When you suffer from cold, you seek out warmth; when 9.15
you are tormented by heat, you wish for the cold; you long for food when you are hungry, and for water when you are thirsty. Where is physical robustness, what is it, how is it, whose is it? So, observing that your body is diseased, do not

tad evam ājñāya śarīram āturaṃ
    bal'|ânvito 'sm' îti na mantum arhasi.
a|sāram a|sv|antam a|niścitaṃ jagaj;
    jagaty a|nitye, balam a|vyavasthitam.
kva Kārtavīryasya bal'|âbhimāninaḥ
    sahasra|bāhor balam Arjunasya tat?
cakarta bāhūn yudhi yasya Bhārgavo
    mahānti śṛṅgāṇy aśanir girer iva.
kva tad balaṃ Kaṃsa|vikarṣaṇo Hares
    turaṅga|rājasya puṭ'|âvabhedinaḥ
yam eka|bāṇena nijaghnivāñ Jarāḥ
    kram'|āgatā rūpam iv' ôttamaṃ jarā.
Diteḥ sutasy' âmara|roṣa|kāriṇaś
    camū|rucer vā Namuceḥ kva tad balam?
yam āhave kruddham iv' āntakaṃ sthitaṃ
    jaghāna phen'|âvayavena Vāsavaḥ.
9.20 balaṃ Kurūṇāṃ kva ca tat tad" âbhavad
    yudhi jvalitvā taras" âujasā ca ye
samit|samiddhā jvalanā iv' âdhvare
    hat'|âsavo bhasmani paryavasthitāḥ.
ato viditvā bala|vīrya|māninām
    bal'|ânvitānām avamarditaṃ balam,
jagaj jarā|mṛtyu|vaśaṃ vicārayan
    bale 'bhimānaṃ na vidhātum arhasi!

imagine that you are replete with bodily well-being. The world is without substance, uncertain, and bodes ill; and since it is impermanent, the physical realm is unreliable.

Where is the might of thousand-armed Árjuna Karta-virya, so proud of his power? Bhárgava cut off his arms in battle as a thunderbolt cuts off a mountain's giant peaks. Where is the strength of Hari who tore apart Kansa and split the jaw of the Horse-King? Jaras struck him down with a single arrow, just as old age eventually strikes down even the rarest beauty. Where is the strength of Námuchi son of Diti, light of the army and provoker of the gods? Furious as death he stood his ground in battle, but Vásava killed
him with a morsel of foam. Where is the strength of the 9.20
Kurus at war, blazing with energy and vigor? Like sacrificial fires stoked with fuel, they turned to ashes, their life-breath ended. Therefore recognize that physical capacity is ground down even in mighty men proud of their strength and valor. Reflect on the world under the sway of old age and death, and take no pride in strength!

balaṃ mahad vā yadi vā na manyase,
kuruṣva yuddhaṃ saha tāvad indriyaiḥ.
jayaś ca te 'tr' âsti mahac ca te balaṃ,
parājayaś ced vitathaṃ ca te balam;
tathā hi vīrāḥ puruṣā na te matā
jayanti ye s'|âśva|ratha|dvipān arīn,
yathā matā vīratarā manīṣiṇo
jayanti lolāni ṣaḍ|indriyāṇi ye.
‹ahaṃ vapuṣmān!› iti yac ca manyase
vicakṣaṇaṃ n' âitad. idaṃ ca gṛhyatām:
kva tad vapuḥ sā ca vapuṣmatī tanur
Gadasya Śāmbasya ca Sāraṇasya ca?
9.25 yathā mayūraś cala|citra|candrako
bibharti rūpaṃ guṇavat svabhāvataḥ,
śarīra|saṃskāra|guṇād ṛte tathā
bibharṣi rūpaṃ, yadi rūpavān asi.
yadi pratīpaṃ vṛṇuyān na vāsasā,
na śauca|kāle yadi saṃspṛśed apaḥ,
mṛjā|viśeṣaṃ yadi n' ādadīta vā,
vapur vapuṣman vada kīdṛśaṃ bhavet.
navaṃ vayaś c' ātma|gataṃ niśāmya yad
gṛh'|ônmukhaṃ te viṣay'|āptaye manaḥ,
niyaccha tac chaila|nad"|īray'|ôpamaṃ
drutaṃ hi gacchaty a|nivarti yauvanam.
ṛtur vyatītaḥ parivartate punaḥ,
kṣayaṃ prayātaḥ punar eti candramāḥ,
gataṃ gataṃ n' âiva tu saṃnivartate
jalaṃ nadīnāṃ ca nṛṇāṃ ca yauvanam.

Whether or not you think your physical prowess great, make war against your senses. Your victory in that arena would be a great strength, but if defeated, your physical strength is futile; for men who conquer enemies well-equipped with horses, chariots and elephants are not considered as heroic as those thoughtful men who conquer the six roving senses.

And it's not clever to believe 'I am handsome!' Ponder this: where are the fine looks, where are the fine bodies of Gada, Shamba or Sárana? If you are beautiful, then the beauty 9.25
you exhibit must exclude any attractive feature resulting from personal care, just as the peacock with its fluttering, glittering tail carries its beauty naturally. O handsome man, describe what your body would be like if its unpleasant parts were not covered with clothes, if it had no contact with water after excretion, or if it were unbathed. Imagining that green youth is integral to you, your mind turns homeward in the expectation of finding pleasurable sensations. Stop it, for youth, like a coursing mountain stream, flows swiftly and does not return.

The seasons pass and come back again, the moon wanes and waxes again, but gone, gone, never to return are the waters of a river and the youth of a man.

vivarṇita|śmaśru valī|vikuñcitaṃ
viśīrṇa|dantaṃ śithila|bhru niṣ|prabham
yadā mukhaṃ drakṣyasi jarjaraṃ tadā
jar'|âbhibhūto vimado bhaviṣyasi.

9.30 niṣevya pānaṃ madanīyam uttamaṃ
niśā|vivāseṣu cirād vimādyati,
naras tu matto bala|rūpa|yauvanair
na kaś cid a|prāpya jarāṃ vimādyati.

yath" êkṣur atyanta|rasa|prapīḍito
bhuvi praviddho dahanāya śuṣyate,
tathā jarā|yantra|nipīḍitā tanur
nipīta|sārā maraṇāya tiṣṭhati.

yathā hi nṛbhyāṃ karapattram īritaṃ
samucchritaṃ dāru bhinatty an|eka|dhā,
tath" ôcchritāṃ pātayati prajām imām
ahar|niśābhyām upasaṃhitā jarā.

smṛteḥ pramoṣo vapuṣaḥ parābhavo
rateḥ kṣayo vāc|chruti|cakṣuṣāṃ grahaḥ
śramasya yonir bala|vīryayor vadho
jarā|samo n' âsti śarīriṇāṃ ripuḥ.

idaṃ viditvā nidhanasya daiśikaṃ
jar"|âbhidhānaṃ jagato mahad bhayam
‹ahaṃ vapuṣmān balavān yuv" êti› vā
na mānam āroḍhum an|āryam arhasi.

When you behold your face grown old—lusterless, lined with wrinkles, with a white mustache, broken teeth and sagging eyebrows—then, beaten by age, you will be free of vanity. A man who drinks hard for days and nights eventu- 9.30
ally sobers up, but a man besotted with his own strength, looks and youth never comes to his senses until he reaches old age. Just as sugar-cane, once all its juice is completely squeezed out, is thrown on the ground to dry it ready for the fire, so does the body, once it has been crushed in the mill of old age and drained of its natural juices, wait to die.

Just as a mighty tree is chopped into segments by two men working a saw, so are these living beings that have risen up toppled by old age in league with day and night. It steals memory, humiliates beauty, ruins sex, seizes speech, hearing and sight, produces fatigue and kills strength and vigor; old age is the matchless enemy of humankind. Acknowledge this great death-indicating danger in the world, known as old age, and do not rise to the ignoble and complacent thought: 'I am lovely, strong and young.'

9.35 ahaṃ mam' êty eva ca rakta|cetasaḥ
śarīra|saṃjñe tava yaḥ kalau grahaḥ,
tam utsṛj' âivaṃ yadi śāmyatā bhaved,
bhayaṃ hy ahaṃ c' êti mam' êti c' ārchati.
yadā śarīre na vaśo 'sti kasya cin
nirasyamāne vividhair upaplavaiḥ,
kathaṃ kṣamaṃ vettum ahaṃ mam' êti vā
śarīra|saṃjñaṃ gṛham āpadām idam?
sa|pannage yaḥ ku|gṛhe sad" â|śucau
rameta nityaṃ pratisaṃskṛte '|bale,
sa duṣṭa|dhātāv a|śucau cal'|âcale
rameta kāye viparīta|darśanaḥ.
yathā prajābhyaḥ ku|nṛpo balād balīn
haraty a|śeṣaṃ ca na c' âbhirakṣati,
tath" âiva kāyo vasan'|ādi|sādhanaṃ
haraty aśeṣaṃ ca na c' ânuvartate.
yathā prarohanti tṛṇāny a|yatnataḥ
kṣitau prayatnāt tu bhavanti śālayaḥ,
tath" âiva duḥkhāni bhavanty a|yatnataḥ
sukhāni yatnena bhavanti vā na vā.

9.40 śarīram ārtaṃ parikarṣataś calaṃ
na c' âsti kiṃ cit param'|ârthataḥ sukham;
sukhaṃ hi duḥkha|pratikāra|sevayā
sthite ca duḥkhe tanuni vyavasyati.
yath" ân|apekṣy' âgryam ap' īpsitaṃ sukhaṃ
prabādhate duḥkham upetam aṇv api,
tath" ân|apekṣy' ātmani duḥkham āgataṃ
na vidyate kiṃ cana kasya cit sukham.

With 'I' and 'mine' you, passionate-minded, are holding on to a faulty conception of the body. Let go of it, if peace is to come about, for 'I' is dangerous, and 'mine' is calamitous. Since no one can control a body eroded by adversities of various kinds, how can it be sensible to suppose that this body, the abode of ill-boding, is 'I' or 'mine'? Only a man who is pleased with a flimsy snake-filled hovel, always dirty and constantly needing repairs, would be perverse enough to enjoy his unclean fluctuating body with its hostile elements. Just as a tyrant forcibly takes the full sum of taxes from his subjects yet fails to protect them, likewise the body takes in full its provisions such as clothes, yet remains anarchic; and just as grass grows easily in the soil but rice only with labor, so unhappiness appears readily but happiness only with effort, if at all. 9.35

There is no real happiness for man, dragging around his painful changeable body; but he assumes he will be happy if he can minimize unhappiness by adopting countermeasures against sorrow. Just as the advent of even a tiny annoyance detracts from a great, longed-for pleasure, so no man experiences any happiness oblivious to the suffering that has befallen him. 9.40

śarīram īdṛg bahu|duḥkham a|dhruvaṃ
phal'|ânurodhād atha n' âvagacchasi.
dravat phalebhyo dhṛti|raśmibhir mano
nigṛhyatāṃ gaur iva śasya|lālasā.
na kāma|bhogā hi bhavanti tṛptaye
havīṃṣi dīptasya vibhāvasor iva;
yathā yathā kāma|sukheṣu vartate
tathā tath" êcchā viṣayeṣu vardhate.
yathā ca kuṣṭha|vyasanena duḥkhitaḥ
pratāpanān n' âiva śamaṃ nigacchati,
tath" êndriy'|ârtheṣv a|jit'|êndriyaś caran
na kāma|bhogair upaśāntim ṛcchati.

9.45 yathā hi bhaiṣajya|sukh'|âbhikāṅkṣayā
bhajeta rogān na bhajeta tat|kṣayam,*
tathā śarīre bahu|duḥkha|bhājane
rameta mohād viṣay'|âbhikāṅkṣayā.
an|artha|kāmaḥ puruṣasya yo janaḥ
sa tasya śatruḥ kila tena karmaṇā.
an|artha|mūlā viṣayāś ca kevalā
nanu praheyā viṣamā yath" ârayaḥ!
ih' âiva bhūtvā ripavo vadh'|ātmakāḥ
prayānti kāle puruṣasya mitratām
paratra c' âiv' êha ca duḥkha|hetavo
bhavanti kāmā na tu kasya cic chivāḥ.

You don't accept that this is the way the body is—unstable and prone to much suffering—because you like the wages of physical action. Restrain your mind, which chases after results, with the halter of steadfastness, as if it were a corn-loving cow! For the enjoyment of sensuality is never sufficient, like offerings into a blazing fire; the longer sense pleasure continues, the greater grows the longing for the sensory realm. And just as a man suffering with leprosy gets no relief from heat, likewise a man of unruly senses who is preoccupied with sensory experience finds no peace in sensual enjoyment.

For as one might cultivate diseases rather than their erad- 9.45
ication through a desire for the pleasures of medication, so through a befuddled desire for the sensory realm one might find pleasure in the body, that recipient of many pains. When a man wishes misfortune on another, that man is thereby deemed an enemy. Surely the sensory realm, the sole root of misfortune, ought to be shunned as a dangerous enemy! Those who are a man's deadly enemies here and now can in time become his friends; but desires, the cause of suffering, are not benign for anybody, neither now nor in the future.

yath" ôpayuktaṃ rasa|varṇa|gandhavad
vadhāya kiṃpāka|phalaṃ na puṣṭaye;
niṣevyamāṇā viṣayāś cal'|ātmano
bhavanty anarthāya tathā na bhūtaye.
tad etad ājñāya vipāpman" ātmanā
vimokṣa|dharm'|ādy upasaṃhitaṃ hitam,
juṣasva me saj|jana|saṃmataṃ mataṃ.
pracakṣva vā niścayam udgiran giram.»

9.50 iti hitam api bahv ap' îdam uktaḥ
śruta|mahatā śramaṇena tena Nandaḥ,
na dhṛtim upayayau na śarma lebhe
dvirada iv' âtimado mad'|ândha|cetāḥ.
Nandasya bhāvam avagamya tataḥ sa bhikṣuḥ
pāriplavaṃ gṛha|sukh'|âbhimukhaṃ na dharme,
sattv'|āśay'|ânuśaya|bhāva|parīkṣakāya
Buddhāya tattva|viduṣe kathayāṃ cakāra.

Saundaranande mahā|kāvye Mad'|âpavādo nāma navamaḥ sargaḥ.

It tastes good, it looks good, it smells good, but eating a *kimpáka* fruit brings death and not nourishment; likewise a giddy man's preoccupation with the sense realm brings misery and not well-being. So with your better nature recognize that my advice, pertaining to liberation, *dharma*, and the like, is good. Let my opinions, shared by wise people, find favor with you. Now speak out and tell me your decision."

Though addressed at length in this salutary fashion by 9.50
the learned ascetic, Nanda did not become steadfast, he did not find peace; like an excessively ruttish elephant, his mind was blinded by lust. Then the monk understood that Nanda's feelings were wavering and that he was focusing on domestic pleasures, not on the *dharma*. So he related it all to the Buddha, the truth-knower, the examiner of the mental dispositions, latent tendencies and emotions of all beings.

End of Canto 9: The Denunciation of Infatuation.

CANTO 10
A LESSON IN HEAVEN

10.1 Śrutvā tataḥ sad|vratam utsisṛkṣuṃ
bhāryāṃ didṛkṣuṃ bhavanaṃ vivikṣum,
Nandaṃ nir|ānandam apeta|dhairyam
abhyujjihīrṣur munir ājuhāva.
taṃ prāptam a|prāpta|vimokṣa|mārgaṃ
papraccha citta|skhalitaṃ su|cittaḥ.
sa hrīmate hrī|vinato jagāda
svaṃ niścayaṃ niścaya|kovidāya.
Nandaṃ viditvā Sugatas tatas taṃ
bhāry"|âbhidhāne tamasi bhramantam,
pāṇau gṛhītvā viyad utpapāta
maṇiṃ jale sādhur iv' ôjjihīrṣuḥ.
kāṣāya|vastrau kanak'|âvadātau
virejatus tau nabhasi prasanne,
anyonya|saṃśliṣṭa|vikīrṇa|pakṣau
saraḥ|prakīrṇāv iva cakravākau.
10.5 tau devadār'|ûttama|gandhavantaṃ
nadī|saraḥ|prasravaṇ'|âughavantam,
ājagmatuḥ kāñcana|dhātumantaṃ
deva'|rṣimantaṃ Himavantam āśu.
tasmin girau cāraṇa|siddha|juṣṭe
śive havir|dhūma|kṛt'|ôttarīye,
agamya|pārasya nirāśrayasya
tau tasthatur dvīpa iv' âmbarasya.

WHEN THE SAGE heard that he was lacking fortitude and intended to give up his excellent observances and return home to see his wife, he summoned the unhappy Nanda in order to offer uplift. Nanda arrived with faltering mind after failing to arrive at liberation's path, and was questioned by the noble-minded one. Bowed down with shame, he spoke of his decision to that decision-knowing modest man. Aware that Nanda was lost in the darkness of ignorance known as "wife," the Súgata planned to extricate him and taking him by the hand flew up into the sky, like a good man lifts up a jewel in the water. 10.1

With their ochre garments they shone like refined gold in the clear sky, like a pair of *chakra·vaka* birds rising from a lake, their wings outstretched to clasp one another. In an 10.5
instant they traveled to the golden-ored Himalayan mountains, imbued with the lovely scent of deodar trees, abounding in rivers, lakes and rushing streams, home to divine seers. They found themselves standing on a pure mountain, as though on an island in the shoreless and unsupported sky. It was inhabited by celestial singers and perfected beings, and was blanketed in smoke from their sacrificial offerings.

śānt'|êndriye tatra munau sthite tu,
sa|vismayaṃ dikṣu dadarśa Nandaḥ
darīś ca kuñjāṃś ca vanaukasaś ca
vibhūṣaṇaṃ rakṣaṇam eva c' âdreḥ.
bahv|āyate tatra site hi śṛṅge
saṃkṣipta|barhaḥ śayito mayūraḥ
bhuje Balasy' āyata|pīna|bāhor
vaiḍūrya|keyūra iv' ābabhāse.
manaḥśilā|dhātu|śil"|āśrayeṇa
pītā|kṛt'|âṃso virarāja siṃhaḥ
saṃtapta|cāmīkara|bhakti|citraṃ
rūpy'|âṅgadaṃ śīrṇam iv' Āmbikasya.*
10.10 vyāghraḥ klama|vyāyata|khela|gāmī
lāṅgūla|cakreṇa kṛt'|âpasavyaḥ
babhau gireḥ prasravaṇaṃ pipāsur
ditsan pitṛbhyo 'mbha iv' âvatīrṇaḥ.
calat|kadambe Himavan|nitambe
tarau pralambe camaro lalambe,
chettuṃ vilagnaṃ na śaśāka bālaṃ,
kul'|ôdgatāṃ prītim iv' ārya|vṛttaḥ.
suvarṇa|gaurāś ca kirāta|saṃghā
mayūra|pitt'|ôjjvala|gātra|lekhāḥ,
śārdūla|pāta|pratimā guhābhyo
niṣpetur udgāra iv' âcalasya.
darī|carīṇām ati|sundarīṇāṃ
manohara|śroṇi|kuc'|ôdarīṇām
vṛndāni rejur diśi kiṃnarīṇāṃ,
puṣp'|ôtkacānām iva vallarīṇām.
nagān nagasy' ôpari devadārūn
āyāsayantaḥ kapayo viceruḥ

But, while the sage stood there with his senses quiet, Nanda's gaze flitted every which way in astonishment at the caves and bowers that embellished the mountain, and at the hermits who guarded it.

For there on a pale far-stretching pinnacle lay a peacock
with its tail feathers narrowed, resembling a bracelet of cat's-
eye gems on the long-reaching muscular arm of Bala. And
a lion with his shoulder yellowed from reclining on a rock
of red arsenic looked like Ámbika's broken silver armlet
variously etched with refined gold. A tiger proceeding in 10.10
stately languid stretches to a mountain stream, his tail curled
over his right shoulder as he prepared to drink, seemed like
a man going down to offer water to his ancestors.

A yak was caught in the overhang of a rustling *kadámba* tree on the Himalayan slope, unable to free his entangled tail, like a man of noble conduct who cannot cut free from an inherited friendship. As though the mountain spewed, there spilled forth groups of golden-bodied mountain tribespeople, their limbs streaked with shining peacock bile like tigers pouncing from their caves. All around appeared clusters of surpassingly lovely cavern-dwelling *kínnaris* with gorgeous hips, breasts and bellies, their hair coiled like creeper flowers.

Monkeys roamed across the mountain disturbing the deodar trees, but finding no fruit on them went away again,
as from powerful men whose favor is fruitless. Among the 10.15

tebhyaḥ phalaṃ n' âpur ato 'pajagmur
modha|prasādebhya iv' ēśvarebhyaḥ.

10.15 tasmāt tu yūthād a|lasāyamānāṃ
niṣpīḍit'|âlaktaka|rakta|vaktrām
śākhā|mṛgīm eka|vipanna|dṛṣṭiṃ
dṛṣṭvā munir Nandam idaṃ babhāṣe:

«kā Nanda rūpeṇa ca ceṣṭayā ca
sampaśyataś cārutarā matā te—
eṣā mṛgī v" âika|vipanna|dṛṣṭiḥ,
sa vā jano yatra gatā tav' êṣṭiḥ?»

ity evam uktaḥ Sugatena Nandaḥ
kṛtvā smitaṃ kiṃ cid idaṃ jagāda,
«kva c' ôttama|strī bhagavan vadhūs te
mṛgī naga|kleśa|karī kva c' âiṣā?»

tato munis tasya niśamya vākyaṃ
hetv|antaraṃ kiṃ cid avekṣamāṇaḥ
ālambya Nandaṃ prayayau tath" âiva
krīḍā|vanaṃ vajra|dharasya rājñaḥ.

troop the sage noticed an indolent female monkey, with one damaged eye and its face red with crushed cochineal. He said to Nanda:

"As you look right round, Nanda, which is in your opinion the more delectable in beauty and mannerisms—this monkey with her damaged eye, or the person who is the object of your desire?"

When the Súgata said this to him, Nanda gave a small smile and replied, "What comparison can there be, Lord, between your sister-in-law, the most excellent of women, and this mischief-making monkey in the trees?"

The sage heard his answer, and with a further motivating illustration in mind he took hold of Nanda just as before and departed for the pleasure garden of the thunderbolt-wielding king.*

ṛtāv ṛtāv ākṛtim eka eke
kṣaṇe kṣaṇe bibhrati yatra vṛkṣāḥ,
citrāṃ samastām api ke cid anye
ṣaṇṇām ṛtūnāṃ śriyam udvahanti.
10.20 puṣyanti ke cit surabhīr udārā
mālāḥ srajaś ca grathitā vicitrāḥ,
karṇ'|ânukūlān avataṃsakāṃś ca
pratyarthibhūtān iva kuṇḍalānām.
raktāni phullāḥ kamalāni yatra
pradīpa|vṛkṣā iva bhānti vṛkṣāḥ,
praphulla|nīl'|ôtpala|rohiṇo 'nye
s'|ônmīlit'|âkṣā iva bhānti vṛkṣāḥ.
nānā|virāgāṇy atha pāṇḍarāṇi,
suvarṇa|bhakti|vyavabhāsitāni,
a|tāntavāny eka|ghanāni yatra
sūkṣmāṇi vāsāṃsi phalanti vṛkṣāḥ.
hārān maṇīn uttama|kuṇḍalāni
keyūra|varyāṇy atha nūpurāṇi—
evaṃvidhāny ābharaṇāni yatra
svarg'|ânurūpāṇi phalanti vṛkṣāḥ.
vaiḍūrya|nālāni ca kāñcanāni
padmāni vajr'|âṅkura|kesarāṇi,
sparśa|kṣamāṇy uttama|gandhavanti
rohanti niṣkampa|talā nalinyaḥ.

Some of the trees there manifest one or other season from
moment to moment, while others wear the combined and
various glory of all six seasons at once. Some trees produce 10.20
exquisite fragrant garlands and wreaths variously interwo-
ven, and flower ornaments so suited to the ear that they
seem to rival earrings. There are trees there that blossom
with red lotuses and shine like lanterns, while others, as
though open-eyed, grow blue, full-blown lotuses.

Multi-hued or white, shimmering with gold thread, unwoven and seamless are the delicate garments that trees there bear as fruit. Pearl necklaces, gems, superb earrings, wonderful armlets, anklets—these are the kind of heaven-suited jewels that trees there bear as fruit. And from the unstirred surfaces of lotus pools grow golden lotuses with stems of cat's-eye gems and diamond shoots and filaments, yet yielding to the touch and intensely fragrant.

10.25 yatr' āyatāṃś c' âiva tatāṃś ca tāṃs tān
vādyasya hetūn suṣirān ghanāṃś ca
phalanti vṛkṣā maṇi|hema|citrāḥ
krīḍā|sahāyās tridaś'|ālayānām.
mandāra|vṛkṣāṃś ca kuśeśayāṃś ca
puṣp'|ānatān koka|nadāṃś ca vṛkṣān
ākramya māhātmya|guṇair virājan
rājāyate yatra sa pārijātaḥ.
kṛṣṭe tapaḥ|śīla|halair a|khinnais
tripiṣṭapa|kṣetra|tale prasūtāḥ,
evaṃvidhā yatra sad" ânuvṛttā
divaukasāṃ bhoga|vidhāna|vṛkṣāḥ.
manaḥśil"|ābhair vadanair vihaṃgā,
yatr' âkṣibhiḥ sphāṭika|saṃnibhaiś ca,
śāvaiś ca pakṣair abhilohit'|ântair,
māñjiṣṭhakair ardha|sitaiś ca pādaiḥ.
citraiḥ suvarṇa|chadanais tath" ânye
vaiḍūrya|nīlair nayanaiḥ prasannaiḥ;
vihaṃgamāḥ śiñjirik'|âbhidhānā
rutair manaḥ|śrotra|harair bhramanti.
10.30 raktābhir agreṣu ca vallarībhir
madhyeṣu cāmīkara|piñjarābhiḥ
vaiḍūrya|varṇābhir upānta|madhyeṣv
alaṃkṛtā yatra khagāś caranti.
rociṣṇavo nāma patatriṇo 'nye
dīpt'|âgni|varṇ'|ôjjvalitair iv' āsyaiḥ,
bhramanti dṛṣṭīr vapuṣ" ākṣipantaḥ
svanaiḥ śubhair apsaraso harantaḥ.
yatr' êṣṭa|ceṣṭāḥ satata|prahṛṣṭā
nir|artayo nir|jaraso vi|śokāḥ,

Assistants to amusement in the gods' abodes, trees aglitter there with gems and gold bear instruments for music, extended in length or pulled taut, hollow or solid.* The coral tree is ruler there, radiant with the qualities of majesty and lording it over the *mandáras* and water-lilies and trees of crimson lotuses that bow under their flowery weight. 10.25

There, in the topsoil of heaven's fields which is tilled by the unwearying plows of asceticism and moral self-restraint, grow these kinds of trees, in compliance always with the provision of enjoyment for the denizens of heaven.

There are birds with beaks the color of red arsenic, crystalline eyes, tawny wings tipped with scarlet, and with claws half crimson, half white. There are other birds too, with limpid eyes blue as cat's-eye gems and shimmering golden feathers; these *shínjirika*s, as they are called, flit about en-
chanting the mind and ear with their trilling. And there are 10.30
birds that wander there arrayed in plumage red at the tip, yellow-gold in the middle and the color of cat's-eye jewels at the end. Other birds, their bright beaks colored like a flaming fire, are known as *rochíshnu*s. They dart about, catching the eye with their beauty and entrancing the *ápsaras*es with their lovely fluting.

Here the merit-makers take their pleasure, doing as they wish, always blissful, free from pain, old age and grief, the splendor of each being low, great or average according to

svaiḥ karmabhir hīna|viśiṣṭa|madhyāḥ
svayaṃ|prabhāḥ puṇya|kṛto ramante.
pūrvaṃ tapo|mūlya|parigraheṇa
svarga|kray'|ârthaṃ kṛta|niścayānām
manāṃsi khinnāni tapo|dhanānāṃ
haranti yatr' âpsaraso laḍantyaḥ.
nity'|otsavaṃ taṃ ca niśāmya lokaṃ
nis|tandri|nidr"|ârati|śoka|rogam,
Nando jarā|mṛtyu|vaśaṃ sad" ārtaṃ
mene śmaśāna|pratimaṃ nṛ|lokam.

10.35 Aindraṃ vanaṃ tac ca dadarśa Nandaḥ
samantato vismaya|phulla|dṛṣṭiḥ;
harṣ'|ânvitāś c' âpsarasaḥ parīyuḥ
sa|garvam anyonyam avekṣamāṇāḥ.
sadā yuvatyo madan'|âika|kāryāḥ
sādhāraṇāḥ puṇya|kṛtāṃ vihārāḥ
divyāś ca nir|doṣa|parigrahāś ca
tapaḥ|phalasy' āśrayaṇaṃ surāṇām.

tāsāṃ jagur dhīram, udāttam anyāḥ,
padmāni kāś cil lalitaṃ babhañjuḥ,
anyonya|harṣān nanṛtus tath" ânyāś,
citr'|âṅga|hārāḥ stana|bhinna|hārāḥ.
kāsāṃ cid āsāṃ vadanāni rejur
van'|ântarebhyaś cala|kuṇḍalāni,
vyāviddha|parṇebhya iv' ākarebhyaḥ
padmāni kāraṇḍava|ghaṭṭitāni.

tā niḥsṛtāḥ prekṣya van'|ântarebhyas
taḍit|patākā iva toyadebhyaḥ,
Nandasya rāgeṇa tanur vivepe
jale cale candramasaḥ prabh" êva.

their former deeds. Here the *ápsaras*es play the flirt, enrapturing the weary minds of ascetics who had decided to buy heaven by first paying the price in ascetic practices. When Nanda saw this world in constant celebration, without languor, sleep, dullness, grief or sickness, he reasoned that the human world, in thrall to age and death and always prone to pain, was comparable to a cremation ground.

Nanda gazed at Indra's forest all around him, his eyes 10.35
wide in amazement; and the *ápsaras*es drew round him, full of joy and eyeing eachother disdainfully. Eternally youthful and occupied solely with lovemaking, they were a communal enjoyment for heaven-dwellers who had earned merit. Taking these heavenly women as lovers was no fault, just an acceptance of the rewards of asceticism.

Some sang in low, some in high tones, some pulled playfully at lotuses, and others danced exuberantly with each other, through their vivid gestures breaking the pearl necklaces on their breasts. The faces of some peeped out from among the woods, their earrings swaying, as lotuses shaken by a *karándava* bird peep out from among their scattered and disordered leaves.

Watching them emerge from the forest interiors like lightning unfurled from clouds, Nanda's body shivered with
passion like moonlight reflected in rippling water. His eyes 10.40
intense with interest, he mentally seized on their divine bodies and teasing gestures as though his passion was aroused

10.40 vapuś ca divyaṃ lalitāś ca ceṣṭās
tataḥ sa tāsāṃ manasā jahāra
kautūhal'|āvarjitayā ca dṛṣṭyā
saṃśleṣa|tarṣād iva jāta|rāgaḥ.
sa jāta|tarṣo 'psarasaḥ pipāsus
tat|prāptaye 'dhiṣṭhita|viklav'|ārtaḥ,
lol'|êndriy'|âśvena mano|rathena
jehrīyamāṇo, na dhṛtiṃ cakāra.
yathā manuṣyo malinaṃ hi vāsaḥ
kṣāreṇa bhūyo malinī|karoti,
mala|kṣay'|ârthaṃ na mal'|ôdbhav'|ârthaṃ
rajas tath" âsmai munir ācakarṣa.
doṣāṃś ca kāyād bhiṣag ujjihīrṣur
bhūyo yathā kleśayituṃ yateta,
rāgaṃ tathā tasya munir jighāṃsur
bhūyastaraṃ rāgam upāninAya.
dīpa|prabhāṃ hanti yath" ândha|kāre
sahasra|raśmer uditasya dīptiḥ,
manuṣya|loke dyutim aṅganānām
antardadhāty apsarasāṃ tathā śrīḥ.
10.45 mahac ca rūpaṃ sv|aṇu hanti rūpaṃ,
śabdo mahān hanti ca śabdam alpam,
gurvī rujā hanti rujāṃ ca mṛdvīṃ;
sarvo mahān hetur aṇor vadhāya.

through thirsting for union with them. He grew thirsty, and tormented by the agitation which governed him, he desired to drink up the *ápsaras*es to alleviate his thirst. Put to shame by desire, that chariot of the mind pulled by the galloping senses-horses, his resolution failed.

Just as a man uses soda to make dirty clothes even dirtier, not to create more dirt but to remove it, so the sage fomented passion in Nanda. And just as a doctor seeks to draw out humoral faults from the body by further paining it, so the sage, intending to destroy passion in him, first brought about a far greater passion. As the radiance of the rising thousand-rayed sun annihilates lamplight in the darkness, so does the glory of the *ápsaras*es obscure the
shine of women in the world of humankind. Great beauty 10.45
destroys small beauty, a great noise destroys a little noise, and a severe sickness destroys a mild sickness; every great cause brings the destruction of a lesser one.

muneḥ prabhāvāc ca śaśāka Nandas
tad darśanaṃ soḍhum a|sahyam anyaiḥ,
a|vīta|rāgasya hi dur|balasya
mano dahed apsarasāṃ vapuḥ|śrīḥ.
matvā tato Nandam udīrṇa|rāgaṃ
bhāry"|ânurodhād apavṛtta|rāgam,
rāgeṇa rāgaṃ pratihantu|kāmo
munir virāgo giram ity uvāca:
«etāḥ striyaḥ paśya divaukasas tvaṃ
nirīkṣya ca brūhi yath" ârtha|tattvam
etāḥ kathaṃ rūpa|guṇair matās te
sa vā jano yatra gataṃ manas te?»
ath' âpsaraḥsv eva niviṣṭa|dṛṣṭī,
rāg'|âgnin" ântar|hṛdaye pradīptaḥ,
sa|gadgadaṃ kāma|viṣakta|cetāḥ
kṛt'|âñjalir vākyam uvāca Nandaḥ:
10.50 «hary|aṅgan" âsau muṣit'|âika|dṛṣṭir
yad|antare syāt tava nātha vadhvāḥ,
tad|antare 'sau kṛpaṇā vadhūs te
vapuṣmatīr apsarasaḥ pratītya.
āsthā yathā pūrvam abhūn na kā cid
anyāsu me strīṣu niśāmya bhāryām
tasyāṃ tataḥ samprati kā cid āsthā
na me niśāmy' âiva hi rūpam āsām.
yathā pratapto mṛdun" ātapena
dahyeta kaś ciṇ mahat" ânalena,
rāgeṇa pūrvaṃ mṛdun" âbhitapto
rāg'|âgnin" ânena tath" âbhidahye.
vāg|vāriṇā māṃ pariṣicya tasmād
yāvan na dahye sa iv' âbja|śatruḥ,

And by the power of the sage Nanda was able to endure that sight unendurable for others, for the bodily splendor of the *ápsaras*es would have burned the mind of a feeble man not free of passion. The dispassionate sage judged that Nanda's passion had turned away from its accommodation with his wife and was aroused for the *ápsaras*es, and intending to repulse passion with passion, he said:

"Look at these heavenly women and after observing them, speak in accordance with the truth of the matter. Do you prefer these women with their beauty and accomplishments, or the person who holds your mind?"

Then with his eyes resting on the *ápsaras*es, his heart burning with the fire of passion and his thoughts stuck in lust, Nanda folded his hands in reverence and stammered out these words:

"Whatever difference there might have been between the 10.50
one-eyed monkey and your sister-in-law, Lord, is the same when your pitiable sister-in-law is set against the lovely *ápsaras*es. Just as previously I did not care for other women when I beheld my wife, so now I have no regard for her when I behold their beauty. Just as somebody warmed by a gentle heat would by burned by a huge fire, so previously I was warmed by a mild passion but am now scorched by this fiery passion.

Therefore sprinkle on me the water of your voice, before I am burned up like the enemy of the water-born,* for passion's fire threatens to consume me right now, like a fire

rāg'|âgnir ady' âiva hi māṃ didhakṣuḥ
kakṣaṃ sa|vṛkṣ'|âgram iv' ôtthito 'gniḥ.
prasīda, sīdāmi, vimuñca mā mune,
vasundharā|dhairya na dhairyam asti me.
asūn vimokṣyāmi, vimukta|mānasa,
prayaccha vā vāg|amṛtaṃ mumūrṣave.

10.55 an|artha|bhogena vighāta|dṛṣṭinā
pramāda|daṃṣṭreṇa tamo|viṣ'|âgninā
ahaṃ hi daṣṭo hṛdi manmath'|âhinā
vidhatsva tasmād agadaṃ, mahā|bhiṣak!
anena daṣṭaḥ madan'|âhinā hi nā
na kaś cid ātmany an|avasthitaḥ sthitaḥ;
mumoha Vodhyor hy acal'|ātmano mano
babhūva dhīmāṃś ca sa Śantanus tanuḥ.
sthite viśiṣṭe tvayi saṃśraye śraye
yathā na yām' îha vasan diśaṃ diśam
yathā ca labdhvā vyasana|kṣayaṃ kṣayaṃ
vrajāmi tan me kuru śaṃsataḥ sataḥ.»
tato jighāṃsur hṛdi tasya tat tamas
tamo|nudo naktam iv' ôtthitaṃ tamaḥ
maha"|rṣi|candro jagatas tamo|nudas
tamaḥ|prahīṇo nijagāda Gautamaḥ:

mounting in the underwood to the trees above. Please, O sage firm as the earth, I am sinking, save me who am without firmness. I will give up my life, O man of liberated mind, unless you grant me in my dying moment the ambrosia of your words.

For I have been bitten in the heart by the snake of lust, 10.55
which has worthlessness for its coils, destruction for its eyes, infatuation for its fangs and dark ignorance for its burning venom. Great physician, prescribe a remedy! For nobody bitten by this snake of lust remains contained in himself; though imperturbable by nature, Vodhyu's mind was stupefied, and wise Shántanu was enfeebled.

I take refuge in you who are established in the best refuge. So that I do not depart from this life to dwell now here, now there, so that I can obtain that abode which is the end of misery—and still continue—take action for me who am your suppliant."

So the moon of the great seers, the dispeller of the world's darkness, Gáutama devoid of darkness spoke, wishing to dispel the darkness in Nanda's heart like the moon dispels the night's rising darkness:

«dhṛtiṃ pariṣvajya, vidhūya vikriyāṃ,
nigṛhya tāvac chruta|cetasī, śṛṇu:
imā yadi prārthayase tvam aṅganā,
vidhatsva śulk'|ârtham ih' ôttamaṃ tapaḥ.

10.60 imā hi śakyā na balān na sevayā
na sampradānena na rūpavattayā
imā hriyante khalu dharma|caryayā.
sacet praharṣaś, cara dharmam ādṛtaḥ.

ih' âdhivāso divi daivataiḥ samaṃ
vanāni ramyāṇy a|jarāś ca yoṣitaḥ
idaṃ phalaṃ svasya śubhasya karmaṇo
na dattam anyena na c' âpy a|hetutaḥ.

kṣitau manuṣyo dhanur|ādibhiḥ śramaiḥ
striyaḥ kadā cidd hi labheta vā na vā.
a|saṃśayaṃ yat tv iha dharma|caryayā
bhaveyur etā divi puṇya|karmaṇaḥ.

tad a|pramatto niyame samudyato
ramasva yady apsaraso 'bhilipsase,
ahaṃ ca te 'tra pratibhūḥ sthire vrate
yathā tvam ābhir niyataṃ sameṣyasi.»

«ataḥ paraṃ paramam» iti vyavasthitaḥ
parāṃ dhṛtiṃ parama|munau cakāra saḥ.
tato muniḥ pavana iv' âmbarāt patan
pragṛhya taṃ punar agaman mahī|talam.

Saundaranande mahā|kāvye Svarga|nidarśano nāma daśamaḥ sargaḥ.

"Embrace resolution, abandon rebelliousness, restrain your ears and heart, then listen: If you desire these women, practice the highest asceticism in this life to pay their bride-
price. For they cannot be won by strength, nor by service, 10.60
not by gifts, not by handsomeness, but only by the practice of *dharma*. If they please you, practice *dharma* diligently.

Life here in heaven together with the gods, the delightful forests and these unaging women are the reward of one's own pure deeds. The reward cannot be given by anyone else, nor is it available without due motivation. On earth, a man may sometimes win women with his exertions—by the use of weapons, for instance—or he may not. But what is beyond doubt is that these celestial women must belong to a man who makes merit through the practice of *dharma*.

So if you wish to win the *ápsaras*es, undertake the disciplinary rules joyfully, attentively and eagerly, and I will stand guarantor that if you are steadfast in your observances you will definitely be united with them."

"Henceforth I will," he said, and fixed his resolve on the supreme sage. Then the sage took hold of him and flying down from the sky like the wind, returned once more to earth.

End of Canto 10: A Lesson in Heaven.

CANTO 11
THE CONDEMNATION OF HEAVEN

II.1 TATAS TĀ YOṢITO dṛṣṭvā
Nando Nandana|cāriṇīḥ,
babandha niyama|stambhe
dur|damam capalaṃ manaḥ.

so 'n|iṣṭa|naiṣkramya|raso mlāna|tāmaras'|ôpamaḥ,
cacāra vi|raso dharmaṃ niveśy' âpsaraso hṛdi.
tathā lol'|êndriyo bhūtvā dayit'|êndriya|gocaraḥ
indriy'|ârtha|vaśād eva babhūva niyat'|êndriyaḥ.
kāma|caryāsu kuśalo, bhikṣu|caryāsu viklavaḥ,
param'|ācārya|viṣṭabdho brahmacaryaṃ cacāra saḥ.
II.5 saṃvṛtena ca śāntena tīvreṇa madanena ca,
jal'|âgner iva saṃsargāc chaśāma ca śuśoṣa ca.
svabhāva|darśanīyo 'pi vairūpyam agamat param,
cintay" âpsarasāṃ c' âiva niyamen' āyatena ca.

prastaveṣv api bhāryāyāḥ priya|bhāryas tath" âpi saḥ
vīta|rāga iv' ôttasthau na jaharṣa na cukṣubhe.
taṃ vyavasthitam ājñāya bhāryā|rāgāt parāṅ|mukham,
abhigamy' âbravīn Nandam Ānandaḥ praṇayād idam:

«aho sadṛśam ārabdhaṃ śrutasy' âbhijanasya ca,
nigṛhīt'|êndriyaḥ svastho niyame yadi saṃsthitaḥ.
II.10 abhiṣvaktasya kāmeṣu rāgiṇo viṣay'|ātmanaḥ
yad iyaṃ saṃvid utpannā n' êyam alpena hetunā.

AFTER SEEING those women who wander in the gardens II.1
of Nándana, Nanda bound his volatile mind, so difficult to tame, to the post of restraint.

He housed the *ápsaras*es in his heart; then, sapless as a wilting lotus and unappreciative of renunciation's taste, he practiced *dharma* unenthusiastically. So it was that Nanda with his restive senses, who had pastured his senses with his lover, now became controlled in his senses through the very power of sensory experience. Skilled in love-making, disturbed by monkish ways, he practiced celibacy propped up by the supreme teacher.

He was soothed by calming restraint and drained by vi- II.5
olent passion, just as one is calmed and dried from a combination of water and fire. Though he had always been handsome by nature, he became very ugly, which resulted as much from his obsession with the *ápsaras*es as from extensive restrictions.

Although Nanda had cherished his wife, he appeared like someone free of passion, and he neither thrilled nor trembled even when his wife was mentioned. Noticing that Nanda had settled down and had turned away from his passion for his wife, Anánda came up to him and affectionately said:

"If your senses are contained, if you are at ease and keeping to the rules, then oh! this is a beginning worthy of
an educated and well-born person. No insignificant cause II.10
could have effected this understanding in a lusty man in the clutches of passion whose nature centered on sense objects.

vyādhir alpena yatnena mṛduḥ pratinivāryate,
prabalaḥ prabalair eva yatnair naśyati vā na vā.
dur|haro mānaso vyādhir balavāṃś ca tav' âbhavat.
vinivṛtto yadi sa te, sarvathā dhṛtimān asi!

duṣkaraṃ sādhv an|āryeṇa, māninā c' âiva mārdavam,
atisargaś ca lubdhena, brahmacaryaṃ ca rāgiṇā.

ekas tu mama saṃdehas tav' âsyāṃ niyame dhṛtau
atr' ânunayam icchāmi, vaktavyaṃ yadi manyase.

11.15 ārjav'|âbhihitaṃ vākyaṃ na ca gantavyam anyathā—
rūkṣam apy āśaye śuddhe rūkṣato n' âiti saj|janaḥ.
a|priyaṃ hi hitaṃ snigdham a|snigdham a|hitaṃ priyam.
dur|labhaṃ tu priya|hitaṃ svādu pathyam iv' āuṣadham.

viśvāsaś c' ârtha|caryā ca sāmānyaṃ sukha|duḥkhayoḥ
marṣaṇaṃ praṇayaś c' âiva mitra|vṛttir iyaṃ satām.
tad idaṃ tvā vivakṣāmi praṇayān na jighāṃsayā.
tvac|chreyo hi vivakṣā me yato n' ârhāmy upekṣitum.

apsaro|bhṛtako dharmaṃ caras' îty abhidhīyase.
kim idaṃ bhūtam āho svit? parihāso 'yam īdṛśaḥ!
11.20 yadi tāvad idaṃ satyaṃ, vakṣyāmy atra yad auṣadham,
auddhatyam atha vaktṝṇām, abhidhāsyāmi tattvataḥ.»

ślakṣṇa|pūrvam atho tena hṛdi so 'bhihatas tadā
dhyātvā dīrghaṃ niśaśvāsa kiṃ cic c' âvāṅ|mukho 'bhavat.

A mild illness can be checked with little effort, but a violent illness is destroyed only with great effort, if at all. Your illness was mental; it was intense and difficult to remove. If it is in remission, you are in every way resolute! Goodness is hard for the ignoble, flexibility for the opinionated, liberality for the avaricious, and celibacy for the lustful.

But I have one doubt concerning your steadfastness in the rules. If you think you can tell me about it, I would welcome
reassurance on this matter. Words spoken sincerely should 11.15
not be otherwise construed—a good man does not judge even harsh speech harshly when the intention behind it is pure. For unpleasant but beneficial advice is a kindness, while pleasant but unhelpful words are not. It is as difficult to find advice that is both pleasing and beneficial as it is to find medicine that is both palatable and effective.

Among decent folk, friendly behavior consists of tolerance, affection, trust, acting in the other's interest, and the sharing of joys and sorrows. So I'd like to talk to you out of affection, and not with the intention of hurting you. My wish is to talk of what is best for you, something that I ought not to disregard.

You are said to be practicing *dharma* to earn the *ápsaras*es.
Well? Is it true? Such a thing would be a joke! If it is true, 11.20
I will prescribe a remedy for it, and if it is just the work of gossip-mongers, I will put the truth around."

Then, wounded in his heart though it was gently done, Nanda brooded awhile, sighed deeply, and turned his face aside.

tatas tasy' êṅgitaṃ jñātvā manaḥ|saṃkalpa|sūcakam,
babhāṣe vākyam Ānando madhur'|ôdarkam a|priyam:
«ākāreṇ' âvagacchāmi tava dharma|prayojanam,
yaj jñātvā tvayi jātaṃ me hāsyaṃ kāruṇyam eva ca.
yath" āsan'|ârthaṃ skandhena kaś cid gurvīṃ śilāṃ vahet
tadvat tvam api kām'|ârthaṃ niyamaṃ voḍhum udyataḥ!
11.25 titāḍayiṣayā dṛpto yathā meṣo 'pasarpati,
tadvad a|brahmacaryāya brahmacaryam idaṃ tava.
cikrīṣanti yathā paṇyaṃ vaṇijo lābha|lipsayā,
dharma|caryā tava tathā paṇya|bhūtā na śāntaye.
yathā phala|viśeṣ'|ârthaṃ bījaṃ vapati kārṣakaḥ,
tadvad viṣaya|kārpaṇyād viṣayāṃs tyaktavān asi.
ākāṅkṣec ca yathā rogaṃ pratīkāra|sukh'|ēpsayā
duḥkham anvicchati bhavāṃs tathā viṣaya|tṛṣṇayā.
yathā paśyati madhv eva na prapātam avekṣate,
paśyasy apsarasas tadvad, bhraṃśam ante na paśyasi.
11.30 hṛdi kām'|âgninā dīpte kāyena vahato vratam
kim idaṃ brahmacaryaṃ te manas" â|brahmacāriṇaḥ?
saṃsāre vartamānena yadā c' âpsarasas tvayā
prāptās tyaktāś ca śataśas. tābhyaḥ kim iti te spṛhā?
tṛptir n' âst' îndhanair agner, n' âmbhasā lavaṇ'|âmbhasaḥ,
n' âpi kāmaiḥ sa|tṛṣṇasya. tasmāt kāmā na tṛptaye.
a|tṛptau ca kutaḥ śāntir? a|śāntau ca kutaḥ sukham?

Noting his changed expression which betrayed the willfulness of his mind, Anánda addressed him in words that were unwelcome but which would have a sweet consequence:

"I understand from your expression your motive in practicing *dharma*, and knowing it, I am moved to both laughter and compassion on your account. Just as someone would carry a heavy rock on his shoulder to use as a seat, likewise you are laboring to uphold the rules of restraint for the sake
of sensual indulgence! Just as a wild ram draws back when 11.25
he is about to charge, likewise this celibacy of yours is undertaken for the sake of sex. Just as businessmen like to buy goods to make a profit, so you practice *dharma* as an article for trade, not to become peaceful. Just as a farmer scatters seed to produce a particular fruit, likewise you have let go of sense objects because of your weakness for them.

You are seeking out suffering with your thirst for sensory experience, as though someone would want to be ill just to enjoy the pleasure of a remedy. Just as a man looking for honey does not notice a precipice, so in your focus on the
*ápsaras*es you do not see your resulting fall. What is this 11.30
celibacy of yours? While your heart is ablaze with the fire of lust, you carry out your observances with your body only, and are not celibate in your mind.

As you continue in the round of birth and death, you have won and lost the *ápsaras*es hundreds of times. Why then this longing for them? A fire is never content with its fuel, nor the ocean with its water, not a lustful man with sensuality. Therefore sensuality cannot deliver satisfaction. Without satisfaction, from where comes peace? Without

a|sukhe ca kutaḥ prītir? a|prītau ca kuto ratiḥ?

riraṃsā yadi te tasmād adhyātme dhīyatāṃ manaḥ;
praśāntā c' ân|avadyā ca n' âsty adhyātma|samā ratiḥ.

11.35 na tatra kāryaṃ tūryais te, na strībhir, na vibhūṣaṇaiḥ;
ekas tvaṃ yatra|tatra|sthas tayā raty" ābhiraṃsyate.

mānasaṃ balavad duḥkhaṃ tarṣe tiṣṭhati tiṣṭhati.
taṃ tarṣaṃ chindhi, duḥkhaṃ hi tṛṣṇā c' âsti ca n' âsti ca;
sampattau vā vipattau vā, divā vā naktam eva vā,
kāmeṣu hi sa|tṛṣṇasya na śāntir upapadyate.
kāmānāṃ prārthanā duḥkhā; prāptau tṛptir na vidyate,
viyogān niyataḥ śoko viyogaś ca dhruvo divi.

kṛtv" âpi duṣkaraṃ karma
svargaṃ labdhv" âpi dur|labham,
nṛ|lokaṃ punar ev' âiti
pravāsāt sva|gṛhaṃ yathā.

11.40 yadā bhraṣṭasya kuśalaṃ śiṣṭaṃ kiṃ cin na vidyate,
tiryakṣu pitṛ|loke vā narake v" ôpapadyate.
tasya bhuktavataḥ svarge viṣayān uttamān api
bhraṣṭasy' ārtasya duḥkhena, kim āsvādaḥ karoti saḥ?

śyenāya prāṇi|vātsalyāt sva|māṃsāny api dattavān,
Śibiḥ svargāt paribhraṣṭas tādṛk kṛtv" âpi duṣkaram.
Śakrasy' ârdh'|āsanaṃ gatvā pūrva|pārthiva eva yaḥ,
sa|devatvaṃ gate kāle Māndhāt" âdhaḥ punar yayau.
rājyaṃ kṛtv" âpi devānāṃ papāta Nahuṣo bhuvi.

peace, from where comes happiness? Without happiness, from where comes joy? And without joy, from where comes bliss?

If you long for that bliss, then focus your mind on your inner self; unequaled is the tranquil and irreproachable bliss of the inner self. With bliss you have no need of music, 11.35
women nor ornaments; bliss will gladden you when you are alone, wherever you happen to be.

As long as thirst remains, mental suffering remains powerful. Abolish that thirst, for suffering and thirst either coexist, or neither exists; in neither good times nor bad, by neither day nor night is peace possible for a man who thirsts after sensual pleasures. The longing for sensual pleasures brings unsatisfactoriness; when they come they deliver no fulfillment, yet when one is deprived of them, as is certain in the hereafter, grief is inevitable.

A man can perform deeds difficult to do and even win heaven so hard to win, but he comes back to the human world, just as a traveler returns home after living abroad.
When no good remains to the descending man, he is reborn 11.40
among the animals, or in the world of the ancestors, or in hell. He falls, visited by sorrow, after enjoying in heaven the most appetizing sense objects—and how does that gratification help him?

In his tenderness for all living things Shibi even gave his own flesh to a hawk, but he fell from heaven even after so difficult a deed. In the olden days King Mandhátri gained half of Indra's throne, but the time of his divinity passed and he went to the lower region again. Though Náhusha

prāptaḥ kila bhujaṅgatvaṃ, n' âdy' âpi parimucyate.
11.45 tath" âiv' Êlivilo rājā rāja|vṛttena saṃskṛtaḥ,
svargaṃ gatvā punar bhraṣṭaḥ kūrmī|bhūtaḥ kil' ârṇave.
Bhūridyumno Yayātiś ca te c' ânye ca nṛpa'|rṣabhāḥ
karmabhir dyām abhikrīya, tat|kṣayāt punar atyajan.
asurāḥ pūrva|devās tu surair apahṛta|śriyaḥ;
śriyaṃ samanuśocantaḥ pātālaṃ śaraṇaṃ yayuḥ.
kiṃ ca rāja'|rṣibhis tāvad asurair vā sur'|ādibhiḥ?
mah'|Êndrāḥ śataśaḥ petur—māhātmyam api na sthiram!
saṃsadaṃ śobhayitv" Āindrīm Upendraś ca tri|vikramaḥ,
kṣīṇa|karmā papāt' ôrvīṃ madhyād apsarasāṃ rasan.
11.50 ‹hā Caitraratha, hā vāpi, hā Mandākini, hā priye!›
ity ārtā vilapanto 'pi gāṃ patanti divaukasaḥ.
tīvraṃ hy utpadyate duḥkham iha tāvan mumūrṣatām;
kiṃ punaḥ patatāṃ svargād ev' ânte sukha|sevinām!
rajo gṛhṇanti vāsāṃsi, mlāyanti paramāḥ srajaḥ,
gātrebhyo jāyate svedo, ratir bhavati n' āsane.
etāny ādau nimittāni cyutau svargād divaukasām,
an|iṣṭān' îva martyānām ariṣṭāni mumūrṣatām.
sukham utpadyate yac ca divi kāmān upāśnatām,
yac ca duḥkhaṃ nipatatāṃ; duḥkham eva viśiṣyate.

reigned even over the gods, he fell to earth. They say he became a snake and is still not free.

Likewise King Ílivila, perfected by his royal conduct, went to heaven but fell again and became, it is said, a turtle in the ocean. Bhuri·dyumna, Yayáti and those other bull-like kings bought heaven with their deeds, but left it again when their merit ran out. The *ásura*s, former divinities, were robbed of their rank by the gods; they took refuge under the earth, jointly grieving for their lost glory. 11.45

But why list examples of royal seers, *ásura*s and gods? Great Indras have fallen in their hundreds—even the most exalted state is not fixed! Upéndra, who covered the world in three strides, graced the court of Indra. When the credit for his deeds was spent, he fell to earth from among the *ápsaras*es, screaming.

The sky-dwellers fall to earth, crying out in regret: 'Oh 11.50
the groves,* oh the lakes, oh the heavenly Ganges,* oh my beloved!'

People at death's door here in this world feel violent sorrow; how much more so the pleasure-addicts when they finally fall from heaven! Their clothes collect dust, their sublime wreaths wither, sweat appears on their bodies, and they take no joy in their station. These are the signs of the imminent fall of the sky-dwellers from heaven, like the unwanted and ominous signs of mortals approaching death. They experience happiness when they savor pleasures in heaven, and suffering when they fall; but it is suffering which predominates.

11.55 tasmād a|sv|antam a|trāṇam a|viśvāsyam a|tarpakam,
vijñāya kṣayiṇaṃ svargam, apavarge matiṃ kuru.
a|śarīraṃ bhav'|âgraṃ hi gatv" âpi munir Udrakaḥ,
karmaṇo 'nte cyutas tasmāt tiryag|yoniṃ prapatsyate.*
maitrayā sapta|vārṣikyā brahma|lokam ito gataḥ,
Sunetraḥ punar āvṛtto garbha|vāsam upeyivān.
yadā c' āiśvaryavanto 'pi kṣayiṇaḥ svarga|vāsinaḥ,
ko nāma svarga|vāsāya kṣeṣṇave spṛhayed budhaḥ?
sūtreṇa baddho hi yathā vihaṃgo
vyāvartate dūra|gato 'pi bhūyaḥ
a|jñāna|sūtreṇa tath" âvabaddho
gato 'pi dūraṃ punar eti lokaḥ.

11.60 kṛtvā kāla|vilakṣaṇaṃ pratibhuvā
mukto yathā bandhanāt,
bhuktvā veśma|sukhāny atītya samayaṃ
bhūyo viśed bandhanam.
tadvad dyāṃ pratibhū|vad ātma|niyamair
dhyān'|ādibhiḥ prāptavān,
kāle karmasu teṣu bhukta|viṣayeṣv
ākṛṣyate gāṃ punaḥ.
antar|jāla|gatāḥ pramatta|manaso
mīnās taḍāge yathā
jānanti vyasanaṃ na rodha|janitaṃ,
svasthāś caranty ambhasi,
antar|loka|gatāḥ kṛt'|ârtha|matayas
tadvad divi dhyāyinaḥ
manyante śivam a|cyutaṃ dhruvam iti,
svaṃ sthānam āvartakam.

Therefore recognize that heaven has no favorable outcome, and is vulnerable, unreliable, unsatisfactory and perishable, and set your mind on emancipation. 11.55

The sage Údraka has attained a disembodied state at the zenith of existence, but when his good deeds expire he will fall from there to an animal womb. By practicing loving-kindness for seven seasons Sunétra went from this world to Brahma's world, but he returned to dwell in a womb again. When even the sovereign dwellers of heaven decay, what wise man would yearn for an ephemeral stay there?

For just as a bird bound by a string flies back again although it has flown far, so do people bound by the string of ignorance return again though they have traveled far.

A prisoner is released when bail has secured him a reprieve 11.60
for a certain time. He enjoys domestic pleasures, but when his time is up he must go to prison again. In the same way a man wins heaven through self-restraint, meditation and so on, as though on bail, but is eventually dragged back to earth again when the sensual pleasures resulting from his good actions have been enjoyed.

Just as fish in a pond carelessly swim into a net and, unaware of the tragedy that will result from their capture, continue to move around happily in the water, so do people in that world believe they have achieved their end. They are engrossed in heaven and believe their own position there to be benign, unfallen and certain, though it is reversible.

taj janma|vyādhi|mṛtyu|vyasana|parigataṃ
matvā jagad idaṃ
saṃsāre bhrāmyamāṇaṃ divi nṛṣu narake
tiryak|pitṛṣu ca.
yat trāṇaṃ nir|bhayaṃ yac chivam a|mara|jaraṃ
niḥ|śokam a|mṛtaṃ
tadd|hetor brahmacaryaṃ cara, jahihi calaṃ
svargaṃ prati rucim.»

Saundaranande mahā|kāvye Svarg'|âpavādo nām'
âikādaśaḥ sargaḥ.

Therefore be aware that this existence—wandering in samsara, perhaps in heaven, or among men, or in hell, or in the animal or ancestor realms—is permeated with the afflictions of birth, sickness and death. So practice abstinence for the sake of that sheltering state which is safe and benign, which is without danger, without aging and dying, sorrowless and deathless, and give up your appetite for that shifting heaven."

End of Canto 11: The Condemnation of Heaven.

CANTO 12
COMPREHENSION

12.1 APSARO|BHṚTAKO dharmaṃ caras' îty atha coditaḥ
Ānandena, tadā Nandaḥ paraṃ vrīḍam upāgamat.
tasya vrīḍena mahatā, pramodo hṛdi n' âbhavat,
a|prāmodyena vimukhaṃ n' âvatasthe vrate manaḥ.
kāma|rāga|pradhāno 'pi, parihāsa|samo 'pi san,
paripāka|gate hetau na sa tan mamṛṣe vacaḥ.
a|parīkṣaka|bhāvāc ca, pūrvaṃ matvā divaṃ dhruvam.
tasmāt kṣeṣṇuṃ pariśrutya bhṛśaṃ saṃvegam eyivān.
12.5 tasya svargān nivavṛte saṃkalp'|âśvo mano|rathaḥ
mahā|ratha iv' ônmārgād a|pramattasya sāratheḥ.
svarga|tarṣān nivṛttaś ca, sadyaḥ svastha iv' âbhavat,
mṛṣād a|pathyād virato jijīviṣur iv' āturaḥ.
visasmāra priyāṃ bhāryām apsaro|darśanād yathā,
tath" â|nityatay" ôdvignas tatyāj' âpsaraso 'pi saḥ.
mahatām api bhūtānām āvṛttir iti cintayan
saṃvegāc ca sa|rāgo 'pi vīta|rāga iv' âbhavat.
babhūva sa hi saṃvegaḥ śreyasas tasya vṛddhaye,
dhātur edhir iv' ākhyāte paṭhito 'kṣara|cintakaiḥ.
12.10 na tu kāmān manas tasya kena cij jagṛhe dhṛtiḥ
triṣu kāleṣu sarveṣu, nipāto 'stir iva smṛtaḥ.

AFTER ANÁNDA had accused him practicing *dharma* as 12.1
a hired laborer for the *ápsaras*es, Nanda was deeply
ashamed. Because of his great shame, there was no pleasure
in his heart, and through lack of pleasure his depressed mind
could not persist in his stated intention. Though chiefly
preoccupied with sensuality and passion, and though he
did not mind being ridiculed, his motivation had matured
to the extent that he could not ignore Anánda's words.

Because his nature was not given to careful inspection,
he had previously considered heaven to be permanent. So
when he heard about its perishability he was profoundly
disturbed. The chariot of his mind, with its horses of in- 12.5
clination, turned back from heaven like a great chariot is
turned back from the wrong path by an attentive charioteer.

When he had turned away from his thirst for heaven, he suddenly seemed to become well, like a sick man who gives up tasty but unhealthy food in his determination to live. Just as he had forgotten about his beloved wife when he gazed on the *ápsaras*es, so also did he forsake the *ápsaras*es, disturbed by the fact of their impermanence. He thought about the return to earth of even the greatest beings, and though he was a passionate man, in his shocked agitation he seemed devoid of passion.

For the shock existed for furthering the increase of Excellence in him, just as, for the grammarians, the root "to
increase" is listed among the verbs after "to exist."* But be- 12.10
cause of passion, constancy, which resembles the indefinite
particle "existing" in that it pertains to the past, the present
and the future, did not in any way take hold of his mind.*

khela|gāmī mahā|bāhur gaj'|êndra iva nir|madaḥ,
so 'bhyagacchad guruṃ kāle vivakṣur bhāvam ātmanaḥ.
praṇamya ca gurau mūrdhnā bāṣpa|vyākula|locanaḥ
kṛtv" âñjalim uvāc' êdaṃ hriyā kiṃ cid avāṅ|mukhaḥ:

«apsaraḥ|prāptaye yan me bhagavan pratibhūr asi,
n' âpsarobhir mam' ârtho 'sti, pratibhūtvaṃ tyajāmy aham.
śrutvā hy āvartakaṃ svargaṃ saṃsārasya ca citratām,
na martyeṣu na deveṣu pravṛttir mama rocate.
12.15 yadi prāpya divaṃ yatnān niyamena damena ca
a|vitṛptāḥ patanty ante, svargasya tyāgine namaḥ!

ataś ca nikhilaṃ lokaṃ viditvā sa|car'|âcaram,
sarva|duḥkha|kṣaya|kare tvad|dharme parame rame.
tasmād vyāsa|samāsābhyāṃ
tan me vyākhyātum arhasi
yac chrutvā, śṛṇvatāṃ śreṣṭha,
paramaṃ prāpnuyāṃ padam.»

tatas tasy' āśayaṃ jñātvā vipakṣāṇ' îndriyāṇi ca,
śreyaś c' âiv' āmukhī|bhūtaṃ, nijagāda Tathāgataḥ:
«aho! pratyavamarśo 'yaṃ śreyasas te purojavaḥ,
araṇyāṃ mathyamānāyām, agner dhūma iv' ôtthitaḥ.
12.20 ciram unmārga|vihṛto lolair indriya|vājibhiḥ,
avatīrṇo 'si panthānaṃ diṣṭyā dṛṣṭy" â|vimūḍhayā!

With stately gait and strong in arm, like a princely elephant out of rut, he came to the guru at an appropriate time to tell him of his disposition. He bowed his head to the guru and folded his hands in reverence, and with tears filling his eyes and his face partially lowered in shame, he said:

"Lord, you stood guarantor for my attainment of the *ápsaras*es. But now I have no need of the *ápsaras*es, and I relinquish your guarantee. For I have heard of the cyclical nature of heaven and of the variety of rebirths in samsara, and neither among men nor among gods does active existence hold any appeal for me. If men must eventually fall 12.15
unfulfilled from a heaven so effortfully obtained through observance of the rules and through training, then homage to the man relinquishing heaven!

Comprehending the entire world with its moving and unmoving parts, I find pleasure in your supreme teaching, which puts an end to all suffering. Could you therefore explain it to me both in detail and in summary, O best of hearers, so that in hearing it I may obtain the supreme station."

The realized one understood his disposition, and that though his senses were still opposed to it, Excellence was now within his sight, and he spoke:

"Oh! This comprehension is the precursor of Excellence arising in you, just as when a firestick is rotated, smoke arises as a precursor of fire. For a long time the frenzied horses of 12.20
the senses have carried you the wrong way. How wonderful that with clear vision you have alighted on the right path!

adya te sa|phalaṃ janma, lābho 'dya su|mahāṃs tava,
yasya kāma|rasa|jñasya naiṣkramyāy' ôtsukaṃ manaḥ.
loke 'sminn ālay'|ārāme nivṛttau dur|labhā ratiḥ;
vyathante hy a|punar|bhāvāt prapātād iva bāliśāḥ.

duḥkhaṃ na syāt sukhaṃ me syād iti prayatate janaḥ,
atyanta|duḥkh'|ôparamaṃ sukhaṃ tac ca na budhyate.
ari|bhūteṣv a|nityeṣu satataṃ duḥkha|hetuṣu,
kām'|ādiṣu jagat saktaṃ. na vetti sukham avyayam.
12.25 sarva|duḥkh'|âpahaṃ tat tu hasta|stham amṛtaṃ tava,
viṣaṃ pītvā yad agadaṃ samaye pātum icchasi.

an|arha|saṃsāra|bhayaṃ mān'|ârhaṃ te cikīrṣitam,
rāg'|âgnis tādṛśo yasya dharm'|ônmukha parāṅ|mukhaḥ.
rāg'|ôddāmena manasā sarvathā duṣkarā dhṛtiḥ,
sa|doṣaṃ salilaṃ dṛṣṭvā pathinena pipāsunā.

īdṛśī nāma buddhis te niruddhā rajas" âbhavat
rajasā caṇḍa|vātena vivasvata iva prabhā.
sā jighāṃsus tamo hārdaṃ yā samprati vijṛmbhate,
tamo naiśaṃ prabhā saurī vinirgīrṇ" êva Meruṇā.

Today your birth bears fruit, today you profit greatly, in that your mind longs for withdrawal though you know the taste of passion. In this world with its liking for the household life, it is hard to take pleasure in abstention from activity; for fools shrink from the prospect of the end of rebirth as from the edge of a cliff.

People are stimulated to effortful activity by the thought that there might be no suffering and that they could be happy, unaware that their happiness is just the absence of major suffering. The world fastens on lust and other desires, which are inimical to us, transitory, and an ongoing cause
of suffering. It does not know imperishable bliss. Having 12.25
drunk poison, you wish to drink a timely antidote; that cup of deathlessness is within your reach, and it destroys all suffering.

Worthy of honor is your intention and its fear of a worthless samsara. You have put that kind of fiery passion behind you; you are facing the *dharma*. Steadfastness is in every respect hard to accomplish when the mind is given to unfettered passion, just as it is hard for a thirsty traveler to maintain self-control when he sees dirty water.

This kind of reasoning was obviously blocked in you by the dust of passion, just as the light of the sun is obscured by a strong gust of dust. Now it spreads out, seeking to dispell the darkness that is your emotionality, just as the sunny radiance put forth by Mount Meru seeks to disperse nocturnal darkness.

12.30 yukta|rūpam idaṃ c' âiva śuddha|sattvasya cetasaḥ
yat te syān naiṣṭhike sūkṣme śreyasi śraddadhānatā!
dharma|cchandam imaṃ tasmād vivardhayitum arhasi,
sarva|dharmā hi, dharma|jña, niyamāc chanda|hetavaḥ.
satyāṃ gamana|buddhau hi, gamanāya pravartate;
śayyā|buddhau ca śayanaṃ, sthāna|buddhau tathā sthitiḥ.

antar|bhūmi|gataṃ hy ambhaḥ śraddadhāti naro yadā,
arthitve sati, yatnena tadā khanati gām imām.
n' ârthī yady agninā vā syāc, chraddadhyāt taṃ na v" âraṇau,
mathnīyān n' âraṇiṃ kaś cit; tad|bhāve sati, mathyate.
12.35 sasy'|ôtpattiṃ yadi na vā śraddadhyāt kārṣakaḥ kṣitau,
arthī sasyena vā na syād, bījāni na vaped bhuvi.

ataś ca ‹hasta› ity uktā mayā śraddhā viśeṣataḥ,
yasmād gṛhṇāti sad|dharmaṃ dāyaṃ hasta iv' â|kṣataḥ.
prādhānyād ‹indriyam› iti, sthiratvād ‹balam› ity ataḥ,
guṇa|dāridrya|śamanād ‹dhanam› ity abhivarṇitā.
rakṣaṇ'|ârthena dharmasya tath" ‹êṣīk" êty› udāhṛtā
loke 'smin dur|labhatvāc ca ‹ratnam› ity abhibhāṣitā.
punaś ca ‹bījam› ity uktā nimittaṃ śreyaso' yadā;
pāvan'|ârthena pāpasya ‹nad" îty› abhihitā punaḥ.

This is surely an appropriate course for your mind when purified in its essence—that you might have confidence in the ultimate, subtle Excellence! Therefore you should cultivate this predilection for the *dharma*, for all factors of existence, *dharma*-knower, necessarily have desire as their cause. For when one has a mind to walk, one undertakes the actions for walking; likewise lying down occurs when one has a mind to lie down, and standing when one has a mind to stand. 12.30

When a man believes there is water underground, and is in need of it, then he digs the earth assiduously. If a man doesn't need a fire, or if he does not believe that fire comes from firesticks, then he would not rotate the firesticks; but when that condition is true, he rotates them. And if a farmer 12.35
did not believe that corn is produced from the earth, or if he had no need of corn, he would not sow seeds in the ground.

That is why I refer to faith particularly as 'the hand,' since it reaches out to the true *dharma* like an unimpaired hand reaches out for a gift. It is described as 'the sense organ' because of its prevalence, and as 'strong' because of its persistence, and as 'wealth' because it allays the impoverishment of virtue. It is declared to be 'the arrow' by reason of its protection of the *dharma*, and it is named 'the jewel' because it is so hard to find in this world. What is more, it is said to be 'the seed,' since it causes the arising of Excellence; again, it is called 'the river' because it cleanses wickedness.

12.40 yasmād dharmasya c' ôtpattau
śraddhā kāraṇam uttamam,
may" ôktā kāryatas tasmāt
tatra tatra tathā tathā.
śraddh"|âṅkuram imaṃ tasmāt saṃvardhayitum arhasi;
tad|vṛddhau vardhate dharmo, mūla|vṛddhau yathā drumaḥ.
vyākulaṃ darśanaṃ yasya dur|balo yasya niścayaḥ,
tasya pāriplavā śraddhā, na hi kṛtyāya vartate.
yāvat tattvaṃ na bhavati hi dṛṣṭaṃ śrutaṃ vā,
tāvac chraddhā na bhavati bala|sthā sthirā vā.
dṛṣṭe tattve niyama|paribhūt'|êndriyasya
śraddhā|vṛkṣo bhavati sa|phalaś c' āśrayaś ca.

Saundaranande mahā|kāvye Pratyavamarśo nāma
dvādaśaḥ sargaḥ.

As faith is the primary factor in the arising of *dharma*, I 12.40
have called it different names on various occasions due to its effects. Therefore you should nurture this shoot of faith; when it grows, *dharma* grows, just as a tree grows when its roots grow. When a man's vision is blurred and he is weak in resolve, his faith wavers, for it is not operating towards its proper outcome.

As long as reality is not seen or heard, faith is not firm or strongly fixed. But when a man's senses are governed by the rules of restraint and he sees reality, then the tree of faith is fruitful and supportive.

End of Canto 12: Comprehension.

CANTO 13
THE CONQUEST OF THE SENSES BY MORAL SELF-RESTRAINT

13.1 ATHA SAṂRĀDHITO Nandaḥ śraddhāṃ prati maha"|rṣiṇ
parisikto 'mṛten" êva yuyuje parayā mudā.
kṛt'|ārtham iva taṃ mene sambuddhaḥ śraddhayā tayā,
mene prāptam iva śreyaḥ sa ca Buddhena saṃskṛtaḥ.
ślakṣṇena vacasā kāṃś cit, kāṃś cit paruṣayā girā,
kāṃś cid ābhyām upāyābhyāṃ sa vininye vināyakaḥ.
pāṃsubhyaḥ kāñcanaṃ jātaṃ viśuddhaṃ nir|malaṃ śuci,
sthitaṃ pāṃsuṣv api yathā pāṃsu|doṣair na lipyate,
13.5 padma|parṇaṃ yathā c' âiva jale jātaṃ jale sthitam,
upariṣṭād adhastād vā na jalen' ôpalipyate,
tadval loke munir jāto lokasy' ânugrahaṃ caran,
kṛtitvān nir|malatvāc ca loka|dharmair na lipyate.
śleṣaṃ tyāgaṃ priyaṃ rūkṣaṃ kathāṃ ca dhyānam eva ca
mantu|kāle cikits'|ârthaṃ cakre, n' ātm'|ânuvṛttaye.
ataś ca saṃdadhe kāyaṃ mahā|karuṇayā tayā,
mocayeyaṃ kathaṃ duḥkhāt sattvān' îty anukampakaḥ.
atha saṃharṣaṇān Nandaṃ viditvā bhājanī|kṛtam,
abravīd bruvatāṃ śreṣṭhaḥ krama|jñaḥ śreyasāṃ kramam.
13.10 «ataḥ prabhṛti bhūyas tvaṃ śraddh"|êndriya|puraḥsaraḥ
a|mṛtasy' āptaye, saumya, vṛttaṃ rakṣitum arhasi.
prayogaḥ kāya|vacasoḥ śuddho bhavati te yathā,
uttāno vivṛto gupto 'n|avacchidras tathā kuru—

SUSTAINED BY the great seer's talk on faith, Nanda was filled with utter joy, as though he had been sprinkled with the elixir of deathlessness. The perfectly enlightened one considered him to have virtually reached the goal by means of faith, while Nanda himself, brought to readiness by the Buddha, felt as though Excellence had already been attained. 13.1

The trainer trained some with gentle words, some with robust speech, and some with both these methods. Just as gold originates in dirt, but is pure, flawless and clean, and though it remains in the dirt it is not soiled by dust-spots, and just as a lotus-leaf originates in water and remains in 13.5
water, but neither from above nor from below is it stained by water, likewise the sage is born in the world and operates as a favor to the world, but because of his perfectedness and spotlessness he is not soiled by any worldly thing. During times of counseling he stayed close or kept away, was kind or severe, and used stories or meditation not to win obedience to himself, but to promote healing.

In his sympathy discerning how he might free sentient beings from suffering, with great compassion he had taken on a bodily form. Now, aware that by gladdening him he had made Nanda a fitting receptacle for instruction, the best of speakers, knower of the gradual path, explained the steps to Excellence.

"In order to reach deathlessness, my friend, you, with 13.10
the faculty of faith as your forerunner, should from now onwards increase the guard on your conduct. So that your physical and verbal acts become pure, they should be upright, open, regulated and without blemish—upright be-

uttāno bhāva|karaṇād, vivṛtaś c' âpy a|gūhanāt,
gupto rakṣaṇa|tātparyād, a|cchidraś c' ân|avadyataḥ.

śarīra|vacasoḥ śuddhau sapt'|âṅge c' âpi karmaṇi,
ājīva|samudācāraṃ śaucāt saṃskartum arhasi.

doṣāṇāṃ kuhan'|ādīnāṃ pañcānām a|niṣevaṇāt,
tyāgāc ca jyotiṣ'|ādīnāṃ caturṇāṃ vṛtti|ghātinām,

13.15 prāṇi|dhānya|dhan'|ādīnāṃ varjyānām a|pratigrahāt,
bhaikṣ'|âṅgānāṃ nisṛṣṭānāṃ niyatānāṃ pratigrahāt,
parituṣṭaḥ śucir mañjuś caukṣayā jīva|sampadā,
kuryā duḥkha|pratīkāraṃ yāvad eva vimuktaye.

karmaṇo hi yathā|dṛṣṭāt kāya|vāk|prabhavād api
ājīvaḥ pṛthag ev' ôkto duḥ|śodhatvād ayaṃ mayā.
gṛha|sthena hi duḥ|śodhā dṛṣṭir vividha|dṛṣṭinā,
ājīvo bhikṣuṇā c' âiva pareṣv āyatta|vṛttinā.

etāvac chīlam ity uktam. ācāro 'yaṃ samāsataḥ;
asya nāśena, n' âiva syāt pravrajyā na gṛha|sthatā.

13.20 tasmāc cāritra|sampanno brahmacaryam idaṃ cara,
aṇu|mātreṣv avadyeṣu bhaya|darśī dṛḍha|vrataḥ.
śīlam āsthāya vartante sarvā hi śreyasi kriyāḥ,
sthān'|âdyān' îva kāryāṇi pratiṣṭhāya vasundharām.

cause of the workings of your true character, open because nothing is hidden, regulated because of the focus on self-government, and without blemish because they are irreproachable.

Purity demands that you refine your manner of making a living to conform to pure physical and verbal acts and also to the seven constituent parts of action.*

By refraining from the five faults such as hypocrisy, by relinquishing the four destroyers of good conduct such as astrology, by refusing to accept those gifts which should be 13.15
avoided, such as living beings, grain, and money, and by accepting the restrictions prescribed for alms-taking, contented, pure and lovely through making your living in a successful and clean manner, counteract suffering until the moment of liberation.

Because of the difficulty in keeping it clean, I have explained making a living separately from actions as they are seen in body and speech. For a householder who subscribes to various doctrines has difficulty in maintaining an uncontaminated doctrine, while a monk who depends for his subsistence on other people has difficulty in keeping his livelihood clean.

Such is what is termed moral self-restraint. To summarize, it is virtuous conduct; were it to disappear, neither true going forth nor true household life would be possible.

Therefore live this renunciant life endowed with virtuous 13.20
conduct, firm in your vowed observances, and seeing danger even in what is only very slightly objectionable. For all actions pertaining to Excellence rest on moral self-restraint,

mokṣasy' ôpaniṣat saumya vairāgyam iti gṛhyatām,
vairāgyasy' âpi saṃvedaḥ, saṃvido jñāna|darśanam.
jñānasy' ôpaniṣac c' âiva samādhir upadhāryatām,
samādher apy upaniṣat sukhaṃ śārīra|mānasam.
praśrabdhiḥ kāya|manasaḥ sukhasy' ôpaniṣat parā,
praśrabdher apy upaniṣat prītir apy avagamyatām.
13.25 tathā prīter upaniṣat prāmodyaṃ paramaṃ matam,
prāmodyasy' âpy a|hṛllekhaḥ ku|kṛteṣv a|kṛteṣu vā
a|hṛllekhasya manasaḥ śīlaṃ t' ûpaniṣac chuci;
ataḥ śīlaṃ nayaty agryam iti śīlaṃ viśodhaya.
śīlanāc chīlam ity uktaṃ, śīlanaṃ sevanād api,
sevanaṃ tan|nideśāc ca, nideśaś ca tad|āśrayāt.
śīlaṃ hi śaraṇaṃ, saumya, kāntāra iva daiśikaḥ;
mitraṃ bandhuś ca rakṣā ca dhanaṃ ca balam eva ca.
yataḥ śīlam, ataḥ, saumya, śīlaṃ saṃskartum arhasi.
etat sthānam anyeṣu ca mokṣ'|ārambheṣu yoginām.
13.30 tataḥ smṛtim adhiṣṭhāya capalāni sva|bhāvataḥ
indriyāṇ' îndriy'|ârthebhyo nivārayitum arhasi,
bhetavyaṃ na tathā śatror n' âgner n' âher na c' âśaneḥ
indriyebhyo yathā svebhyas tair ajasraṃ hi hanyate.

ust as the physical activities of standing and so on take place esting on the ground.

My dear friend, accept that dispassion is the secret of iberation, understanding of dispassion, and knowledge of understanding. Recognize that concentration is the secret of knowledge, and physical and mental bliss of concentration. Understand that complete confidence is the real secret of physical and mental bliss, and that joy is the secret of confidence.

Likewise great rapture is considered the secret of joy, 13.25
and the secret of rapture is a clear conscience in respect of
hings ill-done or undone. But pure moral self-restraint is
he secret of a clear conscience; therefore purify your moral
elf-restraint, for moral self-restraint comes first.

It is said that moral self-restraint comes from moral self-estraining, moral self-restraining comes from practice, practice comes from instruction, and instruction comes from seeking it. For moral self-restraint is a refuge, my friend, like a guide in the wilderness; it is friend, kinsman, protection, wealth and strength. Since this is moral self-restraint, dear friend, you must make it perfect. This is the position adopted by practitioners in their various endeavors for liberation.

Next, establishing mindfulness, hold back those naturally 13.30
estless senses from sensory experience, for one's own senses,
ever injurious, are more to be feared than an enemy, a fire,
a snake or a thunderbolt.

dviṣadbhiḥ śatrubhiḥ kaś cit kadā cit pīḍyate—na vā;
indriyair bādhyate sarvaḥ sarvatra ca sad" âiva ca.
na ca prayāti narakaṃ śatru|prabhṛtibhir hataḥ.
kṛṣyate tatra nighnas tu capalair indriyair hataḥ.
hanyamānasya tair duḥkhaṃ hārdaṃ bhavati vā—na vā.
indriyair bādhyamānasya hārdaṃ śārīram eva ca.

13.35 saṃkalpa|viṣa|digdhā hi pañc'|êndriya|mayāḥ śarāḥ;
cintā|puṅkhā rati|phalā viṣay'|ākāśa|gocarāḥ.
manuṣya|hariṇān ghnanti kāma|vyādh'|ēritā hṛdi,
vihanyante yadi na te tataḥ patanti taiḥ kṣatāḥ.
niyam'|âjira|saṃsthena dhairya|kārmuka|dhāriṇā,
nipatanto nivāryās te mahatā smṛti|varmaṇā.

indriyāṇām upaśamād arīṇāṃ nigrahād iva,
sukhaṃ svapiti v" āste vā yatra tatra gat'|ôddhavaḥ.
teṣāṃ hi satataṃ loke viṣayān abhikāṅkṣatām,
saṃvin n' âiv' âsti kārpaṇyāc chunām āśāvatām iva.
13.40 viṣayair indriya|grāmo na tṛptim adhigacchati,
ajasraṃ pūryamāṇo 'pi samudraḥ salilair iva.

avaśyaṃ gocare sve sve vartitavyam ih' êndriyaiḥ,
nimittaṃ tatra na grāhyam anuvyañjanam eva ca.
ālokya cakṣuṣā rūpaṃ, dhātu|mātre vyavasthitaḥ;
‹strī› v" êti ‹puruṣo› v" êti na kalpayitum arhasi.

Some people are sometimes persecuted by malevolent enemies—or they are not; but at every moment everyone, everywhere, is harried by the senses. And a man slain by an enemy, for example, does not go to hell. But all docile is he pulled there when smitten by his restless senses. One may suffer emotionally when struck by an enemy—or one may not. Yet when harried by the senses, one suffers both emotionally and physically.

For those arrows made of the five senses are smeared with 13.35
the poison of fanciful notions; they have anxious preoccupation for tail-feathers, sensual bliss for arrow-heads, and they range through the space of sensory experience. The hunter Passion fires them into the hearts of men like deer, and if they are not deflected, men fall down wounded. They must be deflected as they rain down by the mighty man who takes his stand in the arena of disciplined conduct, bearing the bow of resolution and wearing the armor of mindfulness.

Wherever he may lay his head, wherever he may take his seat, a man is at ease and free from care when his senses are quiet, as when the enemy is quelled. For there is no fulfillment for those who constantly hanker for sensory experience in the world, like dogs in their hunger, voracious
for more. The village of the senses never has enough of sen- 13.40
sory experience, just as the ocean, though rivers perpetually fill it, never has enough water.

Here in the world the senses must necessarily operate, each in its particular sphere, but there should be no grasping at either the major attributes or the minor details of an object. When seeing a shape with your eyes, pay attention only to its primary elements; do not conceptualize it as

sacet strī|puruṣa|grāhaḥ kva cid vidyeta kaś cana
śubhataḥ keśa|dant'|ādīn n' ânuprasthātum arhasi.
n' âpanetuṃ tataḥ kiṃ cit, prakṣepyaṃ n' âpi kiṃcana;
draṣṭavyaṃ bhūtato bhūtaṃ yādṛśaṃ ca yathā ca yat.
13.45 evaṃ te paśyatas tattvaṃ śaśvad indriya|gocare,
bhaviṣyati pada|sthānaṃ n' âbhidhyā|daurmanasyayoḥ.
abhidhyā priya|rūpeṇa hanti kām'|ātmakaṃ jagat,
arir mitra|mukhen' êva priya|vāk kaluṣ'|āśayaḥ.
daurmanasy'|âbhidhānas tu pratigho viṣay'|āśritaḥ
mohād yen' ânuvṛttena paratr' êha ca hanyate.
anurodha|virodhābhyāṃ śīt'|ôṣṇābhyām iv' ârditaḥ,
śarma n' āpnoti na śreyaś; cal'|êndriyam ato jagat.
n' êndriyaṃ viṣaye tāvat pravṛttam api sajjate,
yāvan na manasas tatra parikalpaḥ pravartate.
13.50 indhane sati vāyau ca yathā jvalati pāvakaḥ,
viṣayāt parikalpāc ca kleś'|âgnir jāyate tathā.
abhūta|parikalpena viṣayasya hi badhyate
tam eva viṣayaṃ paśyan bhūtataḥ parimucyate.
dṛṣṭv" âikaṃ rūpam anyo hi rajyate, 'nyaḥ praduṣyati,
kaś cid bhavati madhya|sthas, tatr' âiv' ânyo ghṛṇāyate.
ato na viṣayo hetur bandhāya na vimuktaye;
parikalpa|viśeṣeṇa saṅgo bhavati vā na vā.
kāryaḥ parama|yatnena tasmād indriya|saṃvaraḥ,
indriyāṇi hy aguptāni duḥkhāya ca bhavāya ca.

'woman' or 'man.' If any perception of a woman or man does occur, don't linger over their hair, teeth and so on as beautiful.

Nothing should be taken away, nothing should be added; whatever the kind of object, it should be seen as it really is.

If, in the realm of the senses, you continuously observe 13.45
what is real, then neither attraction nor aversion will leave a footprint in your mind. Like an enemy with a friendly face, fair of speech but foul at heart, attraction with its pleasing form destroys people of passionate nature. What is termed aversion is the repulsion of a sensory event, to which acquiescence, out of delusion, brings ruin in both this life and the next.

When a man is tormented by likes and dislikes as by cold and heat, he finds no relief, nor does he find Excellence; hence the restlessness of a person's senses. So long as fanciful imaginings do not operate in the mind, the senses, though operational, will not be glued to sensory objects. Just as a 13.50
fire burns when it has both fuel and air, so too does the fire of defilement arise when both sense objects and imaginings about them are present. For a man is imprisoned by unreal imaginings about a sense object, but when he sees that very same sense object as it really is, then he is freed.

Upon seeing one and the same form, one person desires it, another repulses it, yet another remains indifferent, while someone else will feel compassion. It follows that sense objects are not the cause of bondage or liberation; whether attachment arises or not is due to specific imaginings. For this reason you should control your senses with the maxi-

13.55 [...]
tasmād eṣām a|kuśala|karāṇām arīṇāṃ
cakṣur|ghrāṇa|śravaṇa|rasana|sparśanānām
sarv'|âvasthaṃ bhava viniyamād a|pramattaḥ.
m" âsminn arthe kṣaṇam api kṛthās tvaṃ pramādam!»

Saundaranande mahākāvye Śīl'|êndriya|jayo nāma
trayodaśaḥ sargaḥ.

mum of effort, for ungoverned senses make for sorrow and rebirth.

[...]* 13.55

In every situation, therefore, be careful to place restrictions on those enemies—sight, smell, hearing, taste and touch—which produce unwholesome states. Don't be negligent about this even for an instant!"

End of Canto 13: The Conquest of the Senses by Moral Self-Restraint.

CANTO 14
THE INITIAL POINT OF DEPARTURE

14.1 «ATHA SMṚTI|KAVĀṬENA pidhāy' êndriya|saṃvaram,
bhojane bhava mātrā|jño dhyānāy' ân|āmayāya ca.
prāṇ'|âpānau nigṛhṇāti, glāni|nidre prayacchati,
kṛto hy atyartham āhāro vihanti ca parākramam.
yathā c' âtyartham āhāraḥ kṛto 'n|arthāya kalpate,
upayuktas tath" âtyalpo na sāmarthyāya kalpate.
ācayaṃ dyutim utsāhaṃ prayogaṃ balam eva ca
bhojanaṃ kṛtam atyalpaṃ śarīrasy' âpakarṣati.
14.5 yathā bhāreṇa namate laghun" ônnamate tulā
samā tiṣṭhati yuktena, bhojyen' êyaṃ tathā tanuḥ.
tasmād abhyavahartavyaṃ sva|śaktim anupaśyatā.
n' âtimātraṃ na c' âtyalpaṃ meyaṃ māna|vaśād api,
atyākrānto hi kāy'|âgnir guruṇ" ânnena śāmyati
avacchanna iv' âlpo 'gniḥ sahasā mahat" êndhasā.
atyantam api saṃhāro n' āhārasya praśasyate,
an|āhāro hi nirvāti nir|indhana iv' ânalaḥ.
yasmān n' âsti vin" āhārāt sarva|prāṇa|bhṛtāṃ sthitiḥ,
tasmād duṣyati n' āhāro. vikalpo 'tra tu vāryate,
14.10 na hy eka|viṣaye 'nyatra sajyante prāṇinas tathā
a|vijñāte yath" āhāre. boddhavyaṃ tatra kāraṇam.
cikits"|ârthaṃ yathā dhatte vraṇasy' ālepanaṃ vraṇī,
kṣud|vighāt'|ârtham āhāras tadvat sevyo mumukṣuṇā.
bhārasy' ôdvahan'|ârthaṃ ca rath'|âkṣo 'bhyajyate yathā,
bhojanaṃ prāṇa|yātr"|ârthaṃ tadvad vidvān niṣevate.
samatikramaṇ'|ârthaṃ ca kāntārasya yath" âdhvagau

“Next, having closed off the dam of the senses with 14.1
the gate of mindfulness, be measured in your food intake, for the sake of meditation as well as good health. Too much food restricts the in-breath and out-breath, brings fatigue and sleepiness, and destroys one's spirit of enterprise. And just as it is detrimental to eat too much, so is it incapacitating to eat too little. Overly small meals drain the body of its solidity, its healthy glow, its energy, its usefulness and its strength.

Just as the scales go down with a heavy weight and up 14.5
with a light one, but stay level with the correct weight, so does this body with its food. Therefore you should take food with due consideration for your own capacity. Don't apportion yourself too much or too little even if you have a strong opinion on this subject, for when it is weighed down with heavy food, the fire of the body dies down like a small fire all at once covered with a lot of fuel.

Total avoidance of food is not recommended, for a person who doesn't eat is extinguished like a fire without fuel. Since none who bear breath can continue to exist without food, eating is not wrong. However, a choice of foods is not
permitted, for living beings are not so attached to any other 14.10
single sphere of activity as they are to indiscriminate eating. Make sure you understand the reason for this.

A man hopeful of liberation should take food in order to remove hunger, just as a man with an ulcer puts ointment on it to heal it. As a cart-axle is oiled to allow it to bear a heavy weight, so a wise man takes food to enable him to journey through life. In violent desperation parents on a journey might eat the flesh of their child to survive the wilderness;

putra|māṃsāni khādetāṃ dampatī bhṛśa|duḥkhitau;
evam abhyavahartavyaṃ bhojanaṃ pratisaṃkhyayā,
na bhūṣ"|ârthaṃ na vapuṣe na madāya na dṛptaye.

14.15 dhāraṇ'|ârthaṃ śarīrasya bhojanaṃ hi vidhīyate
upastambhaḥ pipatiṣor dur|balasy' êva veśmanaḥ.
plavaṃ yatnād yathā kaś cid badhnīyād dhārayed api,
na tat|snehena yāvat tu mah"|âughasy' ôttitīrṣayā,
tath" ôpakaraṇaiḥ kāyaṃ dhārayanti parīkṣakāḥ,
na tat|snehena yāvat tu duḥkh'|âughasya titīrṣayā.

śocatā pīḍyamānena dīyate śatrave yathā,
na bhaktyā n' âpi tarṣeṇa kevalaṃ prāṇa|guptaye,
yog'|ācāras tath" āhāraṃ śarīrāya prayacchati,
kevalaṃ kṣud|vighāt'|ârthaṃ na rāgeṇa na bhaktaye.

14.20 mano|dhāraṇayā c' âiva pariṇāmy' ātmavān ahaḥ,
vidhūya nidrāṃ yogena niśām apy atināmayeḥ.
hṛdi yat saṃjñinaś c' âiva nidrā prādur|bhavet tava,
guṇavat|saṃjñitāṃ saṃjñāṃ tadā manasi mā kṛthāḥ.
dhātur ārambha|dhṛtyoś ca, sthāma|vikramayor api,
nityaṃ manasi kāryas te bādhyamānena nidrayā.

āmnātavyāś ca viśadaṃ te dharmā ye pariśrutāḥ.
parebhyaś c' ôpadeṣṭavyāḥ, saṃcintyāḥ svayam eva ca.
prakledyam adbhir vadanaṃ, vilokyāḥ sarvato diśaḥ,
cāryā dṛṣṭiś ca tārāsu jijāgariṣuṇā sadā.

14.25 antar|gatair a|capalair vaśa|sthāyibhir indriyaiḥ,
a|vikṣiptena manasā caṅkramyasv' āsva vā niśi.

that's how food should be eaten, with careful reflection, and not for display, nor for one's appearance, nor for self-pride nor amusement.

For food is provided to support the body, just as a prop 14.15
is provided for a dilapidated house on the point of collapse. Just as someone might effortfully construct a boat and even carry it, not because he is so fond of it but because he needs to cross a great flood, likewise clear-sighted men support the body with a means of subsistence, not because they are so fond of it but because they intend to cross the flood of suffering.

Just as a grief-stricken man under duress hands over his goods to his enemy, not out of affection nor because he wants something but solely to safeguard his life, likewise the practitioner of yoga* gives food to his body, not because of greed or affection for his body but solely to remove hunger.

Now, when you have spent the day self-possessed in pur- 14.20
suit of mental concentration, you should shake off sleep and pass the night too in yogic practice. Don't assume that your consciousness at this time is a high quality consciousness, since when you are thus conscious, drowsiness may take shape in your heart. When sleep threatens, always keep in mind the fundamental principles of initiative and determination, strength and courage.

Clearly recite those teachings that you have learned. Teach them to others, and contemplate them yourself. Wet your face with water, look around in all directions, and fix your
eyes on the stars when you intend to stay awake. With your 14.25
senses still, controlled and directed inwards, you should walk or sit at night with a collected mind.

bhaye prītau ca śoke ca nidrayā n' âbhibhūyate,
tasmān nidr"|âbhiyogeṣu sevitavyam idaṃ trayam.
bhayam āgamanān mṛtyoḥ, prītiṃ dharma|parigrahāt,
janma|duḥkhād a|paryantāc chokam āgantum arhasi.

evam|ādiḥ kramaḥ, saumya, kāryo jāgaraṇaṃ prati;
vandhyaṃ hi śayanād āyuḥ kaḥ prājñaḥ kartum arhati?
doṣa|vyālān atikramya vyālān gṛha|gatān iva,
kṣamamaṃ prājñasya na svaptuṃ nistitīrṣor mahad bhayam.

14.30 pradīpte jīva|loke hi mṛtyu|vyādhi|jar'|âgnibhiḥ,
kaḥ śayīta nir|udvegaḥ pradīpta iva veśmani?
tasmāt tama iti jñātvā, nidrāṃ n' āveṣṭum arhasi,
a|praśānteṣu doṣeṣu su|śastreṣv iva śatruṣu.

pūrvaṃ yāmaṃ tri|yāmāyāḥ prayogeṇ' âtināmya tu,
sevyā śayyā śarīrasya viśrām'|ârthaṃ sva|tantriṇā.
dakṣiṇena tu pārśvena sthitay", āloka|saṃjñayā,
prabodhaṃ hṛdaye kṛtvā śayīthāḥ śānta|mānasaḥ.
yāme tṛtīye c' ôtthāya, carann āsīna eva vā
bhūyo yogaṃ manaḥ|śuddhau kurvīthā niyat'|êndriyaḥ.

14.35 ath' āsana|gata|sthāna|prekṣita|vyāhṛt'|ādiṣu
samprajānan kriyāḥ sarvāḥ, smṛtim ādhātum arhasi.
dvār'|âdhyakṣa iva dvāri yasya praṇihitā smṛtiḥ,
dharṣayanti na taṃ doṣāḥ puraṃ guptam iv' ârayaḥ.
na tasy' ôtpadyate kleśo yasya kāya|gatā smṛtiḥ.
cittaṃ sarvāsv avasthāsu bālaṃ dhātr" îva rakṣati.

Sleep cannot overwhelm someone in a state of fear, joy or grief, so focus on these three during the onslaught of sleep. You should derive fear from the fact that death is getting closer, joy from your possession of the *dharma*, and grief from the boundless suffering attendant upon birth.

These are examples of the steps that can be taken to stay awake; for what wise man would waste his life in sleep? It is not right for a wise man anxious to avoid grave peril to go to sleep, side-stepping the reptilian faults as though ignoring snakes in his house. Who could sleep without worry in the 14.30
world of humankind, ablaze with the fires of death, sickness and aging, any more than in a burning house? Therefore acknowledge that sleep is darkness, and do not let it envelop you, since the faults, like heavily armed enemies, are not yet won to peace.

However, after spending the first of the night's three watches in a useful way, a self-controlled man should seek sleep in order to rest his body. Lie down on your right side, remaining conscious of the idea of light, maintaining awareness in your heart and with your mind at peace. Get up in the third watch of the night, and either walking or sitting practice yogic discpline again with pure mind and controlled senses.

Then, remaining aware of all your actions, be mindful 14.35
when you sit, move about, stand still, look, speak and so on. When mindfulness is in place like a gatekeeper at his gateway, then the faults cannot violate you, as enemies dare not attack a well-guarded city. Defilement does not arise in a man who is mindful with regard to his body. Mindfulness

śaravyaḥ sa tu doṣāṇāṃ yo hīnaḥ smṛti|varmaṇā,
raṇa|sthaḥ pratiśatrūṇāṃ vihīna iva varmaṇā.
a|nāthaṃ tan mano jñeyaṃ yat smṛtir n' âbhirakṣati,
nir|ṇetā dṛṣṭi|rahito viṣameṣu carann iva.
14.40 an|artheṣu prasaktāś ca, sv'|ârthebhyaś ca parāṅ|mukhāḥ,
yad|bhaye sati n' ôdvignāḥ—smṛti|nāśo 'tra kāraṇam.
sva|bhūmiṣu guṇāḥ sarve ye ca śīl'|ādayaḥ sthitāḥ,
vikīrṇā iva gā gopaḥ, smṛtis tān anugacchati.
pranaṣṭam a|mṛtaṃ tasya, yasya viprasṛtā smṛtiḥ;
hasta|stham a|mṛtaṃ tasya, yasya kāya|gatā smṛtiḥ.
āryo nyāyaḥ kutas tasya smṛtir yasya na vidyate?
yasy' āryo n' âsti ca nyāyaḥ, pranaṣṭas tasya sat|pathaḥ.
pranaṣṭo yasya san|mārgo, naṣṭaṃ tasy' â|mṛtaṃ padam;
pranaṣṭam a|mṛtaṃ yasya, sa duḥkhān na vimucyate.
14.45 tasmāc caraṃś caro 'sm' îti, sthito 'sm' îti c' âdhiṣṭhitaḥ
evam|ādiṣu kāleṣu smṛtim ādhātum arhasi.

yog'|ânulomaṃ vi|janaṃ vi|śabdaṃ
śayy"|āsanaṃ, saumya, tathā bhajasva;
kāyasya kṛtvā hi vivekam ādau,
sukho 'dhigantuṃ manaso vivekaḥ.
a|labdha|cetaḥ|praśamaḥ sa|rāgo
yo na pracāraṃ bhajate viviktam
sa kṣaṇyate hy a|pratilabdha|mārgaś
carann iv' ôrvyāṃ bahu|kaṇṭakāyām.

guards his thoughts in all circumstances, as a nurse protects a child.

A person lacking the armor of mindfulness is a target
for the faults, as a soldier without armor is a target for
his enemy. The mind unguarded by mindfulness can be
regarded as defenseless, like a blind man stumbling over
rough ground without a guide. When men are attached 14.40
to worthless objects, turn their backs on objects worthy of
them, and fail to shudder at this danger—the reason in these
cases is loss of mindfulness.

When every virtue such as moral self-restraint has settled
on its own patch, mindfulness follows them like a cowherd
goes out after his straying cows. Deathlessness is lost to
him whose mindfulness goes outwards, but when he stays
mindful of his body, he holds deathlessness in his hand.
Where is the noble plan of a man lacking mindfulness? And
if he does not have a noble plan, then he has lost the true
path. When he has lost the true path, the deathless place
disappears for him too; he for whom deathlessness is lost is
not liberated from suffering. Therefore when walking, be 14.45
aware that you are walking, and when standing still, know
that you are standing still. That is how you should maintain
mindfulness at these times and others.

My friend, find a private, quiet place to lie or sit, suitable for the practice of yogic discipline; for once physical solitude is adopted, mental discrimination is easy to reach. The passionate man who cannot find emotional peace and who does not take to solitary ways gets injured, as though walking over thorny ground when he can't locate the path.

a|dṛṣṭa|tattvena parīkṣakeṇa
sthitena citte viṣaya|pracāre
cittaṃ niṣeddhuṃ na sukhena śakyaṃ,
kṛṣṭ'|âdako gaur iva sasya|madhyāt.
an|īryamāṇas tu yath" ânilena
praśāntim āgacchati citra|bhānuḥ,
alpena yatnena tathā vivikteṣv
a|ghaṭṭitaṃ śāntim upaiti cetaḥ.

14.50 kva cid bhuktvā yat tad, vasanam api yat tat parihitaḥ,
vasann ātm'|ārāmaḥ, kva cana vi|jane yo 'bhiramate,
kṛt'|ârthaḥ sa jñeyaḥ, śama|sukha|rasa|jñaḥ kṛta|matiḥ,
pareṣāṃ saṃsargaṃ pariharati yaḥ kaṇṭakam iva.
yadi dvandv'|ārāme jagati viṣaya|vyagra|hṛdaye,
vivikte nir|dvandvo viharati kṛtī śānta|hṛdayaḥ,
tataḥ pītvā prajñā|rasam amṛtavat tṛpta|hṛdayo.
viviktaḥ saṃsaktaṃ viṣaya|kṛpaṇaṃ śocati jagat.
vasañ chūny'|āgāre yadi satatam eko 'bhiramate,
yadi kleś'|ôtpādaiḥ saha na ramate śatrubhir iva,
carann ātm'|ārāmo yadi ca pibati prīti|salilaṃ,
tato bhuṅkte śreṣṭhaṃ tridaśa|pati|rājyād api sukham.»

Saundaranande mahā|kāvya Ādi|prasthāno nāma
caturdaśaḥ sargaḥ.

An enquirer who has not seen reality cannot easily restrain his thoughts when he is placed among the glittering show of sense objects, just as it is hard to drive a bull from corn when he is grazing on farmland. But in solitude, the mind is not stimulated and subsides with little effort, just as a radiant fire subsides when unstirred by the wind.

A man who eats anything at any place, wears any clothes, 14.50
lives in self-sufficiency, who is happy to be anywhere without people and avoids the company of others like a thorn—he is recognized as a determined man of achievement, and knows the taste of the bliss of peace.

The world likes alternatives and is distracted to the core by sensual experience. If a man lives in it in seclusion, indifferent to choice, virtuous and with his heart at peace, then he has sipped the taste of wisdom as if it were the cup of deathlessness and is content at heart. A man of discernment, he grieves for the clinging world as it hoards sensual experience.

If he is glad to always live alone in a deserted spot, if he has as little liking for the sources of defilement as for an enemy, if he lives in self-sufficiency and drinks the water of bliss, then he enjoys a greater happiness than that afforded by Indra's kingdom."

End of Canto 14: The Initial Point of Departure.

CANTO 15
ABANDONING NOTIONS

15.1 «YATRA TATRA vivikte tu,
baddhvā paryaṅkam uttamam,
ṛjuṃ kāyaṃ samādhāya,
smṛty" âbhimukhay" ânvitaḥ,
nās'|âgre vā, lalāṭe vā, bhruvor antara eva vā
kurvīthāś capalaṃ cittam ālambana|parāyaṇam.
sacet kāma|vitarkas tvāṃ dharṣayen mānaso jvaraḥ,
kṣeptavyo n' âdhivāsyaḥ sa vastre reṇur iv' āgataḥ.
yady api pratisaṃkhyānāt kāmān utsṛṣṭavān asi,
tamāṃs' îva prakāśena pratipakṣeṇa tāñ jahi.
15.5 tiṣṭhaty anuśayas teṣāṃ channo 'gnir iva bhasmanā.
sa te bhāvanayā, saumya, praśāmyo 'gnir iv' âmbunā.
te hi tasmāt pravartante bhūyo, bījād iv' âṅkurāḥ;
tasya nāśena te na syur, bīja|nāśād iv' âṅkurāḥ.
arjan'|ādīni kāmebhyo dṛṣṭvā duḥkhāni kāminām,
tasmāt tān mūlataś chindhi, mitra|saṃjñān arīn iva.
a|nityā moṣa|dharmāṇo riktā vyasana|hetavaḥ,
bahu|sādhāraṇāḥ kāmā. barhyā hy āśī|viṣā iva!
ye mṛgyamāṇā duḥkhāya, rakṣyamāṇā na śāntaye.
bhraṣṭāḥ śokāya mahate, prāptāś ca na vitṛptaye.

"IN WHATEVER secluded place you are, sitting with your legs crossed, holding your body erect, keeping mindfulness to the fore, you should settle the restless mind wholly on an area such as the tip of the nose, the forehead, or the space between the eyebrows. If your mind offends you with feverish ideas of passion, do not dwell on them but brush them off, like dust that has collected on your clothing. 15.1

Even though you have let go of the passions as a result of careful examination, destroy them by their opposite, as
darkness is destroyed by light. A tendency towards the pas- 15.5
sions continues to exist, as does a fire covered over with ash. Extinguish this tendency with meditation, dear friend, as fire is extinguished with water. Because of that tendency the passions re-emerge, like shoots from a seed; when it is destroyed they would not exist, just as shoots would not exist if the seed were destroyed.

So observe the sufferings of passionate men arising from their passions, beginning with the acquisition of wealth, and cut them off at the root, as though they were enemies calling themselves friends. For the passions are impermanent, hollow, the cause of unhappiness; they are held in common with many other people, and by their very nature can be easily taken from you. Destroy them like poisonous snakes! When the passions are hunted there is suffering, but no peace in their conservation. Losing them brings great grief, but acquiring them no satisfaction.

15.10 tṛptiṃ vitta|prakarṣeṇa, svarg'|âvāptyā kṛt'|ârthatām,
kāmebhyaś ca sukh'|ôtpattiṃ yaḥ paśyati sa naśyati.
calān a|pariniṣpannān a|sārān an|avasthitān.
parikalpa|sukhān kāmān; na tān smartum ih' ârhasi.

vyāpādo vā vihiṃsā vā kṣobhayed yadi te manaḥ,
prasādyaṃ tad|vipakṣeṇa maṇin" îv' ākulaṃ jalam.
pratipakṣas tayor jñeyo maitrī kāruṇyam eva ca,
virodho hi tayor nityaṃ, prakāśa|tamasor iva.
nivṛttaṃ yasya dauḥśīlyaṃ vyāpādaś ca pravartate,
hanti pāṃsubhir ātmānaṃ sa snāta iva vāraṇaḥ.
15.15 duḥkhitebhyo hi martyebhyo vyādhi|mṛtyu|jar"|ādibhiḥ
āryaḥ ko duḥkham aparaṃ sa|ghṛṇo dhātum arhati?

duṣṭena c' êha manasā bādhyate vā paro na vā,
sadyas tu dahyate tāvat svaṃ mano duṣṭa|cetasaḥ;
tasmāt sarveṣu bhūteṣu maitrīṃ kāruṇyam eva ca
na vyāpādaṃ vihiṃsāṃ vā vikalpayitum arhasi.

yad yad eva prasaktaṃ hi vitarkayati mānavaḥ,
abhyāsāt tena ten' âsya natir bhavati cetasaḥ.
tasmād a|kuśalaṃ tyaktvā kuśalaṃ dhyātum arhasi,
yat te syād iha c' ârthāya param'|ârthasya c' āptaye.
15.20 saṃvardhante hy a|kuśalā vitarkāḥ sambhṛtā hṛdi,
an|artha|janakās tulyam ātmanaś ca parasya ca.
śreyaso vighna|karaṇād, bhavanty ātma|vipattaye;
pātrī|bhāv'|ôpaghātāt tu, para|bhakti|vipattaye.

It is ruinous to perceive contentment in enormous wealth, 15.10
success in the winning of heaven, or the source of happiness
in the passions. The passions are shifting, unreal, without
a core, unstable. The happiness they bring is a figment of
the imagination; pay no attention to them now.

If malicious or aggressive thoughts churn in your mind,
they must be softened with their opposite, as turbid water clears with a jewel.* It's known that loving-kindness
and compassion are their opposite, for they are always in-
compatible, like light and dark. When malice operates in
someone who has renounced bad conduct, he heaps himself
with filth, like an elephant throwing dust over himself after
a wash. For what noble and compassionate person would 15.15
lay further suffering on humanity already suffering from
sickness, death, aging and more?

Another person may or may not be harmed in this world
by a malicious mind, but the maliciously-disposed person's
own mind is burned up straight away; it follows that you
should choose loving-kindness and compassion towards all
living creatures as the alternative to malice and aggression.

Whatever it is that a man continually thinks about, his
mind, through habit, will develop a leaning towards it.
Therefore you must give up what is unwholesome and con-
centrate on the wholesome, since this will work both for
your best interest in this world and for your attainment of
the ultimate goal. When unwholesome thoughts are carried 15.20
in the heart they grow stronger and breed ill for both oneself
and others. Because they act as obstacles to Excellence, they
cause personal failure; and because of the damage done to
the worthy condition, they also lead to the failure in the

manaḥ|karmasv a|vikṣepam api c' âbhyastum arhasi;
na tv ev' â|kuśalaṃ, saumya, vitarkayitum arhasi.

yā tri|kām'|ôpabhogāya cintā manasi vartate,
na ca taṃ guṇam āpnoti bandhanāya ca kalpate.
sattvānām upaghātāya, parikleśāya c' ātmanaḥ,
mohaṃ vrajati kāluṣyaṃ. narakāya ca vartate.
15.25 tad vitarkair a|kuśalair n' ātmānaṃ hantum arhasi,
su|śastraṃ ratna|vikṛtaṃ mṛdd|hato gāṃ khanann iva.

an|abhijño yathā jātyaṃ dahed aguru kāṣṭhavat,
a|nyāyena manuṣyatvam upahanyād idaṃ tathā.
tyaktvā ratnaṃ yathā loṣṭaṃ ratna|dvīpāc ca saṃharet,
tyaktvā naiḥśreyasaṃ dharmaṃ cintayed a|śubhaṃ tathā.

Himavantaṃ yathā gatvā viṣaṃ bhuñjīta n' âuṣadham,
manuṣyatvaṃ tathā prāpya pāpaṃ seveta no śubham.
tad buddhvā pratipakṣeṇa vitarkaṃ kṣeptum arhasi,
sūkṣmeṇa pratikīlena kīlaṃ dārv|antarād iva.

15.30 vṛddhy|a|vṛddhyor atha bhavec cintā jñāti|janaṃ prati.
sva|bhāvo jīva|lokasya parīkṣyas tan|nivṛttaye.
saṃsāre kṛṣyamāṇānāṃ sattvānāṃ svena karmaṇā,
ko janaḥ? sva|janaḥ ko vā? mohāt sakto jane janaḥ.
atīte 'dhvani saṃvṛttaḥ sva|jano hi janas tava,
a|prāpte c' âdhvani janaḥ sva|janas te bhaviṣyati.

loyalties of others. Practice being collected in your mental activities, my friend; and especially do not think unwholesome thoughts.

When a thought in one's mind revolves around enjoyment of the three passions, it does not acquire virtue but produces bondage. Foulness of the mind leads to folly, damages other living beings and brings defilement for oneself. It
leads to hell. Don't harm yourself with unwholesome mus- 15.25
ings, as though a man in digging earth were to fling soil on himself, well-armed and jewel-adorned as he is.*

Just as an ignorant man might burn the best aloe-wood as if it were ordinary firewood, just so is one's human state destroyed by not following this method. And the man who thinks unlovely thoughts while forsaking the unsurpassable *dharma* is like a man who takes away clods of earth from a jewel-island but leaves the jewel behind.

Just like a man who upon reaching the Himalayas swallows poison instead of medicinal herbs is he who wins a human state but serves evil, not goodness. Take cognisance of this, and throw off distracted thinking by means of its opposite, like a wedge is prized out of a piece of lumber by a finer counter-wedge.

Now, you might feel worried about whether your family 15.30
is flourishing or not. You should put a stop to this by examining the true nature of the world of humankind. Among the beings whose own acts drag them through samsara, who is a stranger? Who is family? It's through delusion that people cling to each other. For on the road already traveled, someone who is now family was then a stranger, and on the road to come a stranger will be family.

vihagānāṃ yathā sāyaṃ tatra tatra samāgamaḥ,
jātau jātau tath" āśleṣo janasya sva|janasya ca.
pratiśrayaṃ bahu|vidhaṃ saṃśrayanti yath" âdhvagāḥ,
pratiyānti punas tyaktvā, tadvaj jñāti|samāgamaḥ.

15.35 loke prakṛti|bhinne 'smin na kaś cit kasya cit priyaḥ
kārya|kāraṇa|sambaddhaṃ bālukā|muṣṭivaj jagat.
bibharti hi sutaṃ mātā ‹dhārayiṣyati mām› iti,
mātaraṃ bhajate putro ‹garbheṇ' ādhatta mām› iti.
anukūlaṃ pravartante jñātiṣu jñātayo yadā,
tadā snehaṃ prakurvanti, riputvaṃ tu viparyayāt.

a|hito dṛśyate jñātir, a|jñātir dṛśyate hitaḥ.
snehaṃ kāry'|ântarāl lokaś chinatti ca karoti ca.
svayam eva yath" ālikhya rajyec citra|karaḥ striyam,
tathā kṛtvā svayaṃ snehaṃ saṃgam eti jane janaḥ.

15.40 yo 'bhavad bāndhava|janaḥ para|loke priyas tava—
sa te kam arthaṃ kurute tvaṃ vā tasmai karoṣi kam?
tasmāj jñāti|vitarkeṇa mano n' āveṣṭum arhasi,
vyavasthā n' âsti saṃsāre sva|janasya janasya ca.

‹asau kṣemo janapadaḥ; su|bhikṣo 'sāv; asau śivaḥ.›
ity evam atha jāyeta vitarkas tava kaś cana,
praheyaḥ sa tvayā, saumya. n' âdhivāsyaḥ kathaṃ cana
viditvā sarvam ādīptaṃ tais tair doṣ'|âgnibhir jagat.

Stranger and kinsman embrace each other, some in this birth, some in that, just as birds flock together in the evenings, sometimes here and sometimes there. Just as travelers shelter together in a number of rest-houses, and in leaving them part company again, so it is with a group of family members.

In this world, by nature separate, nobody is truly dear to 15.35
anybody. The world is bound together by cause and effect, like sand held together in your fist. For a mother loves her son with the thought 'He will support me,' and with the thought 'She bore me in her womb,' the son honors his mother. When family members treat each other well, they engender affection, but in the opposite situation they arouse enmity.

A family member may be ill-disposed towards you, while someone unrelated is demonstrably friendly. A man makes or breaks affection because of his different needs. Just as an artist might fall in love with a woman that he has painted himself, so does a man become involved with someone when
he has invented the affection himself. The kinsman whom 15.40
you loved in another life—what does he do for you now, or you for him? So don't let distractions about your family invade your mind, since in samsara there is no abiding difference between family and stranger.

'That country is safe; in that one they give alms generously; that one is happy.' If any such notion should arise in you, shun it, my friend. Do not dwell on it in any way, knowing that the whole world is ablaze with the various fires of defilement.

ṛtu|cakra|nivartāc ca, kṣut|pipāsā|klamād api,
sarvatra niyataṃ duḥkhaṃ. na kva cid vidyate śivam.
15.45 kva cic chītaṃ, kva cid gharmaḥ,
kva cid rogo, bhayaṃ kva cit
bādhate 'bhyadhikaṃ lokaṃ.
tasmād a|śaraṇaṃ jagat.
jarā vyādhiś ca mṛtyuś ca lokasy' âsya mahad bhayam.
n' âsti deśaḥ sa yatr' âsya tad bhayaṃ n' ôpapadyate.
yatra gacchati kāyo 'yaṃ, duḥkhaṃ tatr' ânugacchati.
n' âsti kā cid gatir loke gato yatra na bādhyate.
ramaṇīyo 'pi deśaḥ san su|bhikṣaḥ kṣema eva ca
ku|deśa iti vijñeyo yatra kleśair vidahyate.
lokasy' âbhyāhatasy' âsya duḥkhaiḥ śārīra|mānasaiḥ,
kṣemaḥ kaś cin na deśe 'sti svastho yatra gato bhavet.
15.50 duḥkhaṃ sarvatra sarvasya vartate sarvadā yadā,
chanda|rāgam ataḥ, saumya, loka|citreṣu mā kṛthāḥ.
yadā tasmān nivṛttas te chanda|rāgo bhaviṣyati,
jīva|lokaṃ tadā sarvam ādīptam iva maṃsyate.
atha kaś cid vitarkas te bhaved a|maraṇ'|āśrayaḥ,
yatnena sa vihantavyo vyādhir ātma|gato yathā.
muhūrtam api viśrambhaḥ kāryo na khalu jīvite,
nilīna iva hi vyāghraḥ kālo viśvasta|ghātakaḥ.
balastho 'pi yuvā v'' êti na te bhavitum arhati;
mṛtyuḥ sarvāsv avasthāsu hanti n' âvekṣate vayaḥ.

It's inevitable that suffering exists everywhere, whether from the turning of the cycle of the seasons, or from hunger, thirst and tiredness. Nowhere is happiness found. Some- 15.45
where, cold brings keen distress to man, somewhere heat, somewhere sickness, somewhere danger. The world is therefore shelterless. Aging, sickness and death are most dangerous for mankind. There is no country where that danger doesn't arise.

Where this body goes, it is followed by sorrow. There is no route in the world on which a man is not wounded. Even a safe and delightful country where alms are given generously should be regarded as a flawed country, burned by defilements. The world, stricken by physical and mental suffering, has no safe place to which one could go and be at ease.

Dear friend, since suffering operates in everybody every- 15.50
where and at all times, do not set your passion or your will on the bright things of this world. When your passion and will have turned away from them, you will come to regard the whole world of living beings as burning.

Next, any conception that you might have that isn't grounded in the fact of death should be strenuously fought off, as you would your own illness. Don't trust in life even for a moment, for time slays the trusting man like a tiger lying in wait. The thought that you are young or strong should not exist for you; death kills in all circumstances, without noticing a person's age.

15.55 kṣetra|bhūtam an|arthānāṃ śarīraṃ parikarṣataḥ
svāsthy|āśā jīvit'|āśā vā na dṛṣṭ'|ârthasya jāyate.
nirvṛtaḥ ko bhavet kāyaṃ mahā|bhūt'|āśrayaṃ vahan,
paraspara|viruddhānām ahīnām iva bhājanam?
praśvasity ayam anvakṣaṃ yad ucchvasiti mānavaḥ
avagaccha tad āścaryam a|viśvāsyaṃ hi jīvitam.
idam āścaryam aparaṃ yat suptaḥ pratibudhyate,
svapity utthāya vā bhūyo; bahv|amitrā hi dehinaḥ.

garbhāt prabhṛti yo lokaṃ jighāṃsur anugacchati,
kas tasmin viśvasen mṛtyāv, udyat'|âsāv arāv iva?
15.60 prasūtaḥ puruṣo loke, śrutavān balavān api,
na jayaty antakaṃ kaś cin, n' âjayan n' âpi jeṣyati.
sāmnā dānena bhedena daṇḍena niyamena vā,
prāpto hi rabhaso mṛtyuḥ pratihantuṃ na śakyate.

tasmān n' āyuṣi viśvāsaṃ cañcale kartum arhasi
nityaṃ harati kālo hi sthāviryaṃ na pratīkṣate.
niḥ|sāraṃ paśyato lokaṃ toya|budbuda|durbalam,
kasy' â|mara|vitarko hi syād an|unmatta|cetasaḥ?

tasmād eṣāṃ vitarkāṇāṃ prahāṇ'|ârthaṃ samāsataḥ
ān'|âpāna|smṛtiṃ saumya viṣayī|kartum arhasi.
15.65 ity anena prayogeṇa, kāle sevitum arhasi,
pratipakṣān vitarkāṇāṃ, gadānām agadān iva.

Expectations of well-being or continuing life do not oc- 15.55
ur to a truly seeing man as he drags around his body, that
ield of misfortunes. Who could be happy carrying around
body which hosts the great elements, as though one were
arrying a container full of snakes fighting each other? Life
s unreliable, so consider it a marvel when a man breathes
n and straightaway breathes out again. Another thing of
vonder is that a sleeper wakes up, or that after getting up a
nan later goes to sleep again; for embodied creatures have
nultiple enemies.

Who would trust Death, who with murderous intent
talks people from the womb onwards, any more than one
vould trust an enemy with upraised sword? No man born 15.60
nto the world, though he be learned and mighty, can defeat
Death, maker of ends, nor has ever defeated him, nor will
lefeat him. For impetuous Death, when he arrives, cannot
e countered by diplomacy, gifts, sowing dissent, force or
anctions.

So place no trust in this fleeting life, for time is always
eizing people and need not wait for old age. What sound-
ninded man, seeing the world to be insubstantial and fragile
s a water-bubble, would harbor thoughts of immortality?

So to be brief, dear friend, you should make yourself
roficient in mindfulness of inward and outward breathing
n order to eliminate such fancies.* With this procedure 15.65
ou can adopt countermeasures against such fancies in good
ime, as a medication against sickness.

suvarṇa|hetor api pāṃsu|dhāvako
vihāya pāṃsūn bṛhato yath" āditaḥ,
jahāti sūkṣmān api tad|viśuddhaye.
viśodhya hem'|âvayavān niyacchati.
vimokṣa|hetor api yukta|mānaso
vihāya doṣān bṛhatas tath" āditaḥ,
jahāti sūkṣmān api tad|viśuddhaye.
viśodhya dharm'|âvayavān niyacchati.
krameṇ' âdbhiḥ śuddhaṃ
kanakam iha pāṃsu|vyavahitaṃ
yath" âgnau karmāraḥ
pacati bhṛśam āvartayati ca,
tathā yog'|ācāro
nipuṇam iha doṣa|vyavahitaṃ
viśodhya kleśebhyaḥ
śamayati manaḥ saṃkṣipati ca.
yathā ca sva|cchandād
upanayati karm'|āśraya|sukhaṃ
suvarṇaṃ karmāro
bahu|vidham alaṃkāra|vidhiṣu
manaḥ|śuddho bhikṣur
vaśa|gatam abhijñāsv api tathā
yath"|êcchaṃ yatr'|êcchaṃ
śamayati manaḥ prerayati ca.»

Saundaranande mahā|kāvye Vitarka|prahāṇo nāma
pañcadaśaḥ sargaḥ.

To obtain gold, a dirt-washer discards first the large bits of grit, and then, to refine it further, he discards also the tiny bits of grit. After this cleansing, he retains particles of gold. To obtain liberation, a man of focused mind will likewise abandon first gross faults, and then, to further refine his mind, he abandons also subtle faults. After this cleansing, he retains the constituents of *dharma*.

Just as in this world a goldsmith takes gold that has been washed with water and separated from the dirt in gradual stages, and heats it in the fire and turns it frequently, so the practitioner of yoga, having first cleansed his mind of defilements so that it is completely separated from faults in this world, then makes it calm and concentrated.

And as the goldsmith brings gold to a good state for working at will into various ornaments of many kinds, so too the monk of cleansed mind pacifies his mind, so that it is under his control, and then directs it as he wishes, wherever he wishes among the supernormal faculties."*

End of Canto 15: Abandoning Notions.

CANTO 16
EXPLANATION OF THE NOBLE TRUTHS

16.1 «EVAṂ MANO|DHĀRAṆAYĀ krameṇa
vyapohya kiṃ cit samupohya kiṃ cit,
dhyānāni catvāry adhigamya yogī
prāpnoty abhijñā niyamena pañca:
ṛddhi|pravekaṃ ca bahu|prakāraṃ,
parasya cetaś|carit'|âvabodham,
atīta|janma|smaraṇaṃ ca dīrghaṃ,
divye viśuddhe śruti|cakṣuṣī ca.
ataḥ paraṃ tattva|parīkṣaṇena
mano dadhāty āsrava|saṃkṣayāya,
tato hi duḥkha|prabhṛtīni samyak
catvāri satyāni padāny avaiti—
bādh'|ātmakaṃ duḥkham idaṃ prasaktaṃ;
duḥkhasya hetuḥ prabhav'|ātmako 'yam;
duḥkha|kṣayo niḥsaraṇ'|ātmako 'yaṃ;
trāṇ'|ātmako 'yaṃ praśamāya mārgaḥ.
16.5 ity ārya|satyāny avabudhya buddhyā
catvāri samyak pratividhya c' âiva,
sarv'|āsravān bhāvanay" âbhibhūya,
na jāyate śāntim avāpya bhūyaḥ.
a|bodhato hy a|prativedhataś ca
tattv'|ātmakasy' âsya catuṣṭayasya,
bhavād bhavaṃ yāti na śāntim eti
saṃsāra|dolām adhiruhya lokaḥ.
tasmāj jar"|āder vyasanasya mūlaṃ
samāsato duḥkham avaihi janma;
sarv'|âuṣadhīnām iva bhūr bhavāya
sarv'|āpadāṃ kṣetram idaṃ hi janma.
yaj janma rūpasya hi s'|êndriyasya
duḥkhasya tan n' âika|vidhasya janma

"So by using mental concentration to gradually take a little away and to add a little, the practitioner attains the four meditative states, and then inevitably acquires the five supernormal faculties: all manner of wonderful psychic powers, knowing the movements of the minds of other people, remembering past births from long ago, and divine, purified hearing and sight. 16.1

From then on, by an examination of reality, he positions his mind to destroy the rebirth-producing tendencies,* for it is then that he correctly understands the Four Truths starting with the statement about suffering—this is constant suffering, identifiable with affliction; this is the cause of suffering, identifiable with origination; this is the destruction of suffering, identifiable with escape; and this is the path to peace, identifiable with protection.

16.5
By using his intellect to understand and completely penetrate the Four Noble Truths, and by using meditation to overpower all the rebirth-producing tendencies, he attains peace and is not born again. For in failing to understand and penetrate this tetrad which identifies reality, the world, hoisted in the swing of samsara, goes from existence to existence without finding peace.

In short, you must therefore accept that birth, the root of miseries such as old age, is suffering; for this birth is the field of all adversity, as is the earth for all plants. For the birth of a body endowed with sense faculties is the birth of suffering in all its varieties, and the arising of this excrescence is the arising of death and disease. Food mixed with poison conduces to the loss of life and not to its preservation, whether the food itself be good or bad. Likewise, all birth makes

yaḥ sambhavaś c' âsya samucchrayasya
mṛtyoś ca rogasya ca sambhavaḥ saḥ.
sad v" âpy a|sad v" âpi viṣa|miśram annaṃ
yathā vināśāya na dhāraṇāya,
loke tathā tiryag upary adho vā
duḥkhāya sarvaṃ na sukhāya janma.

16.10 jar"|ādayo n' âika|vidhāḥ prajānāṃ
satyāṃ pravṛttau prabhavanty an|arthāḥ;
pravātsu ghoreṣv api māruteṣu
na hy a|prasūtās taravaś calanti.
ākāśa|yoniḥ pavano yathā hi,
yathā śamī|garbha|śayo hutāśaḥ,
āpo yath" ântar|vasudhā|śayāś ca,
duḥkhaṃ tathā citta|śarīra|yoni.
apāṃ dravatvaṃ, kaṭhinatvam urvyā
vāyoś calatvaṃ, dhruvam auṣṇyam agneḥ,
yathā sva|bhāvo hi tathā sva|bhāvo
duḥkhaṃ śarīrasya ca cetasaś ca.
kāye sati, vyādhi|jar"|ādi duḥkhaṃ,
kṣut|tarṣa|varṣ'|ôṣṇa|himādi c' âiva.
rūp'|āśrite cetasi s'|ânubandhe,
śok'|ârati|krodha|bhay'|ādi duḥkham.
pratyakṣam ālokya ca janma duḥkhaṃ
duḥkhaṃ tath" âtītam ap' îti viddhi.
yathā ca tad duḥkham idaṃ ca duḥkhaṃ
duḥkhaṃ tath" ân|āgatam apy avehi.

16.15 bīja|svabhāvo hi yath" êha dṛṣṭo,
bhūto 'pi bhavyo 'pi tath" ânumeyaḥ.
pratyakṣataś ca jvalano yath" ôṣṇo,
bhūto 'pi bhavyo 'pi tath" ôṣṇa eva.

for sorrow and not happiness, whether the birth be among animals or in the worlds above or below.

All kinds of troubles, old age for instance, will appear 16.10
among mankind as long as life continues; for non-existent trees do not shake even when violent gales blow. As wind is born from the air, as fire lies embryonic in *shami* wood, as water gestates in the earth's interior, so are the mind and body pregnant with suffering. As fluidity inheres in water, solidity in earth, motion in wind, and constant heat in fire, so does suffering inhere in the mind and body. So long as the body exists, there is suffering such as disease and old age, and also hunger, thirst, rain, heat and cold. And when there is a bonded mind dependent on the body, there is suffering such as grief, despair, anger and fear.

Having seen with your own eyes that birth is suffering, understand that past birth was suffering too. Just as that was suffering and this is suffering, be aware that future birth will also be suffering. For just as the inherent nature of a seed is 16.15
obvious here and now, its inherent nature in the past and the future can be inferred. And as there is heat from a fire burning in front of us, so was there also heat in the past and will be in the future.

tan nāma|rūpasya guṇ'|ânurūpaṃ
yatr" âiva nirvṛttir, udāra|vṛtta.
tatr' âiva duḥkhaṃ, na hi tad|vimuktaṃ
duḥkhaṃ bhaviṣyaty, abhavad, bhaved vā.

pravṛtti|duḥkhasya ca tasya loke
tṛṣṇ"|ādayo doṣa|gaṇā nimittam
n' âiv' ēśvaro, na prakṛtir, na kālo,
n' âpi svabhāvo, na vidhir yadṛcchā.
jñātavyam etena ca kāraṇena
lokasya doṣebhya iti pravṛttiḥ.
yasmān mriyante sa|rajas|tamaskā,
na jāyate vīta|rajas|tamaskaḥ.

icchā|viśeṣe sati tatra tatra
yān'|āsan'|āder bhavati prayogaḥ.
yasmād atas tarṣa|vaśāt tath" âiva
janma prajānām iti veditavyam.

16.20 sattvāny abhiṣvaṅga|vaśāni dṛṣṭvā,
sva|jātiṣu prīti|parāṇy atīva,
abhyāsa|yogād upapāditāni
tair eva doṣair iti tāni viddhi.
krodha|praharṣ'|ādibhir āśrayāṇām
utpadyate c' êha yathā viśeṣaḥ,
tath" âiva janmasv api n' âika|rūpo
nirvartate kleśa|kṛto viśeṣaḥ.
roṣ'|âdhike janmani tīvra|roṣa,*
utpadyate rāgiṇi tīvra|rāgaḥ,
moh'|âdhike moha|bal'|âdhikaś ca,
tad|alpa|doṣe ca tad|alpa|doṣaḥ.

There where psycho-physical existence grows in conformity to its characteristics, right there, O man of noble conduct, is suffering, for without it suffering will not exist, did not exist, could not exist.

The reason for this suffering during one's active life in the world is not a God, not nature, not time, not the inherent nature of things, not predestination, not accident, but the hosts of faults such as desire. You must understand thereby that man's active life continues because of its faults. It follows that people who are subject to passion and mental darkness die repeatedly, while someone free from passion and mental darkness is not born again.

An action such as going or sitting occurs whenever there is a particular volition to that effect. Therefore understand that the birth of living creatures is likewise forced by volition.

Having seen that living beings are ruled by attachment, 16.20
entirely engrossed in pleasure-seeking among their own kind, know that because of their engagement in these habits they will be reborn with those very faults. Just as the distinctive character of embodied individuals arises because of their anger, joy and so on, so does their distinctive defilement-created character develop in various formats in future births too. Violent hatred arises in the future birth of someone given to hate, violent lust in someone who was lustful, a very powerful delusion in someone given to delusion, and a lesser fault in someone whose fault was less than these.

phalaṃ hi yādṛk samavaiti sākṣāt
tad|āgamād bījam avaity atītam;
avetya bīja|prakṛtiṃ ca sākṣād
an|āgataṃ tat|phalam abhyupaiti.
doṣa|kṣayo jātiṣu yāsu yasya,
vairāgyatas tāsu na jāyate saḥ.
doṣ'|āśayas tiṣṭhati yasya yatra,
tasy' ôpapattir vi|vaśasya tatra.
16.25 taj janmano n' âika|vidhasya, saumya,
—tṛṣṇ"|ādayo—hetava ity avetya,
tāṃś chindhi, duḥkhād yadi nirmumukṣā.
kārya|kṣayaḥ kāraṇa|saṃkṣayādd hi,
duḥkha|kṣayo hetu|parikṣayāc ca.
śāntaṃ śivaṃ sākṣi|kuruṣva dharmam,
tṛṣṇā|virāgaṃ layanaṃ nirodhaṃ
sanātanaṃ trāṇam a|hāryam āryam,
yasmin na jātir, na jarā, na mṛtyur,
na vyādhayo, n' â|priya|samprayogaḥ,
n' êcchā|vipanna priya|viprayogaḥ;
kṣemaṃ padaṃ naiṣṭhikam a|cyutaṃ tat.
dīpo yathā nirvṛtim abhyupeto
n' âiv' âvaniṃ gacchati n' ântarikṣam,
diśaṃ na kāṃ cid vidiśaṃ na kāṃ cit,
sneha|kṣayāt kevalam eti śāntim,
evaṃ kṛtī nirvṛtim abhyupeto
n' âiv' âvaniṃ gacchati n' ântarikṣam,
diśaṃ na kāṃ cid vidiśaṃ na kāṃ cit,
kleśa|kṣayāt kevalam eti śāntim.

When someone considers which kind of fruit is in front of him, he can, based on its origin, determine what seed it was in the past; and when someone considers the nature of a seed in front of him, he knows what the future fruit of that seed will be. When a man has destroyed faults in certain forms of existence, thanks to that dispassion he is not reborn in those forms again. When he harbors a latent tendency to a fault in that form, rebirth in that form is forced on him.

So be aware, my friend, of the causes—desire, for example 16.25
—of the many types of birth, and if you seek freedom from suffering, cut them off. For the destruction of an effect follows from the utter destruction of its cause, and the destruction of suffering follows from the destruction of its cause. Set *dharma** before your eyes, which is peaceful and benign, with no passion for desire, a resting place, a cessation, an eternal, irremoveable, and noble protection, in which there is no birth, no old age, no death, no sicknesses, no association with anything unpleasant, no failure of wishes and no separation from anything pleasant; it is an ultimate, unfallen state of ease.

Just as a light which is extinguished does not travel to the earth or the sky, nor to the directions or any intermediate directions but, because its oil is used up, merely ceases, so he who has reached nirvana travels not to the earth, not to the sky, nor to any of the directions or intermediate directions, but, because his defilements have ended, just attains peace.

16.30 asy' âbhyupāyo 'dhigamāya mārgaḥ
prajñā|tri|kalpaḥ praśama|dvi|kalpaḥ.
sa bhāvanīyo vidhivad budhena
śīle śucau tri|pramukhe sthitena.

vāk|karma samyak saha|kāya|karma,
yathāvad ājīva|nayaś ca śuddhaḥ—
idaṃ trayaṃ vṛtta|vidhau pravṛttaṃ,
śīl'|āśrayaṃ karma|parigrahāya.

satyeṣu duḥkh'|ādiṣu dṛṣṭir āryā
samyag vitarkaś ca parākramaś ca—
idaṃ trayaṃ jñāna|vidhau pravṛttaṃ,
prajñ"|āśrayaṃ kleśa|parikṣayāya.

nyāyena saty'|âbhigamāya yuktā
samyak smṛtiḥ samyag atho samādhiḥ—
idaṃ dvayaṃ yoga|vidhau pravṛttaṃ,
śam'|āśrayaṃ citta|parigrahāya.

kleś'|âṅkurān na pratanoti śīlaṃ
bīj'|âṅkurāt kāla iv' âtivṛttaḥ.
śucau hi śīle puruṣasya doṣā
manaḥ sa|lajjā iva dharṣayanti.

16.35 kleśāṃs tu viṣkambhayate samādhir
vegān iv' âdrir mahato nadīnām;
sthite samādhau hi na dharṣayanti
doṣā bhujaṅgā iva mantra|baddhāḥ.

prajñā tv a|śeṣeṇa nihanti doṣāṃs,
tīra|drumān prāvṛṣi nimnag" êva.
dagdhā yayā na prabhavanti doṣā,
vajr'|âgnin" êv' ânusṛtena vṛkṣāḥ.

The means to reach it is the path* of threefold wisdom 16.30
and twofold peace. It should be cultivated as instructed by a wise man abiding in the pure threefold moral self-restraint.

Right verbal and bodily actions, and making one's living in a pure and suitable manner—these three occur in the ordinance on behavior, and are a basis for moral self-restraint in order that one's actions may be circumscribed. The noble doctrine concerning the Truths of suffering etc., as well as right thought and effort—these three occur in the ordinance on knowledge, and are a basis for wisdom in order that one's defilements may be annihilated. Right mindfulness conjoined to the plan for the discovery of the truth, and right concentration—these two occur in the ordinance on yogic practice, and are a basis for peace in order that one's thoughts may be circumscribed.

Moral self-restraint does not grow offshoots of defilement, just as a season which has passed does not grow shoots from a seed. Given that his moral self-restraint is pure, the faults of a man venture only timidly to attack his mind.
But concentration casts off the defilements like a mountain 16.35
casts off the mighty torrents of rivers; for the faults, like snakes transfixed by a magic formula, do not venture to attack a man who is fixed in concentration. And wisdom destroys faults without a remainder, as a river in the rainy season destroys the trees on its bank. Faults burned up by it cannot prevail, like trees burned up by the fire ensuing from a thunderbolt.

tri|skandham etaṃ pravigāhya mārgaṃ
praspaṣṭam aṣṭ'|âṅgam a|hāryam āryam,
duḥkhasya hetūn prajahāti doṣān,
prāpnoti c' âtyanta|śivaṃ padaṃ tat.
asy' ôpacāre dhṛtir ārjavaṃ ca
hrīr a|pramādaḥ praviviktatā ca,
alp'|êcchatā tuṣṭir a|saṃgatā ca
loka|pravṛttāv a|ratiḥ kṣamā ca.

yāthātmyato vindati yo hi duḥkhaṃ
tasy' ôdbhavaṃ tasya ca yo nirodham,
āryeṇa mārgeṇa sa śāntim eti,
kalyāṇa|mitraiḥ saha vartamānaḥ.

16.40 yo vyādhito vyādhim avaiti samyag
vyādher nidānaṃ ca tad|auṣadhaṃ ca,
ārogyam āpnoti hi so 'cireṇa,
mitrair abhijñair upacaryamāṇaḥ.
tad vyādhi|saṃjñāṃ kuru duḥkha|satye
doṣesv api vyādhi|nidāna|saṃjñām
ārogya|saṃjñāṃ ca nirodha|satye
bhaiṣajya|saṃjñām api mārga|satye.

tasmāt pravṛttiṃ parigaccha duḥkhaṃ,
pravartakān apy avagaccha doṣān;
nivṛttim āgaccha ca tan|nirodhaṃ,
nivartakaṃ c' âpy avagaccha mārgam.
śirasy atho vāsasi sampradīpte,
saty'|âvabodhāya matir vicāryā,
dagdhaṃ jagat satya|nayaṃ hy a|dṛṣṭvā
pradahyate samprati dhakṣyate ca.

On penetrating this clear and irremovable noble path, with its three divisions and eight branches, one abandons the faults, which are the causes of suffering, and reaches the state of utter happiness. Ancillary to it are firmness, sincerity, modesty, heedfulness and solitude, minimal wishfulness, contentment, freedom from forming attachments, patience, and no fondness for active life in the world.

He who discovers the true nature of suffering, and its arising and cessation will, proceeding together with wise friends, reach peace by the noble path. The sick man who 16.40
understands his disease correctly, and its cause and its remedy will, when tended by knowledgeable friends, soon win good health. So with regard to the Truth about suffering, think of suffering as a disease; with regard to the faults, consider them as the cause of illness; concerning the Truth of cessation, think of it as good health, and as for the Truth about the path, regard it as the remedy.*

Therefore accept that active life is suffering, and understand faults as being related to active life; recognize cessation of suffering to be the ceasing of active life, and know the path as being related to cessation. Though your head and clothes be on fire, direct your mind towards the comprehension of the Truths, for in its failure to perceive the doctrine of the Truths, the world was burned, is burning now, and will burn in the future.

yad" âiva yaḥ paśyati nāma|rūpaṃ
kṣay" îti, tad darśanam asya samyak;
samyak ca nirvedam upaiti paśyan,
nandī|kṣayāc ca kṣayam eti rāgaḥ.

16.45 tayoś ca nandī|rajasoḥ kṣayeṇa
samyag vimuktaṃ pravadāmi cetaḥ.
samyag vimuktir manasaś ca tābhyāṃ,
na c' âsya bhūyaḥ karaṇīyam asti.

yathā|svabhāvena hi nāma|rūpaṃ
tadd|hetum ev' âsta|gamaṃ ca tasya,
vijānataḥ paśyata eva c' âhaṃ
bravīmi samyak kṣayam āsravāṇām.

tasmāt paraṃ saumya vidhāya vīryaṃ,
śīghraṃ ghaṭasv āsrava|saṃkṣayāya
duḥkhān a|nityāṃś ca nir|ātmakāṃś ca
dhātūn viśeṣeṇa parīkṣamāṇaḥ.

dhātūn hi ṣaḍ bhū|salil'|ânalādīn
sāmānyataḥ svena ca lakṣaṇena
avaiti yo n' ânyam avaiti tebhyaḥ,
so 'tyantikaṃ mokṣam avaiti tebhyaḥ.

When someone sees that psycho-physical existence is imbued with decay, his insight is correct; with this correct vision he becomes disinterested in worldly objects and from the ending of pleasure in worldly objects his passion comes to an end. I declare that the mind is completely liberated 16.45
by the ending of these two things—passion, and pleasure in worldly objects. When the mind is perfectly free of these two things, there is nothing further that one must do. For I proclaim the total annihilation of rebirth-producing tendencies in a man who knows and sees psycho-physical existence just as it is, and its cause and its disappearance.

Therefore apply your utmost energy, dear friend, and be quick to strive for the eradication of the rebirth-producing tendencies, investigating in particular the elements, which are full of suffering, impermanent and without self. For the man who understands the six elements of earth, water, fire and so on in their general and particular characteristics, and who understands that there is nothing else apart from them, attains utter freedom from them.

kleśa|prahāṇāya ca niścitena
kālo 'bhyupāyaś ca parīkṣitavyaḥ;
yogo 'py a|kāle hy an|upāyataś ca
bhavaty an|arthāya, na tad|guṇāya.

16.50 a|jāta|vatsāṃ yadi gāṃ duhīta
n' âiv' āpnuyāt kṣīram a|kāla|dohī;
kāle 'pi vā syān na payo labheta,
mohena śṛṅgād yadi gāṃ duhīta.

ārdrāc ca kāṣṭhāj jvalan'|âbhikāmo
n' âiva prayatnād api vahnim ṛcchet;
kāṣṭhāc ca śuṣkād api pātanena,
n' âiv' âgnim āpnoty an|upāya|pūrvam.

tad|deśa|kālau vidhivat parīkṣya,
yogasya mātrām api c' âbhyupāyam,
bal'|â|bale c' ātmani sampradhārya,
kāryaḥ prayatno na tu tad|viruddhaḥ.

pragrāhakaṃ yat tu nimittam uktam
uddhanyamāne hṛdi tan na sevyam,
evaṃ hi cittaṃ praśamaṃ na yāti
[- - -]nā vahnir iv' êryamāṇaḥ.

śamāya yat syān niyataṃ nimittaṃ
jāt'|ôdbhave cetasi tasya kālaḥ,
evaṃ hi cittaṃ praśamaṃ niyacchet
pradīpyamāno 'gnir iv' ôdakena.

When someone has formed a resolve to abandon the defilements, he should carefully consider the correct time and method to do so; for even yogic discipline can lead to failure, not success, if practiced at the wrong time or in the
wrong way. A man milking a cow at the wrong time, when 16.50
her calf is not yet born, will get no milk; and even at the right time, he would get no milk if, in ignorance, he were to milk her by the horn. A man wanting a fire will not get one from damp wood, even if he tries; and even laying on dry wood, he won't get a fire if he uses the wrong method.

Having considered the time and place for yogic practice, as prescribed, and also its extent and method, and after reflecting on your own strengths and weaknesses, make an effort, avoiding anything which conflicts with them.

The meditational technique known to promote energy should not be practiced when one's spirits are excited, for thus the mind, like a fanned fire [...], does not become peaceful. When the mind is excited, it is the time for the meditational technique prescribed for tranquillity, for thus the mind, like a blazing fire doused by water, subsides into peace.

16.55 śam'|āvahaṃ yan niyataṃ nimittaṃ
sevyaṃ na tac cetasi līyamāne,
evaṃ hi bhūyo layam eti cittam
an|īryamāṇo 'gnir iv' âlpa|sāraḥ.

pragrāhakaṃ yan niyataṃ nimittaṃ
layaṃ gate cetasi tasya kālaḥ,
kriyā|samarthaṃ hi manas tathā syān
mandāyamāno 'gnir iv' êndhanena.

aupekṣikaṃ n' âpi nimittam iṣṭaṃ
layaṃ gate cetasi s'|ôdbhave vā,
evaṃ hi tīvraṃ janayed an|artham
upekṣito vyādhir iv' āturasya.

yat syād upekṣā niyataṃ nimittaṃ
sāmyaṃ gate cetasi tasya kālaḥ,
evaṃ hi kṛtyāya bhavet prayogo
ratho vidhey'|âśva iva prayātaḥ.

The meditational technique prescribed for bringing tranquillity should not be practiced when the mind is depressed, for thus the mind, like a little unfanned fire, sinks still further into depression. When the mind is depressed, it is time for the meditational technique prescribed for energy, for thus the mind, like a slow-burning fire plied with fuel, becomes useful. 16.55

The meditational technique of equanimity is not recommended when the mind is either over-excited or depressed, for this may produce serious mishap, like the neglected disease of a sick man. When the mind is in equilibrium, it is time for the meditation prescribed for equanimity, for thus it can apply itself to its job, like a chariot setting off with well-trained horses.

rāg'|ôddhava|vyākulite 'pi citte,
maitr'|ôpasaṃhāra|vidhir na kāryaḥ;
rāg'|ātmāko muhyati maitrayā hi
snehaṃ kapha|kṣobha iv' ôpayujya.

16.60 rāg'|ôddhate cetasi dhairyam etya
niṣevitavyaṃ tv a|śubhaṃ nimittam,
rāg'|ātmako hy evam upaiti śarma
kaph'|ātmako rūkṣam iv' ôpayujya.

vyāpāda|doṣeṇa manasy udīrṇe
na sevitavyaṃ tv a|śubhaṃ nimittam,
dveṣ'|ātmakasya hy a|śubhā vadhāya
pitt'|ātmanas tīkṣṇa iv' ôpacāraḥ.

vyāpāda|doṣa|kṣubhite tu citte
sevyā sva|pakṣ'|ôpanayena maitrī;
dveṣ'|ātmano hi praśamāya maitrī
pitt'|ātmanaḥ śīta iv' ôpacāraḥ.

moh'|ânubaddhe manasaḥ pracāre
maitr'|â|śubhā c' âiva bhavaty a|yogaḥ;
tābhyāṃ hi saṃmoham upaiti bhūyo
vāyv|ātmako rūkṣam iv' ôpanīya.

moh'|ātmikāyāṃ manasaḥ pravṛttau
sevyas tv idaṃ|pratyayatā|vihāraḥ;
mūḍhe manasy eṣa hi śānti|mārgo
vāyv|ātmake snigdha iv' ôpacāraḥ.

When the mind is disordered due to the excitement of passion, the prescription for cultivating loving-kindness should not be followed; for a man of passionate nature is debilitated by loving-kindness, like a patient with a phlegm imbalance using oil treatments.* When the mind is stirred 16.60
up by passion, one should find stability and practice the impurity meditation, for that is how a man of passionate nature finds relief, like a patient with a phlegm condition using astringent treatments.

When the mind is agitated by the fault of malice, the impurity meditation should not be undertaken, for the impurity meditation destroys a hate-filled man, like treatment with acids in the case of a patient with a bile condition. But when the mind is disturbed by the fault of malice, the loving-kindness meditation should be practiced with reference to one's own position; for loving-kindness calms a hate-filled man, like treatment with cooling remedies for a patient with a bile condition.

When the activities of the mind are related to delusion, neither the loving-kindness nor the impurity meditation is suitable; for a deluded man is further dazed by these two, like a patient with a wind condition treated with astringents. When the activities of the mind are confused in nature, an analysis of causality should be undertaken; for this is the path to peace for a deluded mind, like treatment with oils in the case of a patient with a wind condition.

16.65 ulkā|mukha|stham hi yathā suvarṇaṃ
suvarṇa|kāro dhamat' îha kāle
kāle pariprokṣayate jalena
krameṇa kāle samupekṣate ca.
dahet suvarṇaṃ hi dhamann a|kāle;
jale kṣipan saṃśamayed a|kāle;
na c' âpi samyak paripākam enaṃ
nayed a|kāle samupekṣamāṇaḥ.
sampragrahasya praśamasya c' âiva
tath" âiva kāle samupekṣaṇasya
samyaṅ nimittaṃ manasā tv avekṣyaṃ,
nāśo hi yatno 'py an|upāya|pūrvaḥ.»
ity evam a|nyāya|nivartanaṃ ca
nyāyaṃ ca tasmai Sugato babhāṣe;
bhūyaś ca tat tac caritaṃ viditvā,
vitarka|hānāya vidhīn uvāca.
yathā bhiṣak pitta|kaph'|ânilānāṃ
ya eva kopaṃ samupaiti doṣaḥ
śamāya tasy' âiva vidhiṃ vidhatte,
vyadhatta doṣeṣu tath" âiva Buddhaḥ.

In this world a goldsmith at times blows the gold placed in the furnace, at times uses water to sprinkle it, and at times watches it. For in blowing at the wrong time he might burn the gold; casting it into water at the wrong time he would make it cool down; and in merely observing it at the wrong time, he might not bring it to perfect readiness. Likewise the correct meditational subject of an energy, calm or equanimity meditation should at times be mentally reviewed, for even diligence is destructive if it is accompanied by the wrong method." 16.65

In this way the Súgata spoke to him concerning right method and the retreat from the wrong method; and knowing all the various behavioral types, he gave further instructions for abandoning opinionated thought. Just as a doctor prescribes a treatment to alleviate whichever among the humors of bile, phlegm and wind has become irritated, so too has the Buddha prescribed concerning the faults.

16.70 «ekena kalpena sacen na hanyāt
sv|abhyasta|bhāvād a|śubhān vitarkān,
tato dvitīyaṃ kramam ārabheta;
na tv eva heyo guṇavān prayogaḥ.
an|ādi|kāl'|ôpacit'|ātmakatvād
balīyasaḥ kleśa|gaṇasya c' âiva,
samyak|prayogasya ca duṣ|karatvāc,
chettuṃ na śakyāḥ sahasā hi doṣāḥ.
aṇvyā yath" âṇyā vipul'|âṇir anyā
nirvāhyate tad|viduṣā nareṇa,
tadvat tad ev' â|kuśalaṃ nimittaṃ
kṣipen nimitt'|ântara|sevanena.
tath" âpy ath' âdhyātma|nava|grahatvān
n' âiv' ôpaśāmyed a|śubho vitarkaḥ;
heyaḥ sa tad|doṣa|parīkṣaṇena,
sa|śvāpado mārga iv' âdhvagena.
yathā kṣudh|ārto 'pi viṣeṇa pṛktaṃ
jijīviṣur n' êcchati bhoktum annam,
tath" âiva doṣ'|āvaham ity avetya
jahāti vidvān a|śubhaṃ nimittam.
16.75 na doṣataḥ paśyati yo hi doṣaṃ
kas taṃ tato vārayituṃ samarthaḥ?
guṇaṃ guṇe paśyati yaś ca yatra
sa vāryamāṇo 'pi tataḥ prayāti.
vyapatrapante hi kula|prasūtā
manaḥ|pracārair a|śubhaiḥ pravṛttaiḥ,
kaṇṭhe manasv" îva yuvā vapuṣmān
a|cākṣuṣair a|prayatair viṣaktaiḥ.

"If one cannot destroy impure thoughts by this first 16.70
method, because they have become so habitual, then one should try a second way; but the good practice should certainly not be given up. The faults cannot be cut off all of a sudden, partly because the powerful mass of defilements has by nature been accumulating from beginningless time, and partly because the correct practice is so difficult to do.

Just as a man expert in such matters removes a large pin by means of smaller pin, likewise one should drop an ineffective meditational subject by focusing on a different one. Even so, an impure thought might not subside because of the individual's inexperience; it should then be abandoned by an examination of its faults, like a traveler leaves a road beset by wild beasts. Just as a man who wants his life to continue avoids eating poisoned food even when he is starving, so too does a wise man leave aside an impure meditation, knowing that it brings corruption.

When a man does not see a fault as a fault, who is able to 16.75
restrain him from it? But a man who sees the virtue in virtue moves towards it despite being restrained. For nobly-born men are ashamed of the continuing impure movements of their minds, like a handsome and spirited young man is ashamed of unsightly and badly-finished chains round his neck.

nirdhūyamānās tv atha leśato 'pi
tiṣṭheyur ev' â|kuśalā vitarkāḥ;
kāry'|ântarair adhyayana|kriy"|ādyaiḥ
sevyo vidhir vismaraṇāya teṣām.
svaptavyam apy eva vicakṣaṇena
kāya|klamo v" âpi niṣevitavyaḥ;
na tv eva saṃcintyam a|san nimittaṃ
yatr' âvasaktasya bhaved an|arthaḥ.
yathā hi bhīto niśi taskarebhyo
dvāraṃ priyebhyo 'pi na dātum icchet,
prājñas tathā saṃharati prayogaṃ
samaṃ śubhasy' âpy a|śubhasya doṣaiḥ.

16.80 evaṃ|prakārair api yady upāyair
nivāryamāṇā na parāṅ|mukhāḥ syuḥ,
tato yathā|sthūla|nibarhaṇena
suvarṇa|doṣā iva te praheyāḥ.
druta|prayāṇa|prabhṛtīṃś ca tīkṣṇāt
kāma|prayogāt parikhidyamānaḥ,
yathā naraḥ saṃśrayate tath" âiva
prājñena doṣeṣv api vartitavyam.
te ced a|labdha|pratipakṣa|bhāvā
n' âiv' ôpaśāmyeyur a|sad|vitarkāḥ,
muhūrtam apy a|prativadhyamānā
gṛhe bhujaṃgā iva n' âdhivāsyāḥ.
dante 'pi dantaṃ praṇidhāya kāmaṃ,
tālv|agram utpīḍya ca jihvay" âpi,
cittena cittaṃ parigṛhya c' âpi,
kāryaḥ prayatno, na tu te 'nuvartyāḥ.

kim atra citraṃ yadi vīta|moho
vanaṃ gataḥ svastha|manā na muhyet.

However, unwholesome thoughts may persist to a small extent, though they are being shaken loose; they should be obliterated by taking up different methods, such as study and work. A man of clear vision could even resort to sleep, or to physical exhaustion; but he should absolutely not meditate on a bad subject, dependence on which might bring negative consequences. For just as a man fearful of thieves does not like to open his door at night, even to friends, likewise a wise man expels the activity of pure and impure thoughts alike, due to their faults.

If they are being restricted by these kinds of method, 16.80
yet are not reversed, then they must be discarded, like the impurities in gold, by removing them according to their coarseness. Just as a man weary of excessive love-making will, for example, go for a brisk walk, so should the wise man proceed in relation to the faults. If those bad thoughts do not subside because their counteragent cannot be found, still they must not be tolerated even for a moment without being repulsed, like snakes in the house. Make an effort—grit your teeth if you like, press your tongue against the top of the palate, hold your mind with the mind—but never comply with them.

It's hardly surprising that a man free of ignorance who has retired to the forest in full mental health should be undeluded. A man unshaken when challenged in his heart by

ākṣipyamāṇo hṛdi tad|vitarkair
na kṣobhyate yaḥ sa kṛtī, sa dhīraḥ.

16.85 tad ārya|saty'|âdhigamāya pūrvaṃ
viśodhay' ânena nayena mārgam,
yātrā|gataḥ śaktru|vinigrah'|ârthaṃ
rāj" êva lakṣmīm a|jitāṃ jigīṣan.

etāny araṇyāny abhitaḥ śivāni
yog'|ânukūlāny a|jan'|êritāni
kāyasya kṛtvā praviveka|mātraṃ
kleśa|prahāṇāya bhajasva mārgam.

Kauṇḍinya|Nanda|Kṛmil'|Âniruddhās,
Tiṣy'|Ôpasenau, Vimalo 'tha Rādhaḥ,
Vāṣp'|Ôttarau Dhautaki|Moharājau,
Kātyāyana|Dravya|Pilindavatsāḥ,

Bhaddāli|Bhadrāyaṇa|Sarpadāsa|,
Subhūti|Godatta|Sujāta|Vatsāḥ,
Saṃgrāmajid Bhadrajid Aśvajic ca,
Śroṇaś ca Śoṇaś ca sa|Koṭikarṇaḥ,

Kṣem"|Ājito Nandaka|Nanda|mātāv,*
Upāli|Vāgīśa|Yaśo|Yaśodāḥ,
Mahāhvayo Valkali|Rāṣṭrapālau,
Sudarśana|Svāgata|Meghikāś ca,

16.90 sa|Kapphinaḥ Kāśyapa Auruvilvo,
mahā|Mahākāśyapa|Tiṣya|Nandāḥ,
Pūrṇaś ca Pūrṇaś ca sa Pūrṇakaś ca,
Śonāparāntaś ca sa Pūrṇa eva,

Śāradvatīputra|Subāhu|Cundā,
Kondeya|Kāpya|Bhṛgu|Kuṇṭhadhānāḥ,
sa|Śaivalau Revata|Kauṣṭhilau ca,
Maudgalya|gotraś ca Gavāṃpatiś ca—

uch thoughts is a complete man, a steadfast man. Therefore 16.85
o obtain the Noble Truths, first cleanse the path by this
nethod, as a king desiring to conquer unconquered riches
irst clears the road when he goes on an expedition to subdue
is enemy. These gracious forests around us are not teeming
vith people and are suited to yogic discipline. Give your-
elf enough solitude, and follow the path to abandon the
lefilements.

Kaundínya, Nanda, Krímila and Anirúddha, Tishya and
Jpaséna, Vímala and Radha, Vashpa, Úttara, Dháutaki and
Aoha·raja, Katyáyana, Dravya and Pilínda·vatsa, Bhaddáli,
Bhadráyana, Sarpa·dasa, Subhúti, Go·datta, Sujáta, Vatsa,
angrámajit, Bhádrajit, and Áshvajit, Shrona, Shona Koti·
arna, Kshema, Ájita, the mothers of Nándaka and Nanda,
Jpáli, Vagísha, Yashas and Yashóda, Maháhvaya, Válkalin
nd Rashtra·pala, Sudárshana, Svágata and Méghika, Ká- 16.90
phina, Káshyapa of Uruvílva, Maha·káshyapa the Great,
ishya, Nanda, the two Purnas as well as Púrnaka and Pur-
a Shonaparánta, the son of Sharádvati, Subáhu, Chunda,
Kondéya, Kapya, Bhrigu, Kuntha·dhana, Sháivala, Révata
nd Káushthila, and Maudgalyáyana and Gavam·pati—

yaṃ vikramaṃ yoga|vidhāv akurvaṃs
tam eva śīghraṃ vidhivat kuruṣva.
tataḥ padaṃ prāpsyasi tair avāptaṃ
sukh'|āvṛtais tvaṃ niyataṃ yaśaś ca.
dravyaṃ yathā syāt kaṭukaṃ rasena
tac c' ôpayuktaṃ madhuraṃ vipāke,
tath" âiva vīryaṃ kaṭukaṃ śrameṇa
tasy' ârtha|siddhyā madhuro vipākaḥ.
vīryaṃ paraṃ kārya|kṛtau hi mūlaṃ,
vīryād ṛte kācana n' âsti siddhiḥ.
udeti vīryād iha sarva|sampan,
nir|vīryatā cet sakalaś ca pāpmā.

16.95 a|labdhasy' â|lābho,
niyatam upalabdhasya vigamaḥ.
tath" âiv' ātm'|âvajñā
kṛpaṇam adhikebhyaḥ paribhavaḥ,
tamo nis|tejastvaṃ
śruti|niyama|tuṣṭi|vyuparamaḥ
nṛṇāṃ nir|vīryāṇāṃ
bhavati vinipātaś ca bhavati.
nayaṃ śrutvā śakto
yad ayam abhivṛddhiṃ na labhate,
paraṃ dharmaṃ jñātvā
yad upari nivāsaṃ na labhate,
gṛhaṃ tyaktvā muktau
yad ayam upaśāntiṃ na labhate—
nimittaṃ kausīdyaṃ
bhavati puruṣasy' âtra na ripuḥ.
a|nikṣipt'|ôtsāho
yadi khanati gāṃ vāri labhate,

that courage which they showed in the practice of yoga, be quick do the same, as instructed. Then you will certainly attain the state, and the glory, that those blissful ones reached.

Just as a substance may be pungent in flavor yet when eaten ripe may prove to be sweet, so an endeavor may be hard in its execution but when it ripens through the accomplishment of its aims, prove to be sweet. Endeavor is paramount, for it is the foundation of doing what needs to be done, and without endeavor there would be no accomplishment at all. All success in the world arises from endeavor, and if there were no endeavor evil would be complete.

Men without endeavor won't acquire what has not yet 16.95
been acquired, and they are bound to lose what has been acquired. They experience self-contempt, wretchedness, the scorn of their superiors, mental darkness, lack of brilliance, and a loss of learning, restraint and contentment; a great fall awaits them. When a competent person hears the method but makes no progress, when he knows the supreme *dharma* but wins no higher estate, when he leaves his home but finds no peace in freedom—the reason for this is his own laziness, and not an enemy.

A man obtains water when he digs the ground with unceasing perseverance, and he produces fire from firesticks by continually rubbing them together. And those who apply

prasaktaṃ vyāmathnañ
    jvalanam araṇibhyāṃ janayati.
prayuktā yoge tu
    dhruvam upalabhante śrama|phalaṃ,
drutaṃ nityaṃ yāntyo
    girim api hi bhindanti saritaḥ.
kṛṣṭvā gāṃ paripālya ca śrama|śatair
    aśnoti sasya|śriyaṃ;
yatnena pravigāhya sāgara|jalaṃ
    ratna|śriyā krīḍati;
śatrūṇām avadhūya vīryam iṣubhir
    bhuṅkte narendra|śriyaṃ
tad vīryaṃ kuru śāntaye viniyataṃ
    vīrye hi sarva|rddhayaḥ.»

Saundaranande mahā|kāvya Ārya|satya|vyākhyāno nāma ṣoḍaśaḥ sargaḥ.

themselves to yogic discipline are sure to win the reward of their exertions; for rivers that run swiftly and continously can erode even a mountain.

When a man has plowed the soil and protected it with infinite pains he earns a bounteous crop of corn; after laboring to plumb the ocean's waters he glories in his wealth of jewels; and when his arrows have driven off an enemy force, he enjoys royal sovereignity. So strive for peace, for all progress surely lies in endeavor."

End of Canto 16: Explanation of the Noble Truths.

CANTO 17
THE ATTAINMENT OF DEATHLESSNESS

17.1 ATH' ÂIVAM ādeśita|tattva|mārgo,
Nandas tadā prāpta|vimokṣa|mārgaḥ;
sarveṇa bhāvena gurau praṇamya
kleśa|prahāṇāya vanaṃ jagāma.
tatr' âvakāśaṃ mṛdu|nīla|śaṣpaṃ
dadarśa śāntaṃ taru|ṣaṇḍavantam
niḥ|śabdayā nimnagay" ôpagūḍhaṃ
vaiḍūrya|nīl'|ôdakayā vahantyā.
sa pādayos tatra vidhāya śaucaṃ,
śucau śive śrīmati vṛkṣa|mūle,
mokṣāya baddhvā vyavasāya|kakṣāṃ
paryaṅkam aṅk'|âvahitaṃ babandha.
ṛjuṃ samagraṃ praṇidhāya kāyaṃ,
kāye smṛtiṃ c' âbhimukhīṃ vidhāya,
sarv'|êndriyāṇy ātmani saṃnidhāya,
sa tatra yogaṃ prayataḥ prapede.
17.5 tataḥ sa tattvaṃ nikhilaṃ cikīrṣur,
mokṣ'|ânukūlāṃś ca vidhīṃś cikīrṣan,
jñānena lokyena śamena c' âiva
cacāra cetaḥ|parikarma|bhūmau.
saṃdhāya dhairyaṃ, praṇidhāya vīryaṃ,
vyapohya saktiṃ parigṛhya śaktim,
praśānta|cetā niyama|stha|cetāḥ;
svasthas tato 'bhūd viṣayeṣv an|āsthaḥ.

So, HAVING had the path to reality pointed out to him, Nanda arrived at liberation's path; with his whole heart he paid homage to the guru and set out for the forest in order to abandon the defilements. There within a grove of trees he saw a peaceful clearing of soft dark grass, enfolded by a silent stream whose waters flowed beryl-blue. 17.1

He washed his feet there, and at a tree root, pure, auspicious and glorious, he girded himself with the resolve to win liberation and sat with his legs crossed and his hands in his lap.* Holding his body completely straight, directing his attention toward his body, and centering all his senses on himself, he began yogic practice in earnest.

Wanting to experience reality in its entirety, and with 17.5
the intention of carrying out the prescribed practices conducive to liberation, he used ordinary worldly knowledge and peacefulness to move into the stage in which the mind is prepared. Fastened to firmness, applying endeavor, repelling clinging and embracing capability, his peaceful thoughts rested within the rules of restriction; and being now healthy, he became indifferent to sensory experience.

ātapta|buddheḥ prahit'|ātmano 'pi.
sv|abhyasta|bhāvād atha kāma|saṃjñā,
paryākulaṃ tasya manaś cakāra,
prāvṛṭsu vidyuj jalam āgat" êva.
sa paryavasthānam avetya sadyaś,
cikṣepa tāṃ dharma|vighāta|kartrīm,
priyām api krodha|parīta|cetā
nārīm iv' ôdvṛtta|guṇāṃ manasvī.
ārabdha|vīryasya manaḥ|śamāya,
bhūyas tu tasy' â|kuśalo vitarkaḥ,
vyādhi|praṇāśāya niviṣṭa|buddher
upadravo ghora iv' ājagāma.
17.10 sa tad|vighātāya nimittam anyad,
yog'|ânukūlaṃ kuśalaṃ prapede,
ārtāyanaṃ kṣīṇa|balo bala|sthaṃ
nirasyamāno balin" âriṇ" êva.
puraṃ vidhāy' ânuvidhāya daṇḍaṃ,
mitrāṇi saṃgṛhya, ripūn vigṛhya,
rājā yath" āpnoti hi gām a|pūrvāṃ
nītir mumukṣor api s" âiva yoge.
vimokṣa|kāmasya hi yogino 'pi
manaḥ puraṃ, jñāna|vidhiś ca daṇḍaḥ;
guṇāś ca mitrāṇy, arayaś ca doṣā,
bhūmir vimuktir yatate yad|artham.

Though burning zeal was in his mind and urgency in his inner self, a lustful thought occurred to him as a result of his long-standing habits. It made his mind turbulent, like lightning striking water during the rainy season. He discarded that thought, obstacle-maker to *dharma* that it was, when he suddenly became aware of the impediment, as an excitable man throws off a loved but pushy woman when his mind is encompassed by anger.

But as he was commencing his endeavor to pacify his mind, again an offensive thought occurred to him, like a severe new symptom appearing in a man whose faculties are preoccupied with fighting off an existing disease. To elimi- 17.10
nate it, he started another subject of meditation, wholesome and favorable to yogic practice, as an enfeebled man harrassed by a forceful enemy sets out for a secure refuge for the oppressed.

When it comes to yogic practice, a man seeking liberation must adopt a policy like that of a king who wins previously unconquered territory by fortifying his city, administering justice, gathering allies and repulsing enemies. For the mind of the liberation-seeking practitioner is his citadel, and the rules for gaining knowledge are his system of justice; his virtues are his allies, his fault his enemies, and liberation the new land for which he labors.

sa duḥkha|jālān mahato mumukṣur,
vimokṣa|mārg'|âdhigame vivikṣuḥ,
panthānam āryaṃ paramaṃ didṛkṣuḥ,
śamaṃ yayau kiṃ cid upātta|cakṣuḥ.
yaḥ syān niketas tamaso '|niketaḥ
śrutv" âpi tattvaṃ sa bhavet pramattaḥ,
yasmāt tu mokṣāya sa pātra|bhūtas,
tasmān manaḥ sv'|ātmani saṃjahāra.

17.15 sambhārataḥ pratyayataḥ svabhāvād
āsvādato doṣa|viśeṣataś ca,
ath' ātmavān niḥsaraṇ'|ātmataś ca,
dharmeṣu cakre vidhivat parīkṣām.
sa rūpiṇaṃ kṛtsnam a|rūpiṇaṃ ca
sāraṃ didṛkṣur vicikāya kāyam;
ath' â|śuciṃ duḥkham a|nityam a|svaṃ
nir|ātmakaṃ c' âiva cikāya kāyam.
a|nityatas tatra hi śūnyataś ca
nir|ātmato duḥkhata eva c' âpi,
mārga|pravekeṇa sa laukikena
kleśa|drumaṃ saṃcalayāṃ cakāra.
yasmād a|bhūtvā bhavat' îha sarvaṃ,
bhūtvā ca bhūyo na bhavaty avaśyam,
sa|hetukaṃ ca kṣayi|hetumac ca,
tasmād a|nityaṃ jagad ity avindat.
yataḥ prasūtasya ca karma|yogaḥ,
prasajyate bandha|vighāta|hetuḥ
duḥkha|pratīkāra|vidhau sukh'|ākhye,
tato bhavaṃ duḥkham iti vyapaśyat.

Wishing to be free of the great net of suffering, hoping to gain access to the road to liberation, wanting to see the sublime noble path, he attained some measure of insight, and grew peaceful. Heedless is the unhoused man who has heard the truth, yet houses ignorance; but since Nanda had become a vessel fit for liberation, he gathered his mind into his own self.

Self-contained, he carried out the recommended inves- 17.15
tigation into all phenomena, with reference to their prerequisites, their causes, their inherent nature, how they are experienced, their particular faults, and their termination. He examined the body with the intention of viewing its entire material and immaterial substance; and he observed that the body was not pure, that it was prone to suffering, impermanent, without properties, and without self. From his perception of the body as impermanent, empty, without a self, and also as suffering, by this most excellent ordinary worldly path he shook the tree of defilements.

Since everything that exists here and now did not exist before, and that having come into existence it will necessarily not exist in the future, and since it is dependent on a cause and yet that cause wanes, Nanda concluded that the world is impermanent.

Because karma is joined to a living being, and since the cause of bondage and destruction is linked to that drug for counteracting suffering which is called pleasure, Nanda saw that existence entails suffering.

17.20 yataś ca saṃskāra|gataṃ viviktaṃ,
na kārakaḥ kaś cana vedako vā,
sāmagryataḥ sambhavati pravṛttiḥ,
śūnyaṃ tato lokam imaṃ dadarśa.
yasmān nirīhaṃ jagad a|svatantraṃ,
n' āiśvaryam ekaḥ kurute kriyāsu,
tat tat pratītya prabhavanti bhāvā
nir|ātmakaṃ tena viveda lokam.
tataḥ sa vātaṃ vyajanād iv' ôṣṇe,
kāṣṭh'|āśritaṃ nirmathanād iv' âgnim,
antaḥ|kṣiti|sthaṃ khananād iv' âmbho,
lok'|ôttaraṃ vartma dur|āpam āpa.
saj|jñāna|cāpaḥ smṛti|varma baddhvā,
viśuddha|śīla|vrata|vāhana|sthaḥ,
kleś'|âribhiś citta|raṇ'|âjira|sthaiḥ
sārdhaṃ yuyutsur vijayāya tasthau.
tataḥ sa bodhy|aṅga|śit'|ātta|śastras,
samyak|pradhān'|ôttama|vāhana|sthaḥ,
mārg'|âṅga|mātaṅga|vatā balena,
śanaiḥ śanaiḥ kleśa|camūṃ jagāhe.
17.25 sa smṛty|upasthāna|mayaiḥ pṛṣatkaiḥ
śatrūn viparyāsa|mayān kṣaṇena,
duḥkhasya hetūṃś caturaś caturbhiḥ
svaiḥ svaiḥ pracār'|āyatanair dadāra.

Since individuality is produced by conditions, and there 17.20
is no maker or thinker, and individual activity arises from a network of causes, Nanda saw that this world is empty.

Since the world is not self-dependent and has no power to set things in motion, and no one exercises sovereignity in actions, and since states of existence arise in dependence on all sorts of things, he understood that the world was without self.

Then, like feeling a cool breeze from fanning oneself during the hot season, or like getting fire that is latent in wood by rubbing sticks together, or like finding underground water by digging for it, he reached the hard-to-reach supramundane path.*

With his bow of true knowledge, binding on his armor of mindfulness, standing in his chariot of pure vows of moral self-restraint, he stood determined to fight for victory against his enemy, the defilements, which were ranged in the battlefield of his mind. Holding the sharp weapon of the constituents of enlightenment, and standing on the excellent chariot of well-directed effort, with his army which consisted of the elephants of the constituents of the path, he
gradually penetrated the ranks of the defilements. With the 17.25
arrows of the four foundations of mindfulness, each with its own range of application, in an instant he burst apart the four enemies which consist of distorted views, the causes of suffering.*

āryair balaiḥ pañcabhir eva pañca
cetaḥ|khilāny a|pratimair babhañja,
mithy"|âṅga|nāgāṃś ca tath"|âṅga|nāgair
vinirdudhāv' âṣṭabhir eva so 'ṣṭau.
ath' ātma|dṛṣṭiṃ sakalāṃ vidhūya,
caturṣu satyeṣv a|kathaṃkathaḥ san,
viśuddha|śīla|vrata|dṛṣṭa|dharmo,
dharmasya pūrvāṃ phala|bhūmim āpa.

sa darśanād ārya|catuṣṭayasya,
kleś'|âika|deśasya ca viprayogāt,
pratyātmikāc c' âpi viśeṣa|lābhāt,
pratyakṣato jñāni|sukhasya c' âiva,
dārḍhyāt prasādasya, dhṛteḥ sthiratvāt,
satyeṣv a|saṃmūḍhatayā caturṣu,
śīlasya c' â|cchidratay" ôttamasya,
niḥ|saṃśayo dharma|vidhau babhūva.

17.30 ku|dṛṣṭi|jālena sa viprayukto
lokaṃ tathā|bhūtam avekṣamāṇaḥ
jñān'|āśrayāṃ prītim upājagāma
bhūyaḥ prasādaṃ ca gurāv iyāya.

yo hi pravṛttiṃ niyatām avaiti
n' âiv' ânya|hetor iha n' âpy a|hetoḥ,
pratītya tat tat samavaiti tat tat—
sa naiṣṭhikaṃ paśyati dharmam āryam.
śāntaṃ śivaṃ nir|jarasaṃ virāgaṃ,
niḥśreyasaṃ paśyati yaś ca dharmam,
tasy' ôpadeṣṭāram ath' ārya|varyaṃ
sa prekṣate Buddham avāpta|cakṣuḥ.

With his five incomparable noble powers he broke up the five barren places of the mind,* and with his eight elephants which were the constituents of the right path he drove off the eight elephants which were the constituents of the wrong path.* Shaking off the theory of the self completely, entertaining no doubts about the Four Truths, clear in his duty with regard to the pure vows of moral self-restraint, he reached the stage of the first fruit of the *dharma*.*

From his insight into the noble fourfold doctrine, from disconnecting from part of the defilements, from his personal attainment of distinction, from his perception of the bliss experienced by those who know, from the strength of his tranquillity, from the constancy of his resolve, from his clarity regarding the Four Truths, and from his lack of blemish in his supreme moral self-restraint he freed himself from uncertainty in the prescriptions of *dharma*. Loosed 17.30
from the net of wrong views and discerning the world as it really is, he experienced joy founded on knowledge, and felt still greater gratitude toward his guru.

For he who understands that while a particular activity in the here and now is not caused by something else, it is also not without cause, and who recognizes that everything is dependent on a variety of things*—he sees the ultimate noble *dharma*. And he who sees that *dharma* is tranquil, benign, without age or passion, and unexcelled, and sees that its teacher, Buddha, is the best of the noble ones—he has won insight.

yath" ôpadeśena śivena mukto
rogād a|rogo bhiṣajaṃ kṛta|jñaḥ,
anusmaran paśyati citta|dṛṣṭyā
maitryā ca śāstra|jñatayā ca tuṣṭaḥ,
āryeṇa mārgeṇa tath" âiva muktas
Tathāgataṃ tattva|vid ārya|sattvaḥ,
anusmaran paśyati kāya|sākṣī
maitryā ca sarva|jñatayā ca tuṣṭaḥ.
17.35 sa nāśakair dṛṣṭi|gatair vimuktaḥ,
paryantam ālokya punar bhavasya,
bhaktvā ghṛṇāṃ kleśa|vijṛmbhiteṣu,
mṛtyor na tatrāsa na dur|gatibhyaḥ.
tvak|snāyu|medo|rudhir'|âsthi|māṃsa|
keś'|ādin" âmedhya|gaṇena pūrṇam
tataḥ sa kāyaṃ samavekṣamāṇaḥ;
sāraṃ vicinty' âṇv api n' ôpalebhe.
sa kāma|rāga|pratighau sthir'|ātmā
ten' âiva yogena tanū cakāra;
kṛtvā mah"|ôraska|tanus tanū tau,
prāpa dvitīyaṃ phalam ārya|dharme.
sa lobha|cāpaṃ parikalpa|bāṇaṃ
rāgaṃ mahā|vairiṇam alpa|śeṣam
kāya|svabhāv'|âdhigatair bibheda
yog'|āyudh'|âstrair a|śubhā|pṛṣatkaiḥ.
dveṣ'|āyudhaṃ krodha|vikīrṇa|bāṇaṃ
vyāpādam antaḥ|prasavaṃ sapatnam,
maitrī|pṛṣatkair dhṛti|tūṇa|saṃsthaiḥ
kṣamā|dhanurjyā|visṛtair jaghāna.
17.40 mūlāny atha trīṇy a|śubhasya vīras
tribhir vimokṣ'|āyatanaiś cakarta,

Just as a healthy man who was delivered from illness by successful treatment in his gratitude forms a mental picture of his doctor, and in remembering him, is delighted by his kindness and scientific knowledge, likewise a man liberated by the noble path, who knows reality and possesses the noble truth, is witness to the realized one, and in remembering him is delighted by his loving-kindness and omniscience.

Liberated from destructive views, seeing the end of re- 17.35
birth, feeling compassionate repugnance at the extent of the defilements, he feared neither death nor rebirth in the lower realms. Then he perceived that the body was filled with a host of impurities such as skin, sinew, fat, blood, bone, flesh and hair; and in reflecting on its substance, he found not even an atom that was real. Firm in himself, and using the same yogic practice, he minimized the obstacles, desire and hate; himself broad-chested, he made them small, and so obtained the second fruit of the noble *dharma*.

That small remainder of the great enemy passion, which has longing for its bow and imaginings for its arrows, he shattered with his own arsenal of the weapons of yogic practice, the arrows of impurity meditation obtained through seeing the real nature of the body. He killed his adversary, malice, which drives one from within, which has hatred for its weapon and anger for its scattering arrows, with his own arrows of loving-kindness, kept in a quiver of constancy and dispersed by the bow-string of tolerance.

Then he, the hero, cut away the three roots of impurity 17.40
with the three supports of liberation, like a noble man cuts down three bow-bearing enemies at the head of their army

camū|mukha|sthān dhṛta|kārmukāṃs trīn
arīn iv' âris tribhir āyas'|âgraiḥ.
sa kāma|dhātoḥ samatikramāya
pārṣṇi|grahāṃs tān abhibhūya śatrūn,
yogād anāgāmi|phalaṃ prapadya;
dvār' îva nirvāṇa|purasya tasthau.

kāmair viviktaṃ malinaiś ca dharmair
vitarkavac c' âpi vicāravac ca,
viveka|jaṃ prīti|sukh'|ôpapannaṃ
dhyānaṃ tataḥ sa prathamaṃ prapede.
kām'|âgni|dāhena sa vipramukto
hlādaṃ paraṃ dhyāna|sukhād avāpa,
sukhaṃ vigāhy' āpsv iva gharma|khinnaḥ,
prāpy' êva c' ârthaṃ vipulaṃ daridraḥ.

tatr' âpi tad|dharma|gatān vitarkān,
guṇ'|âguṇe ca prasṛtān vicārān,
buddhvā manaḥ|kṣobha|karān a|śāntāṃs,
tad|viprayogāya matiṃ cakāra.
17.45 kṣobhaṃ prakurvanti yath" ōrmayo hi
dhīra|prasann'|âmbu|vahasya sindhoḥ,
ek'|âgra|bhūtasya tath" ōrmi|bhūtāś
citt'|âmbhasaḥ kṣobha|karā vitarkāḥ.
khinnasya suptasya ca nirvṛtasya
bādhāṃ yathā saṃjanayanti śabdāḥ,
adhyātmam aik'|âgryam upāgatasya
bhavanti bādhāya tathā vitarkāḥ.

with three metal-tipped arrows.* In order to pass entirely beyond the sphere of desire, he had overpowered those enemies who attack from behind, and through yogic practice he had won the fruit of not returning to earth; now he stood as though at the gateway to the city of nirvana.

Then he entered the first level of meditation,* in which passion and the tainted constituents of reality are absent. It consists of an initial and a sustained application of the mind to its object, is born of discernment, and is imbued with happiness and bliss. Saved from the burns of passion's fire, he experienced great rapture through the bliss of meditation, like the pleasure of a heat-exhausted man when he dives into water, or like the delight of a pauper finding fabulous wealth.

He realized that even at this stage the initial application of concentration to the constituents of reality, as well as the sustained application of concentration to a consideration of their virtues and flaws, are not conducive to peace but make undulations in the mind. He decided to break away from
them. For just as waves make ripples in a river bearing calm, 17.45
limpid water, waves of thought make ripples in the waters of the one-pointed mind. And just as noises disturb an exhausted person who is sleeping peacefully, so do thoughts become an irritant for someone who has reached inner one-pointedness.

ath' â|vitarkaṃ kramaśo '|vicāram
ek'|âgra|bhāvān manasaḥ prasannam,
samādhi|jaṃ prīti|sukhaṃ dvitīyaṃ
dhyānaṃ tad ādhyātma|śivaṃ sa dadhyau.

tad dhyānam āgamya ca citta|maunaṃ,
lebhe parāṃ prītim a|labdha|pūrvām.
prītau tu tatr' âpi sa doṣa|darśī
yathā vitarkeṣv abhavat tath" âiva.

prītiḥ parā vastuni yatra yasya
viparyayāt tasya hi tatra duḥkham;
prītāv ataḥ prekṣya sa tatra doṣān
prīti|kṣaye yogam upāruroha.

17.50 prīter virāgāt sukham ārya|juṣṭaṃ
kāyena vindann atha samprajānan,
upekṣakaḥ sa smṛtimān vyahārṣīd;
dhyānaṃ tṛtīyaṃ pratilabhya dhīraḥ.

yasmāt paraṃ tatra sukhaṃ sukhebhyas
tataḥ paraṃ n' âsti sukha|pravṛttiḥ;
tasmād babhāṣe śubha|kṛtsna|bhūmiṃ
par'|âpara|jñaḥ param' êti maitryā.

Then he gradually entered the second level of meditation, which has no initial or sustained application of the mind to its object. Born of concentration and calm due to mental one-pointedness, it is joyfully blissful and endowed with inner delight. And in reaching that level of meditation in which the mind is silent, he experienced a profound joy which he had never felt before. But in that joy too he noticed a flaw, just as he had with regard to thoughts. For he who takes profound joy in anything will also find unsatisfactoriness in it, because of the possibility of its alteration; so noticing the flaws in joy, he undertook yogic practice to destroy joy.

Through his non-attachment to joy he then discovered 17.50
the physical bliss enjoyed by the noble ones, and with full comprehension he passed the time in equanimity, attentive and steady; and he attained the third level of meditation. Bliss does not operate beyond this level, since the bliss here is greater than any other bliss. Therefore the knower of the lower and the higher called it the stage of the entirely lovely, supreme through loving-kindness.

dhyāne 'pi tatr' âtha dadarśa doṣaṃ
mene paraṃ śāntam an|iñjam eva—
ābhogato 'p' îñjayati sma tasya
cittaṃ pravṛttaṃ sukham ity ajasram.
yatr' êñjitaṃ, spanditam asti tatra,
yatr' âsti ca spanditam, asti duḥkham.
yasmād atas tat sukham iñjakatvāt
praśānti|kāmā yatayas tyajanti.

atha prahāṇāt sukha|duḥkhayoś ca
mano|vikārasya ca pūrvam eva,
dadhyāv upekṣā|smṛtimad viśuddhaṃ
dhyānaṃ tath" â|duḥkha|sukhaṃ caturtham.

17.55 yasmāt tu tasmin na sukhaṃ na duḥkhaṃ,
jñānaṃ ca tatr' âsti tad|artha|cāri;
tasmād upekṣā|smṛti|pāriśuddhir
nirucyate dhyāna|vidhau caturthe.

dhyānaṃ sa niśritya tataś caturtham,
arhattva|lābhāya matiṃ cakāra,
saṃdhāya maitraṃ balavantam āryaṃ
rāj" êva deśān a|jitāñ jigīṣuḥ.
ciccheda kārtsnyena tataḥ sa pañca
prajñ"|âsinā bhāvanay" ēritena
ūrdhvaṃ|gamāny uttama|bandhanāni
saṃyojanāny uttama|bandhanāni.
bodhy|aṅga|nāgair api saptabhiḥ sa
sapt' âiva citt'|ânuśayān mamarda,
dvīpān iv' ôpasthita|vipraṇāśān
kālo grahaiḥ saptabhir eva sapta.

But since he considered the highest to be peaceful and without fluctuation, he detected a flaw even in meditation at this level—that his mind fluctuated continuously due to modulations in the workings of bliss. Where there is fluctuation, there is motion, and where there is motion, there is suffering. Because of this fluctuation, ascetics who strive for peace give up that bliss.

Then, because he had just given up bliss and suffering as well as alteration of the mind, he attained the fourth level of meditation, which is pure, free from happiness and sorrow,
and endowed with equanimity and mindfulness. Since there 17.55
is no bliss or sorrow at this level, knowledge lives here at one with its object; therefore in the description of the fourth level of meditation it is said that there is purification of equanimity and mindfulness.

With the support of the fourth level of meditation, he made up his mind to win the worthy state, as a king joins with a mighty and noble ally when he wishes to conquer unconquered territories. With the sword of wisdom wielded through meditation, he completely severed the final five upper bonds, the last ties to rebirth.* With his seven elephants of the constituents of enlightenment he also trampled down the seven negative predispositions of the mind,* as Time with the seven planets tramples down the seven continents when their destruction is due.

agni|drum'|ājy'|âmbuṣu yā hi vṛttiḥ
kabandha|vāyv|agni|divākarāṇām,
doṣeṣu tāṃ vṛttim iyāya Nando
nirvāpaṇ'|ôtpāṭana|dāha|śoṣaiḥ.
17.60 iti tri|vegaṃ tri|jhaṣaṃ tri|vīcam
ek'|âmbhasaṃ pañca|rayaṃ dvi|kūlam
dvi|grāham aṣṭāṅgavatā plavena
duḥkh'|ārṇavaṃ dus|taram uttatāra.
arhattvam āsādya sa sat|kriy"|ârho
nir|utsuko niṣ|praṇayo nir|āśaḥ
vi|bhīr vi|śug vīta|mado vi|rāgaḥ;
sa eva dhṛty" ânya iv' ābabhāse.
bhrātuś ca śāstuś ca tay" ânuśiṣṭyā
Nandas tataḥ svena ca vikrameṇa
praśānta|cetāḥ paripūrṇa|kāryo
vāṇīm imām ātma|gatāṃ jagāda:
«namo 'stu tasmai Sugatāya, yena
hit'|âiṣiṇā me karuṇ"|ātmakena
bahūni duḥkhāny apavartitāni
sukhāni bhūyāṃsy upasaṃhṛtāni.
ahaṃ hy an|āryeṇa śarīra|jena
duḥkh'|ātmake vartmani kṛṣyamāṇaḥ,
nivartitas tad|vacan'|âṅkuśena,
darp'|ānvito nāga iv' âṅkuśena.
17.65 tasy' ājñayā kāruṇikasya śāstur
hṛdi|stham utpāṭya hi rāga|śalyam
ady' âiva tāvat su|mahat sukhaṃ me
sarva|kṣaye kiṃ bata nirvṛtasya!
nirvāpya kām'|âgnim ahaṃ hi dīptaṃ
dhṛty|ambunā pāvakam ambun" êva;

That process by which fire, trees, ghee and water are
extinguished, uprooted, burned and dried up by clouds,
wind, fire and the sun—Nanda applied that process to the
faults. Thus with his eightfold boat he crossed the hard-to- 17.60
cross ocean of suffering, which has three streams, three fish,
three waves, one body of water, five streams, two shores
and two crocodiles. With no yearning, no affection, no
expectation, no fear, no grief, no pride, no passion, he was
worthy of honor on reaching the worthy state; though it
was him, he seemed different because of his steadfastness.

Through the guidance of his brother and teacher and through his own valor, Nanda had accomplished what was to be done, and with tranquil mind he inwardly gave praise:

"Homage be to him, the Súgata, who in his compassionate striving for my well-being turned away many sorrows
and brought great joy. For I was being pulled down the path
of suffering by ignoble physicality, but I was turned back,
hooked by his words, as a proud elephant is turned back
with a hook. The arrow of lust that was lodged in my heart 17.65
was pulled out under the direction of the compassionate
teacher. Immense bliss is mine right now, and oh! my peace
in the annihilation of it all!

Just as I would put out a fire with water, I have extinguished the burning fire of passion with the water of steadfastness; now I have come to utter rapture, like someone

hlādaṃ paraṃ sāmpratam āgato 'smi,
śītaṃ hradaṃ gharma iv' âvatīrṇaḥ.
na me priyaṃ kiṃ cana, n' â|priyaṃ me;
na me 'nurodho 'sti, kuto virodhaḥ.
tayor a|bhāvāt sukhito 'smi sadyo,
him'|ātapābhyām iva viprayuktaḥ.
mahā|bhayāt kṣemam iv' ôpalabhya,
mah"|âvarodhād iva vipramokṣam,
mah"|ārṇavāt pāram iv' â|plavaḥ,
san bhīm'|ândhakārād iva ca prakāśam,
rogād iv' ārogyam a|sahya|rūpād,
ṛṇād iv' ân|ṛṇyam an|anta|saṃkhyāt,
dviṣat|sakāśād iva c' âpayānaṃ,
durbhikṣa|yogāc ca yathā subhikṣam,
17.70 tadvat parāṃ śāntim upāgato 'haṃ
yasy' ânubhāvena vināyakasya.
karomi bhūyaḥ punar|uktam asmai
namo namo 'rhāya Tathāgatāya.
yen' âhaṃ girim upanīya rukma|śṛṅgaṃ
svargaṃ ca plavaga|vadhū|nidarśanena,
kām'|ātmā tri|diva|carībhir aṅganābhir
nirkṛṣṭo yuvati|maye kalau nimagnaḥ.
tasmāc ca vyasana|parād anartha|paṅkād
utkṛṣya krama|śithilaḥ karīva paṅkāt;
śānte 'smin virajasi vijvare viśoke
sad|dharme vitamasi naiṣṭhike vimuktaḥ.

slipping into a cool lake during the summer heat. There is nothing at all that is pleasant or unpleasant for me; I am not enamored of anything, and even less am I hostile to anything. In the absence of these two I am straightaway joyful, like one who is spared extremes of cold and heat.

Like finding safety from great danger, like release from imprisonment, like reaching the futher shore of the great ocean without a boat, like light after terrible darkness, like recovery from an unendurable sickness, like solvency after incalculable debt, like escape from an enemy presence, like
plentiful alms after a dearth of alms, likewise I have come to 17.70
utmost peace through the power of the teacher. Again and repeatedly I do homage, homage to him, the worthy one, the realized one.

By him I was taken to the golden-peaked mountain and to heaven, where, lustful for the women who wander the triple heaven, and sunk in the evil comprised of young women, I was dragged out of that condition by his example of the female monkey. I was dragged from the worst of predicaments, the worthless slime, like a feeble-footed elephant from the mud; now I am liberated into this good *dharma*, which is peaceful, ultimate, without passion, without fever, without grief, and without mental darkness.

tam̩ vande param anukampakam̩ maha”|rṣim̩,
mūrdhn” âham̩ prakṛti|guṇa|jñam āśaya|jñam,
sambuddham̩ daśa|balinam̩ bhiṣak|pradhānam̩,
trātāram̩. punar api c’ âsmi sam̩natas tam!»

mahā|kāvye Saundaranande ’|mṛt’|âdhigamo nāma
saptadaśaḥ sargaḥ.

I bow my head to the supremely compassionate one, the great seer, knower of the qualities of nature, knower of the disposition of beings, the perfectly enlightened, holder of the ten powers, best of physicians, my rescuer. Again I bow to him!"

End of Canto 17: The Attainment of Deathlessness.

CANTO 18
HIS INSTRUCTIONS REVEALED

18.1 ATHA DVIJO bāla iv' āpta|Vedaḥ,
kṣipraṃ vaṇik prāpta iv' āpta|lābhaḥ,
jitvā ca rājanya iv' âri|sainyaṃ,
Nandaḥ kṛt'|ârtho gurum abhyagacchat.
draṣṭuṃ sukhaṃ jñāna|samāpti|kāle,
gurur hi śiṣyasya guroś ca śiṣyaḥ,
«pariśramas te sa|phalo may' îti»;
yato didṛkṣ" âsya munau babhūva.
yato hi yen' âdhigato viśeṣas tasy'
ôttam'|âṅge 'rhati kartum ijyām
āryaḥ sa|rāgo 'pi kṛtajña|bhāvāt.
prakṣīṇa|mānaḥ kim u vīta|rāgaḥ?
yasy' ârtha|kāma|prabhavā hi bhaktis
tato 'sya sā tiṣṭhati rūḍhamūlā.
dharm'|ânvayo yasya tu bhakti|rāgas
tasya prasādo hṛday'|âvagāḍhaḥ.
18.5 kāṣāya|vāsāḥ kanak'|âvadātas,
tataḥ sa mūrdhnā gurave praṇeme,
vāt'|ēritaḥ pallava|tāmra|rāgaḥ
puṣp'|ôjjvala|śrīr iva karṇikāraḥ.
ath' ātmanaḥ śiṣya|guṇasya c' âiva
mahā|muneḥ śāstṛ|guṇasya c' âiva
saṃdarśan'|ârthaṃ sa na māna|hetoḥ
svāṃ kārya|siddhiṃ kathayāṃ babhūva.

SUCCESSFUL as a twice-born youth who has mastered the Vedas, as a businessman who has turned a quick profit, as a warrior king who has conquered an enemy army, Nanda then approached the guru. For at the time when knowledge has been perfected, it is pleasant for the teacher to see the student, and for the student to see the teacher, each with the thought "your striving has borne fruit through me"; and so he wished to see the sage. 18.1

For a noble one, even when he is passionate, should pay homage, bowing his head, out of gratitude to the person through whom he has gained something special. How much more should a man do so when he is without passion and his pride at an end? When a person's devotion springs from wealth or lust, its roots remain in those things. But when his passion for devotion follows *dharma*, then tranquillity enters his heart.

Shining like gold in his ochre garments, he bowed his head to the guru, like a wind-stirred *karnikára* tree with its shoots coppery crimson and its flowers radiantly blazing. Then he spoke of his own success in his task, not out of conceit, but to fully demonstrate the characteristics of a pupil in himself, and the characteristics of a teacher in the great sage. 18.5

«yo dṛṣṭi|śalyo hṛday'|âvagāḍhaḥ
prabho bhṛśaṃ mām atudat su|tīkṣṇaḥ.
tvad|vākya|saṃdaṃśa|mukhena me sa
samuddhṛtaḥ, śalya|hṛt" êva śalyaḥ
kathaṃkathā|bhāva|gato 'smi yena
cchinnaḥ sa, niḥ|saṃśaya, saṃśayo me.
tvac|chāsanāt sat|patham āgato 'smi
su|deśikasy' êva pathi pranaṣṭaḥ.
yat pītam āsvāda|vaś'|êndriyeṇa
darpeṇa kandarpa|viṣaṃ may" āsīt
tan me hataṃ tvad|vacan'|âgadena,
viṣaṃ vināś" îva mah"|âgadena.
18.10 kṣayaṃ gataṃ janma nirasta|janman
sad|dharma|caryām uṣito 'smi samyak.
kṛtsnaṃ kṛtaṃ me kṛta|kārya kāryaṃ;
lokeṣu bhūto 'smi na loka|dharmā.
maitrī|stanīṃ, vyañjana|cāru|sāsnāṃ,
sad|dharma|dugdhāṃ, pratibhāna|śṛṅgām,
tav' âsmi gāṃ sādhu nipīya tṛptas,
tṛṣ" êva gām, uttama, vatsa|varṇaḥ.
yat paśyataś c' âdhigamo mam' âyaṃ
tan me samāsena mune nibodha,
sarva|jña kāmaṃ viditaṃ tav' âitat
svaṃ t' ûpacāraṃ pravivakṣur asmi.
anye 'pi santo vimumukṣavo hi
śrutvā vimokṣāya nayaṃ parasya,
muktasya rogād iva rogavantas
ten' âiva mārgeṇa sukhaṃ ghaṭante.

"The arrow of wrong views that was plunged into my heart, O Lord, had struck me forcibly and was extremely sharp. It was extracted by the forceps of your words, like an arrow removed by a surgeon. The doubt which made me full of questions and opinions has been excised, O you who are without doubts. Because of your instruction I have arrived at the true path, like a lost man who finds his way through the directions of a good guide. That love-poison that I drunk in my pride when my senses were ruled by relishing was eradicated by the antidote of your words, like a deadly poison eradicated by a powerful antidote.

Birth has been destroyed for me, O remover of birth, and 18.10
I live entirely in the practice of the good *dharma*. I have completely finished what was to be done, O task-accomplisher; I exist in the world but am free of its phenomena. I have drunk from the cow of your speech which has udders of loving-kindness, the lovely dewlap of substance, milk of the good *dharma*, and horns of inspiration. I am rightly contented, O excellent one, as a little calf drinks from a cow, due to thirst, and is satisfied.

O sage, listen to a summary of my achievement when I saw clearly, for I would personally like to talk of my course of treatment, though I suppose you know it already, all-knowing one. For when they hear that someone has been guided to liberation, other good men hoping for liberation will also strive for happiness by the same route, just as sick people, when they hear of someone's deliverance from sickness, strive for relief by the same method.

urvy|ādikāñ janmani vedmi dhātūn,
n' ātmānam urvy|ādiṣu teṣu kiṃ cit;
yasmād atas teṣu na me 'sti saktir.
bahiś ca kāyena samā matir me.
18.15 skandhāṃś ca rūpa|prabhṛtīn daś'|ârdhān
paśyāmi yasmāc capalān a|sārān
an|ātmakāṃś c' âiva vadh'|ātmakāṃś ca—
tasmād vimukto 'smy a|śivebhya ebhyaḥ.
yasmāc ca paśyāmy udayaṃ vyayaṃ ca
sarvāsv avasthāsv aham indriyāṇām,
tasmād a|nityeṣu nir|ātmakeṣu
duḥkheṣu me teṣv api n' âsti saṅgaḥ.
yataś ca lokaṃ sama|janma|niṣṭhaṃ
paśyāmi niḥ|sāram a|sac ca sarvam,
ato dhiyā me manasā vibuddham,*
‹asm' îti› me n" êñjitam asti yena.
catur|vidhe n'|âika|vidha|prasaṅge
yato 'ham āhāra|vidhāv a|saktaḥ;
a|mūrchitaś c' āgrathitaś ca tatra.
tribhyo vimukto 'smi tato bhavebhyaḥ.
a|niścitaś c' â|pratibaddha|citto
dṛṣṭa|śrut'|ādau vyavahāra|dharme,
yasmāt sam'|ātm" ânugataś ca tatra,
tasmād visaṃyoga|gato 'smi muktaḥ.»

I know that the elements of earth and so on are present in birth, and that in these elements such as earth there is no self at all; that is why I do not cling to them. I think
in the same way about my body and what is outside it. I 18.15
can see that the five constituents of human identity such as material form are fickle, without substance, without self, murderous—so I am free of these pernicious things.* And since I behold a rising up and falling away in all aspects of the senses, impermanent, without self, and unsatisfactory as they are, I have no attachment for them either.

Since I can see that in all the world birth is equivalent to death, without substance and without reality, my mind has awoken from thought, so that I have no inclination to think 'I exist.' Attachment to the four kinds of food* takes many forms, but I do not cling to them; I am not fooled or fettered by them. Therefore I am free of the three realms of existence. Since my mind is unshackled and I do not depend on aspects of ordinary life such as what is seen and heard, but engage in those actions while I myself remain in equilibrium, I am therefore separate from them, and free."

18.20 ity evam uktvā guru|bāhumānyāt
sarveṇa kāyena sa gāṃ nipannaḥ,
praverito lohita|candan'|âkto
haimo mahā|stambha iv' ābabhāse.
tataḥ pramādāt prasṛtasya pūrvaṃ
śrutvā dhṛtiṃ vyākaraṇaṃ ca tasya,
dharm'|ânvayaṃ c' ânugataṃ prasādaṃ,
megha|svaras taṃ munir ābabhāṣe.
«uttiṣṭha, dharme sthita śiṣya|juṣṭe!
kiṃ pādayor me patito 'si mūrdhnā?
abhyarcanaṃ me na tathā praṇāmo,
dharme yath" âiṣā pratipattir eva.
ady' âsi su|pravrajito jit'|ātmann
aiśvaryam apy ātmani yena labdham.
jit'|ātmanaḥ pravrajanaṃ hi sādhu,
cal'|ātmano na tv a|jit'|êndriyasya.
ady' âsi śaucena pareṇa yukto
vāk|kāya|cetāṃsi śucīni yat te
ataḥ punaś c' â|prayatām a|saumyāṃ
yat, saumya, no vekṣyasi garbha|śayyām.
18.25 ady' ârthavat te śrutavac chrutaṃ tac
chrut'|ânurūpaṃ pratipadya dharmam.
kṛta|śruto vipratipadyamāno
nindyo hi nir|vīrya iv' ātta|śastraḥ.

So saying he laid his whole body on the ground out of 18.20
reverence for the guru, seeming like a great fallen column of
gold tinged with saffron. The sage heard of the constancy of
Nanda, who had recently come forth from carelessness, and
of his discriminating analysis, and of his clarity concerning
the logic of *dharma*, and when he had listened to this, he
spoke in a voice like the clouds:

"O you who abide in the *dharma* so cherished in a pupil,
stand up! Why do you lie with your head at my feet?
Your prostration does not honor me as much as your entry
into the *dharma*. Self-conqueror, today your departure from
home is successful, since you have thereby won sovereignity
over yourself. Departure from home is perfected in someone who has conquered himself, but not in a flighty man
of unconquered senses. Today you are joined to supreme
purity, since your speech, body and mind are clean, and
because after this you will not again enter that impure, un-
gentle bed that is the womb. Today you have learned that 18.25
which is purposeful and learned, and you have followed the
dharma according to that learning. For he who has perfect
learning and acts contrary to it is blameworthy, like a man
with a sword but no courage.

aho, dhṛtis te '|viṣay'|ātmakasya,
yat tvaṃ matiṃ mokṣa|vidhāv akārṣīḥ!
‹yāsyāmi niṣṭhām!› iti bāliśo hi
janma|kṣayāt trāsam ih' âbhyupaiti.
diṣṭyā dur|āpaḥ kṣaṇa|saṃnipāto
n' âyaṃ kṛto moha|vaśena moghaḥ!
udeti duḥkhena gato hy adhastāt
kūrmo yuga|cchidra iv' ârṇava|sthaḥ.
nirjitya Māraṃ yudhi dur|nivāram,
ady' âsi loke raṇa|śīrṣa|śūraḥ.
śūro 'py a|śūraḥ sa hi veditavyo
doṣair a|mitrair iva hanyate yaḥ.
nirvāpya rāg'|âgnim udīrṇam adya
diṣṭyā sukhaṃ svapsyasi vīta|dāhaḥ!
duḥkhaṃ hi śete śayane 'py udāre
kleś'|âgninā cetasi dahyamānaḥ.
18.30 abhyucchrito dravya|madena pūrvam,
ady' âsi tṛṣṇ"|ôparamāt samṛddhaḥ;
yāvat sa|tarṣaḥ puruṣo hi loke
tāvat samṛddho 'pi sadā daridraḥ.
ady' âpadeṣṭuṃ tava yukta|rūpaṃ
Śuddhodhano me nṛ|patiḥ pit" êti;
bhraṣṭasya dharmāt pitṛbhir nipātād
a|ślāghanīyo hi kul'|âpadeśaḥ.
diṣṭy" âsi śāntiṃ paramām upeto
nistīrṇa|kāntāra iv' āpta|sāraḥ!
sarvo hi saṃsāra|gato bhay'|ārto
yath" âiva kāntāra|gatas tath" âiva.

What constancy in you, who are not sense-based, in that you have set your mind on what is prescribed for liberation! For only a foolish person in the world thinks 'I will pass into oblivion!' and so comes to fear the end of rebirth. How wonderful that you met the right moment, so hard to come by, and that it was not wasted under the sway of delusion! For a man who has gone to the lower realms struggles to rise, like a turtle in the ocean swimming up to a hole in a yoke. Having conquered Mara, who is so hard to stop in battle, you are a hero in the world today, first rank in combat. For even a hero is not considered heroic if he is struck down by the foe-like faults.

How wonderful that today you have extinguished the raging fire of passion, and will sleep unfevered and at ease! For a man who is being burned in his mind by the fire of the defilements sleeps fitfully, even in a sumptuous bed.
Previously you stood out for your pride in your possessions, 18.30
but today, because your thirst has stopped, you have fabulous wealth; for even a moneyed man is poor in the world as long as he thirsts. Today it is right for you to point to King Shuddhódana as your father; for bringing attention to one's family is not commendable in someone who has fallen from the *dharma* on which his ancestors had settled. How wonderful that you, like a man who has come through the wilderness and found riches, have reached supreme tranquillity! For all who are in samsara are prey to danger, just like people in the wilderness.

āraṇyakaṃ bhaikṣa|caraṃ vinītaṃ
draksyāmi Nandaṃ nibhṛtaṃ kad" êti,
āsīt purastāt tvayi me didṛkṣā.
tath" âsi diṣṭyā mama darśanīyaḥ!
bhavaty a|rūpo 'pi hi darśanīyaḥ
sv|alaṃkṛtaḥ śreṣṭhatamair guṇaiḥ svaiḥ,
doṣaiḥ parīto malinī|karais tu
su|darśanīyo 'pi virūpa eva.

18.35 adya prakṛṣṭā tava buddhimattā,
kṛtsnaṃ yayā te kṛtam ātma|kāryam.
śrut'|ônnatasy' âpi hi n' âsti buddhir
n' ôtpadyate śreyasi yasya buddhiḥ.
unmīlitasy' âpi janasya madhye
nimīlitasy' âpi tath" âiva cakṣuḥ,
prajñā|mayaṃ yasya hi n' âsti cakṣuś
cakṣur na tasy' âsti, sa|cakṣuṣo 'pi.

duḥkha|pratīkāra|nimittam ārtaḥ
kṛṣy'|ādibhiḥ khedam upaiti lokaḥ.
ajasram āgacchati tac ca bhūyo
jñānena yasy' âdya kṛtas tvay" ântaḥ.
‹duḥkhaṃ na me syāt, sukham eva me syād!›
iti pravṛttaḥ satataṃ hi lokaḥ,
na vetti tac c' âiva tathā yathā syāt.
prāptaṃ tvay" âdy' â|sulabhaṃ yathāvat.»

ity evam|ādi sthira|buddhi|cittas
Tathāgaten' âbhihito hitāya
staveṣu nindāsu ca nir|vyapekṣaḥ.
kṛt'|âñjalir vākyam uvāca Nandaḥ:

18.40 «aho, viśeṣeṇa, viśeṣa|darśiṃs,
tvay" ânukampā mayi darśit" êyam!

I had previously wanted to see you, wondering when I would see you settled, tamed to the forest life of the mendicant. How wonderful for me that you are now so pleasing to behold! For even an uncomely man is pleasing to behold when he is well-adorned with his own most excellent virtues, but a man, even a handsome man, is truly ugly when he is encompassed by befouling faults.

Today your intelligence is superlative, for through it your 18.35
task is entirely complete. For even an outstandingly learned man has no intelligence if his intelligence does not give rise to Excellence. Likewise among the open-eyed, it is the man with closed eyes who may have sight, for a man whose sight does not consist of insight has no sight, though he have good eyes.

The afflicted masses exhaust themselves in work such as plowing to counteract suffering. Suffering returns continually, but through your knowledge you have put an end to it today. 'May I have no suffering, just happiness!' With this aim, people are constantly busy, but how it might come about they do not know. You have today rightly obtained what is hard to obtain."

When the realized one said this and more for the sake of his welfare, Nanda remained steady in mind and heart, unaffected by praise or criticism. He folded his hands in reverence and spoke:

"Oh, you have shown me compassion with distinction, 18.40
you who see distinctions! Because of it I have, against my will, been saved from the danger of samsara, O Lord, when

yat kāma|paṅke bhagavan nimagnas
    trāto 'smi saṃsāra|bhayād a|kāmaḥ.
bhrātrā tvayā śreyasi daiśikena
    pitrā phala|sthena tath" âiva mātrā,
hato 'bhaviṣyaṃ yadi na vyamokṣyaṃ
    sārthāt paribhraṣṭa iv' â|kṛt'|ârthaḥ.

śāntasya tuṣṭasya sukho viveko
    vijñāta|tattvasya parīkṣakasya;
prahīṇa|mānasya ca nir|madasya
    sukhaṃ virāgatvam a|sakta|buddheḥ.

ato hi tattvaṃ parigamya samyaṅ,
    nirdhūya doṣān, adhigamya śāntim,
svaṃ n' āśrayaṃ samprati cintayāmi,
    na taṃ janaṃ, n' âpsaraso na devān.

I had been submerged in the slime of lust. I would have failed, like a man who falls behind his caravan and wins no fortune, if I had not been liberated by you, my brother and guide to Excellence, by my father who is established in the fruit, and also by my mother.

Solitude is delightful for a man who is calm and contented, who has an understanding of reality and who makes careful investigations; and the absence of amorous love is delightful for a man who has put pride aside, who is without lust, and whose mind does not cling. So I have perfectly understood reality, I have expelled my faults and I have found peace! Now I do not think of my own home, my wife, the *ápsaras*es or the gods.

idaṃ hi bhuktvā śuci śāmikaṃ sukhaṃ,
na me manaḥ kāṅkṣati kāma|jaṃ sukham,
mah"|ârham apy annam a|daivat'|āhṛtaṃ
divaukaso bhuktavataḥ sudhām iva.
18.45 aho 'ndha|vijñāna|nimīlitaṃ jagat,
paṭ'|ântare paśyati n' ôttamaṃ sukham!
su|dhīram adhyātma|sukhaṃ vyapāsya hi,
śramaṃ tathā kāma|sukh'|ârtham ṛcchati.
yathā hi ratn'|ākaram etya dur|matir
vihāya ratnāny a|sato maṇīn haret,
apāsya sambodhi|sukhaṃ tath" ôttamaṃ
śramaṃ vrajet kāma|sukh'|ôpalabdhaye.
aho hi sattveṣv ati|maitra|cetasas
Tathāgatasy' ânujighṛkṣutā parā!
apāsya yad dhyāna|sukhaṃ mune paraṃ,
parasya duḥkh'|ôparamāya khidyase.
mayā nu śakyaṃ pratikartum adya kiṃ
gurau hit'|âiṣiṇy anukampake tvayi?
samuddhṛto yena bhav'|ârṇavād ahaṃ
mah"|ârṇavāc cūrṇita|naur iv' ōrmibhiḥ.»
tato munis tasya niśamya hetumat
prahīṇa|sarv'|āsrava|sūcakaṃ vacaḥ
idaṃ babhāṣe vadatām an|uttamo
yad arhati śrīghana eva bhāṣitum:
18.50 «idaṃ kṛt'|ârthaḥ param'|ârtha|vit kṛtī.
tvam eva dhīmann abhidhātum arhasi,
atītya kāntāram avāpta|sādhanaḥ
su|daiśikasy' êva kṛtaṃ mahā|vaṇik.
avaiti Buddhaṃ nara|damya|sārathiṃ

For having tasted this pure, peaceful bliss, my mind does
not crave lust-born pleasures, just as, after tasting divine
nectar, the mind of a heaven-dweller does not crave even
the finest earthly fare that is not eaten by the gods. Oh, 18.45
the world is blinkered by the blindness of its knowledge,
and does not see that in a different garment there is utter
bliss! It throws away the security of inner happiness, and
labors instead for sensual gratification. Just as a simpleton
would come to a mine and carry off semi-precious stones
of no value whilst leaving behind the jewels, so might a
man labor to win sensual gratification whilst discarding the
supreme bliss of perfect enlightenment.

How wonderfully kind is the favor shown to living beings by the realized one, in the extraordinary benevolence of his mind! O sage, you lay aside supreme meditational rapture, and work for the cessation of the suffering of others. You have entirely pulled me out of the sea of existence, like a man rescued from the great ocean when his boat has been battered by waves. What could I possibly do now in return for you, my well-wishing, compassionate guru?"

Then the sage, peerless among speakers, listened to his reasoned speech that indicated his lack of all rebirth-producing tendencies, and said what a Buddha Shri·ghana* ought to say:

"You have achieved your goal, you know the ultimate 18.50
truth, you are successful. Wise man, it is proper for you to
say this, just as it is proper for a great merchant who has
passed through the wilderness and acquired a fortune to declare what his good guide has done for him. O worthy man,
since even a man who has seen the truth, whose mind is at

kṛtī yath" ârhann upaśānta|mānasaḥ
na dṛṣṭa|satyo 'pi tath" âvabudhyate,
pṛthag|janaḥ kiṃ bata, buddhimān api.
rajas|tamobhyāṃ parimukta|cetasas
tav' âiva c' êyaṃ sadṛśī kṛta|jñatā;
rajaḥ|prakarṣeṇa jagaty avasthite
kṛta|jña|bhāvo hi kṛta|jña dur|labhaḥ.
sa|dharma, dharm'|ānvayato yataś ca te
mayi prasādo 'dhigame ca kauśalam.
ato 'sti bhūyas tvayi me vivakṣitaṃ
nato hi bhaktaś ca niyogam arhasi.
avāpta|kāryo 'si, parāṃ gatiṃ gato,
na te 'sti kiṃ cit karaṇīyam aṇv api.
ataḥ paraṃ, saumya, car' ânukampayā,
vimokṣayan kṛcchra|gatān parān api.
18.55 ih' ârtham ev' ārabhate naro 'dhamo,
vimadhyamas t' ûbhaya|laukikīṃ kriyām;
kriyām amutr' âiva phalāya madhyamo,
viśiṣṭa|dharmā punar a|pravṛttaye.
ih' ôttamebhyo 'pi mataḥ sa t' ûttamo
ya uttamaṃ dharmam avāpya naiṣṭhikam
a|cintayitv" ātma|gataṃ pariśramaṃ
śamaṃ parebhyo 'py upadeṣṭum icchati.
vihāya tasmād iha kāryam ātmanaḥ
kuru, sthir'|ātman, para|kāryam apy atho.
bhramatsu sattveṣu tamo|vṛt'|ātmasu
śruta|pradīpo niśi dhāryatām ayam.
bravītu tāvat puri vismito janas,
tvayi sthite kurvati dharma|deśanāḥ,
‹aho bat' āścaryam idaṃ vimuktaye

peace and whose goal is accomplished, does not understand the Buddha, the charioteer of men who need to be tamed, still less so does the man in the street, clever though he may be. O grateful man, this awareness of what has been done for you is worthy of you, whose heart is freed from passion and darkness; for gratitude is hard to find while the world abides in its excess of passion.

Dharma-endowed man, from following *dharma*, confidence in me and skill in achievement are yours. I would like to ask more of you, for you are modest and devoted, and worthy of a calling. Your task is complete, you have traveled the high path, and there is nothing, not even the smallest thing, left for you to do. From now on wander with compassion, delivering others who are also in trouble.

An inferior man works towards goals here in the world, 18.55
the next man for both this world and the other world; the average man acts for reward in the hereafter, but the man of superior character works for the cessation of active life. However, the man who is considered better than the best in the world is he who has obtained the supreme and ultimate *dharma* and wishes to guide others to tranquillity, without thinking of the trouble to himself. Therefore give up doing things for yourself here in the world, O you who are firm in yourself, and do things for others. Let this lantern of learning be carried among living beings enveloped in dark ignorance who roam in the night.

Just let the astonished people in the city say, when you stand giving instruction in *dharma*, 'Goodness! It's amazing that this man, who was a libertine, gives talks on liberation!' When your wife at home hears about your stability of

karoti rāgī yad ayaṃ kathām!› iti.
dhruvaṃ hi saṃśrutya tava sthiraṃ mano
nivṛtta|nānā|viṣayair mano|rathaiḥ,
vadhūr gṛhe s" âpi tav' ânukurvatī,
kariṣyate strīṣu vi|rāgiṇīḥ kathāḥ.
18.60 tvayi parama|dhṛtau niviṣṭa|tattve
bhavana|gatā na hi raṃsyate dhruvaṃ sā—
manasi śama|dam'|ātmake vivikte
matir iva kāma|sukhaiḥ parīkṣakasya.»
ity arhataḥ parama|kāruṇikasya śāstur
mūrdhnā vacaś ca caraṇau ca samaṃ gṛhītvā;
svasthaḥ, praśānta|hṛdayo, vinivṛtta|kāryaḥ,
pārśvān muneḥ pratiyayau vi|madaḥ kar" îva.
bhikṣ"|ârthaṃ samaye viveśa sa puraṃ
dṛṣṭīr janasy' ākṣipan.
lābh'|âlābha|sukh'|âsukh'|ādiṣu samaḥ,
svasth'|êndriyo niḥ|spṛhaḥ.
nirmokṣāya cakāra tatra ca kathāṃ
kāle janāy' ârthine,
n' âiv' ônmārga|gatān parān paribhavann
ātmānam utkarṣayan.
ity eṣā vyupaśāntaye na rataye
mokṣ'|ârtha|garbhā kṛtiḥ.
śrotṝṇāṃ grahaṇ'|ârtham anya|manasāṃ
kāvy'|ôpacārāt kṛtā.
yan mokṣāt kṛtam anyad atra hi mayā
tat kāvya|dharmāt kṛtaṃ
pātuṃ tiktam iv' āuṣadhaṃ madhu|yutaṃ,
hṛdyaṃ kathaṃ syād iti.

mind, now that its desires for the various sense-objects have been turned away, she too is sure to follow your example, and speak of dispassion to her women. Since your firmness 18.60
is paramount and you have penetrated the real nature of things, she will certainly not enjoy being in the palace—just as when the mind of a careful examiner is discerning, tranquil and subdued in its nature, his thoughts find no enjoyment in sensuality."

So with his head he grasped the words and feet together of the worthy one, the supremely compassionate teacher; and sound in himself, his heart at ease, his task ended, he left the sage's side like an elephant free of rut. At the appropriate time he entered the city for alms, catching the eye of the people. Staying the same in gain or loss and in happiness and sadness alike, he was free of longings, with his senses in sound health. There in due course he spoke of deliverance to people in need of it, not disparaging those on the wrong path nor vaunting himself.

This composition on the subject of liberation is for calming the reader, not for his pleasure. It is fashioned out of the medicine of poetry with the intention of capturing an audience whose minds are on other things. Thinking how it could be made pleasant, I have handled in it things other than liberation, things introduced due to the character of poetry, as bitter medicine is mixed with honey when it is drunk.

prāyeṇ' ālokya lokaṃ viṣaya|rati|paraṃ
mokṣāt pratihataṃ,
kāvya|vyājena tattvaṃ kathitam iha mayā
mokṣaḥ param iti.
tad buddhvā śāmikaṃ yat tad avahitam ito
grāhyaṃ na lalitaṃ;
pāṃsubhyo dhātu|jebhyo niyatam upakaraṃ
cāmīkaram iti.

Saundaranande mahā|kāvya Ājñā|vyākaraṇo nām'
âṣṭādaśaḥ sargaḥ.

ārya|Suvarṇākṣī|putrasya Sāketakasya bhikṣor ācārya|bhadant'|
Âśvaghoṣasya mahā|kaver mahā|vādinaḥ kṛtir iyam.

Seeing that the world generally holds the pleasure of sensory experience uppermost and is resistant to liberation, I, holding liberation to be paramount, have described the truth in the guise of poetry. Knowing this, that part which relates to peace should be carefully extracted from it, not the entertaining part; serviceable gold necessarily comes from ore-born dust.

End of Canto 18: His Instructions Revealed.

This is the composition of the Venerable Ashva·ghosha of Sakéta, noble son of Suvarnákshi, monk, teacher, great poet and eloquent speaker.

NOTES

Bold *references are to the English text;* ***bold italic*** *references are to the Sanskrit text. An asterisk (*) in the body of the text marks the word or passage being annotated.*

1.15 **soma juice**: a ritual narcotic drink used in sacrifices.

1.36 **Dauṣmanti**: a patronymic more usually appearing as Dauṣyanti or Dauṣyanta, and referring to Duṣyanta the father of Bhárata.

1.39 **their actions being meritorious**: an illustration of the law of a karma; good deeds will inevitably produce good results at some point in the future.

1.40 **dharma, wealth and pleasure**: three legitimate life aims in Hindu thought.

1.44 The **six permitted occupations** of a brahmin are studying, teaching, performing sacrifices, conducting sacrifices on behalf of others, giving charitable gifts and receiving charitable gifts.

2.53 These mythical **elephants** support the earth on their backs.

2.59 **god of love**: Kama.

3.11 **Vínaya**: the disciplinary code followed by monastics.

3.27 **the first fruit**: the first of four stages in the attainment of liberation.

3.39 **many were stream-entrants**: they had attained the first stage, or the first fruit of the path, of *dharma*.

4.5 **the loveliest. . . men**: the Sanskrit verse contains a pun on the names of the couple: *sundarī* means beautiful and *nanda* means happy.

4.13 **vishéshaka**: a mark on the forehead made with sandal.

4.18 **he resembled. . . breeze**: as Nanda bends down, his hair loosens and the flowers in it fall out, so that his head seems to expand. The comparison is possibly to the Cobra's Saffron plant, which continually sheds filaments of pollen.

4.20 **tamála paste**: juice from the leaf of the *Xanthochymus pictorius* plant, used for cosmetics.

4.35 *saced*: "if," Buddhist usage. See also verses 10.60, 13.43, 15.3 and 16.70.

4.46 **the ten powers**: the Buddha is said to possess ten special faculties, such as knowing the consequences of all actions.

5.8 *kakṣyāṃ mahato*: amended from JOHNSTON's *kakṣyā/mahato*. *kakṣyāṃ* is taken in the sense of the staff of the inner apartment. According to 4.26, they were unaware of the Buddha's arrival.

5.9 **to remind us of the time**: the disciplinary code prohibits eating meals after midday.

5.12 **reward in the world**: by the law of karma a meritorious act such as carrying the Buddha's bowl will have a favorable consequence.

5.15 **the dirt of the defilements**: unwholesome qualities (*kleśa*) which defile the mind.

5.35 Anánda is also known as **the sage of Vidéha**, his native area.

5.40 **samsara**: the ongoing cycle of birth, death and rebirth to which all beings are subject until they attain liberation.

6.6 **banged her feet against the palace stairs**: unable to bear the sight of Súndari's sorrow, the maid intends to slip away quietly, but her own distress makes her inadvertently knock noisily against the stairs.

6.10 *upopaviṣṭā*: an archaic form.

6.22 *doṣato gāḥ*: this is a conjecture, but it is supported as idiomatically authentic by *Rāmāyaṇa* 6.93.13.

6.24 *digdha*: a poisoned arrow.

6.25 *rodan'/āroṣita/rakta/dṛṣṭiḥ*: *āroṣita* probably corresponds to Pāli *rosita*, "smeared, anointed."

6.26 **like a fallen Padma Lakshmi without her lotus**: the goddess Lakshmi is also known as Padma. Presumably, a statue of the goddess has fallen over, thus depriving her of the lotus on which she customarily sits or stands.

6.27 ***prakoṣṭhe***: dual neuter, normally masculine.

6.32 ***prabhṛtīś***: emended from *prabhṛtīṃ* (suggestion by HARUNAGA ISAACSON).

6.32 **vina**: the Indian lute.

6.46 ***na sa nirvṛtaḥ syāt***: also, he would not attain nirvana.

7.2 **flower-bannered god**: Kama, god of love.

7.17 **taught twice over**: the Sanskrit word *guru* means both a family elder (in this case older brother) and a religious teacher.

7.32 ***Dilipasya***: possibly Dilīpa rather than Dilipa is intended, though the metre does not accommodate the heavy syllable.

8.10 ***tad***: emended from *yad.*

8.17 ***nadī/taṭāt***: emended from *nadī/talāt.*

8.15 **fooled by the sound of singing**: enticing deer with music was a recognized hunting ploy.

9.12 The four physical **elements**, earth, water, fire and wind, are the primary qualities of all material things, including the human body.

9.13 **mantras**: a potent verbal formula or charm.

9.45 ***tat/kṣayam***: emended from *tat/kṣamam.*

10.9 ***Āmbika***: the name is a conjecture.

10.18 **The thunderbolt-wielding king**: Indra.

10.25 **extended in length. . . solid**: this probably refers to stringed instruments, drums, wind instruments and percussive instruments of a solid material such as brass.

10.53 **enemy of the water-born**: *Abja* is also the day lotus, whose enemy is the moon which distils cooling liquid. Another possibility is to follow JOHNSTON's reading of *abja/ketuḥ*, he whose banner is the fish, the god Kama.

11.50 **Oh the groves**: this translates the Sanskirt ***Caitraratha***, since the groves and gardens of heaven are cultivated by Chitra·ratha.

11.50 **the heavenly Ganges**: Mandākini was the name of the river Ganges in heaven before it fell to earth.

11.56 Verses 11.56–57 are omitted from JOHNSTON's edition.

12.9 **the root "to increase"**: in the *Dhātupāṭha*, Pāṇini's lexicon of Sanskrit verbal roots, the root *edh* "to increase" occurs immediately after the root *bhū*, "to exist."

12.10 **the indeclinable particle "existing"**: the word ***asti*** is considered an example of an indeclinable particle or *nipāta*.

13.13 **manner of making a living. . . constituent parts of action**: These are outlined in 3.30–34. In the context of mendicancy, making a living refers to the monk's acceptance of alms.

13.55 JOHNSTON does not supply the text for this verse as he considers it spurious.

14.19 **yoga**: a set of disciplinary practices intended to increase self-control.

15.12 **as turbid water clears with a jewel**: it was held that certain jewels had the power to miraculously purify muddy water.

15.25 **jewel-adorned as he is**: Nanda is adorned with the three jewels of Buddhism: the Buddha, the *dharma*, and the community of monastics.

15.64 **mindfulness of inward and outward breathing**: paying sustained attention to the in- and out-breath as a way of building concentration is considered a core Buddhist meditation practice.

15.69 The five **supernormal faculties** are listed in 16.2.

16.3 **rebirth-producing tendencies**: the tendencies which bind a person to rebirth are known as *āsravas*. They are the desire for sensory experience, the desire for continued existence, holding views, and spiritual ignorance.

16.22 ***tīvra|roṣa***: emended from *doṣ'|âdhike janmani tīvra|doṣa.*

16.26 **dharma**: used here as a synonym for nirvana.

16.30 **the path**: the path to liberation consists of eight categories of correct modes of living; it is the subject of verses 16.31–36.

16.41 **So with regard to the Truth. . . remedy**: Buddhism's Four Noble Truths are listed with a medical analogy.

16.59 **When the mind is disordered. . . using oil treatments**: this and the following five verses refer to the three humors—phlegm, bile and wind—of ayurvedic medicine.

16.89 ***mātāv***: an atypical form in compounds for *mātṛ*.

17.3 **his hands in his lap**: conjecture for *aṅk'|âvahitam*.

17.22 **supramundane path**: a term used to mark a breakthrough that occurs when the mind focuses on the unconditioned nirvana.

17.25 **The four foundations of mindfulness** are the contemplation of the body, feeling, mind and mental objects. The four **distorted views** are to regard as permanent that which is impermanent, to regard as pleasant that which is unsatisfactory, to regard as having a self that which has no self, and to regard as pure that which is impure.

17.26 The **five incomparable noble powers** are faith, endeavor, mindfulness, concentration and wisdom. The **five barren places** are doubt concerning the Buddha, the *dharma*, the community of monastics or the disciplinary code, and anger.

17.26 **constituents of the right path. . . the wrong path**: the categories of the eightfold path and their opposites.

17.27 **the stage of the first fruit**: the first of four stages to liberation. Nanda attains the four stages at 17.27, 17.37, 17.41 and 17.57–62 respectively.

17.31 **everything is dependent on a variety of things**: here Nanda understands the doctrine of dependent origination.

17.40 **The three supports of liberation** are the conditionless, the desireless, and emptiness. The **three roots of impurity** are desire, hatred and delusion.

17.42 **first level of meditation**: Nanda undertakes a set of meditative attainments called the *dhyānas* (17.42–56), abandoning each level of meditation for a progressively higher one as he detects subtle faults in it.

17.57 **five upper bonds**: Nanda destroys the last five of the ten fetters (*saṃyojana*) which tie beings to the cycle of rebirth.

17.58 The seven **constituents of enlightenment** (*bodhy/aṅga*) are mindfulness, the investigation of *dharma*, endeavor, rapture, tranquillity, concentration and equanimity, while the **seven negative predispositions of the mind** are lust, holding a grudge, speculative opinion, doubt, pride, craving for continued existence, and ignorance.

18.15 **five constituents of human identity**: the five *skandhas*, the processes that combine to make up a human being, are corporeality, sensation, perception, mental formations and consciousness.

18.17 ***vibuddham***: emended from *vibaddham.*

18.18 **four kinds of food**: four types of material and mental nutriment that feed rebirth.

18.49 **Shri·ghana**: rare epithet for the Buddha.

GLOSSARY OF COMMON NAMES AND EPITHETS

ÁDITYAS a group of sun gods

AIRÁVATA name of Indra's elephant, and supporter of the world's eastern quarter

ANÁNDA one of the best-known of the Buddha's disciples; also known as the sage of Vidéha

ÁPSARASES a class of beautiful semi-divine women

ARÁDA one of the Buddha's teachers

ÁRJUNA KARTA·VIRYA is the first of several mighty heroes mentioned in verses 9.17–20 who were vanquished despite their strength

ÁSURAS a class of demons

BHÁRATA son of Shakúntala and King Dushyánta, and raised in the hermitage of the sage Kanva

BODHISATTVA the Buddha prior to his enlightenment

BRAHMA the creator god

BRAHMIN a member of the priestly caste

BUDDHA "awakened one," epithet of Siddhártha (or Sarvártha·siddha) Gáutama after he attains nirvana; Nanda's older half-brother

CHAKRA·VÁKA the ruddy sheldrake, a species of waterbird that signifies conjugal love in Sanskrit literature

CHITRA·RATHA a *gandhárva* who cultivates the beautiful gardens of heaven

DHARMA the doctrine expounded by the Buddha which leads to liberation

DUSHYÁNTA a king, husband of Shakúntala and father of Bhárata

GANDHÁRVAS a class of semi-divine beings famed for their music-making; sometimes lovers of the *ápsaras*es

GARGYA a poor brahmin who became the preceptor of Rama

GÁUTAMA the clan which produced both Nanda and the Buddha

GAYA town where the Buddha attained liberation

GIRI·VRAJA "mountain-fenced," the name of the capital of Mágadha

HIRÁNYA·RETAS "Golden-semen" is the first of many gods, sages and kings listed in 7.25–45, all of whom desired various women

IKSHVÁKU dynasty in northern India into which the Buddha was born

INDRA chief of the gods, and bearer of a number of epithets

KÁKSHIVAT GÁUTAMA a Vedic sage renowned as a teacher

KANDÁRPA another name for Kama, the god of love

KANVA sage in whose hermitage Bhárata was raised

KÁPILA GÁUTAMA a sage, and legendary founder of the city Kápila·vastu

KÁPILA·VASTU the city in which Nanda lives, and where the Buddha was born

KARÁNDAVA an aquatic bird

KARMA past deeds which influence one's present situation

KASHI another name for the city of Varánasi

KÁSHYAPA one of the seven great seers of ancient times

KAUNDÍNYA the Buddha's first convert, who heads the list of the chief disciples given in 16.87–91.

KAUTSA previous clan of the Ikshváku dynasty before Kápila becomes the clan guru

KÍNNARA (M) / KÍNNARI (F) / KÍMPURUSHA (M) mythical mountain-dwelling beings famed for their beauty.

KSHATRIYA caste of warriors and the aristocracy

LAKSHMI goddess of good fortune

MÁITHILI another name for Sita, daughter of the king of Míthila

MÁNDARA sacred mountain, residence of various deities

MANU first man and progenitor of the human race

MARA personification of evil and the passions and representative of death. He tempts the Buddha-to-be to abandon his quest for liberation.

MARUTS minor storm deities and attendants of Indra

MERU sacred golden mountain at the center of the world

NANDA the Buddha's half-brother and hero of the *Saundarananda*

NÁNDANA gardens of heaven frequented by the *ápsarases*

RAMA son of King Dasha·ratha and hero of the *Rāmāyaṇa*

RAMBHA an *ápsaras*

RATI one of the wives of Kama, god of love

SARVÁRTHA·SIDDHA "successful in all his goals," the Buddha's given name

SHAKÚNTALA mother of Bhárata, famously cursed not to be remembered by her husband Dushyánta

SHAKA kind of tree

SHAKRA another name for Indra, chief of the gods

SHAKYA the clan of the founders and inhabitants of Kápila·vastu

SHALA a valuable timber tree

SHALVAS name of a people whose king, along with various other returners to civilian life, is mentioned in verse 7.51

SHÁNTANU legendary king who pined for the love of a ferryman's daughter

SHASTRA learned treatises

SHIBI king who famously gave part of his own flesh to a hungry hawk. He heads the list (11.42–49 and 11.56–57) of legendary figures whose stay in heaven was temporary no matter how meritorious their deeds.

SHUDDHÁVASA a heavenly realm of great purity

SHUDDHÓDHANA king of Kápila·vastu and father of Nanda and the Buddha

SÚGATA "the well-gone," epithet of the Buddha

SÚNDARI "Beauty," Nanda's wife

TATHÁGATA the realized one, "who has gone thus," epithet of the Buddha

TÚSHITA the heavenly realm where the Buddha-to-be resided prior to his last birth

ÚDRAKA one of the Buddha's teachers

VÁISHRAVANA another name for Kubéra, god of wealth

VALMÍKI legendary author of the *Rāmāyaṇa*, and sage in whose hermitage Sita's sons were raised.

VASÍSHTA one of the seven great seers of ancient times, and appearing in the *Rāmāyaṇa* as keeper of the Wishing Cow

VEDAS four collections of oral teachings and hymns forming the basis of Hindu religions

VEDÁNGA six auxiliary disciplines used in the interpretation of the Vedas

INDEX

Sanskrit words are given in the English alphabetical order, according to the accented CSL pronuncuation aid. They are followed by the conventional diacritics in brackets.

THE CLAY SANSKRIT LIBRARY

The volumes in the series are listed here in order of publication.
Titles marked with an asterisk* are also available in the
Digital Clay Sanskrit Library (eCSL).
For further information visit www.claysanskritlibrary.org

1. The Emperor of the Sorcerers (*Bṛhatkathāślokasaṃgraha*) (vol. 1 of 2) by *Budhasvāmin*. Sir James Mallinson
2. Heavenly Exploits (*Divyāvadāna*). Joel Tatelman
3. Maha·bhárata III: The Forest (*Vanaparvan*) (vol. 4 of 4)* William J. Johnson
4. Much Ado about Religion (*Āgamaḍambara*) by *Bhaṭṭa Jayanta*. Csaba Dezső
5. The Birth of Kumára (*Kumārasaṃbhava*) by *Kālidāsa*. David Smith
6. Ramáyana I: Boyhood (*Bālakāṇḍa*) by *Vālmīki*. Robert P. Goldman
7. The Epitome of Queen Lilávati (*Līlāvatīsāra*) (vol. 1 of 2) by *Jinaratna*. R.C.C. Fynes
8. Ramáyana II: Ayódhya (*Ayodhyākāṇḍa*) by *Vālmīki*. Sheldon I. Pollock
9. Love Lyrics (*Amaruśataka, Śatakatraya & Caurapañcāśikā*) by *Amaru, Bhartṛhari & Bilhaṇa*. Greg Bailey & Richard Gombrich
10. What Ten Young Men Did (*Daśakumāracarita*) by *Daṇḍin*. Isabelle Onians
11. Three Satires (*Kaliviḍambana, Kalāvilāsa & Bhallaṭaśataka*) by *Nīlakaṇṭha, Kṣemendra & Bhallaṭa*. Somadeva Vasudeva
12. Ramáyana IV: Kishkíndha (*Kiṣkindhākāṇḍa*) by *Vālmīki*. Rosalind Lefeber
13. The Emperor of the Sorcerers (*Bṛhatkathāślokasaṃgraha*) (vol. 2 of 2) by *Budhasvāmin*. Sir James Mallinson
14. Maha·bhárata IX: Shalya (*Śalyaparvan*) (vol. 1 of 2)* Justin Meiland

15. Rákshasa's Ring (*Mudrārākṣasa*)*
by *Viśākhadatta*. Michael Coulson
16. Messenger Poems (*Meghadūta, Pavanadūta & Haṃsadūta*)
by *Kālidāsa, Dhoyī & Rūpa Gosvāmin*. Sir James Mallinson
17. Ramáyana III: The Forest (*Araṇyakāṇḍa*)
by *Vālmīki*. Sheldon I. Pollock
18. The Epitome of Queen Lilávati (*Līlāvatīsāra*) (vol. 2 of 2)
by *Jinaratna*. R.C.C. Fynes
19. Five Discourses on Worldly Wisdom (*Pañcatantra*)*
by *Viṣṇuśarman*. Patrick Olivelle
20. Ramáyana V: Súndara (*Sundarakāṇḍa*) by *Vālmīki*.
Robert P. Goldman & Sally J. Sutherland Goldman
21. Maha·bhárata II: The Great Hall (*Sabhāparvan*)
Paul Wilmot
22. The Recognition of Shakúntala (*Abhijñānaśākuntala*) (Kashmir Recension) by *Kālidāsa*. Somadeva Vasudeva
23. Maha·bhárata VII: Drona (*Droṇaparvan*) (vol. 1 of 4)*
Vaughan Pilikian
24. Rama Beyond Price (*Anargharāghava*)
by *Murāri*. Judit Törzsök
25. Maha·bhárata IV: Viráta (*Virāṭaparvan*)
Kathleen Garbutt
26. Maha·bhárata VIII: Karna (*Karṇaparvan*) (vol. 1 of 2)
Adam Bowles
27. "The Lady of the Jewel Necklace" & "The Lady who Shows her Love" (*Ratnāvalī & Priyadarśikā*) by *Harṣa*.*
Wendy Doniger
28. The Ocean of the Rivers of Story (*Kathāsaritsāgara*) (vol. 1 of 7)
by *Somadeva*. Sir James Mallinson
29. Handsome Nanda (*Saundarananda*)*
by *Aśvaghoṣa*. Linda Covill
30. Maha·bhárata IX: Shalya (*Śalyaparvan*) (vol. 2 of 2)*
Justin Meiland
31. Rama's Last Act (*Uttararāmacarita*) by *Bhavabhūti*.
Sheldon Pollock. Foreword by Girish Karnad

32. "Friendly Advice" (*Hitopadeśa*) by *Nārāyaṇa* &
"King Víkrama's Adventures" (*Vikramacarita*). Judit Törzsök

33. Life of the Buddha (*Buddhacarita*)
by *Aśvaghoṣa*. Patrick Olivelle

34. Maha·bhárata V: Preparations for War (*Udyogaparvan*) (vol. 1 of
Kathleen Garbutt. Foreword by Gurcharan Das

35. Maha·bhárata VIII: Karna (*Karṇaparvan*) (vol. 2 of 2)
Adam Bowles

36. Maha·bhárata V: Preparations for War (*Udyogaparvan*) (vol. 2 of
Kathleen Garbutt

37. Maha·bhárata VI: Bhishma (*Bhīṣmaparvan*) (vol. 1 of 2)*
Including the "Bhagavad Gita" in Context
Alex Cherniak. Foreword by Ranajit Guha

38. The Ocean of the Rivers of Story (*Kathāsaritsāgara*) (vol. 2 of 7)
by *Somadeva*. Sir James Mallinson

39. "How the Nagas were Pleased" (*Nāgānanda*) by *Harṣa* &
"The Shattered Thighs" (*Ūrubhaṅga*) by *Bhāsa*.*
Andrew Skilton

40. Gita·govínda: Love Songs of Radha and Krishna (*Gītagovinda*)*
by *Jayadeva*. Lee Siegel. Foreword by Sudipta Kaviraj

41. "Bouquet of Rasa" & "River of Rasa" (*Rasamañjarī & Rasataraṅgiṇī*) by *Bhānudatta*. Sheldon Pollock

42. Garland of the Buddha's Past Lives (*Jātakamālā*) (vol. 1 of 2)*
by *Āryaśūra*. Justin Meiland

43. Maha·bhárata XII: Peace (*Śāntiparvan*) (vol. 3 of 5)*
"The Book of Liberation" (*Mokṣadharma*). Alexander Wynne

44. The Little Clay Cart (*Mṛcchakaṭikā*) by *Śūdraka*.
Diwakar Acharya. Foreword by Partha Chatterjee

45. Bhatti's Poem: The Death of Rávana (*Bhaṭṭikāvya*)*
by *Bhaṭṭi*. Oliver Fallon

46. "Self-Surrender," "Peace," "Compassion," and "The Mission of the Goose": Poems and Prayers from South India (*Ātmārpaṇastuti, Śāntivilāsa, Dayāśataka & Haṃsasaṃdeśa*) by *Appayya Dīkṣita, Nīlakaṇṭha Dīkṣita & Vedānta Deśika.* Yigal Bronner & David Shulman
Foreword by Gieve Patel
47. Maha·bhárata VI: Bhishma (*Bhīṣmaparvan*) (vol. 2 of 2)* Alex Cherniak
48. How Úrvashi Was Won (*Vikramorvaśīya*) by *Kālidāsa* Velcheru Narayana Rao & David Shulman
49. The Quartet of Causeries (*Caturbhāṇī*) by *Śūdraka, Śyāmilaka, Vararuci & Īśvaradatta.* Csaba Dezső & Somadeva Vasudeva
50. Garland of the Buddha's Past Lives (*Jātakamālā*) (vol. 2 of 2)* by *Āryaśūra.* Justin Meiland
51. Princess Kadámbari (*Kādambarī*) (vol. 1 of 3) by *Bāṇa.* David Smith
52. The Rise of Wisdom Moon (*Prabodhacandrodaya*)* by *Kṛṣṇamiśra.* Matthew T. Kapstein
Foreword by J.N. Mohanty
53. Maha·bhárata VII: Drona (*Droṇaparvan*) (vol. 2 of 4)* Vaughan Pilikian
54. Maha·bhárata X & XI: Dead of Night & The Women (*Sauptikaparvan & Strīparvan*).* Kate Crosby
55. Seven Hundred Elegant Verses (*Āryāsaptaśatī*)* by *Govardhana.* Friedhelm Hardy
56. Málavika and Agni·mitra (*Mālavikāgnimitram*) by *Kālidāsa.* Dániel Balogh & Eszter Somogyi